THE THIRD TRAVELER

Stephen L Graf

Copyright © 2024 Stephen L Graf

All rights reserved

The characters and events portrayed in this book are fictitious. Any similarity to real persons, living or dead, is coincidental and not intended by the author.

No part of this book may be reproduced, or stored in a retrieval system, or transmitted in any form or by any means, electronic, mechanical, photocopying, recording, or otherwise, without express written permission of the publisher.

ISBN-13: 9798879447651

Cover design by: Jeffrey Wood
Library of Congress Control Number: 2024904393
Printed in the United States of America

For my mother and father.

I would like to thank my intrepid readers, my father, Edward L. Graf Jr., and my sister-in-law, Suzanne Graf. Thanks to Katherine Summers for her excellent proofreading skills. I'd also like to thank John Oakes for his sage advice on the title. Finally, thanks very much to Jeff Wood for his hard work and patience in designing the cover art.

Who is the third who walks always beside you?
When I count, there are only you and I together
But when I look ahead up the white road
There is always another one walking beside you
Gliding wrapt in a brown mantle, hooded
I do not know whether a man or a woman
—But who is that on the other side of you?

T.S. ELIOT

THE THIRD TRAVELER

Antarctica, February 1912

The explorers couldn't hear their own grunts over the howling wind. Seventy-two degrees of frost combined with a howling 30-mph wind made it feel like -78 Fahrenheit. A human body, left completely exposed to such elements, would die from hypothermia in a matter of minutes. Ciaran and Lieutenant Wellesley had been marching without break for nearly two hours. Strapped into harnesses like a pair of draft oxen, they dragged behind them a sledge that carried everything standing between them and a hasty death. There was the tent, tools, some extra clothes, the primus stove, and the little bit of food and oil that remained. Not much. Not nearly enough to sustain two nearly starving men through superhuman exertions. But it'd do if Lieutenant Wellesley's calculation was correct, and they were indeed within a three-day march from the next supply depot. The rations went further since they'd lost Owens, but that gain was negated by the fact that the going was much slower with only two men pulling the sledge.

Their margin for error had been razor thin the entire return journey. Missing a depot, or any delays caused by storms would spell near-certain doom. Ciaran tried not to think about that. He was just an ordinary seaman while Lieutenant Wellesley was an officer. Ciaran left that type of worry to the Lieutenant. Still, he helped prepare the food for all of their meals. Ciaran knew exactly how much food and heating oil remained and how far it would take them. He simply preferred not to think about it.

The increase in wind was another concern. Ciaran had seen this before, it was going to blizz. The only question was how violent the storm would be, and how long it'd last. The Lieutenant obviously sensed the looming weather front, and that was why they continued to push forward in the face of a strong headwind after already eclipsing their normal ten-hour allotment of marching. Ciaran tried to block out every message his body was sending him: the agony that started in the sole of his left foot and shot halfway up that leg each time he took a step, the discomfort his shoulders and back felt from the harness, the hunger that gnawed at his stomach, and the thirst that'd turned his tongue and lips to leather. In fact, he tried to block out everything except the job at hand. Ciaran feared he might lie down in the snow and just give up were he to think about how many hours of man-hauling remained before they reached the next depot, and then how many more weeks after that to finally return to the safety of base camp. Instead, he narrowed the scope of what lay before him, shrinking his universe to one step. Once he'd taken that step, his universe became the next step, and so on.

Ciaran almost never glanced over at the Lieutenant to his right. The Lieutenant's labored breathing, and the occasional bumping of their shoulders assured Ciaran that the Lieutenant was there, that he wasn't alone. Otherwise, with his eyes focused solely on the ground directly before him, he might've slipped into the belief that he was the last man on Earth, that no one else remained. Only…there was another. At least, there seemed to be. When Ciaran was facing forward, his eyes focused straight ahead, it seemed as if he could see a third, cloaked in brown, walking along with them to his left. But each time he turned to see whom it might be, the figure evanesced. He'd almost asked the Lieutenant about it on several occasions, but Ciaran reckoned the Lieutenant had enough to concern him without fretting that his partner had gone soft in the head. Yet, Ciaran couldn't shake the feeling of a third presence accompanying them.

Could it have been Owens? No, that was impossible. They'd lost Owens coming down the Beardmore Glacier several weeks earlier. They'd stopped in what had looked like a safe spot to camp for the night. As they were pitching the tent and setting up the campground, Owens, while reaching for a tent pole, had stepped on a crevasse that had been concealed by a thin layer of snow. Ciaran witnessed the whole thing. One moment Owens was there, the next moment he wasn't. It happened so fast Owens didn't even have time to cry out. But as soon as the ground gave way beneath him, Owens knew exactly what was about to befall him. Ciaran had seen the stricken look of recognition that crossed Owen's rugged face as the crust of frost beneath him cracked and gave way. That look haunted Ciaran. Owens had locked gazes with Ciaran, silently pleading with his eyes for something far beyond Ciaran's power to give. No one else had seen the look and Ciaran had told no one about it, but he knew it was something he'd carry with him for the rest of his life. Of course, at the moment it didn't appear as if that was going to be a very long haul.

No one heard Owens land—that's how deep the crevasses were. Some of them went down for miles, burrowing deep into the crust of the earth. Ciaran thought of a comment made by his countryman, the great Antarctic explorer Ernest Shackleton: "What the ice gets, the ice keeps." The ice was keeping Owens. They called down to Owens for nearly an hour, but he never responded. Ciaran had pleaded with Lieutenant Wellesley to allow him to go down on a rope and search for Owens. But the Lieutenant decided it was too dangerous—they couldn't afford to lose another man. It was the right call, but the Lieutenant had taken that one hard.

He blamed himself for Owens' death. It was his command—Owens was his responsibility. *Of them which thou gavest me have I lost none.* No, not quite none.

What about Hanes? The young aristocrat had been the fourth in the final party. He'd been included in the polar party to tend to the ponies that carried most of their provisions for the journey out. They'd lost the last of the ponies going up Beardmore Glacier during the journey out. The Lieutenant wouldn't allow them to butcher the ponies' remains for some necessary meat. He'd said it was inhumane. Perhaps, but not nearly as inhumane as the hunger they'd endured on their return journey.

They'd lost Hanes about a week earlier. One night, he'd told Ciaran and the Lieutenant that he was heading outside the tent and that he might be a while. But he never returned. Both Ciaran and Lieutenant Wellesley knew exactly what Hanes was up to. They couldn't bear to look at him or at each other when he announced it, ashamed of their tacit endorsement of his suicide. Hanes was in bad shape—he could barely walk. Ciaran had caught a look at Hanes's feet while he was removing his boots one night a week earlier. They were both completely black—frostbitten to the point that they were already turning gangrenous. If Hanes could somehow have been saved in the state he was, the formerly dashing Royal Marine officer was going to lose both of his legs at the knees. At best.

Hanes also suffered from the disease which threatened them all, the name of which no one dared utter: scurvy. Scurvy had taken far more lives on polar expeditions than the ice, the erratic weather, or the unforgiving terrain. While they all had it, Hanes's scurvy was much more advanced than that of Ciaran or the Lieutenant. Hanes knew he wouldn't make it back to the base; he probably wasn't going to make it to the next supply depot. His destroyed feet and general lack of strength had prevented Hanes from helping haul the sledge the final few days before his disappearance. Instead, he simply staggered along beside it. Even without carrying anything, Hanes was constantly falling behind, often to the point where he was completely out of sight, forcing him to catch up when Ciaran and the Lieutenant stopped to rest. The only thing keeping Hanes going was his unbounded courage and fierce pride. But the human body, no matter how tough and muscular it may appear on the outside, is a frail thing—mortally threatened by relatively minor changes in temperature, constantly preyed upon by hunger and thirst, and brought down by microbes far too small to be seen by the eye. An iron will can only carry a body so far. Hanes had reached the breaking point. When he did break there'd only be two choices: leave him to die alone on the ice or haul him on the sledge. A gaunt shadow of the jaunty former soldier who'd first reported for the mission, Hanes nevertheless still weighed close to eleven stone with clothes. Ciaran and the Lieutenant were already struggling to pull two hundred and forty pounds of supplies. Another hundred and fifty pounds might break them.

Hanes decided not to force Ciaran and the Lieutenant to make that choice. Fully aware that hauling him would mean all three of their deaths, Hanes gave them the last two things left in his power to give. First, he traded what little remained of his life for theirs. Hanes's death would give Ciaran and the Lieutenant life, or at least the chance of it. They all knew that, even if no one dared say it aloud. And, who knows, maybe in a less noble moment the Lieutenant and Ciaran had secretly hoped that Hanes wouldn't catch up with them on one of those instances when he'd strayed behind on the march. The instinct that preserves human life had perhaps inspired in the two healthier members of the party the wish that the ice would take Hanes as it had Owens. The second thing Hanes had given Ciaran and the Lieutenant, something that couldn't be measured in heartbeats or respirations, something greater still than the gift of life to those two particular men, was clean consciences. In that icy hell, Hanes figuratively took water and washed their hands of his fate. Using what little bit of strength was left in him to drag himself out of the tent in the middle of the night, he'd crawled off like a cat to die on its own.

Their search for Hanes the next morning turned up nothing. Just like Owens, the ice had claimed him and it wasn't giving him back. Lieutenant Wellesley held a brief memorial service which he ended by saying, "What more can I say of Hanes than he was an Englishman?" Ciaran, being an Irishman himself, felt that there was a good bit more the Lieutenant could've said, but kept his peace.

It was equally impossible that the third whom Ciaran was now seeing could've been Hanes, at least not the living Hanes that they'd known. A healthy man couldn't have survived one night exposed without a sleeping bag and tent, let alone a week. And Hanes wasn't healthy. He'd been more dead than alive when he'd staggered out of the tent. So, if it wasn't a complete figment of his imagination, Ciaran was perplexed as to whom or what this third presence might be. At least it gave him something to take his mind off of the mountain of troubles confronting them and the slew of aches and pains to which his body had fallen prey.

County Kerry, August 1910

Bridget stopped at the top of the hill to catch her breath. The short walk into the village had never tired her before and she couldn't understand why she felt so done-in on this day. She was nearly twenty, but she suddenly felt as if she were the ancient Cathleen Ni Houlihan. She gazed out at the farmland spread out in the valley below her, patches of lush green separated by low, gray stone walls. At times like this with the sun shining down lending the earth a kind of golden sheen, an almost heavenly glaze, she could understand why people could love this god-forsaken island. She looked at David Patrick's farm. It was a small patch of tilled land amidst a sea of green grass. Michael Dwyer had been buying all of the farms in the area and turning them into grazing land for sheep. Her father was one of the last holdouts. Indeed, the changes had forced David Patrick to add another foot of stone to the low wall that surrounded three sides of his property in order to keep the sheep from climbing over and digging up his spuds. The rear of his property was bordered by a small stream from which the family took their drinking, cooking, and bathing water. In the well-worn dirt behind the cottage stood a necessary house and an enclosed area where the chickens could roam free during the day.

The cottage itself was small, containing only two rooms. The walls were composed of stone and turf, with a roof of thatched straw. When he was just a boy, David Patrick had helped his father build it. They were only tenant farmers then, this being well before the Land Act had made sufficient funds available to Bridget's grandfather to purchase the land. As the eldest male child, David Patrick had inherited the farm upon her grandfather's death. Since he'd taken ownership of the cabin—for it was more cabin than house—David Patrick had re-thatched the roof only once, and that was well before Bridget had been born. Given the number of leaks that were beginning to spring open each time it rained—which was practically every day in Ireland—it seemed a re-thatching was coming due. From the chimney trailed a thin wisp of smoke.

*

"There you are," her mother said as Bridget pushed in the wooden front door. "I was about to give up on you entirely, so I was. Have you brought the flour?"

"I have," Bridget produced a small burlap sack from the bag slung over her shoulder and handed it to her mother.

"What kept you, colleen?"

Bridget dropped into a thatched chair at the rough-hewn wooden table in the center of the room. Heaving a sigh, she replied, "Dunno, Mam. I'm destroyed with the walking today."

"It'd be that extra weight you're carrying."

"Weight?"

"Aye, you've gained half a stone these past two months, so you have. What you're in need of is more activity."

"I don't see how more activity is going to make me less knackered. Besides, between cleaning the Murphys' house, helping out around here, and sewing at night, I'd say I get quite enough activity."

"You young people. Always complaining about a little hard work."

Hoping to change the topic, Bridget asked, "Where's Da?"

At that moment, David Patrick O'Shea walked in the front door whistling. Nodding toward him, Eithne muttered, "Speak of the devil, and he doth appear."

David Patrick removed a cloth cap to reveal a balding pate. His cheeks were flushed and a grin was plastered across his ruddy face as he walked over to Bridget. "Look Eithne," he said as he kissed Bridget's cheek, "it's the Rose of Tralee, come to visit the O'Sheas."

Bridget blushed and fidgeted.

Eithne, years past the point of being amused by David Patrick's antics, set down the bowl she was stirring and demanded: "And where have you been?"

"I was just helping Sean Ryan…"

"Sure," Eithne cut in bitterly, "helping him dispose of

some of his poteen."

"No," David Patrick responded, aggrieved—or at least appearing so. "I was helping him repair his still. As you know, it sits on the border of our property. I have a responsibility to ensure it's safe."

"Responsibility!" Eithne snorted. "Thanks so much for attending to our safety! And I don't suppose there was a sup taken after you'd fulfilled your responsibility?"

"It would've been impolite of me to turn it down."

"I've never seen a soul whose nice manners led him to taking on a feed of whiskey so often as yourself."

David Patrick held up his right hand, the index finger and thumb almost pressed together, and replied, "I took just a smahan."

"Aye, smahans such as yours caused Noah to build an ark."

Recognizing that there was no way he was ever going to win this argument, David Patrick turned his attention to Bridget. "Are you after stopping in the village?"

"Aye."

"Any word from himself at all?"

Bridget shook her head glumly: "Not since they left New Zealand."

David Patrick stood up, a bit wobbly, walked over to Bridget and patted her on the shoulders affectionately. "Ah, now, don't take it so hard. I'm sure he intends to write. That lad's got his hands full, love."

"I suppose."

"How long 'til they return?"

"He said they'd be gone at least two years, maybe three or four."

"I wouldn't be waiting around on that lad if I were you," Eithne interjected. "A lot can happen in three or four years, so it can. Besides, you're almost twenty. Better to find someone who's here now. A bird in hand, as the saying goes."

"I don't want anyone else, Mam, I only want Ciaran. Besides, I promised I'd wait for him."

"But why wait on someone when you don't even know if he'll come back at all?"

"Now Eithne," David Patrick interrupted. "We agreed we wouldn't talk about such things, remember?"

"Whisst, you," Eithne responded. "This is something our daughter needs to hear."

"He's coming back, Mam."

"There's no way of knowing that for certain. And if he does come back, he may not be the same. A hard place like that can change a man, so it can."

"If it changes him, I'll love him all the more."

"Easy enough that is to say now. He could come back broken—sickly, lame, missing limbs. A place like that is pitiless."

"As are you!" Bridget shot back, but the catch in her voice betrayed her.

"All right, Eithne, that's enough. Give the girl some peace."

"That's fine," Eithne remained unrepentant. "Three or four years is a power of time to wait. We'll see how you feel in a year."

"It'll be exactly the same as how I feel now, Mammy. That's not going to change. Ciaran's the only one I want. There's no one else in the world for me but Ciaran."

"Now don't say that, Asthore," David Patrick interjected. "I can understand you waiting. Wait your two or three or four years if you like. But don't close your heart to anything in case something changes in the that time," David Patrick paused to perform the sign of the cross, then added, "world without end."

"Something may change in that time, that's out of my control. But I won't. If I can't have Ciaran, I don't want anyone."

David Patrick and Eithne both shook their heads, but for different reasons.

Hell's Kitchen, July 1936

The stifling air in the second-floor gym reeked of musty leather and stale sweat. There were three large windows along the far wall that were closed with the blinds pulled in spite of the nearly one hundred-twenty-degree heat inside the poorly ventilated room. The staccato beats of skipping ropes and speed bags filled the air like a metronome, providing a steady rhythm to a hive of otherwise disparate activity and noise. Dominating the center of the room was a full-sized ring. Supposedly it was the same ring in which Dempsey fought Firpo at the Polo Grounds when the champ was rescued by the infamous "long count." But that was a rumor no one seemed capable of either completely verifying or dispelling.

Adjacent to a door which led to the dark, cramped locker room hung three heavy bags, all of which were being pounded by fighters. On the opposite side of the room was a small platform covered by an enormous plywood board on which fighters skipped rope and shadow boxed. Along the windowed wall were four speed bags of various sizes, also all in use. The wall opposite that was covered by framed black and white photos of fighters and yellowing fight cards. In the ring, two lightweights sparred. Standing on the ring apron overseeing the action within the ring was Paddy Byrnes, a small, trim, man in his late thirties with thinning hair and a pair of ears which looked like ragged chew toys and were three sizes too large for his head.

The owner of the gym, Jake Scanlan, bald with a gut that his oversized suit couldn't conceal, walked into the room chewing a cigar. "Hey Paddy!" he called.

"Yeah, Jake?" Paddy replied, never taking his eyes off of the fighters circling one another in the ring.

"Where the hell's Davy Boy?"

"He's not here," Paddy replied, his voice betraying an only slightly watered-down Irish brogue.

"I can see that, dammit! Where is he?"

"Dunno."

"Look at me when I'm talkin' to ya, dammit! I'm not holdin' no conversations with the back of your head."

A frown clouded Paddy's usually cheery features. "Stop dancing about the two of yez and get to it," he barked at the fighters in the ring. Turning to face Jake, he replied evenly, "What can I do for yeh, Jake?"

"For starters ya can tell me where the hell Davy is. He's fightin' Carvallo in a week."

"I told yeh, I don't know where he is. We called his place and his landlady said he was out—said he hadn't been there in two days."

"Then go find him, godammit. He's fightin' for the middleweight champeenship of the goddam planet in one week and his ass needs to be in the gym. These chances don't come along twice."

"I'm training Moretti at the moment, Jake. He's fighting on the undercard."

"I don't give two shits about Moretti," Jake snapped. Moretti paused from his sparring to eye him. "No offense Tony, ya got a lot of heart, but you're a ham and egger and that's all you'll ever be, and ya know it."

Paddy stared at Jake in disbelief. Moretti shook his head, his face concealed by ill-fitting headgear, touched gloves with his opponent and continued sparring.

"There's not gonna be a goddam undercard without Davy," Jake pointed out. "Davy's the show. Period."

"What do yeh want me to do about it, Jake?"

"I just told ya, ya goddam thick mick!" Jake exploded. "Go find Davy and drag his ass in here if ya have to. I don't care if he's in the middle of a two-day bender. Pour a pot of coffee down his throat and lace the mitts on him."

"But I told yeh, he's not home. I aleady checked."

"I heard ya. Check the bars around his neighborhood. And what the hell's the name of that floozy he hangs out with?"

"He hangs out with a lot of floozies, Jake. Yeh'll have to be a bit more specific than that."

"The blonde bimbo. She dances at Radio City, I think."

"Oh, Rita."

"Yeah, that's the dame. Check with her. See if she's seen him."

Paddy hopped nimbly to the floor. An associate trainer, a man in his late twenties with thick, dark hair and a flattened-out nose, was standing there holding the water bottles. "Keep an eye on 'em, Tommy" Paddy said to him. "Make sure Moretti doesn't drop his left."

Tommy nodded to Paddy and climbed onto the ring apron in time to ring the bell to end the round.

*

Rita's place was located just off of Times Square, about ten blocks from Scanlan's Gym, which was situated in the heart of Hell's Kitchen. An eight-story, brick building that'd once been an upscale hotel before the turn of the century, it was now a dilapidated weekly boarding house for people who were either down on their luck or didn't want a lot of questions asked. It was a place where a man and woman could stay together without having to produce a marriage certificate. The front desk clerk—a slovenly man with an Eastern European accent wearing only a sleeveless t-shirt and sweating profusely in spite of a fan that was directed right at him—provided Paddy with Rita's room number in exchange for a small bribe. The elevator was out of service, so Paddy was forced to climb six flights of stairs. By the time he'd reached her floor, Paddy had broken a healthy sweat. The lightbulb to the only light fixture in the sixth-floor hallway had either burned out or been stolen, so Paddy was forced to pick his way down the darkened corridor like a cat burglar, pausing at every door to try to make out the room number. The floorboards creaked as he walked, and at one point he felt something small and furry scuttle past him. Shuddering, he hoped it was a cat. He knew better.

Paddy found Rita's room at the end of the hall and paused before the entrance. Placing his ear against the peeling paint of the thin, wooden door, Paddy could hear snatches of a softly spoken conversation over a radio playing big band music. He couldn't tell if the male voice he heard was Davy, but it was worth a try. Without saying anything, Paddy rapped his knobby knuckles firmly against the door three times and listened for a reaction. There was a burst of anxious whispering; then the room became quiet.

After a moment, Paddy cleared his throat and said, "I know yer in there, Rita. I'm after hearing yeh talking."

There was another burst of whispering, then a gratingly nasal female voice responded, "I ain't here...I mean Rita ain't here. That is, you got the wrong place, mister."

"Ah, now Rita, I know it's yerself. I'd recognize that mellifluous voice anywhere. It's Paddy Byrnes, Davy's trainer. I'm looking for himself."

More whispering. "He says he ain't here. I mean..."

She was cut off by an angry voice. Paddy stood back and smiled. Moments later, the door flung open. Framed by the doorway was Davy Boy with only a towel wrapped around his narrow waist. Seeing Davy's wavy dark blonde hair and his chiseled body, Paddy was reminded that he'd often thought that Davy should've gotten into the pictures rather than the fight game. The diva had the personality for it. Davy could've made money off his looks. In the fight game, a pretty face like that would only incentivize his opponents to ugly him up. Catching sight of Paddy, a dark look crossed Davy's face, but the playful gleam remained in his blue eyes.

"What the hell do you want, Paddy?" Even though he'd left Ireland at the age of two and a half, a hint of a brogue was still discernible in Davy's voice.

"Wonderful to see yeh as well, Davy," Paddy replied with a chuckle. Seeing Rita on the rumpled double bed behind Davy, the covers pulled up to her neck, Paddy touched his cloth cap and said, "Rita."

Rita nodded, trying to summon all of the dignity the situation would allow, and replied, "How's tricks, Paddy?"

"Grand, grand. Of course, things would be a bit better if my fighter would turn up for his training session."

"You can just forget about that now, Paddy. I ain't going," Davy responded, still blocking the door.

Paddy looked at him quizzically.

Davy stepped back and nodded for Paddy to enter. "You may as well come in. I don't need the entire building in on my business."

Central Park, April 1947

The ship was an old-fashioned two-masted schooner, the kind that used to sail the high seas in colonial days. Although it was less than one-hundredth the scale of an actual sea-going vessel, the detailing was impressive. The one-piece sails were a thin, white canvas, pliable enough to actually catch wind and move the ship. The entire ship was made of white pine, unlike the real schooners whose ribbing, hulls, and various other parts had to be made of denser, tougher wood. But the model ship didn't have to withstand gales in the North Atlantic, or monsoons in the South Pacific, it only had to survive a breezy afternoon at the Central Park Boat Pond.

Percy, a shy, wispy ten-year-old, had worked on the model boat at the kitchen table of Aunt Martha's tiny apartment in midtown the entire winter. He'd saved his allowance for nearly a year to purchase the model kit, along with the glue, paints, and tools necessary to complete it. After testing the ship in Aunt Martha's bathtub, Percy was confident it was sea-worthy. But this would be its first sojourn into open waters. After school, Percy had returned to Aunt Martha's place to retrieve the boat. Then he rode the subway up to the 72nd Street station and walked down West 72nd to the park entrance. Upon entering the park, Percy followed the path by the southern finger of the lake, past Cherry Hill and Bethesda Terrace, until he came to the Conservatory Water. Aunt Martha didn't have a bag big enough to transport the ship, so he carried it pressed tightly against his chest like the Magi bearing gifts to the Christ child.

There was a good breeze for sailing, but the sky was overcast and there were some ominous-looking clouds along the western horizon. At least a dozen boats were out on the water when Percy arrived. People in ones and twos surrounded the little concrete-bordered pond, monitoring the progress of their vessels like concerned parents. On the eastern end of the pond stood a dilapidated, low wooden building that served as the Central Park Model Yacht Club. Percy slowly made his way around the pond, looking for the best location from which to launch his tiny ship. He'd been here many times both with Aunt Martha and by himself to watch the miniature yachts sail. There was something about the hobby that captured his imagination. It was like a portal to another world—a world beyond cramped efficiency apartments in run-down tenement buildings, beyond schools monitored by mean-spirited teachers in which the bullies seemed to outnumber the victims. Sailing opened his imagination to a world marked by exotic ports, unexplored lands, and adventure. Percy was sure such a world lay out there somewhere, but when he gazed out his window at night all he saw was the dingy dining room of the family who occupied the apartment in the building across the alley from his.

After several minutes of searching, he stopped at a spot which afforded a good view of the entire pond and where he wasn't too close to any of the other boat owners. Kneeling at the edge of the pond, he paused to glance behind himself. Percy's presence had caught the attention of an old man wearing a weathered, but neatly pressed, gray flannel suit and black wide-brimmed fedora seated on the bench directly behind him. The old man, leaning forward on his cane, smiled and gave Percy the thumbs-up. Percy blushed, fumbled to return the thumbs-up and quickly turned back to the pond. Following a final visual once-over, he hoisted the ship onto the edge of the pond. Carefully placing the boat atop the gently rippling water, Percy whispered, "I dub thee HMS Dauntless."

Giving it a gentle shove, Percy watched the tiny ship glide smoothly out toward open waters. He held his breath as the sails caught the breeze and filled. In a moment it shot out toward the middle of the pond. Puffing with pride and having no one with whom to share his accomplishment, Percy turned to look at the old man, who grinned and gave him another thumbs-up. Glancing around the pond, he saw pairs of fathers and sons also monitoring the progress of their boats. How often he'd envied those boys, but not today. He may not have had a father, but he had a ship—a ship every bit as good as theirs, albeit smaller and less expensive than most of the other boats navigating the pond. But it was *his* ship; he'd built it all from scratch with his own two hands. How many other boys there could say as much?

Aunt Martha couldn't accompany him—she'd had to work that afternoon. Had she been there, she may have gasped in surprise at the small smile of pride and satisfaction that enlivened his usually sullen features as the HMS Dauntless caught the wind and shot out toward the middle of the pond.

County Kerry, November 1910

"How long's it been?" Eleanor asked as she chopped carrots for stew. In her late teens with brown eyes and curly auburn hair, Eleanor had been schoolmates with Bridget and was nearly her match in beauty. Eleanor worked as a live-in cook for the Murphys, sleeping in a tiny room on the ground floor off of the pantry. The living arrangement rendered a romantic life outside of work challenging for Eleanor. As a result, she took great interest in other people's love lives, Bridget's in particular.

"Going on three months," Bridget replied, scrubbing the polished wooden floor of the Murphys' kitchen on her hands and knees. The Murphys had the largest house of any Catholic family in their small, rural village. Although the Murphys' place was by no means a "big house," it was a mansion compared to the O'Shea family homestead. A two-story wood-frame building with a slate roof and lots of windows, it contained a kitchen, a sitting room, and three bedrooms—one for Mr. and Mrs. Murphy, and the other two shared by their six children. Mr. Murphy owned a thriving supplies store in the village.

"Has herself figured it out yet?"

"No, but she soon will," Bridget paused to wipe her brow with her forearm. The protuberance of her belly couldn't be detected through the loose white blouse she was wearing, but she'd already had to give up wearing some of her tighter-fitting smocks. Bridget wasn't only trying to conceal it from her parents, but from the Murphys, as well. She was afraid that if the Murphys discovered she was in a family way they might put her out. And, in her current compromised condition, Bridget didn't believe she'd be able to find another job given the great preponderance of crawthumpers in their tiny village. Going back to scrubbing, Bridget added, "Mam's always on about my weight."

"What'll she do when she finds out?"

"Have a heart attack and then make a shaughraun out of me over the shame of it."

"Sure, your da won't allow that to happen?"

"He won't want it to happen, I reckon, but my da doesn't have the final say in our wee house."

"Have you thought about going to London to get it taken care of?"

"That's a mortal sin. I'd rather incur Mam's wrath than God's."

"But having the baby out of holy wedlock is a sin in God's eyes, as well."

"I can't win." Bridget paused from scrubbing again, this time to wipe the tears away from her eyes with her forearm. "Still, I'm not going to London. The child is Ciaran's. I could never do that to something that's a part of him."

"So, you're certain it's Ciaran's?"

"Don't be cheeky."

"Sorry. How many times did you…?"

"Once—the night before he shipped out."

"Only once?"

"That's all it takes."

"Where?"

Bridget paused from scrubbing again and looked at Eleanor curiously. "What do you mean 'where'? Surely, you know where."

"Don't be daft, Bridgey," Eleanor laughed. "I mean in

what place did the two of you…?"

"Oh," Bridget giggled. "In a pile of hay in his da's barn. There was a cow next to us mooing the entire time. It wasn't the most romantic—not the way you'd dream it'd happen."

"No, there wouldn't be any cows in my fantasies. So, it's love?"

"Aye."

"What's that like? I've never loved a lad as far as I know."

"You'd know if you had. It's wonderful and awful at the same time. It's like you're being given the most delicious drink in the world and that drink is drowning you. Thinking of him makes me feel happy and contented, and at the same time, it terrifies me."

"Why terrifies? Are you afraid you'll lose him?"

"Yes, but not to another girl."

"To what then?"

"Ice."

"Sure, he's coming back. It'll all be grand, you'll see."

"I keep having this dream—it's a nightmare, really. He's all alone, trapped out in the ice somewhere. He's sick and he's hungry, and he keeps calling out to me. I'm there, I can hear him. But there's a storm on and the snow is falling so hard I can see no more than a foot in front of me. I call back to him, but I know he can't hear me. He just keeps calling for me over and over, but we never find each other. Then, after a while, the calling stops…"

Bridget dropped her scrub brush and placed her face in her hands. Eleanor left the carrots and potatoes and rushed over to her. Kneeling on the wet wooden floor beside her, Eleanor threw her arms around Bridget and said, "It's just a dream, love. It doesn't mean a thing. It's just your fears getting the better of you while you're asleep and can't defend yourself from them. Sure, he's coming home. Your Ciaran's coming home to you."

Bridget sniffled and looked at Eleanor, "Do you think?"

"It'll be grand, love. You'll see. He'll come back and you can get married and the two of you will raise that little one you have coming. It'll all be grand."

Bridget nodded uncertainly and brushed the tears from her eyes with the back of her hand.

*

A steady rain was falling outside of the O'Shea's snug home, transforming the gloaming into a murky gray. Around back, the chickens had taken to the shelter of their coop for the night. Overhead, a thick blanket of clouds obscured both the setting of the sun and the rising of the moon. Bridget paused before the door for several minutes, allowing the rain to fall on her while she gathered up her strength. Taking a deep breath, she turned the knob and pushed in the door to find Eithne at the stove, preparing supper. Bridget shook the rain off of herself as best she could before crossing the threshold, then she made a beeline for the stove to warm herself.

"Mam," she said, avoiding eye contact.

Eithne merely grunted in return.

Bridget rubbed her wet hands together over the large, black, cast-iron stove. "Where's Da?"

"Your guess is as good as mine."

After warming herself, Bridget sat down and removed her shoes. Eithne studied Bridget out of the corner of her eye as her daughter removed her cloak and hung it near the stove to dry. Following several minutes of silence, Eithne cleared her throat and said, "I was having a chat with Mrs. Rourke at the market today."

"Is that so?" Bridget responded absent-mindedly. "How is Mrs. Rourke? Did she have any good gossip for you?"

"Not gossip, as such. She had something interesting to say about you."

"About me? What on Earth could that woman possibly have to say about me?"

"She said she saw you getting sick behind the Murphy's pantry three different mornings last week."

"Why is she hanging about behind the Murphy's house?" Bridget responded defensively.

"She wasn't hanging about. She was passing by on the road on her way to the village. Don't change the topic. Why were you getting sick?"

"I don't know." Bridget tugged at a curl the rain had brought out from her long, dark brown hair. "I haven't been feeling well lately, that's all."

"This doesn't have anything to do with all of that weight you've gained?"

"Weight? What weight?"

"You've put on nearly a stone. Don't pretend you don't know what I'm talking about, girl. Lying is a mortal sin, so it is."

"It's a venial sin, Mam."

"It depends on the lie," Eithne replied haughtily. "Lying to your mother is a mortal sin. Father McGuire told me."

"Father McGuire told you no such thing," Bridget responded wearily. Whenever her mother wanted to make a point that would be beyond refute, she claimed that it came from their parish priest, Father McGuire. Eithne wholeheartedly accepted Church dogma, believing the word of the Church, and its human representatives, to be infallible—even if that word hadn't actually come from either.

"Is it a liar you're calling me?" Eithne was quickly becoming indignant.

Before Bridget could reply the door opened and in walked a whistling David Patrick. Oblivious to what he'd intruded upon, he removed his jacket and cloth cap and shook the rain from them. Then he headed to the stove to warm himself, blithely querying, "How's my two favorite lasses in the world?"

Neither Eithne nor Bridget responded. They just sat there glowering at one another.

"Grand, is it then?" David Patrick chuckled, sitting at the table and removing a pipe from his coat pocket. After placing a pinch of tobacco in it he took a few puffs. Calmly, he inquired, "So, what is it that I've happened upon?"

"Mauve Rourke told me that she'd seen herself," she paused to nod at Bridget, "getting sick behind the Murphy's house three times this past week."

"What of it?" David Patrick demanded, more bemused than irritated by the situation. "Who cares what the ol' ownshucks says? Is she taking on the role of village doctor in addition to her duties as town gossip?"

"It was in the morning," Eithne replied with finality.

"Eh?" David Patrick looked confused momentarily. Eithne nodded knowingly to emphasize her point. After a moment, a light of recognition entered David Patrick's eyes: "Oh. Ahhhh..."

Turning to Bridget, he asked gently, "Well, what is it, Asthore? Time will easily make a liar of you on this one. You may as well tell us now. Are you?"

Eyes downcast, Bridget replied in a tone just above a whisper, "It's true, Da, I am."

"Is it..."

Before David Patrick could finish his question Bridget interjected, "It's Ciaran's."

David Patrick stood and walked over to Bridget. Standing behind her, he placed his hand lovingly on her shoulder and said, "I'm sure this situation will resolve itself when the lad returns."

"And if he doesn't return?" Eithne demanded savagely.

Bridget burst into tears. Glaring at Eithne, David Patrick responded, "There's no call for that sort of talk, woman." He placed both hands on Bridget's heaving shoulders and rubbed them gently, saying, "He'll be back, sure as I'm standing here."

"Even if he does make it back," Eithne continued, unperturbed by David Patrick's looks of chastisement, "Herself has already told us it'd be at least two years, maybe even three or four, before he makes it home. How are we to explain our daughter being in a family way with no father to speak of?"

A twinkle in his eye, David Patrick suggested, "Immaculate conception?"

Eithne shot to her feet, incensed, "You're going to bring Christ's own curse down on the lot of us with your blasphemies, David Patrick O'Shea!"

David Patrick shrugged, "It worked for Mary."

"I'm at Mass each Sunday and every Holy Day of obligation, so I am. I go to confession every Saturday, even when I have nothing to confess. I say my rosary every night, I follow every command in the Bible..."

"Yes," David Patrick interjected, "all but one: 'Love thy neighbor as you love yourself.'"

Not put off by David Patrick's criticism, Eithne exclaimed, "I'm not going to be cast into the eternal flame for your transgressions, David Patrick O'Shea." Nodding to Bridget, she added, "Or those of the duchess there, either." Snatching her rosary beads from the table and, looking up to heaven, Eithne exclaimed, "Please don't punish me, Oh Lord, for the sins of this blasphemer, or the fornications of this whore of Babylon."

Bridget burst into tears anew at Eithne's last comment. David Patrick shook his head and chuckled, "It seems to me, if I remember correctly, that Bridget isn't the only one in this room to fornicate before she was married, Eithne."

"How dare you!" Eithne exploded.

"I was just trying to introduce the pot to the kettle."

Tears filled Eithne's eyes. She choked back a sob and asked, "What'll we do about the shame of it? No doubt Mauve Rourke has already told half the village, and the other half will soon know."

Eithne dropped into a chair and burst into tears of her own. "What'll we do?"

"We'll raise that child as if it were our own until Ciaran is able to come back and take his place as father and head of household. No child born out of love can be a bad thing, I don't care what sharp-tongued serpents like Mauve Rourke say." Walking over to Eithne, David Patrick comforted her: "It'll be grand, love. This'll all work out."

Eithne sniffled and looked up, a gleam of hope in her

eyes, "Yes, maybe it will work out. Maybe the Holy Ghost will take pity on us and cause her to miscarry."

Hell's Kitchen, July 1936

There was one stuffed, straight-back chair in the room and it was buried under Davy's clothes. Davy scooped up the jacket, pants, white dress shirt and underwear and tossed them carelessly on the bed. Then he waved Paddy toward the seat. Paddy looked at Davy, puzzled at the formalities, then sat down. Because of the angle of the afternoon sun shining through the open window, Paddy found himself forced to squint and look away. "Out with it. What's keeping yeh from training, Davy?"

Davy sat on the edge of the bed in front of Paddy, thereby screening him from the sun. He took a deep breath and paused a moment, thereby heightening the impact of what was to come. As he waited for Davy's reply, Paddy listened to the traffic rushing by on the West 42nd Street below. Leaning in until he was almost face to face with Paddy, in a voice that sounded like a stage whisper, Davy said, "I had the dream again."

"The dream?"

"Yeah," Davy leaned back as though he were Moses presenting the tablets on Mt. Sinai, "the dream."

"Dream?" Rita demanded in her nasal voice. "What dream?"

Both men ignored her.

"Might I ask a question of yeh, Davy?" Paddy inquired after a moment.

"What?"

"How many times does this make it that yeh've had the

dream?"

Davy leaned back and rubbed his chin for a moment, pondering. As he did so, Rita interjected in a louder and, somehow, even more whiny voice, "*What* dream?"

Paddy and Davy continued to ignore her. Davy responded to Paddy, "Twelve and a half."

"Twelve and a half?" Paddy couldn't help chuckling.

"This is serious, you sawed-off Leprechaun."

"I didn't mean to laugh, Davy. It's just twelve and *a half*?"

Pulling the duvet about her as she sat up in bed, Rita demanded in a voice that was almost a scream, "What dream?"

Looking back over his shoulder at her, Davy replied, "Clam up, Rita. Can't you see we're talking?" Turning back to Paddy, he continued, "That's right—half. I started to have the dream one time but got woke up in the middle."

Paddy did his best to wipe any sign of bemusement from his face. Looking at Davy seriously, he said, "Listen, Davy, if yeh've had the dream twelve and a half times and it hasn't come true yet..."

"It didn't come true the first eleven and a half times," Davy interrupted. "I just had the last one."

"Fair enough. But if yeh already had it eleven and a half times and it hasn't come to pass, then doesn't that tell yeh that it's never going to happen? It's just a dream, not some sort of premonition."

"What it tells me is that since I've gone eleven and a half times without it happening, then that makes it that much more likely to happen this time."

"That's not the way math works, Davy," Paddy replied

patiently.

"What're you talking about, Pads?"

"The odds of it happening are the same every time—slim to none. The odds don't increase just because yeh've had the dream a few more times."

"Of course it means that it's more likely," Davy straightened up, indignant. "It becomes more likely to happen every time I have the dream…"

"WHAT DREAM?" Rita shouted.

"Stop yapping, Rita!" Davy replied, annoyed. Turning to Paddy, Davy stood up and said, "Don't you tell me about mathematics, Paddy Byrnes. Don't forget, I made it through the ninth grade. You barely finished grammar school."

"All right," Paddy held up his hands. "I didn't come here to argue with yeh about math or who is more educated than who…"

"Whom!" Rita interjected.

"Shut up, Rita!" Davy and Paddy responded in unison this time.

"I know why you came, Paddy" Davy said, walking over and opening the door. "So you can just fuck off outa here. I ain't fighting Carvallo. Not after I had the dream. Tell Jake Scanlan he can shove the fight up his fat ass!"

"Nobody said anything about yeh fighting Carvallo. I just want yeh to come down to the gym and break a little sweat. Yeh don't even gotta spar. I just think that if yeh'd work out, yeh'd feel much better." Paddy glanced at the empty liquor bottles scattered around the room. "Plus," he added, "I don't think it'd hurt none to sweat out some of that booze. Yeh smell like John Jameson's piss."

"I don't know, Pads," Davy wavered, "Rita and me had some plans for the day…"

"Rita and I," she corrected him, "and just go, you big ape. I can't bear the sight of your ugly mug anymore!"

Davy looked and Paddy and shrugged, "Okay, let's go to the gym."

Paddy nodded to the clothes on the bed. "Yeh might want to get dressed first."

"Oh yeah," Davy grinned. "I almost forgot."

As Paddy exited the room, Davy turned to Rita, who was leaning against the headboard with the duvet pulled up to her neck. "I'll be back in a few hours, Rita."

"Oh no you will not," Rita nearly shouted at him. "No one tells me to shut up!"

Davy shrugged and turned to follow Paddy out. As he was about to exit the room, Rita picked up what appeared to be a military medal of some sort that had fallen on the bed. Tossing it at Davy, she cried, "And take your stupid World's Biggest Jerk medal with you!"

Catching it, Davy frowned and said, "Be careful with that! It's an antique."

"Disappear, you louse!"

After pulling the door to behind himself, Davy turned to Paddy, shook his head and said, "Women." After inspecting the medal, he dropped it in his jacket pocket.

Central Park, April 1947

A sudden storm ripped apart the previously peaceful afternoon sky, sending most of the boaters scurrying for cover as soon as they were able to recover their vessels. Raindrops the size of grapes poured from the sky so that it felt almost like standing under a waterfall. Percy's ship ran aground on the opposite shore from where he stood, so he sprinted around the pond to retrieve it. With the rain pounding down, some of the model yacht owners had taken the additional step of wading out to retrieve their ships. The area around the pond emptied of people quickly. As he bent down to carefully scoop out his ship, Percy glanced across the water toward the bench the old man had occupied, but it was abandoned. Firmly pressing the ship against his chest, he didn't worry about the pond water rolling off of it onto his jumper since it was already soaked.

Drenched to the bone before he'd even departed the Conservatory Water area, Percy made his way toward the 72nd street station. The sudden downpour had cleared the pathways and sidewalks and allayed his main concern—that someone might accidentally bump into the model ship. The inside of the subway station was another matter. It was packed with people who'd scurried underground to avoid the rain. The air in the station was thick and sultry from the rain and unseasonable heat. Cradling the ship protectively in his arms, Percy carefully navigated the bustling crowd. Arriving at his platform, Percy picked his way toward the far end where it wasn't so crowded. Leaning against a wall, he dripped rainwater onto the filthy concrete floor and tried to catch his breath. With a garbage can screening his side, Percy kept a vigil for the hordes of unheedful commuters who paced the platform like racehorses in blinders. He'd spent too much time, money and effort in building the ship to have it accidentally damaged by careless pedestrians.

When his train arrived, he found a seat in the corner of a car. Both the ship and Percy survived the subway journey intact. Twenty minutes later, Percy emerged onto 47th street. The rain had ceased and the clouds had already parted, revealing a friendly sun. He was still soaked to the bone, though, and his shoes squished with every step he took.

As he was passing his elementary school on the last leg of his journey homeward, he finally encountered difficulty. The trouble came in the worst possible form: four of his classmates from school. Seeing the little pack appear before him on the sidewalk just outside the main gate to his school, Percy whispered under his breath, "Crap."

He stopped and tried to pivot, hoping they hadn't spotted him. But it was too late. "Look!" shouted the largest and meanest member of the group who, owing to those qualifications, also served as their leader. "It's Pussy Kelly."

His flunkies chortled in appreciation of his agile wit.

Glancing at the group nervously, Percy gulped and replied, "Hello, Marty."

Marty's round, pock-marked face curled into a sneer. "It speaks," he scoffed to his cronies, drawing another round of dutiful cackles. As he stepped closer to Percy, the height disparity between the two boys became apparent. Marty stood a full head taller than Percy, the difference being at least partially explained by the fact that Marty had been held back two grades. Nodding at the model ship cradled in Percy's arms, Marty demanded, "Watcha got there, Pussy?"

Percy glanced down at the ship and hugged it tightly to his chest. Although Percy realized the answer was self-evident, even to someone of Marty's limited intellectual capacities, he felt a response of some sort was requisite. Not wanting to risk further antagonizing his tormentor, Percy replied, "A model ship."

"A model ship, huh? Lemme see it."

Percy looked at Marty with frightened eyes, clutching at the ship like a doe protecting its kits.

"Come on, Percy," Marty adopted a more friendly, cajoling tone. "Lemme see it. I won't hurt it, honest."

Percy scanned the faces of the boys in the group, searching in vain for an ally. Finding none, he reluctantly handed the ship to Marty. "Be careful, please. It's delicate."

Marty snatched the ship from Percy and snapped, "I told ya I wouldn't hurt it, didn't I?" Marty looked at the boat admiringly, then whistled and asked, "You make this yourself?"

"Yes."

"That's some fine craftsmanship. Ain't it, boys?"

Marty turned and held the boat up for his toadies to see and they all aped, "Fine craftsmanship!"

Turning back to Percy, Marty asked, "This barge got a name?"

Percy nodded and replied in a voice just above a whisper, "The HMS Dauntless."

"HMS Dauntless?" Marty echoed Percy questioningly. "Naw that ain't right. I think the name of this here tub is the Titanic."

Marty turned to the next largest boy in the group, a dark-haired, dark-eyed boy named Michael with whom Percy had once been friends. Michael wasn't naturally as mean or stupid as the rest, but he was desperate to please his leader, and that made him even more dangerous. Handing the ship to Michael, Marty said, "This looks like the Titanic to ya, don't it, Mikey?"

Michael accepted the boat, surreptitiously shooting Percy an apologetic look for what they both understood was about to happen. "Yeah," he said, moving the ship up and down in the air as though it were riding heavy waves, "just like the Titanic."

Percy gave Michael a pleading look, but he ignored it. Michael held his hand to his forehead as though he were a ship's lookout gazing out to sea, and then remarked, "Oops, iceberg dead ahead!"

With that he slammed the ship onto the sidewalk, smashing it into a thousand pieces. The other two members of the group, the Pinto brothers, howled in appreciation.

Marty nodded to the Pintos and they circled behind Percy, who was gaping at the fragments of his ship in disbelief. Each of the Pintos grabbed one of Percy's arms. Marty then nodded to Michael who took one step forward and dug a vicious uppercut into Percy's midsection. Percy let out a surprised, "Oof!" as the punch drew all of the air out of him. The Pintos released his arms and he dropped to the sidewalk and retched as though he were going to vomit.

Marty leaned down until he was almost nose-to-nose with Percy and snarled, "See? I told ya I wouldn't hurt it."

"Act of God," Michael said, looking a little frightened by what he'd done.

"Yeah," Marty chimed in, apparently liking the sound of that, "act of God. Weren't nothin' nobody coulda done about it! Didn't ya know this is iceberg country, Pussy?" Turning back to his crew, he said, "Let's beat it."

As they were walking away, the younger Pinto brother began to sing, "Oh, they built the ship Titanic..."

The others gleefully joined in. As the group rounded the corner out of sight, Percy, lying on the sidewalk trying to catch his breath, heard the older Pinto shout, "Kerplunk! It sunk!"

Percy lay on the rain-soaked sidewalk gazing through a kaleidoscope of tears at the smashed wreckage that had once been the HMS Dauntless. As he thought of the countless hours spent building the ship, and the further hours working odd jobs to buy the materials, the tears began to slide out of his eyes and drop sideways onto the dirty sidewalk. He knew men weren't supposed to cry, but he wasn't a man. A man stood up for himself. He didn't do anything—just stood there gawking while they destroyed his ship. What would he tell Aunt Martha?

County Kerry, November 1910

Cnoc na Piseog was the epicenter of supernatural activity for the village and its surrounding area. According to legend, a powerful king of the Tuatha Dé Danann—supernatural beings who inhabited Ireland in ancient times—had been driven, along with his tribe, into this mountain by the Milesians in that dark era many ages before St. Patrick brought the one true faith to Ireland. Since that time, the Tuatha Dé Danann, an immortal race, had ruled within the mountain, venturing out from time to time to dance in the moonlight or to abduct mortals to serve them. Legend had it that their king possessed a vast vault overflowing with silver, gold and jewels. According to local lore, some years earlier three brothers had ventured into the mountain seeking that treasure, never to be heard from again. Of course, all of this was open to debate, including whether or not Cnoc na Piseog even qualified as a mountain. Standing only about a thousand feet above sea level, it rolled gently into the surrounding valleys on three sides, with only one side being relatively steep. That was the side that faced the village, and Bridget's father's farm. In the spring and summer, the slopes were covered in lush grass. The pinnacle of the mountain was rounded and perennially bare, like a monk's tonsure. As the years passed and the cautionary tales concerning its inhabitants faded somewhat, the mountaintop gradually evolved into a popular lovers' haunt and picnic spot owing to its breathtaking views.

A blanket spread out beneath them, Bridget and Eleanor sat on a grassy patch overlooking the steep side. From that position, they could gaze down on their valley and village.

Divided into neat, nearly square parcels of farmland, from above the valley resembled a checkerboard. Actually, it was more like half of a checkerboard as the other half of the valley had been converted into grazing land for sheep by Michael Dwyer. At the far end of the valley stood their little village, appearing miniscule and unimportant from their lofty vantage point. Comprised of approximately sixty buildings, the majority of the residences resembled Bridget's. There were a few two-story wooden structures with slate roofs. The tallest building, situated in the center of the village, was the Church of Ireland cathedral that serviced the ten percent of the town's population that was Protestant. The Catholic church, which served the other ninety percent, was a ramshackle sod building with a collapsing thatch roof located on the outskirts of town. The juxtaposition of the two houses of worship served as a stark reminder the oppressive Penal Law days—gone, perhaps, but not forgotten.

It was an unseasonably warm and sunny late autumn afternoon. The smell of falling leaves wafted up to them through the crisp, clear air. Behind them, near the center of the bare mountaintop, was a cairn that most visitors mistakenly attributed to the mountain's mythological inhabitants but which had actually been erected a mere dozen years earlier by some young men from their village after winning the county junior hurling championship. The remnants of their picnic were scattered about the blanket. Leaning back on her elbows, Bridget's legs were splayed out in front of her, and a prominent baby bump was visible through her white dress. A green shawl was wrapped around her shoulders against the wind. The breeze tousled her long brown hair. Eleanor, in a brown house dress and worn leather boots, sat on the blanket beside Bridget, propping herself on one elbow against the now-empty picnic basket. The sun had just passed its high point and, it being their off day, the two had nowhere else to go.

Stretching out into a position of maximum comfort,

Eleanor remarked, "It's grand not to be cooking the Murphys' meals or scrubbing their floors, isn't it? Although, I suppose it might be worse. At least we don't have to work for Protestants."

"Aye," Bridget replied, absently staring at a withered dandelion nearby. Gently plucking it out of the soil so as to not disturb its fluffy, white globe, she raised it to her face to study it.

"Where are you today, girl? Off in the wilds of Antarctica again?"

Bridget didn't respond to the question. Instead, she blew on the dandelion, watching the feathery seeds scatter to the winds. Once the stem was bare, she tossed it away. Turning to Eleanor, she asked, "Do you ever wonder what it'd be like to live someplace else?"

"What do you mean? Like the Antarctic? I didn't think anything could survive there, it's too cold." Realizing what she'd just said, Eleanor quickly added, "I mean long-term."

"I'm not talking about the South Pole, Eleanor. I'm not a bloody penguin. I mean have you ever thought about what life would be like in America or Australia, or even England? Lots of Irish go to those places."

"I don't know about Australia—too far away and too many criminals. But it might be fun to live in a big city like New York or London."

"I've cousins in New York. They say you couldn't pay them to return here, even for a visit."

"Maybe," Eleanor replied, doubtfully. Then, waving at the valley spread out beneath them, she added, "Still, it is beautiful here."

"When the sun shines—which isn't often."

"Not only when the sun shines. It can be beautiful when it's raining on a spring day. Or on a summer day, just after it's finished raining and the sun starts to peak out and shine on everything while it's cool and sparkly and fresh."

"What about the people?"

"What of them? Most of the people around here are good, decent types. The Catholics anyway, and maybe some of the Protestants as well. It's possible."

"You don't have them staring at you, whispering behind your back when you pass them on the road."

"That's just because of your, em, situation. That will end when Ciaran gets back."

"Even if it were to end when Ciaran got back, that wouldn't change that it happened. That it continues to happen. And that it'll only get worse once my child is born."

"Could it be that, perhaps, you're just being too sensitive? Maybe it's not so bad as you think."

"Maybe so," Bridget answered doubtfully. After a short pause, she asked, "What about the superstition, then?"

"What superstition?"

"What superstition? Are you serious? How about the fact that most people around here believe that fairies live in this very mountain?" For emphasis, Bridget patted the ground beside herself.

"Fairies *do* live in this mountain."

"Don't tell me you believe in that nonsense!"

"Whisst, girl, be careful what you say. Especially here, of all places." Eleanor sat up and glanced around herself uneasily.

"And if I'm not careful about what I say?"

"It's told that Eileen O'Connor was saying the same type of thing right before she disappeared."

"Disappeared? I heard she ran off with an English soldier."

"That's precisely what they want you to believe. They're crafty like that."

"Who?"

"Who? —so asks herself! The Good People, of course."

"Da was right," Bridget replied, exasperated. "This country is full of superstitious ninnies."

"Superstitious it may be, I don't know. Whatever you call it, do you think these stories would've lasted this long if there wasn't a wee kernel of truth to be found in them?"

"I give up!" Bridget threw her hands up in the air.

"Good," Eleanor's eyes shifted nervously again, "this isn't the place to be debating such matters."

Behind them, a thrush alighted on a rock and began warbling a melancholy tune. Bridget lay on her back and gazed up at the brilliant, azure sky. A fat cloud that vaguely resembled a pregnant sow slowly floated past. After following it with her eyes for several minutes, she mused, "I wonder if the sky's the same."

"What's that?" Eleanor glanced over. Seeing Bridget stretched out, she lay herself down again and looked up at the sky.

"I wonder if the sky is the same down there at the South Pole as it is here."

"I would think so." Eleanor plucked a long blade of grass

and placed it between her lips. "But, then again, I heard the sun doesn't set for months down there in the summer, and it doesn't rise for months in the winter. So, who knows?" After a few moments pause she added, "Have you heard from himself at all?"

"I got a short note from him about a month ago from when they ported in South Africa."

"Have they made it to Antarctica yet?"

"I'm not sure. Possibly."

"Have you told him..." she trailed off.

"I'm going to. It's my intention. But I just can't seem to force myself to sit down and write that letter."

"You should write him soon. He deserves to know. And who knows? Maybe, when he finds out, it may cause him to not volunteer for any of the more dangerous missions, like actually going to the Pole."

"Maybe," Bridget answered. Then she seemed to get lost in thought.

A few moments of silence passed. In an effort to draw Bridget back out, Eleanor asked, "What will you do, I mean the two of you, when he gets back?"

"That's a long way away, but I imagine we'll get married and settle down."

"Do you think he'll stay in the Royal Navy?"

"I don't know. It's not something we discussed."

"It's a dangerous job, even when they're not off trying to find the South Pole. There's a lot of unrest on the continent at the moment. They say war might not be far off, and if there is a war, you can rest assured the bloody English will have to get involved."

"Why wouldn't they? They're always mucking about in other people's business."

"Of course, if those lads do make it to the Pole, Ciaran could be famous."

"I suppose so."

"You don't think if he got famous he might not want to, you know, take advantage of that?"

"Ciaran?" Bridget shot back, sitting up and looking Eleanor in the eye. "My Ciaran's not like that. He's as true as the day is long."

"Of course, I wasn't trying to imply anything." Eleanor sat up as well. "I can see how it might be nice to be married to a famous lad. Glamorous, I suppose."

"If nothing else, it'd beat scrubbing the Murphys' floors."

They both giggled uncontrollably, but then went quiet again for a few moments. A breeze tussled Bridget's hair. "You know," she remarked, "I read one time that all of the wind and storms we get up here actually originate down in the Antarctic."

"Is that so?"

"'Tis. Sometimes I like to think about how a wind that touched him down there might have made its way across the equator, over the Atlantic, and all the way to our wee village so that it could touch me, too. That comforts me—makes me feel that maybe he's not so far away after all."

A strong breeze blew across the top of the mountain and Bridget wrapped her arms around herself, as though giving it a hug. Eleanor smiled and looked away.

Antarctica, February 1912

The snow was blowing at them sideways at nearly 50 mph by the time Ciaran and the Lieutenant halted their march for the day. Once the Lieutenant had chosen a site on which to camp, they went about their work methodically. Each man knew exactly what needed to be done, they'd followed the same routine every evening for more than three months. Both men had been forced to take on more responsibilities as their group dwindled. Owing to sickness, exhaustion and the fact that they were two men doing the work of four, the time to set up camp had more than doubled as compared to when they initially embarked upon their return journey, relatively strong and healthy, with the full four-man team. The first task entailed pitching the tent. Supported by five bamboo poles, the canvas tent consisted of an inner and an outer component, one layered over top of the other for insulation. The tent was then made fast by means of ropes and stakes driven deep into the hard permafrost using a mallet carried for just that purpose.

The provisions were unloaded from the sledge into the tent, and everything was stowed away securely. Then they set up the primus stove. Running on paraffin, a type of kerosene, the small brass pressurized burner operated like a blow torch, emitting a steady flame. A small, seemingly inconsequential piece of equipment, the primus was every bit as important in providing a barrier between them and a quick death as were their cold weather gear, the tent, and the sleeping bags. Without the primus, there'd be no drinking water. At the bottom of the Earth, in a desolate land where everything seemed upside down, it stood to reason that a desert dryer than the Sahara sat atop a sheet of freshwater ice more than one mile thick, the layers of which measured not in years but in epochs. It was a barren, windswept land, completely unsuitable for human habitation. For that matter, it was unfit to sustain any sort of biological life except, perhaps, microscopic mites and lice. It was a land where nighttime was gauged not in hours, but in months, and that long night was galloping ever closer.

Lieutenant Wellesley lifted the brass canister containing the paraffin, held it to his ear and shook it. The slosh of liquid fuel was barely perceptible. He set the can down and uttered in voice that was not much more than a hoarse whisper, "The paraffin's nearly gone. Every can was filled to the brim when we depoted them on the journey out. But every one that we've recovered on the return has been at least one third empty. I don't understand it."

"Angel's share," Ciaran croaked.

"The Angel's share should only account for five-percent evaporation. We've lost far more than that. If I didn't know better, I'd say some of those lads from the earlier return parties were skimming."

"No sir, them lads 'ud sooner die of thirst than take any of ours and leave us short."

"You're right," the Lieutenant replied, forcing a smile. After placing a small funnel in the brass tank of the primus stove, he lifted the can of paraffin again, screwed off the cap, and began to carefully pour the contents into the funnel. When the tank was nearly full, he stopped and screwed the lids back on both containers. Igniting the flame, he took a chunk of ice he'd carried into the tent for that purpose and dropped it in a tin pot. The pot was then hung over the flame.

Waiting for the ice to melt, the two men removed their boots. Ciaran shifted his body to screen the Lieutenant's vision, and then carefully peeled off the thick woolen sock from his left foot. It was damp from blood. Ciaran's three smallest toes were blackened and swollen like burnt marshmallows. He poked at the middle one gingerly, wincing in pain at the slightest touch.

"How are those toes?" the Lieutenant asked from over

his shoulder.

"They're grand, sir," Ciaran lied.

"Let's have a look."

Ciaran pivoted his lower body, placing his feet on the open space of the tent floor between his sleeping bag and that of the Lieutenant. The Lieutenant examined Ciaran's feet with the impassive curiosity of a physician. He'd studied medicine at university before the urge to see the world had gripped him and he signed on as a midshipman on the *HMS Worcester*, a training ship that primarily prepared officers for the Merchant Navy. While on the Worchester, he'd won a cadetship to the Royal Navy and his career was launched. He leaned in close enough to whiff the scent of incipient gangrene, and commented matter-of-factly, "If they get much worse, I'm going to have to amputate."

"That's all right, sir. I'll still have seven more left."

"That's the spirit. How much do they hurt?"

"Only when I touch them, sir. When we're on the march I hardly notice them."

The Lieutenant nodded. He knew Ciaran was lying—that those toes were probably bringing tears of pain to his eyes every step the indomitable Irishman took. On the march, the frigid temperatures would do little to numb the pain. But the Lieutenant also knew that short of amputating there was only so much he could do for Ciaran out here. So, they both pretended Ciaran was telling the truth when he claimed that the toes didn't hurt. The Lieutenant pulled his shirttails out from under his heavy woollen sweater. Lifting Ciaran's foot like it was a newborn baby, Lieutenant Wellesley guided the foot under his shirt, wincing momentarily when the ice-cold appendage touched his bare chest. "We need to get the blood flowing in there again. I need you in working order. I don't have the strength to pull both the sledge and you."

Ciaran nodded. He allowed the Lieutenant to play the mother hen, even though the Lieutenant was only twelve years his elder. At twenty-one years of age, Ciaran had been the baby of the expedition. Because he wasn't a polar veteran, the Lieutenant hadn't intended to include Ciaran in the polar party. But when illness opened a spot on that team, two factors weighed in Ciaran's favor: his infallible optimism and his capacity for outworking everyone who'd shipped with them. Optimism was a key quality for a perilous mission where the outcome was far from assured. A negative attitude would infect a party far more quickly than scurvy. As to the work ethic, Ciaran had been brought up on a farm in County Kerry, the second youngest of six brothers. His father had once told him, "You may not be as strong or as fast as the other lads, but the one thing you can do is outwork them. When you see the others start to drop from exhaustion, that's when you work harder. When other lads' backs are bowed and tongues are hanging out, you stand straight as a poker, smile and ask for more." It'd been the guiding principle in Ciaran's life. Since his father's bit of a farm was too small to split up, it'd go to Tiernach, his eldest brother. Consequently, Ciaran enlisted in the Royal Navy when he was fourteen years old. The work ethic and his positive attitude were what'd landed him on this mission, the allure of which was double pay and a quick promotion upon return. Not to mention fame, should they be successful. While the risks had been suitably abstract when he'd signed on, Ciaran now understood why so many incentives had been offered. They'd lost three men to various mishaps at the base camp and one more during the sea voyage south. They'd already lost half of their final party, and there was no telling if all three of the four-man support parties had returned to base camp intact. The odds of failure were now alarmingly real, and failure meant one thing only at this point. Ciaran had made a vow to himself that if death came for him, it'd be in the harness, not in his sleeping bag.

With his foot trapped under the Lieutenant's sweater, Ciaran had nothing to do but watch the chunk of solid ice slowly liquefy in the tin pot. As he did so, he thought about the third figure he'd seen marching alongside them earlier that day. Was it an arctic mirage? Fata Morganas were common in the polar regions where large sheets of ice have uniformly low temperatures. But Fata Morganas are seen out on a far horizon, not strolling along beside you. Could it be that he was slipping? Men on polar excursions had been known to be driven mad by the long polar night. Milton Janey, one of the lower deck hands, had gone barmy back at base camp during the polar night that preceded the polar party's journey south and had to be sent home on the relief ship. But it was still summer now, and autumn's first nightfall was nearly a month away, so polar madness couldn't explain this third presence. Ciaran thought of Hanes. Hanes had gone a bit soft in the head the last day or two before he'd taken that long walk off into the icy embrace of eternity. Madness was one of the hallmarks of the end stages of scurvy. Ciaran glanced at the burn on the back of his hand that he'd gotten from the primus a week earlier. It had not yet begun to heal—a sure sign of scurvy. Glancing at the Lieutenant again, Ciaran decided to keep the knowledge of their mysterious marching companion —this third traveler— to himself, at least for the time being.

After several minutes of silence, Lieutenant Wellesley, who came from an upper-class family and considered long gaps in conversation a failure of breeding, mused, "I feel a bit like the ancient mariner."

Ciaran grunted in response.

"You know: 'Water, water everywhere'…"

"But not a drop to drink," Ciaran finished the line for him.

"You know the poem, Creagh?"

"Aye, sir. Lord Hanes had a book of Coleridge with him that he used to let me thumb through from time to time. Only this ain't water around us everywhere. And it ain't ice neither, properly speaking. This is another form of matter, altogether."

"Yes," the Lieutenant responded thoughtfully, "quite."

New York, April 1947

Percy was still lying on his side weeping when the man approached. The man was short and trim, with gray hair on the sides of his head and the incipient bald spot on top covered by a cloth cap pulled down almost to his eyebrows. The man's brown eyes, usually bright and mirthful, had a look of concern as he bent down to examine Percy.

"Are yeh alright, lad?" he asked in a slightly watered-down Irish accent.

The sobs caught in his throat preventing speech. Percy pushed himself into a seated position and nodded. The man looked at him skeptically, and then nodded back. Waving at the pieces of model ship scattered about the sidewalk, he asked, "What happened?"

"I tripped and fell, Mr. Patrick."

"Yeh did at that," Mr. Patrick nodded sympathetically. "Let's get yeh back on yer feet." Leaning over, Mr. Patrick hoisted Percy to a standing position and then dusted him off. "No fractures? No open wounds?"

Percy shook his head.

"All right, then. I think yeh may just survive. Now let's see about that boat of yers."

A sob escaped against his will: "It can't be fixed, Mr.

Patrick."

"Sure, nothing's ever so banjaxed that it can't be fixed so long as yer willing to put in the time and effort."

Mr. Patrick removed his checkered, flannel jacket and spread it on the still-wet sidewalk. Then he began to pick up the wreckage of the ship and place it on the jacket. Percy stood there, his hands in his pockets, watching. After a moment, Mr. Patrick turned to him and asked, "Are yeh going to help or just stand there gawking?"

Percy began retrieving pieces and placing them on the jacket. When they'd recovered all of the pieces, Mr. Patrick dropped to a knee, placed his hands on Percy's shoulders, and, looking him in the eyes, asked, "Do yeh want me to tell the principal what them lads done on yeh?"

A frightened look gripped Percy's face, he quickly shook his head: "I...I fell. No one did anything to me."

"Yeh can drop the act, son. I saw the whole thing. I just couldn't get out here quick enough to stop it. So, what do yeh say? Shall I go to the principal?"

Percy vigorously shook his head, "They'll blame me."

"That's true," Mr. Patrick replied, rubbing his chin. "So, what do we do then?"

Percy meekly shrugged.

"Let me ask yeh a question, son. Did yer da ever teach yeh how to defend yerself?"

"Da?"

"Yer father."

"I never met my father. I don't even know who he was."

"What about yer mam? Did she ever teach you to fight?"

"My mother?" Percy asked. When Mr. Patrick nodded, Percy wondered, "A mother teaching a boy how to fight?"

"What's so odd about that? One of the greatest fighters I ever saw was taught to fight by his mam. Women are tough, son, a lot tougher than men. Yeh'll learn that someday."

"My mother died when I was a baby. I live with my Aunt Martha. Aunt Martha doesn't believe in fighting. She says the Christian thing to do is to turn the other cheek."

"True. But we've seen how well that worked out for Christ."

Percy stared at him, shocked. Mr. Patrick ignored it. He gently picked up the edges of his jacket and lifted it like a sack. "I've seen yeh about the schoolyard. What's yer name, son?"

"It's Percy, sir."

"Percy, eh? That's a fine name. Percival was a knight of the round table—one of only three knights to see the Holy Grail. Did yeh know that?"

"No, sir."

"It's good to know about ourselves, Percy. When we know about ourselves, the rest of the world doesn't seem so mysterious."

Percy nodded.

"Do yeh know the little shed in the back of the school grounds?"

"Yes, sir."

"That's my workshop. Why don't yeh stop by there tomorrow after classes let out and we'll see about making this ship of yers seaworthy again."

"Yes, sir," Percy replied with a hint of a smile.

"Good lad," Mr. Patrick patted him on the shoulder. "And while we're at it, maybe we can see about teaching yeh how to take care of yerself a bit, eh?"

Percy nodded. Mr. Patrick began to walk away. Glancing over his shoulder at Percy, who was still standing in the same place, he said, "Keep yer chin up, Percy." He thought about it for a moment, then added, "Except, of course, when yer fighting."

County Kerry, March 1911

The shrieks of agony pierced the still night air. Bouncing around the low hills that surrounded the little valley, they rose toward the heavens where they were met with indifference. David Patrick stood in front of the tiny cottage, light spilling out of the crack of the door behind him. Above, a thin crescent moon and an aggregation of stars beyond count shone down from a clear sky. With an extinguished pipe gripped tightly between his teeth, he tried to appear nonchalant. Each new scream shattered his portrait of placidity, causing David Patrick to squeeze the cloth cap that he'd long ago ripped from his head. He could hear Eithne's stern voice ordering their daughter to "Push, colleen."

The doula could also be heard encouraging Bridget, but in much gentler terms, "That's it, love. Almost there!"

Almost where? thought David Patrick. She'd been saying the same thing for hours and they still weren't anywhere. What he wanted more than anything was to escape to Sean Ryan's for a sup of poteen big enough to last him until this whole situation sorted itself. He didn't recall Bridget's birth being so difficult and protracted. Of course, that time he'd snuck off to the pub with his father-in-law, John Kavanagh. When they'd returned many hours later—properly bollixed—Bridget had already entered the world. Back then, Eithne was much more demure and didn't say a word about it. Of course, she didn't need to. Her mother, Catherine, had lit into David Patrick and John Kavanagh as if they were dried out fags. They were lucky to have retained any hide whatsoever after she'd finished. But it'd been worth it.

David Patrick hoped it'd all be over before Sean Ryan closed up shop for the night. He wished the father was here so he could take him for a glawsheen the way old John had taken him. But he supposed Ciaran had his hands full. According to his last letter, they were to begin their attempt for the Pole at the beginning of summer. Of course, summer down there occurred during wintertime in the north, as everything was upside down in that part of the world. Ciaran was a sound man. David Patrick had no doubt that Ciaran would make everything right when he returned. He'd marry Bridget and give a name to that wee one that was on its way. But what if he didn't make it back? Many had lost their lives already chasing after the dream of the pole. The Antarctic was ungodly hard country, not like Ireland where a bit of rain was the worst you had to worry about when it came to weather.

Eithne seemed certain that Ciaran wouldn't make it. She was so convinced, in fact, that she'd insisted they go confront old Creagh and demand that one of his other lads make this good. He had four other eligible bachelors, with only the eldest spoken for. Fortunately, David Patrick had been able to talk her out of that one. All Eithne was worried about was appearances —how this thing made *her* look. For Bridget, no one but Ciaran would do. Eithne didn't agree with David Patrick that just talking about Ciaran not coming back could jinx the lad. She claimed that was all superstition. *Superstition,* he chuckled to himself. And this from the woman who believed unreservedly in the wee folk and banshees.

It became very quiet within the cottage for a moment. David Patrick shifted nervously from foot to foot. Perhaps it was just the eye of the storm and the labor would continue all night. Gazing up at the crescent moon, he wondered again how much longer Sean Ryan would be serving. Then he heard a distinct slapping sound, followed by a piercing wail. Only it wasn't Bridget crying this time, nor was it Eithne. This was an all-new voice. He heard the doula say, "It's a beautiful, healthy baby boy!"

David Patrick let out a sigh of relief, made a hurried sign of the cross, said a quick Pater Noster and threw in a few Hail Marys for good measure. He stuffed his cap in his coat pocket and, reaching into the other pocket, retrieved his sack of tobacco and filled his pipe. Fishing a box of wooden matches out of his trouser pocket, he lit the tobacco with an unsteady touch. Raising his trembling hand to eye level so that he could study it, David Patrick arched an eyebrow and took a puff of the pipe. After holding the smoke in his lungs an extra few beats, he exhaled and watched it float up toward the starry sky. In spite of his overwhelming desire to get to Sean Ryan's before he stopped pouring, David Patrick was in no hurry to rush into the cottage. He wanted to ensure that they had time enough to clean the mess before he made his entrance. He'd only seen its aftermath once before, but he distinctly recalled childbirth being a gory business.

Once he'd finished his pipe, he tapped out the ashes and stashed it in his coat pocket. Then he pushed in the front door and stepped into the cottage. Entering the bedroom, he saw Bridget sitting up in the bed holding the wee lad. Although she looked destroyed with the effort, she positively beamed as she gazed on the child. There almost seemed to be an aura around her, like in those stained-glass depictions of the saints that David Patrick had seen in the Galway cathedral as a boy. Beside her stood Eithne, who, like Bridget, glowed. David Patrick couldn't recall the last time he'd seen his wife looking so pleased and contented. Possibly, not since Bridget's birth. The doula worked at the foot of the bed, cleaning and straightening things.

Upon seeing him, Bridget called to David Patrick in a voice worn raw with screaming, "Come see your wee grandson."

David Patrick carefully picked his way across the cottage, avoiding a large stain adjacent to the bed where the cord had been cut. When he reached the bedside, he recalled how unlike older babies that newborns appear. The wee lad's skin seemed kind of gray and filmy, his eyes were nothing but slits, and his head was conical from resting in the birth canal. But he possessed a fine, thick head of curly blond hair and a strong voice, and David Patrick was quite certain the lad was the most beautiful thing he'd ever clapped eyes on. He immediately dissolved into tears. When he was finally able to compose himself, David Patrick leaned over, gently kissed Bridget on the head, saying, "He's beautiful, Asthore. Have you thought of a name?"

"I'm going to name him Ciaran David, after his da and his gran-da," Bridget replied, beaming.

"That's a grand name," David Patrick replied, wiping the tears from the corners of his eyes. "He'll be tall and strong and brave, just like his da."

"And intelligent and kind, just like his gran-da," Bridget added.

Eithne appeared to be so delighted by the birth that it didn't even seem to upset her to be left out. "He's a lovely wee cherub," she chimed in. "So he is."

David Patrick smiled. He'd held out hopes that the birth of the child would change Eithne's attitude toward it. It was easy enough to dislike the idea of a baby because it was inconvenient or possibly embarrassing. But it was quite hard to actually dislike a baby when it was living and breathing and crying for attention right in front of you. It'd take some kind of monster to dislike an actual baby, and David Patrick was certain that his wife was no monster in spite of her other faults. Of course, they all had faults, they were only human. He had his, too. Indeed, he was about to give in to one of them.

"How are you, Asthore?" he asked Bridget.

"Knackered, but never better."

David Patrick caught the doula's attention. His eyes asked: "Is she?"

The doula smiled, nodded and continued cleaning.

"Grand, grand," David Patrick stuffed his hands in his pants pockets and glanced around. He cleared his throat and said, "You seem to have things under control here. I think I might nip off to share the blessed news with the neighbors before it's too late."

"By 'the neighbors' you wouldn't happen to mean Sean Ryan, would you?" Eithne prodded him.

"Well, he is our closest neighbor. I suppose it'd be rude to not share our good fortune with Sean and the others."

"And by 'the others' you'd be referring to whatever pótaire and meisceoir happen to be hanging about Sean Ryan's shebeen?"

David Patrick gave her a hangdog look.

"Oh, go on, then," Eithne relented. "It's not every day one gets to celebrate the birth of a grandchild. Just don't you be buying any rounds!"

David Patrick lit up: "Thanks, love! I won't!" Realizing he needed to be gone before Eithne changed her mind he threw his arm over Bridget's shoulder and said, "He's a lovely wee lad, Asthore. I couldn't be prouder!"

Then he winked at the doula and was gone before Eithne could change her mind.

*

Neither an inn nor a pub, Ryan's wasn't even a place of business from a legal perspective. Ryan's was the type of establishment that would've been classified a speakeasy during the United States' Prohibition era, but in Ireland was referred to as a shebeen. Consisting of only the converted front room of a farmhouse, Sean Ryan peddled therefrom the poteen whiskey he distilled in a shed located on the boundary separating his property from that of David Patrick. Produced in pot-still from potatoes and treacle, Ryan's poteen was clear, had an alcoholic content that usually hovered around 70%, a smell that brought tears to the eyes, and a taste that most closely resembled a low-grade petrol. And he couldn't make enough of it.

Ryan's was still open for business when David Patrick strolled in. The place was tiny, with seating for only eight people. There was a makeshift wooden bar with several low wooden stools in front of it, all of which Sean Ryan had crafted by hand himself. The liquor was kept under the bar, out of sight. There was also a small, round table with four chairs. On the front wall was a picture window that always remained curtained to thwart prying eyes. The only decoration was a poorly executed oil painting of the Blessed Virgin in a rough, wooden frame. Sean Ryan, a man in his fifties with thick, curly gray hair and furtive, brown eyes sat on a stool behind the bar. Seated before the bar were two of David Patrick's neighbors: Larry Doyle and Tim O'Reilly. Upon David Patrick's entrance, they all mumbled a half-hearted greeting.

"This round's on me, lads, I'm a gran-da!"

The offer of free alcohol perked up the crowd. Doyle, nearly twenty years younger than the other three, stood up and clapped David Patrick on the back and said, "Congratulations!"

O'Reilly, who'd attended hedge school together with David Patrick and Sean Ryan, shook David Patrick's hand and said, "Sure, that's grand news. Grand!"

Ryan produced a cowbell that he kept behind the bar for special occasions and rang it. Immediately, his wife, Sarah, screeched from the other room, "I thought I told you not to ring that accursed thing, Sean Ryan!"

Ryan shouted back over his shoulder in an equally loving tone, "Davy O'Shea just became a gran-da and that's worth giving the old bell a wee tinkle or two."

"Oh, right so," Sarah replied in a contrite tone. "Just don't go ringing it any more, then. I'm saying my devotions." As an afterthought, she shouted, "Congratulations David Patrick. Give my best to Eithne."

"I will, indeed. Thank you, Sarah" David Patrick called to the wall, grinning.

Sean Ryan pointed backwards with his thumb in the direction of his wife, rolled his eyes and shook his head. He then produced an earthenware jug of poteen from beneath the bar, placed it on the counter and said, "Me best batch. I only pour it on special occasions."

"Sure, didn't you just pour my taiscaum out of that same cruiskeen?" O'Reilly asked.

"Be still, omadhaun," Ryan snapped. "That was a different jug entirely."

"You just poured mine out of it, too" Doyle chimed in. "Don't I recognize that chip on the handle?"

"Both of yez shut yer gobs ye gassy eejits! It's a different jug I tell yez!"

"Do you see how he treats his customers?" O'Reilly asked David Patrick, feigning offense. "Sure, Grimes the taxman treats me better than that."

"That's because he doesn't have to listen to yer whinging!" Sean Ryan retorted. "With Grimes yeh pay yer bill and get out."

"I'll be honest boys-a-dear, the child birthing has put a powerful thirst on me," David Patrick inserted. "I don't care what jug Sean Ryan pours from so long as he pours it now."

Sean Ryan set out four clean glasses and began to pour. When he'd finished, they all raised their glasses. David Patrick said, "To me newborn grandson, Ciaran David, may he grow to be as intrepid as his young father and as wise as his old granda!"

"Grandchildren are gifts of God," said O'Reilly.

"A new life begun, like father, like son," added Doyle.

Ryan completed the round of toasts by saying, "Sláinte!"

With that, they all downed the contents of their glasses in one gulp.

David Patrick shuddered involuntarily at the strength of the drink and said, "That's grand poteen, Sean, me-lad. If it doesn't kill you, it's sure to liven you up. Another round, if you will."

"Speaking of fathers," O'Reilly said, lighting his pipe, "Who is the father? I didn't even know your Bridget had gotten married."

"She didn't. The father is her fiancée, Ciaran Creagh."

"Ah. Isn't that old Luke Creagh's youngest?"

"Second youngest, I think."

"When are they to be married?"

"As soon as he gets back."

"Gets back from where?" Doyle inquired.

"Are yeh serious, man?" Sean Ryan asked, nonplussed.

Doyle glanced at the others uncertainly, but then nodded.

"The bloody South Pole!"

"Stop coddin' me, will you?"

"Do yeh not read the newspapers?" Sean Ryan persisted.

"I read *The Freeman's Journal.*"

"Have yeh heard nothing of Wellesley's attempt to reach the South Pole? It was all over the papers when they set sail a few months back?"

"Would it be an English undertaking, then?

"It is."

"I wouldn't have paid any mind to that. The only thing I want to hear about from England is when they're setting sail from here." Turning to David Patrick, Doyle asked, "So is your son-in-law-to-be in the Royal Navy?"

"Aye," David Patrick nodded.

"How do you feel about that?"

"It's honest work and God knows there's none of that to be found around here. Old Creagh's wee farm is going to his eldest, Tiernach. What do you suggest he do?"

Doyle shrugged, unprepared for follow-up questions, "Dunno, he could go to America, I suppose. Or join the priesthood."

"Fair enough," David Patrick laughed, "But had he

chosen either of those paths, we wouldn't be standing here now having a drink to celebrate the birth of me grandson."

"Calm yourself, boyo," O'Reilly said to Doyle. "I know old Creagh and he has no great love for the red stomachs. But a lad's gotta make his way in life and that's a fact."

"Besides," Sean Ryan added, "if they actually make it to the Pole, that's sure to bring honor to Ireland in general, and to our wee town in particular."

Doyle looked doubtful: "If they make it."

Hell's Kitchen, July 1936

Davy Boy circled lightly to his left, patiently searching for an opening. Suddenly he stopped, took half a step forward, dipped his left shoulder and dug a vicious left hook into his opponent's liver. The opponent, a tall, lean light heavyweight, emitted an involuntary grunt followed closely by his mouthpiece. The mouthpiece spiraled to the canvas flooring of the ring and bounced to the right as the light heavyweight doubled over in pain. Davy Boy positioned himself for a follow up hook to the head when Paddy banged the bell, urgently shouting: "Time!"

The light heavyweight remained bent over, holding his side and gasping for breath. Davy Boy walked over, patted his opponent on the head, asking, "You all right?"

Without straightening up, the light heavyweight grimaced and gasped, "Just took the wind outa me."

"Good round, Joey," Davy held out his glove for the light heavyweight to touch.

Joey nodded half-heartedly and raised his right fist to touch Davy's glove while remaining doubled-over.

"My God, Tommy," Paddy whispered to the associate

trainer, "Davy's murdering the body. Joey's gonna be pissing blood. Can yeh imagine what he'd look like if he hadn't been on the piss these past three nights?"

Tommy shook his head and climbed into the ring to attend to the light heavyweight. Davy, wearing black high-top boxing shoes and tattered Kelly-green satin shorts, sauntered to the corner, appearing not the least bit winded, and remarked mater-of-factly, "That makes eight rounds, Paddy. You got anyone else for me?"

Paddy climbed onto the ring apron. He removed Davy's headgear and then his mouthpiece. He rinsed off the mouthpiece over the spit bucket with a water bottle, then held the bottle up to Davy's lips for a drink. "That's enough sparring for today. Go find Barney and get a rubdown before showering."

Davy nodded, then Paddy removed his sixteen-ounce sparring gloves, revealing hands wrapped tightly in cloth bandages. Davy stepped through the ropes, descended the three steps onto the floor and was walking toward the locker room when a gaggle of reporters burst into the gym. One of them, *The Post*'s beat reporter, Al Cerbek, spotted Davy from across the gym and shouted, "There he is!"

As a body the group quickly covered the length of the gym and trapped Davy near the speed bags. Cerbek, in a tattered gray sports coat with an equally tattered gray fedora covering his bald pate, arrived first. Stepping in front of Davy to block his path, Cerbek asked, "Any response to what Carvallo said?"

"What Carvallo said?" Davy repeated, perplexed.

"This is a closed gym!" Paddy rushed down from the ring apron and stepped between Davy and the reporters, demanding, "Who said yeh could come in here?"

"Jake called me," Cerbek replied casually, chewing on an extinguished cigar.

"He called me, too," said Stan Edelstein from *The Daily News*.

"He called all of us," a third reporter in the back of the group chimed in.

Paddy turned his head and bellowed in the direction of Scanlan's office, "Jake!"

"What'd Carvallo say?" Davy asked.

Paddy put his hand on Davy's forearm and said, "Don't pay any mind to them, Davy. Go find Barney." But Davy didn't budge, awaiting a response to his question.

"He said they're gonna carry you out of the ring on a stretcher when he gets done with you," Cerbek responded provocatively.

"JAKE!" Paddy bellowed, louder still this time.

"Whadaya mean?" Davy asked, perplexed. "I thought we cancelled that fight, Paddy."

"Cancelled the fight?" several of the reporters shouted.

Paddy glanced over his shoulder into the ring where the associate trainer was still checking on the light heavyweight. "Tommy!" Paddy shouted. "Here! Now!"

"Has the fight been cancelled?" Cerbek demanded.

Paddy ignored the small mob before him. Tommy arrived in a second and Paddy directed him to "Take Davy to Barney and see that he gets rubbed down."

Tommy nodded and grasped Davy by the elbow. Davy held his ground, demanding: "What's this all about, Pads? I thought…"

"Rubdown! NOW!" Paddy interrupted Davy, and then shoved him toward the locker room. Davy allowed himself to be dragged away without further debate. Paddy turned in the other direction and bellowed, "JAKE!" right into Jake's face as he approached from the office.

"Jesus, Paddy," Jake exclaimed, rubbing a finger in his ear, "ya nearly broke my goddam eardrum. What is it?" Seeing the reporters, Jake smiled and suddenly became ingratiating, "How's tricks, fellas? Glad ya could make it."

"So yeh did call 'em?" Paddy asked.

"Of course, I did. These boys sell tickets," Jake winked and nodded at the reporters. "And we still have tickets to sell."

"So, the fight's still on?" Cerbek asked, pen in right hand and pad of paper in the left.

"Of course, the fight's still on. Who told ya otherwise?"

"Davy was acting like the fight had been called off."

"He musta been puttin' ya on. It's that crazy mick sense of humor—nobody understands it, not even them. Rest assured, nobody called off nothing." Jake was at his smoothest. "We're fighting Carvallo on Saturday night come hell or high water. Ya can print this one, boys—Davy Boy could beat Carvallo with one arm tied behind his back. Did ya get a look at the shape he's in? He looks like a goddammed Greek god!"

While the reporters all nodded and scribbled in notebooks, Paddy grabbed Jake by the elbow and said, "Can I speak with yeh, Jake? Alone."

"It can't wait?" Jake asked, incredulous.

"No."

Jake turned to the reporters, "This is Davy Boy's trainer, Paddy Byrnes. You fellas know Paddy, right?"

Several of the reporters nodded and Edelstein said, "Paddy 'the Flame' Byrnes."

"Looks more like a flicker now," Cerbek cracked.

"Speaking of flames," Paddy walked over to Cerbek, removed the stogie from his lips, threw it to the wooden floor and ground it to mush with his right shoe, "there's no smoking in this gym."

"It wasn't even lit!" Cerbek shot back, throwing his arms in the air.

"Give us a moment, boys," Jake said, holding his index finger in the air. "Old Paddy's gonna give me a training update and then I'll give you fellas the straight scoop. No bull."

Jake led Paddy back to his office and closed the door behind him. The chipped white paint on the walls of the tiny office was covered with yellowing fight bills. Jake took a seat behind a desk that was overflowing with folders and paperwork. Sitting in his wooden, swivel chair, Jake propped his feet on the desk and demanded, "Okay, what's so goddammed important?"

"Yeh gotta get those reporters outa here and yeh gotta stop talking about the fight in front of Davy."

"What the hell are ya talkin' about, Paddy? We got a goddam champeenship fight in less than a week and I can't talk about it around him? What gives?"

Paddy placed his hands on the desk, leaned forward, and confided, "He had the dream again, Jake."

"Dream? What dream?"

"*The* dream."

Jake stared at him blankly for a moment. Then he slapped his forehead, running his hand back through his thinning hair. "*The* dream—wonderful! How many times has he had that goddammed dream, anyways?"

"Twelve and a half."

"Twelve and a *half*? How do you have half a goddammed dream?"

"He woke up in the middle of one, I think," Paddy shrugged.

Jake stood up and started pacing the room. "What'd he say?"

"He said he's not fighting."

"Not fighting?" Jake bellowed. Noticing the door to his office was ajar, Jake walked over and closed it. Then he continued in a quieter, but no less agitated tone, "You listen to me, Paddy. You tell that stupid goddam potato-eater that if he don't fight Saturday, he's never fightin' in this town again, AND he's gonna have to learn to walk again."

"What's that supposed to mean, Jake?"

"It means there's some heavy goddam-hitters interested in this fight. Guys that none of us wanna cross. This fight's gotta go off."

"Jaysus, Jake, what've yeh got yerself mixed up in?"

"I haven't got mixed up in nothing, Paddy. It's the goddam fight game. You, of all people, should understand that."

Paddy studied Jake for a moment, then replied, "Calm yerself, Jake. Davy's fighting Carvallo. He may not know it now, but he's fighting. We just gotta treat this situation delicately. Don't be talking about the fight in front of him and for God's sake don't be bringing any reporters around him."

"I got a fight to sell!"

"Not if Davy doesn't fight."

Jake rubbed his forehead, as though trying to ward off a migraine. "All right, we don't talk about it in front of him. But, I'm gonna have a couple of my boys keep an eye on him. He tried scramming before the Williams fight the last time he had that goddam dream. We nearly had to cancel it."

"Aye, that's a good idea. And Tommy or I will fetch him for his workouts and escort him home after. The fight's in six nights. If we can stay on top of this, we'll be grand."

"How's he lookin'?"

"Brilliant. Yeh'd never know he just came off a three-day bender. He sparred four lads today and I'm fairly certain he broke the ribs of two of 'em."

"Good, good," Jake put his arm around Paddy in a paternal manner. "This is the big chance for all of us, Paddy, not just Davy. This is our chance—you and me—to have a shot at the big time. Ya just missed it as a fighter, but ya got a second go as a trainer. These opportunities don't come down the pike every day. We gotta make sure we take our best swing at it."

Paddy nodded: "Aye."

Antarctica, February 1912

Although they were traveling across a sea of frozen freshwater, it may as well have been sand. If a member of the party were to pick up a chunk of ice and place it into his mouth to melt, rather than transforming the ice to water, the man would be left with an unslaked thirst and a painfully ulcerated mouth. The delicate skin on the interior of the mouth would split open from the intense cold well before body heat would begin to thaw the ice. It'd do less damage, and would quench the thirst equally, to simply fill the mouth with salt. Without the primus stove, there was no water. The role of the primus in creating water also meant that they could only drink when they were camped. They couldn't fill a canteen for the march because by the time they tried to take a drink the contents would've already transformed into a solid block of ice. So, in addition to the pains of their exertions they also suffered from dehydration during those long hours on the march. With each tortured step they took toward home base, their parched throats burned with thirst and their tongues and the walls of their mouths felt like tanned leather.

Once the primus had completely melted the ice in the tin pot, Ciaran and the Lieutenant greedily gulped the water down and were able once again to speak in their normal voices. At that point, the Lieutenant broke out their rations. Since the loss of Owens and Hanes they'd been on full rations, something that'd been impossible when the team was still intact. Barring weather delays, Ciaran and the Lieutenant would be able to remain on full rations for the duration of their return journey. One day's rations included cocoa powder, sugar cubes, tea, biscuits and butter, as well as chocolate, cereals, and raisins from time to time. The foundation of the daily nutrition on the march was pemmican—a concentrated mixture of protein and fat that was a staple for all polar explorers at the time. The taste of the pemmican could vary greatly depending upon the ingredients used, with the flavor ranging from something resembling a fatty meatloaf on the positive end to greasy sawdust on the negative. To make it more palatable, the Lieutenant and Ciaran would break the pemmican into bite-sized pieces, add the butter and water, and then cook it as a stew over the primus stove. Sometimes they'd add the cocoa powder and sugar for the sake of variety, but not often because when they did that they were left with nothing to sweeten their after-supper tea.

When the meal had fully cooked, the Lieutenant ladled it onto their plates. Ciaran had noticed that since it'd become just the two of them the Lieutenant would always give him a slightly larger share of the food. He'd pointed it out to the Lieutenant a couple of times, but realized he'd never win that argument and eventually simply accepted the larger portion. Picking up his plate, Ciaran watched the steam waft from the hot stew to the ceiling of the tent. The smell emanating from it probably would've made him nauseous had the plate been offered to him back home. Pemmican stew didn't taste quite as bad as it smelled, but it did make him long for the relative gastronomical delights of a ship's galley. Ciaran might've expected the food on the march to taste better given the fact that they were always literally on the verge of starvation. But it didn't. While the hunger that constantly gnawed at his stomach made him happy to have anything to eat, he nonetheless couldn't help dreaming of his mam's boxty, or better still a nice mince pie. Occasionally, when the pemmican stew was particularly disgusting, Ciaran would wonder if they shouldn't just cook and eat their boots. It couldn't have tasted any worse.

After the initial pangs of hunger were sated, the Lieutenant remarked, "I feel like I know you better than I know my own brother, Creagh. Yet I know next to nothing of your personal life."

"Nothing much to know, sir," Ciaran grinned between mouthfuls of stew.

"Do you have any siblings?"

"Aye, sir, I'm the second youngest of six brothers. And yeh, sir?"

"Just the one brother. Nigel. As the elder son, he's set to take over Father's firm, that's why I went into service in the Royal Navy. What caused you to enlist?"

"I suppose it wasn't too different, sir. Me oldest brother, Tiernach, is going to inherit our da's farm. There's no work to be had in Ireland. So, it was enlist or go to America. I decided I wanted to see the world, so I enlisted."

"Mission accomplished, Creagh. You're seeing the world now. Maybe not the parts you wanted to see, however."

"Begging yer pardon, but yeh'd be wrong there, sir. This is exactly what I wanted to see. I wanted to see things that no man ever saw before, nor might ever see again."

"I'm with you there, Creagh. This is my third time on the ice, though my first time leading a mission. I can't properly explain to people back home why I love it so much. They don't understand. They just see it as a cold and desolate place."

"It's true, it is cold and desolate, sir. But there's a beauty here that can take yer breath away. Sometimes I wonder if God didn't make this place so harsh so that there'd be one place on earth that'd remain untroubled by we humans—a place that He alone could enjoy. If yeh think about it, sir, we're seeing through God's own eyes down here. We're seeing things that only God Himself sees."

"I didn't realize you were so religious, Creagh."

"I'm not, sir. At least, not in the conventional sense. It's just there's something about this place, I don't know quite how to put it into words. Some would call this place God-forsaken, but I see it as just the opposite. I see God in every inch of it."

The Lieutenant stared at Ciaran in wonder. "There's more to you than I ever imagined, Creagh."

Shoveling a spoonful of pemmican stew into his mouth, Ciaran grinned and shrugged.

"I know you're not married, but is there a girl waiting for you back home?"

"Aye, sir. Bridget's her name. The most beautiful girl in County Kerry. We're sort of engaged to be engaged. We'd be engaged proper if I could've only afforded the price of a ring."

"Well, congratulations, old man," the Lieutenant said, clapping Ciaran on the shoulder fraternally. "All the more incentive for us to get back. And with the money you'll earn from this expedition, you'll be able to buy her a fine ring."

"I've plenty of incentive, sir. But sometimes incentive ain't enough. Sometimes yeh just need luck, if yeh follow me, sir."

"I do. That's why I brought you on the polar party, Creagh. I wanted that luck of the Irish with us."

Ciaran grinned again through failing teeth and a mouthful of partially chewed pemmican stew.

"We'll be quite famous if we make it back you know, Creagh. Celebrities, I dare say."

"We may be at that, sir."

"What do you plan to do when you get back? Will you remain in the Royal Navy?"

"I suppose I'll decide that when we get home, sir. Plenty of time for that decision, yet."

"True, true. You're a good sailor and a sound fellow, and I can assure you that you'll have my support for any promotions that come around should you stay in."

"Thank yeh, sir. I guess I've been playing with this idea that I got from Owens."

"God rest his soul" the Lieutenant interjected.

Ciaran did a quick sign of the cross. "Anyway, Owens' plan was to use the money and fame he got from this mission to open a pub back in Cardiff."

"I didn't know that."

"It was all he'd talk about to anyone who'd listen. Just

to the lads on the lower deck, of course, sir. He wouldn't have troubled yerself or any of the other officers with his pipe dreams."

"I may be an officer, but I'm also a man. The same as him and the same as you, Creagh. I would've loved to hear about his pub. It would've been a raucous establishment, knowing its proprietor."

"I reckon it would've been at that, sir."

They were quiet for a moment, honoring the memory of Owens. Then the Lieutenant prodded Ciaran, "So you're thinking about opening a pub yourself now?"

"I thought I might just borrow Owens' idea since he won't be around to open his own. Just a quiet, little pub. I actually know a place, it has a big hearth. I figure I could just sit in front of a fire, summer and winter, drinking stout and getting fat."

"That sounds like a wonderful idea, Creagh. I'll be certain to visit you and buy you a pint once it's up and running."

"That'd be an honor, sir."

"No, Creagh, the honor will be all mine. It truly will."

New York, April 1947

The shed was small, the interior being only ten feet by ten feet. The profusion of items contained therein made it seem smaller still. There were all of the tools of the trade: handsaws, hammers, screwdrivers, wrenches and plyers hung from hooks on the wall above a wooden work bench that stretched the length of one side. Brooms, mops, buckets, shovels, rakes and the like were jammed against another wall. Along the wall opposite the work bench stretched a low, Army surplus cot, covered by a gray wool blanket with a lumpy pillow at the head. An old Army foot locker rested on the ground at its foot. There was a broken chair that used to belong to a teacher positioned in front of the workbench. The wall above it was lined with shelves containing various cleaning products. In the corner, past the foot locker, was a big wooden barrel filled with sawdust used for cleaning up vomit. Since the wooden shed had no windows and was illuminated only by a camping lantern hung from a rafter, it was always layered in shadows, regardless of the time of day or the weather.

There was a knock at the thin door. Mr. Patrick rose from the workbench and opened it. Sunshine along with the shouts and laughter of children leaving school for the day streamed in. Percy stood on the threshold, peeking into the shed uncertainly.

"Yeh made it," Mr. Patrick said with a smile. Stepping back to allow Percy to enter, Mr. Patrick waved him in, saying, "Come in, come in."

Percy had to squint when he stepped inside and glanced around. Noticing the cot along the wall to his left, he asked, "Do you live here?"

"No, no, I just keep the bunk for the nights I have to work past when the trains stop running."

Percy nodded warily: "I can only stay for half an hour. Aunt Martha is expecting me."

"Of course. Wouldn't want to keep Aunt Martha waiting. We won't finish in half an hour, but we can get started." He pointed to the work bench. The pieces of the ship were spread out on one half of it. "There she is."

Percy looked at it glumly, "I forgot how bad it was. Where do we even start?"

"I'd say we'll have to approach it the way a shipbuilder would. We start with the big parts first and save the smaller details for last. I found some pine that might work for the hull," he pointed to some short boards stacked on the other end of the work bench. "Of course, it'll have to be sawed and sanded into shape. That'll take some time, but if you want to do it, we can do it."

"I want to do it."

They set to work. The hull had remained mostly intact, but there was a big crack along the bottom ridge and a chunk was missing from the stern. The crack was simple: they glued it back together and placed the ship in a vice to ensure a tight seal. The jagged hole in the stern was another matter. Using a jigsaw, Mr. Patrick began to cut out a neat square around the rent. Percy gasped, "What're you doing?"

"That hole's too ragged. I'm just cleaning it up so we can fit a replacement piece in there nice and snug."

A gleam of understanding entered Percy's eyes as he nodded. Using a tape measure, Mr. Patrick took the dimensions of the now-square hole in the stern. Nodding at the collection of boards stacked on the end of the bench, he said to Percy, "Pick us a good one."

Percy moved to the end of the bench and began to examine the candidates. Serious as a judge, Percy picked up and eyed every piece of wood in the pile. After going back and comparing several, he chose the board that he thought best matched the grain of the stern. Walking back to Mr. Patrick, Percy extended his selection. Accepting it, Mr. Patrick eyed it discriminatingly, then remarked, "Good choice."

Placing the board in a vice, Mr. Patrick proceeded to saw out a piece to fill the hole in the stern. When he finished, Mr. Patrick handed the small square of pine to Percy and asked him to, "See if it fits."

Percy took the square and gingerly slipped it into the hole in the stern. It fit so snugly that Percy thought they should just leave it where it was. But Mr. Patrick tapped it out so that they could sand and shape it.

*

They'd been working in silence for nearly twenty minutes when Mr. Patrick asked, "So, why'd them lads go after yeh yesterday?"

Percy shrugged, uncomfortable with the line of questioning.

Mr. Patrick persisted, "Did yeh say something to them?"

"No, they're just bullies. Well, Marty is anyway. The others are his stooges—they do whatever he says."

"Has this Marty character picked on yeh before?"

"Sure, lots of times."

"Did yeh tell yer auntie about it?"

Percy nodded.

"What'd she say to do?"

"She told me to tell them to leave me alone."

"Did yeh?"

"Yes."

"What happened?"

"Marty beat me up."

"Of course, he did."

"Why?"

"The second yeh told 'em to leave yeh alone, they knew yeh wasn't going to fight back. They only want to pick on yeh if they're sure yeh won't fight back. If yeh fight back, even if yeh lose, they'll move on to the next victim. Do yeh know why?"

"Because they'll respect me for standing up for myself?"

Mr. Patrick burst out laughing, "Do yeh honestly think a bunch of dung-brained little gobshites like that crew is capable of a sentiment as high-minded as respect? Feck no—excuse me language, I get carried away when I talk about these things—they'll move on 'cause yeh hurt 'em, even if it's just a wee bit. They'd rather pick on someone who's not a threat to hurt 'em at all. So, they'll find someone weaker still."

"Standing up to them won't stop them from being bullies, it'll just move them on to another kid?"

"Yeh can't change human nature with one beating, Percy. But at least the next unlucky lad won't be yeh."

"But I don't want that. I don't want them bullying anyone."

Mr. Patrick paused from working on the boat for a moment, sat back and studied Percy, "Yeh got a good heart, Percy—just like yer namesake, Percival. Percival wasn't the strongest or most confident of the knights of the roundtable. He wasn't a Lancelot or a Galahad. But he was the bravest, do yeh know why?"

"Uh-uh," Percy shook his head.

"Lancelot and Galahad never experienced fear because they always knew they'd win no matter what. But Percival, even though he was frightened, he stood up and fought for what he believed was right. He fought his hardest even though he didn't always win." Mr. Patrick paused and rubbed his chin. "This bully of yers, there is a way to stop him altogether from being a bully."

"What is it?"

"Yeh gotta give him such a licking that he won't ever wanna fight again. Do yeh think yeh could do that?"

"What about his friends?"

"Don't worry about them other poguemahones. When they see yeh destroy their leader they won't want any parts of yeh. It's pack instinct. When the leader goes down, the pack runs—yeh can rely on it."

Percy nodded thoughtfully.

After a few moments, Mr. Patrick followed up, "Do yeh think yeh can do it?"

"No, I don't. I'm scared." He paused for a moment, then added, "But I don't want him picking on me anymore, and I don't want him picking on anyone else, either."

Mr. Patrick patted Percy on the shoulder: "Yer a sound lad. Just like Percival."

County Kerry, May 1911

Bridget rocked the cradle and hummed a lullaby while her mother prepared supper. Smells of kale and potatoes boiling and onions being chopped suffused the little cottage. The tiny home seemed even snugger now that there were four bodies occupying it, even if one of them weighed less than a stone. The door swung open and David Patrick strolled in, his lips forming an announcement. But he was cut off before he could begin by both Bridget and Eithne urgently placing their index fingers to their lips. Glancing at the baby sleeping in the cradle, he nodded.

Pulling the cloth cap from his head, he shoved it into his coat pocket and walked over to Eithne, who was seated at the head of the table cutting an onion. Leaning over, David Patrick said in a voice just above a whisper, "I'm just after talking with

Sean Ryan..."

Eithne interrupted him by waving her hand violently in front of her face, as though brushing away something offensive, and replied, "I can smell that."

"Come on, woman," David Patrick pulled back, a wounded look on his face, "I've something serious to discuss with you."

"Are you saying you haven't taken any drink?"

"No," he rubbed his chin thoughtfully, "I'm not saying that. We may have partaken of a smahan while we discussed this, but it's nothing to do with what I want to tell you."

Eithne stopped chopping the onion momentarily and turned to face David Patrick, "All right, you've got my attention. What grand issue was brought before Parliament today?"

"Sean Ryan told me that in the fall, after we bring in our crops, he's going to help me drain that acre of bogland in the corner of our lot that runs down to the creek."

"You'll do no such thing," Eithne stated flatly.

"But why not?" David Patrick raised his voice a little too much, causing both Eithne and Bridget to glare at him. Lowering his tone to just above a whisper, he asserted, "The only use we're getting of that property right now is the occasional brick of turf for the fire. Sean Ryan said it'd be good land for spuds if we could just drain that standing water into the creek."

"You know why you can't drain that bog, so you do, David Patrick O'Shea."

"Is it the wee folk?"

"The Good People have a rath in it, as well you know. If

you were to dig up that rath it wouldn't go well for yourself nor for Sean Ryan, neither."

"You can't expect me to leave a chunk of land as large as that unused."

"You've left it unused this long."

Nodding toward the baby, David Patrick replied, "That's because we didn't have a need for the extra income that it might produce."

"If it's money for raising that wee one that's needed," Eithne remarked, not bothering to muffle her voice, "then herself can get off of her high horse and go find someone to marry her."

"Hush, now. No sense in upsetting the girl, she's enough to worry about with the wee one. Besides, she has a man. Ciaran will make that right when he returns."

Eithne went back to chopping the onion. "Well, if old Creagh's boy is going to make it right, then we've nothing to worry about. Why talk about draining bogs?"

"Because we don't know when he'll be back to do that and it's now that we're in need of money."

Eithne stopped chopping again and turned to look David Patrick in the eye, "You'll leave it alone if you know what's best for you."

"Simply because you think there may be fairies living on it?"

"There *are* fairies living on it."

"Have you ever seen them?"

"Not here, no. But when we were lasses, Aideen and meself saw one near the foot of Beenoskee on holiday in Dingle."

"And what did this magical fellow look like?"

"He was a fine man, so he was. Beautiful, only wee."

"Are you sure it wasn't some class of dwarf that you saw?"

"No, this lad couldn't have been more than six inches tall. He was leaning against a dandelion sleeping when we came upon him."

"And Aideen saw this tiny fellow as well?"

"She was the one who first spotted him and pointed him out to me."

"Both batty as loons," David Patrick muttered to himself.

"What was that?"

"I said: did either of you have a word with the wee archduke?"

Eithne studied David Patrick for a moment, but decided to let it go. "No, when he realized he was after being seen, he vanished entirely, so he did."

"So how can you be sure you saw him?"

"My eyes don't need my ears to confirm what they already know. And your derision, David Patrick O'Shea, is not going to convince me that I didn't see that which I know I did."

"Fair enough, but have you ever seen any on our property?"

"No, but they're there. Mauve Rourke said there's a fairy road that leads right into that bog, and Agnes Ahearn said she saw a troop of them marching along it on a full moon one night, so she did."

"Is it on the testimony of the two biggest blatherskites in County Kerry that I'm not permitted to make use of me own field?"

"Watch your language, David Patrick O'Shea." Eithne paused to glare at him, and then continued, "Just keep in mind it may be your field, but it's theirs, too. And it was theirs first. The Good People don't take kindly to their places being interfered with. Do you remember John O'Day? All he did was cross one of their roads—he simply walked over it—and they took him, so they did. And him only thirty-nine years of age."

"Daft woman, what're you on about? John O'Day choked to death on a chicken bone! Everyone knows that."

"Aye, the day after he trod over one of their roads."

"How is this country ever going to join the modern world if we go on believing in banshees and Leprechauns and fairies and the like?"

"No one said anything about Leprechauns."

"And what does Father McGuire have to say about your belief in the wee folk? It's paganism, it is."

"God created the Good People, just as He created you and me," Eithne replied, unflappable. "Fallen angels they are."

"Heaven must be a cramped place altogether if the entire heavenly host stand no more than half a foot tall."

"Blasphemer!"

"There's no point in arguing with you. You're not constrained by the rules of logic and reason."

"Logic and reason can't constrain everything at work in this world," Eithne retorted flatly. Then she went back to work, chopping the onion.

David Patrick shook his head, walked to other side of the table and took a seat next to Bridget. Leaning over, he whispered, "Any word from himself at all?"

"A letter arrived in the post today."

"Don't leave me in suspense. Have they made the Pole yet?"

"They hadn't left for it yet when he sent the letter."

"Hadn't left yet? It's been...what?" David Patrick leaned back and thought for a moment. "Let's see, little Ciaran is almost two months old, and his da left nine months before that. It's been eleven months already."

"Aye, but it took them a little over six months just to sail down there. They didn't arrive until January and there wasn't enough summer left to make a run for the Pole then, and it's far too cold to be trying it during the winter months."

"If you were to ask me, I'd say it's far too cold there during the summer, as well."

"I agree, but there you have it. They have to wait until the start of the next summer down there. They'll begin their attempt in November."

"Six more months before they even leave? Did he say at all what they'll be doing to pass the time?"

"They spent the last couple months of the summer past transporting supplies to depots they set up along the route."

"Transporting? How?"

"They used ponies to drag some of it, but it sounds like they dragged most of it themselves."

"That sounds awful. When can we expect them back from the Pole?"

"They won't return to their home base until February, or possibly March if things go poorly."

"Next year?"

Bridget nodded: "If their relief ship can get out I'd say we'll find out what's become of them when the rest of the world does after it makes the papers. But if their relief ship can't get in or out, it could be an additional year before we have any word at all."

"1913?"

Bridget nodded again.

"Did you write himself about his responsibilities as I asked?" Eithne broke in, nodding toward the baby.

"I did, Mam. But he won't get that letter until the relief ship returns in November. Hopefully, the ship gets there before the polar party embarks."

"And what if they don't come back?"

Bridget looked stricken. David Patrick walked over to Bridget and put his hands on her shoulders. "There's no need for talk like that, Eithne. Ciaran's coming back, of that you can be sure."

"Am I the only one who sees that we need to be practical about this matter?" Eithne complained. "There's a chance he won't make it back, so there is. A pretty fair chance if you were to ask me. What becomes of our daughter and the wee one if he doesn't? I'll wager there exist no survivor benefits for fiancées and illegitimate children."

Bridget looked away, not wanting to give Eithne the satisfaction of seeing just how successful her comment had been. David Patrick rubbed Bridget's shoulders. "We're not talking about that, Eithne," he said in a quiet, firm voice. "But I will say this, no matter what happens, our Asthore and her wee lad will always have a place in our home so long as I'm alive. Now let's have no more talk of this. Can't you see it's upsetting herself?"

"She's not the only one who's upset in this wee house, David Patrick O'Shea. I'm tired of seeing Mauve Rourke and Agnes Ahearn whispering every time I pass."

"Pay that gaggle of cailleachs no mind, Eithne," David Patrick responded. "They're probably just whispering about the wee folk they're after seeing traipsing about me bog."

"True for you," Eithne responded with a glare at David Patrick, "but I can't simply ignore what Father McGuire has to say on the matter."

"And what would Father McGuire have to say on the matter at all?"

"He said a child should have a mother and a father."

"And so he does. Only the father is off discovering the South Pole at the moment. When he returns little Ciaran David will have a mother and father to love and raise him. Father McGuire should already know as much."

"God doesn't like things that don't appear proper."

"He doesn't seem to like much of anything altogether. That is, if I were to believe everything yourself tells me."

"Blasphemer!"

Antarctica, February 1912

Locating the supply depot was very much like trying to find the proverbial needle in a haystack. Buried under an enormous cairn of snow, the depot was marked by only a small, red pennant which fluttered atop a fifteen-foot flagpole that'd been sunk into the cairn. There were no natural landmarks that could lead the returning parties to it—it was one tiny red triangle awash in a vast sea of gently undulating white. In an effort to mark their path, they'd dropped empty tin cans along the outward march like Hansel and Gretel scattering bread crumbs. However, all of those markers had been buried by the snowstorms that'd passed through the area during the two months that'd intervened.

They'd faced the exact same obstacles in locating the other depots but had nevertheless found them all. More troubling than the challenge in locating the depot was the rapidly deteriorating physical condition of both the Lieutenant and Ciaran. With more than two hundred miles of hard country remaining between them and home base, Ciaran couldn't help but notice that the Lieutenant had weakened visibly since commencing their return journey a month earlier. On this day, in particular, Ciaran had become aware of having to shoulder more of the burden of hauling the sledge. At times, it'd felt like he was the only one pulling. Ciaran's hope was that the Lieutenant's lack of vigor was mainly attributable to hunger, and that the stores at the depot would restore him. Deep down he knew better.

*

He'd witnessed the Lieutenant pulling out one of his own molars the night before. The Lieutenant had waited until it appeared Ciaran was sleeping. But they didn't sleep any more, not really. It was too cold and too uncomfortable, and they each had too many aches and pains to get the rest they so desperately needed. As a result, throughout the night, they'd alternate between fitful slumber and tortured consciousness. Ciaran had been dreaming of the third that he'd seen shadowing their steps. During his waking hours, Ciaran had interpreted the third traveler as a benign, even comforting, presence. In the dream it wasn't. Even in the dream Ciaran was unable to obtain a straight-on view of the spectral third member of their party. Yet he somehow sensed that in this dream the third traveler represented death. Within the folds of its black, flowing cloak (it was coal black instead of brown in his dream), it carried both Hanes and Owens. Now it was stalking Ciaran and the Lieutenant. Dogging their every step, it watched and waited like a vulture. As this deathly dream-third drew closer, Ciaran thought that he could hear it calling out to them in a hollow, raspy voice. Its tone was oddly soothing, yet the sound of it made the hairs on the back of Ciaran's neck stand up. It murmured, "Take comfort. There's no need to struggle any more. You're already dead."

Ciaran had awoken with a start. In spite of the fact that the temperature within the tent hovered just over the freezing point, the inside of his sleeping bag was drenched with sweat. Could the dream have been true? He couldn't help but wonder. Was it possible that they'd already died and now their spirits were fighting their way through some class of purgatory, just like the Christian Brothers had told him about back in grade school? Had the Lieutenant and himself left their frozen bodies somewhere behind them, strewn on the ice of the Polar Plateau? Or, perhaps they'd all plunged into that crevasse along with Owens, bringing the entire party's story to a full stop.

Ciaran's eyes snapped open in time to see the Lieutenant reach into the back of his mouth and pluck out a tooth. There'd been no need of a dentist's pliers in extracting this molar, nor did the extraction require any visible strain. The Lieutenant may as well have been retrieving an egg from a basket. Holding the freshly plucked tooth up to the light from the midnight sun that penetrated the two layers of tenting, the Lieutenant studied it as though he were a jeweler examining a diamond for defects. When the Lieutenant glanced his way, Ciaran clapped his eyes shut and feigned sleep. Seeing the Lieutenant remove his tooth should've been horrifying to Ciaran on some level. Yet, at that moment, it was oddly reassuring. After all, dead men don't pull their own teeth.

Trying to preserve the illusion of sleep, Ciaran rendered his breathing slow and rhythmic. He didn't want the

Lieutenant to know he'd spied on him during that deeply private moment any more than he wanted to discuss his dream of the third. Fortunately, the existential crisis had passed for Ciaran. He decided that the dream of the third being death was just that, and nothing more. He was reasonably convinced of it, anyway.

As he pondered the entire situation further Ciaran realized that the Lieutenant's dental issue, being real, was much more alarming than some nightmare-induced metaphysical dilemma. The loss of teeth was one of the hallmarks of the end stage of scurvy, and they both knew it. Ciaran understood that talking about it wasn't going to make it any better, so he decided to pretend it'd never happened. The only remedy for their current problems was a successful return to base camp. Or death. Either way, it wasn't worth discussing. So, Ciaran went on pretending to sleep while the Lieutenant pretended that he hadn't caught Ciaran staring, wide-eyed, at him.

*

As both men lay wide awake with eyes screwed shut, Ciaran contemplated their situation. Forced into being really truthful with himself, Ciaran realized that from a health perspective he wasn't all that much better off than the Lieutenant. Every tooth in his head was loose, as well. If the two ever made it back to civilization he could see himself ending up like the old sea dogs he'd seen in the Royal Navy whose smiles contained more gaps than teeth. Or maybe the naval dentists would decide to just pull the lot—whatever teeth might remain after this adventure—and give him a bad set of dentures. In any event, his teeth were the least of Ciaran's concerns. Worrying about his teeth in this situation was like fretting that the deck of a foundering ship hadn't been swabbed properly. Not only had the three toes on his left foot not improved, the blackness had spread to the remaining two.

The Lieutenant hadn't amputated the toes as he'd threatened. But Ciaran suspected that was because the Lieutenant no longer possessed the strength requisite to finish the job. It was just as well, the tiny amount of morphine they were carrying wouldn't have been sufficient for a job like that. Furthermore, for the remainder of the journey Ciaran would've been forced to march on an actively bleeding stump. The advancing case of scurvy from which Ciaran suffered wouldn't have allowed the wound to heal properly until they were back at the home base where he could obtain appropriate medical attention, nutrition, and rest in a bed with clean bandages.

While their physical deterioration was alarming, it was not yet irreversible for either man. Granted, if they ever made it back to civilization, they'd both move forward minus some teeth and digits—possibly fewer appendages, as well, depending on how quickly the gangrene progressed. They'd both be appreciably worse for the wear. But neither man had yet reached the point of no return if each could just press on and survive.

Of more immediate concern was the fact that it'd blizzed the preceding two days, trapping them in the tent. During the journey out, the entire party had been halted by a blizzard for nearly three days and it'd actually been a welcome respite for most of the men. They were able to rest in their sleeping bags, allowing them to recover from the strain of man-hauling and to catch up on some much-needed sleep. But on the homeward trek with supplies running slim and bodies becoming sicker and weaker by the day, any time lost to a storm could ultimately mean the difference between life and death.

*

When the weather had finally broken, Ciaran and the Lieutenant found themselves even further behind schedule with supplies running critically low. In fact, they'd burned the last of their paraffin preparing breakfast that morning.

So, while they still carried a few morsels of food, there'd be no water until they found the supply depot. Fortunately, the depot was close because without water they might be able to finish the day and perhaps push on for a bit the next day, but they wouldn't get far.

It wasn't yet midday, they'd been on the march for close to five hours and Ciaran's mouth already burned with thirst. As he struggled against the harness, fighting for every inch of icy ground, Ciaran wished that they'd taken the time to mark the depots more carefully during the outward march. However, there was nothing to be done about that now.

It was impossible to search for the depot on the march because their hot breath was constantly fogging up their goggles. So, as they began to approach the area where the Lieutenant reckoned the depot should be, they were forced to stop more and more frequently to make a visual search for the pennant marking the depot. Because the land they were traversing was basically flat on all sides, there was no higher ground that they could seek for a superior vantage point. On the positive side of the ledger, it stood to reason that the cairn should be more prominent against a flat backdrop. Most days they'd try to squeeze out an extra mile or two on the march. But on this day finding the depot was all that mattered. Once it'd been located, they'd stop for the night. If they could just locate it.

After having made six fruitless stops, Ciaran was beginning to become concerned that they may've overshot their mark. The Lieutenant stopped. Ciaran didn't notice at first because the Lieutenant had been pulling so little that day that his stopping had almost no appreciable effect on their efforts. Plus, when they were in the harness, each man, like a racehorse in blinders, was singularly focused on the ground directly in front of himself. Ciaran stopped when he heard the Lieutenant croak, just barely audible over the howling wind,

"Halt, Creagh!"

Ciaran stopped and glanced over at the Lieutenant—his face was completely invisible behind the hood, scarf and snow goggles. The Lieutenant nodded at him and added, "Let's have another look."

Ciaran unbuckled the harness. There was an immediate flood of relief to the burning, aching muscles in his shoulders, chest and arms. He paused a moment to allow the blood to rush back into these areas and for the ache to dissipate. Glancing over, Ciaran noticed that the Lieutenant was having difficulty disengaging himself from the harness. Ciaran turned and, without a word, freed the Lieutenant from his harness. Then Ciaran stepped away from the sledge, placed his hand against his brow like a sailor in the crow's nest and scanned the white monotony that stretched out endlessly before them.

Recalling that whenever they'd located the other depots earlier on their return journey, they invariably discovered that they'd shot wide of their mark to the westward, Ciaran focused his visual search eastward. He'd pick out a sector and make a visual sweep—first west to east, then he'd go over the same patch again searching south to north. When he happened to spot the red pennant, he felt the need to blink several times and then refocus in order to ensure the glare of light on the snow wasn't playing tricks on him. But there it was, sure enough, the red pennant marking the depot, fluttering valiantly about a mile to the northeast. The storms had dumped a tremendous amount of snow on the cairn, and only three or four feet of the fifteen-foot flagpole from which the pennant waved now protruded above the snow line.

They'd been off in their calculations by about half a mile to the west and another mile short. That actually wasn't bad given what they were working with. Since Antarctica was unmapped at that point—and even if it had been, there existed no landmarks to steer by on the polar plane—they were forced to navigate using dead reckoning. The effectiveness of this method was compromised by a couple of factors, however. First, their sledge meter, which was supposed to automatically record their distance traveled, had broken during their outward journey. This forced them to count paces, a far less accurate method of recording distance. Keeping track of a pace count was no easy task while also hauling a heavy sledge through thick snow in poor weather conditions. Second, compasses were useless so close to the magnetic pole. Instead, they used a theodolite for direction. Often employed by surveyors, the theodolite was a cumbersome and complicated instrument which measured angles in horizontal and vertical planes. Because of the amount of time and effort it took to set up and read the theodolite, they typically only took readings twice a day—in the morning before embarking, and when they stopped for tea in the afternoon. Steering by the theodolite alone, it was amazing that they were able to come within half a mile of their target longitudinally after ten days marching. Had they been off by an additional half a mile, they might never have located the depot.

"I see it, sir!" Ciaran shouted hoarsely. He pointed with his right hand toward the tiny, red speck that was just visible through the sun's glare off of the snow.

The Lieutenant, twenty paces to Ciaran's right searching in the other direction, turned and ran to Ciaran. Or, at least he came as close to running as his bulky finnesko boots and poor physical condition would allow. When he got to Ciaran's side, he panted, "Where?"

Ciaran pointed to the tiny red triangle fluttering in the heavy wind. When he did so, he thought how lucky they were that the flagpole had not blown over or they assuredly would've been lost. "There, sir."

The Lieutenant took a couple paces forward in the

direction Ciaran had pointed and squinted. Shaking his head, he said, "I don't see it."

Ciaran looked at him. When they'd set out, the Lieutenant had been a youthful-looking man in his early thirties. Now, after three months of trekking, he looked at least two decades older. His shoulders were stooped from the months in the harness and he appeared several inches shorter than when they'd set out. Like Ciaran, he'd lost about twenty pounds owing to a combination of strenuous labor and insufficient nutrition. The Lieutenant's face was wan and deeply lined from care and the effects of the harsh environment in which they'd survived for the past several months. Finally, he had a thick beard that was already betraying more than a few gray hairs, and the parts of his face not covered by the beard were coated in a thick layer of grime from not having bathed since they embarked on their march to the Pole several months earlier. Minus the beard, which he still wasn't able to grow, Ciaran realized that he undoubtedly looked just as dirty and haggard.

"Sure, it's there, sir," Ciaran said, considering that the Lieutenant's diminished eyesight was another sign of advanced scurvy.

"Well done, Creagh," the Lieutenant said, slapping Ciaran on the shoulder. "What do you say we go get ourselves some tea?"

Ciaran grinned and nodded. They both climbed back into the harness, which felt much lighter now.

As they were making that final trudge to the depot, Ciaran turned his head to the left and, out of the corner of his eye, caught a sideways glimpse of the other who'd been traveling with them. He still hadn't said anything to the Lieutenant about their third traveler, but secretly Ciaran was relieved to see their mysterious companion. Aside from his dream the previous night, he hadn't seen the third in nearly four days, counting the two they'd been laid up owing to the snowstorm. As usual, its cloak was brown, not the deathly black of his dream, and Ciaran now felt the presence of the third to be oddly reassuring. Perhaps rather than death, it was a guardian angel watching over them. Ciaran had been raised Catholic, but hadn't practiced that or any religion since enlisting in the Royal Navy. Still, the idea of a guardian angel was comforting and Ciaran clung to that. But his thoughts quickly shifted back to the depot and the bounty contained therein.

*

Designated the 87 Degree depot because of its latitudinal position, it was the penultimate supply dump on their journey home. The final depot, One Hundred Stone Depot (named for the combined weight of supplies contained therein), had been prepared the previous fall, after their arrival in the Antarctic. The 87 Degree depot, like all of the others with the exception of the One Hundred Stone Depot, had been laid during their journey out, a few months earlier. Back in November, sixteen souls divided into four-man teams had set out from the base camp, roughly 900 miles northeast of the Pole. At predetermined locations, the three support teams had peeled off, one-by-one, and headed back to the base camp. Ciaran and the Lieutenant knew that the other parties had all returned at least this far without loss, as they'd been left notes in each of the depots by the various return party leaders. The 87 Degree Depot consisted of a ten-man tent, sunk into the permafrost, with walls of snow built around it to protect it from the elements. Inside, stacked in neatly packed and well-organized crates, was the food needed to carry them to the One Hundred Stone Depot, which would then provide them with the supplies to finish the final leg to home base. The Lieutenant inventoried the supplies while Ciaran unloaded and secured the sledge. Each depot contained just enough supplies to get them to the next depot. It had to be this way because the supplies in the depots had all been man-hauled out, and they didn't have the manpower or equipment to carry a surplus. The Lieutenant had planned out the supply chain down to the last detail before they'd embarked from base camp. He'd included just enough supplies to give them some wiggle-room in case of inclement weather, but it's impossible to foresee every contingency that might arise on a mission like this.

There was no need to pitch a tent since they'd be sleeping inside the depot. So once he'd finished unloading the sledge Ciaran was able to start preparing the evening meal using their new supplies. After setting up the primus stove, he grabbed a bottle of paraffin and unscrewed the cap. Glancing into the bottle, Ciaran looked up and said, "This bottle's about a third empty, sir."

"I know," Lieutenant Wellesley replied, "they all are."

"Do yeh reckon the bottles have leaks?"

"It seems unlikely that they'd all leak precisely the same amount. Besides, if there were a leak, it'd all have leaked by now."

"What could it be?"

The Lieutenant shook his head and shrugged. "The corks may not have been sealed off completely, causing some of it to evaporate. But we should lose two or three percent over the course of a few months, not one third. It's beyond me, I must say."

"We'll just have to continue being careful about how much we use is all, sir."

"Yes, but we have to eat. We have to drink. We can only hope that we don't experience any more unexpected delays."

"Aye," Ciaran responded quietly. They both already knew that wasn't going to happen.

Hell's Kitchen, July 1936

Paddy and Tommy stood next to the ring, watching Davy Boy finish up with his fifth sparring partner of the day. He'd gone ten rounds. Paddy ran the clock and only about half the rounds had been the standard three minutes. As for the other five rounds, some were as short as two minutes and others were five minutes or longer. Paddy manipulated the clock in this manner in order to simulate a boxer's uneven sense of time progression during a fight. For a fighter, time was malleable owing to conditioning and the ebb and flow of a fight among other factors. This deviation from the standard three-minute round during sparring drove Davy crazy, but it wasn't his call. After years in the fight game as both a fighter and a trainer, Paddy understood implicitly that some rounds felt longer than others and that's just the way it was.

Paddy never took his eyes off of Davy, studying his every move, always searching for the little flaws that can turn fatal against a top opponent. Periodically he'd ask Tommy how much time was left in the round. Halfway through the final round, he shouted, "Yer too far outside, Davy. Get inside his jab and stay there, damn it!"

Davy didn't outwardly acknowledge the comment, but within seconds he'd slipped inside his much-taller sparring partner's reach and was working the body.

"That's it!" Paddy encouraged him.

Jake, chewing a lit cigar, ambled up behind Paddy and asked, "How's he lookin'?"

Without turning to look at him, Paddy snapped, "I thought I told yeh not to smoke them stogies of yers in the gym, Jake."

"A little smoke ain't gonna hurt nobody," Jake replied, nevertheless removing the cigar from his mouth, grinding it out against a pillar, and dropping the half-smoked butt into his jacket pocket. "Besides, they should get used to it for their fights. The Garden's gonna be smokier than Pittsburgh come Saturday night. Now answer my question."

At that moment, Davy dug a left hook into his opponent's midsection, causing the man to grimace and drop his elbows to protect his body. Davy immediately sprang up out of his crouch and unleashed a hook to the chin that caused his sparring partner to drop to the canvas like a marionette whose strings had been released.

Paddy quickly rang the bell, shouting, "Time!"

Davy placed his gloves on his hips and looked down at his opponent with concern. Paddy turned to Tommy and said, "Get the salts and make sure Bobby's okay."

Tommy nodded and reached under the stairs to the ring and pulled out a black medical bag. Removing the smelling salts, he grabbed a towel and a water bottle, and bounded up the stairs into the ring.

As Bobby tried to push himself up onto his elbows, Davy squatted down and patted him on the shoulder, advising, "Take it easy, Bob. Here comes Tommy."

Bob nodded blearily and eased his head back down onto the canvas.

Turning around to face Jake, Paddy asked, "Does that answer yer question?" Turning back to the ring, he shouted, "Get over here, Davy!"

Davy nodded, patted Bobby on the shoulder and said, "Good round." Then he stood up and climbed out of the ring. He stopped in front of Paddy, who quickly removed his sparring gloves and headgear. Paddy patted Davy on the cheek and said, "Good work, Davy. Give me five rounds on the speed bag and then see Barney for a rubdown."

Davy nodded and began to walk away.

"Davy!" Paddy called after him.

"Yeah?"

"Yeh don't leave here without seeing me first, got me?"

Davy waved him off and walked to the smallest, fastest speed bag and began to rhythmically pound on it wearing hand-wraps only.

"So's he ready to go or what?" Jake persisted once he and Paddy were alone.

In the ring behind Paddy, Tommy waved the smelling salts under Bobby's nose causing him to immediately sit up. Once he was upright, Tommy gingerly removed his headgear and gloves before helping him to his feet. Tommy then bounded through the ropes. He stopped on the ring apron and stepped on the bottom rope and pulled up the middle rope for Bobby to climb through. Then he helped Bobby, who was still wobbly, down the ring steps.

Seeing the two descend the steps, Paddy called to Tommy, "Have Barney check him out, then go keep an eye on Davy. Don't let Davy outa yer sight!"

Tommy nodded and guided Bobby toward the locker room. As they worked their way through the hive of activity in the gym, several of the fighters who'd been keeping an eye on the action in the ring, stopped to pat Bobby on the shoulder and offer him words of encouragement.

Nodding toward the shambling Bobby, Paddy asked Jake, "That doesn't answer yer question?"

Jake sneered, "That don't answer squat. That dope's lost his last five fights. Dropping some out of shape, punch-drunk, heavy bag with legs ain't the same as mixing it up with the middleweight champeen of the world."

"He sparred five different guys today. He dropped four of them. Two he dropped with body shots. He's boxing beautifully. His timing's perfect. He's not missing any openings, even the little ones. He's even moving his head, weaving and demonstrating a little defense. I wouldn't want to get in there with him."

"But you're a washed-up featherweight, not the undisputed middleweight champeen of the world. Is he ready for Carvallo?"

"As far as the boxing goes, he's as ready as he'll ever be. That little bender he went on didn't set him back one bit. But with Davy, the question is never if the body will be ready, or even the spirit, it's the head yeh gotta worry about with that lad."

"Is it that dream nonsense?"

"Aye, it's the dream."

"Does he know the fight's still on—that he's fightin' for the title Saturday night?"

"He knows, but he doesn't like to hear about it, or talk about it."

"How're ya gonna discuss strategy if ya can't talk about the fight?"

"I been talking strategy with him all along, only I been talking about it in the abstract."

"Abstract?"

"Like, for instance: 'If someone with a reach advantage

like yerself was to fight Carvallo, they'd want to keep him at the end of the jab all night. Don't let him inside to batter the body with hooks.' That sort of thing."

Jake slapped himself in the forehead, "We got a champeenship fight in four nights and we can't even talk to our fighter about it? What that boy needs is a psychiatrist."

"What he needs is a priest."

Jake shook his head, "You Irish and your goddam witch doctors."

"I'm serious, Jake. I can take him to confession. I did that a couple times before when he had the dream and it seemed to calm him down."

"What the hell are ya waitin' for? Get him to a witch doctor. Purge him of his goddam sins, bathe his eternal fuckin' soul in light, and get his goddam head straight! Why didn't ya think of this before?"

Paddy shrugged, "Davy ain't the only one preparing for his first title bout."

"Listen, Paddy, the only thing ya gotta worry about now is makin' sure your fighter shows up for the fight. I want ya or Tommy with him 24/7. Ya sleep with him, ya eat with him, ya travel with him. If he's gotta take a shit, then ya gotta get in the can with him and read him the funny papers. Got me?"

"What about all these other lads in here that need trained, Jake?"

"Don't worry about these goddam ham-and-eggers. Frankie and Maurice can train them. Or they can train themselves. I don't give two shits about the rest of these has-beens and never-will-bes. There's one fighter in this stinkin' joint that can get me my champeenship and he don't wanna fight because of a goddam dream! Ya stay on him, Paddy. Got me?"

"Don't leave him alone. Got it."

Paddy began to walk away, but Jake grabbed his shoulder and pulled him back, adding, "One more thing, Paddy."

Paddy arched his eyebrows.

Jake stepped in close to Paddy, glanced around to ensure no one was close enough to hear, then said, "Not a word of this dream nonsense to no one, got me?"

"I got yeh, Jake."

"The press would have a field day with this. Plus, the bookies would probably shut down all the action on the fight, and we wouldn't want that, would we?"

"No, we wouldn't want that, Jake."

"Bein' able to place a bet on a fight is what makes it interestin' to most fellas. What we're offerin' is entertainment, excitement. And part of what makes it entertainin' or excitin' for a lot of fight fans is bein' able to place a little wager on the outcome—have a little skin of their own in the game."

"Where are yeh going with this, Jake? Yeh wouldn't happen to have a bet down on the fight, now would yeh?"

"Me? No, of course not. But there are people who have made it known to me that they will be bettin' on the fight— powerful people that we don't wanna upset."

Paddy squared up and scrutinized Jake, "What're yeh saying, Jake? Yer not gonna come to us the night of the fight and ask Davy to take a dive or anything like that?"

"No, no, ya got me all wrong, Paddy. These people ain't tryin' to put in a fix, they just wanna ensure that as much money as possible comes in on both fighters. Nobody's takin' no dives. This is my title shot, too, ya know."

"Good, 'cause I know Davy and Davy ain't taking no dives for nobody. Even if somebody were to promise to put a bullet in him right after the fight if he didn't, he'd tell 'em 'Nuts to yeh,' and go out and fight even harder. And if this fight's gonna be rigged, yeh need to let me know right now because I'm walking if it is. I ain't gonna be a part of any of that shite."

"That's why ya didn't get a shot at the title when ya was fightin'. Ya never played ball."

"And I still won't. So, if this fight is gonna be rigged in any kinda way, yeh gotta let me know now, Jake. Cause I won't be a part of it."

"Set your mind at ease, Paddy. No one's fixing nothin'. Just don't go mentionin' that goddam dream to no one, and don't let Davy outa your sight. We need him at the Garden Saturday night ready to fight. We're gonna take that goddam title, Paddy. I can feel it in my gut. Davy's gonna be champ by the end of the night come Saturday."

County Kerry, May 1912

David Patrick called Ciaran David the "little Viking" because of his wavy blond hair, his blue eyes, and the fact that he was taller than any child his age that David Patrick had ever seen. Only fourteen months old, he was already walking and running. He was playing football in the front garden with Eithne, kicking around a makeshift ball that Eithne had sewn from old cloth scraps and filled with hay. As he approached, David Patrick couldn't help but notice Eithne's smile—a smile that'd been absent for many years prior to little Ciaran David's arrival. David Patrick picked his way down the hill through rows of tilled earth sprinkled with potato seeds. When he got within earshot, he paused to remove his pipe from his coat pocket and then stuffed the folded-up newspaper that he was carrying into the emptied pocket. From his other pocket he removed his pouch of tobacco, filled the pipe, and then returned the tobacco to its place. Finally, he removed his matches from his trouser pocket. Lighting the pipe, he took a hard pull, drawing the smoke deep into his lungs. Tossing the expended matchstick away, he returned the box of matches to his trousers. He sighed, simultaneously exhaling a long wisp of smoke, and continued down the hill toward Eithne.

At his approach, Ciaran David cut loose a kick that sailed majestically over Eithne's head coming to a rest at David Patrick's feet. Fielding the ball, he gave it a hard return kick forcing little Ciaran to run after it, laughing.

"You're finished early," Eithne commented.

"Aye," David Patrick responded, taking another pull on the pipe which was clamped tightly between his teeth. He seemed lost in thought.

"Where were you working?"

The question stirred him from his short reverie: "The new field."

"I thought I told you not to talk to me about that."

"You asked, I answered. You've nothing to worry about from that field, though. Sean Ryan and meself were all over it when we cleared it and again when I plowed it. No rath was to be found anywhere, nor did we see any wee roads."

"Of course, you didn't. Aren't I after telling you such things are hidden from the eyes of mortals?"

"If they're hidden from our eyes, how do we know they exist at all?"

"How do we know God exists?"

David Patrick looked at little Ciaran David kicking the ball around the yard and laughing. He glanced at the sun beginning to spread out a tangerine red over the mountains to the west. He looked at the wildflowers coming into bloom. Then, waving his hands around himself expansively, he responded, "There's evidence of God everywhere. But what evidence do we have of the so-called 'Good People' aside from wee lads reclining against toadstools appearing before impressionable young lasses?"

"It was a dandelion, and I'll thank you to watch your tone, David Patrick O'Shea. You can taunt me if you wish, but you'll regret making light of the Good People, so you will. Just because you haven't seen them doesn't mean they don't exist. I'll wager you haven't seen a tiger either, but you're not going to stand here and debate the existence of tigers with me."

"No, but if I haven't seen a tiger, lots of other people have."

"And there's many have seen the Good People."

"The difference is: lots of *sane* people have seen tigers. The only people to see wee folks are besotted old biddies such as your ones, Mauve Rourke and Agnes Ahearn." David Patrick paused for a moment and was about to take a puff of his pipe when he quickly added, "Present company excepted, of course."

Eithne glared at him for a moment, then said, "You're incorrigible, David Patrick O'Shea. I don't know why I bother talking to you at all."

"Listen, Eithne," David Patrick said, removing the newspaper from his coat pocket, "I've something serious to whisper to you. Is herself home?"

"No, she hasn't yet returned from the Murphys'. Why do you ask?"

David Patrick opened the newspaper. The headline on the front page read: "Wellesley's Polar Party Reported Missing

—Believed Lost." As he handed it to Eithne, he commented, "Sean Ryan brought that out to me in the field. It's today's paper."

"Was our Bridget's Ciaran part of that polar party?"

"That's what the article says. It was him, Wellesley, and two other lads on the final party that traveled to the Pole that was lost."

"Is it possible that they might find them?"

"I suppose it's possible. Most of the group that originally sailed down there is staying at their base camp for another winter so they can go look for them in the spring. But if they don't turn up before then, there's not much hope they'll find them alive."

"World without end," Eithne put her hand to her head. "What're we going to do about that wee lad?"

"We'll take care of him and raise him like he was our own—which he is."

"A lad needs a da, and herself needs a man, so she does. Minus a husband, that wee one is just a…"

"Don't say it," David Patrick intoned sternly.

"I say we go to old Creagh right now and demand one of his other lads marry our Bridget to make this right. We should've done it from the start."

"We'll do no such thing—you know his position. He said he wouldn't acknowledge Ciaran David as any kin to him until it came from Ciaran's lips. Now it looks like that might never happen."

"I knew those foolish men were doomed from the start. Who goes traipsing off to the South Pole, I ask you?"

"Now let's not get into all that. I admired the lad for it.

It takes a lot of courage to march off into the unknown with only what you can carry to sustain you."

"Mad is what I call it. What kind of man goes off on a dangerous adventure like that when he's got a girl and a wee one back home to look after?"

"He didn't know about the wee one. We can't fault him for that."

"If you leaven the dough and place it in an oven, you shouldn't be surprised when a loaf of bread emerges."

"That kind of talk is of little use now. Besides, if memory serves, she's not the only one to have leavened the dough before seeing a priest."

"How dare you!" Eithne became incensed. "I told you not to talk of that again. Besides, this is all your fault."

"How do you reckon that?"

"I told you no good could come of digging up that bog! The Good People don't suffer mortals to tinker with what's theirs."

"Are you saying the wee folk, enraged at me for digging up their rath, traveled all the way to the South Pole to exact punishment when I'm out working in that field every day?"

"Their reach is long."

"It'd need to be so since their bodies are no taller than me hand."

"Whisst, you. Don't make things worse. Just be thankful it wasn't you they settled their vengeance on."

"You can't seriously believe…"

Eithne interrupted him, "Whisst! Here comes herself."

At that moment, Bridget pushed open the little gate that

led into their front garden.

"What'll you say to her?" Eithne whispered.

David Patrick shrugged: "The truth. She'll learn it soon enough. She may as well learn it from them that love her best."

Seeing Bridget, little Ciaran David forgot about the ball and made a teetering beeline for her—each step of his mad dash being in direct defiance of gravity. Bridget let the bag she was carrying over her shoulder slip to the ground, then she dropped to one knee and caught him as he arrived. Wrapping the boy in her arms, she kissed the top of his head and said, "How's my little man?"

"Mammy!" he giggled with delight.

After several moments, still hugging Ciaran David tightly, Bridget looked up at David Patrick and Eithne. Eithne avoided her glance and David Patrick failed miserably at smiling. Bridget's face clouded over: "What's wrong with the two of you? You act as if someone…"

She checked herself in mid-sentence. Standing, she locked eyes with David Patrick who was forced to squint and look away owing to the rays of the setting sun shining over Bridget's shoulder. She pleaded, "Da?"

"I'm sorry, Asthore." David Patrick opened the paper for Bridget to see.

She took a few steps forward to better read the headline. Then she paused for a moment, as if trying to get her bearings. In a voice just above a whisper she said, "But he didn't know if he'd be included in the final polar party…" She trailed off.

"He was," David Patrick replied gently.

"But all it says is the party is lost. Maybe they'll find them. Maybe he's all right."

David Patrick smiled weakly and nodded. From over his shoulder, Eithne interjected, "I wouldn't get my hopes up, colleen. It's well time to be thinking of the future, so it is."

"Future?" Bridget uttered absently, looking right through Eithne. She stared over the creek that bounded their little farm, past Cnoc na Piseog, beyond the narrow confines of the island on which she was born. Not stopping there, her gaze sailed over oceans, crossed the equator, and swept down snow-covered mountains and plains that no human eye had yet glimpsed. They searched a desert made of frost for one frail body, drowning in a sea of ice. "Future?" she repeated. "There's no future without Ciaran."

She turned away from David Patrick and Eithne. Facing the setting sun, its rays pierced her eyes creating a kaleidoscope of red and orange. The earth suddenly seemed less stable. Her heart separated from her body and flew to a land where the blood pumping through it would freeze solid in a matter of minutes. Her head felt lighter than air and somehow disconnected from her body. *Polar Party Reported Missing.* They were just words and words cannot hurt. They were nothing more than sounds whose meaning had been agreed upon thus granting them signification. But who agreed upon them? In reality, they were nothing more than sounds—arbitrary, meaningless sounds. How could mere sounds end a world?

Polar Party Reported Missing. Everything began to spin. The next thing Bridget knew she was on the ground in a heap. Ciaran David threw his tiny body over hers and was crying over and over, "Mammy! Mammy!"

Then the darkness closed around her like a warm blanket. She welcomed the darkness. She yearned for the void. *Polar Party Reported Missing.* They were just words. Meaningless sounds. Yet they were meaningless sounds that contained the power to tear apart a world like the wrath of

God.

New York, April 1947

The makeshift heavy bag was really nothing more than an old Army duffle bag, stuffed with sawdust. Suspended by a short chain from a beam that ran the length of the ceiling in the old shed, the bottom of the bag came to Percy's waist when he faced it. Mr. Patrick had removed the loose buckles and taped over all of the zippers in order to protect Percy's hands. To give the bag some space to swing, he'd cleared the floor in the front half of the shed.

"Are yeh lefty or righty?" Mr. Patrick squatted down so he was face-to-face with Percy. Percy looked back at him blankly, so he added, "What hand do yeh write and eat with?"

"Right," Percy replied, holding it up.

"Orthodox" Mr. Patrick commented. Percy responded with another blank stare, so Mr. Patrick explained, "That's what they call right-handed fighters—orthodox. Lefties are called southpaws. Southpaws are more awkward and have a lot more hitches in their style, so righties are easier to train."

Percy nodded, not really having understood any of what Mr. Patrick had said.

"Okay, first things first, let's see yeh make a fist."

Percy half-heartedly balled his right hand into a fist, only he'd tucked his thumb inside the fingers. "That's the way to break yer thumb," Mr. Patrick said. He squatted down and unpeeled the fingers and repositioned the thumb, explaining, "The thumb goes on the outside, resting against the index and middle fingers, like this. When yeh go to hit someone, make sure to squeeze your hand shut as tight as yeh can. Otherwise, yer liable to injure yer hand."

Percy nodded.

"Let's see it."

Percy balled his right hand into a proper fist.

"That's the stuff," Mr. Patrick said, patting Percy's fist.

Straightening up, Mr. Patrick turned and grabbed some worn bag gloves off of the work bench. He handed them to Percy. "Put these on."

Percy pulled on the gloves. They swallowed his little fists and extended nearly to his elbows. "A bit on the large side, I suppose," Mr. Patrick mused, "but they'll have to do. We gotta protect those hands."

Percy nodded again, clearly unsure of what was happening.

"Now let's get yeh situated. Yeh want to stand left foot forward with your left shoulder facing the bag. Yeh never square up to yer opponent, yeh always wanna give him as small a target as possible."

Mr. Patrick turned Percy around until he was in a proper boxing stance, more or less. Then he continued, "Don't stand flatfooted," nodding to Percy's feet. "Yeh want to be on the balls of yer feet so yeh can move easier, but at the same time yeh don't want to stand up too high and offer too easy of a target. So yeh keep yer knees bent and sort of crouch down." He demonstrated, then walked behind Percy and pushed him into position.

"Okay, the last thing is: yeh want to keep yer hands up so yeh can block any punches yer opponent might throw. Hold the left nice and high, maybe six inches in front of yer face." Mr. Patrick grabbed Percy's left hand and moved it into place. "The right hand yeh position alongside yer face, almost touching the jaw."

Mr. Patrick stepped back and looked at Percy, who was doing his best to maintain the stance. "Grand, grand," Mr. Patrick said encouragingly. "Now that yeh know how to stand, I'm gonna teach yeh how to punch. There's really only four different kinds of punches. For an orthodox fighter like yerself, that's the left jab, right cross, left hook, and uppercut. We're not gonna worry about the uppercut for now, that's a tricky one to learn and a wee bit too advanced for our purposes. The other three are all yeh'll really need in a street fight, anyway, so we'll focus on them."

"The first punch is the jab. What yeh do is step forward with yer left foot, and at the same time push yer left fist straight out as far as it'll go, turning it over from sideways to flat when you reach your target."

Mr. Patrick snapped several jabs into the bag. Then he stepped back and said, "Yer turn."

Percy practiced throwing jabs for several minutes with Mr. Patrick observing him closely, stopping to correct or encourage him from time to time. "That needs a little work," Mr. Patrick said, "but let's move on to the straight right. This is a power punch so it's the one yeh really want to learn. In a boxing match, everything builds off of the jab. The jab is what a boxer uses to get inside his opponent's defenses, and it'll score points with the judges. But there's no judges in a street fight. Yeh either win or yeh catch a beating, so yeh wanna lead with yer best punch in a street fight. Usually with righties that's the right hand."

As he spoke, he demonstrated the motions of the punch. "First of all, yeh need a solid base because all of the power with a right comes from yer legs. If yeh just throw arm punches at him, there'll be nothing behind 'em and it won't hurt him. Yeh start by driving off of yer right foot." He squatted down and demonstrated the thrust that the back leg provided. "Then the power moves up yer body. Yeh pivot at the waist, start driving the punch with yer back muscle, let it shift to yer right shoulder, then drive it straight at yer opponent, turning the fist over about halfway through."

Mr. Patrick hammered several powerful rights into the makeshift bag, causing sawdust to fly up out of the top of the duffle bag.

Waving the sawdust that was floating down away from his face, Percy asked, "Did you ever box, Mr. Patrick?"

"A long time ago," Mr. Patrick responded, wiping perspiration from his forehead with his sleeve.

"Were you any good?"

"Well, that's not a fair question to ask me. I'd say yeh should probably ask someone who saw me fight if I was any good, but I don't know if yeh could find any at this point. So, I guess I'll just have to say that I could take care of meself. Now quit stalling and get back to work. Let's see some rights."

Percy threw some half-hearted punches that bounced harmlessly off of the bag. After watching him repeat this half a dozen times, Mr. Patrick stopped him. "Listen, Percy," he said, "we ain't playing patty-cakes here. Yeh gotta throw the punch with bad intentions. Yeh gotta throw it like yer angry at someone."

"But I'm not angry at anyone," Percy pleaded.

"No?" Mr. Patrick replied. "Let me show yeh something." He steered Percy over to the work bench. Percy's model yacht was there, still mostly in pieces, though they'd made some headway with their repairs. "That don't make yeh angry?"

Percy didn't respond, he merely looked at the ground, seeming embarrassed.

"What's the matter, lad?"

"Aunt Martha says people should never fight, no matter what. She said only animals fight. People should be able to resolve their problems without resorting to violence."

Mr. Patrick smiled, "Well, in a perfect world that'd be true. Unfortunately, we don't live in a world like that. There's bullies out there, and all classes of bad people. Walking away may seem like the noble thing to do, but it's pretty hard to walk away when someone's foot is planted on yer neck. Sometimes yeh gotta be brave and say, *I'm gonna stand up for meself, come what may.* Just like yer namesake, Percival."

"But I'm not brave like that. I'm afraid."

"There's no bravery without fear. The most courageous fighter I ever knew used to be terrified to step in the ring."

"But how can you be scared and brave at the same time?"

"If yer not just a wee bit scared then yer just foolhardy or crazy or some kinda eejit. Bravery means yer scared but yeh do what needs to be done anyhow, in spite of the fear."

"But how do you do that? When I get scared, I can't do anything. Sometimes I can't even think."

"That's natural, Percy. Fear is..." he paused to think for a moment, then continued, "it's like a great frost that traps us within it. If we let the fear get the better of us, then it freezes us and we're useless. We can't act because the fear has turned us to ice. But if we look within ourselves, there's a fire burning deep inside that can thaw that ice. This fire is in all of us and has been since whatever begot us crawled out of the primordial ooze. Everything courageous that's ever been done in the history of mankind is in all of us. We just need to find the spark to release it."

"But what's the spark? Where do I find it?"

Mr. Patrick tapped on Percy's heart, saying, "It's in there, lad. Yeh just gotta let it out. Now take another look at the wreckage that was yer ship and let me see yeh throw that right hand again."

Percy glanced over at the pieces of his model yacht spread out across the work bench. A subtle change came over his face. It shifted almost imperceptibly from resignation to anger. He turned back to the bag and glared at it. Assuming his stance, he dug in his rear foot and let loose with a straight right that shook the bag.

"There yeh go!" Mr. Patrick cried, clapping his hands, "Do it again!"

Percy repeated the punch, harder than the previous time.

"That's it!" Mr. Patrick encouraged him, "Again! Again!"

Percy began unloading rights on the makeshift bag that had it dancing on its chain. Mr. Patrick studied Percy's face as he did so. After a few moments, he arched his eyebrow and studied Percy's features more closely. Percy, meanwhile, had begun to add lefts and was wailing on the bag with both hands, a look of fierce determination gripping his face.

Antarctica, February 1912

Ciaran and Lieutenant Wellesley had traveled for three days since leaving the 87 Degree Depot. The first day out the weather was clear with almost no wind and they made good time. The extra rations they'd consumed the night before seemed to have restored the Lieutenant and he was once again pulling his weight in the harness. But by the second day he'd started to slip. He was still pulling, but Ciaran could feel that it wasn't as much. He'd lost even more strength by the third day, and that night another storm blew through. This was the worst storm they'd seen yet: seventy-mile-per-hour winds and driving snow added to frigid conditions that were becoming colder by the day. Winter was approaching and they were still, according to Lieutenant Wellesley's calculations, roughly one hundred and sixty miles from home base. That would be about thirteen days of marching assuming favorable weather conditions and a team that was at full strength, both in terms of manpower and physical health. Neither of those conditions obtained.

At the same time, they didn't have to necessarily make it the full way back to base camp. Before embarking on their journey south, Lieutenant Wellesley had left instructions stipulating that if the final polar party hadn't returned to base camp by the first of March a search party, including a dog team and a physician, was to travel to One Hundred Stone Depot and await them there. March 1st was less than a week away. With only sixty miles left to travel to the One Hundred Stone Depot, if the current storm would break sometime soon, they might actually meet the relief party there. However, there were a lot of "ifs" involved in that proposition and as Ciaran and the Lieutenant had discovered, things in this region rarely worked out the way one hoped or planned.

*

It was the morning of the fourth day out of 87 Degree Depot and, trapped in their tent by the blizzard, Ciaran and the Lieutenant had just finished their breakfast. While tent-bound the protocol was to only consume half-rations. They continued this practice in spite of the surplus of rations that the loss of Owens and Hanes had created. *Better safe than sorry*, the Lieutenant had said. After opening the tent flaps and peeking outside in order to confirm that hurricane conditions continued to prevail—a check that was rendered essentially superfluous by the clamor of the wind battering their tent—the Lieutenant had made the decision to wait it out another day.

"Tomorrow," Lieutenant Wellesley said, buttoning up the tent flap. "We'll start again tomorrow for sure."

"Aye, sir," Ciaran responded, internally noting how yellow the Lieutenant's complexion had become. He wondered if he was yellowing as well. Undoubtedly, he was. The previous day Ciaran had lost his first tooth to scurvy. More were sure to follow if they didn't make it back to base camp soon. Of course, a little yellow skin and some loose teeth were the least of his problems. The blackness of the toes on his left foot had begun to spread up the foot. Ciaran realized that he would almost certainly have to lose the entire foot if they made it back to camp. He just hoped he could walk on it long enough to get there.

"How's that foot doing?" the Lieutenant asked.

"Grand," Ciaran lied. They were both lying to each other about their physical conditions and they both knew it. Yet each had resolved to accept the lies and to not probe any deeper. What was the point? Truth wasn't some magic balm. They were both dying—the one a little more quickly than the other—and they both understood that, whether they cared to admit it or not. The Lieutenant was already on the figurative precipice, gazing into the abyss. Ciaran didn't lag far behind. Yet even now they could still be saved—both of them—and restored—mostly—if they could just reconnoiter with the relief party at the One Hundred Stone Depot.

*

How many perils had they braved? How often had they given the slip to certain death? Now both men had to ask themselves if they'd stood tall in the face of danger and deprivation, surmounting every challenge, only to go down to creeping disease and slow starvation. It didn't seem right. But nothing had seemed right since that fateful day nearly two months earlier when, after more than two months of grueling man-hauling, the four-man final polar party consisting of Ciaran, Lieutenant Wellesley, Hanes and Owens, had arrived at what the Lieutenant believed to be the Pole. Situated atop the polar plateau, a barren, windswept plain which stands nearly ten thousand feet above sea level, there was nothing to distinguish the actual Pole from the miles of relentless white surrounding it on all sides. At a latitude of ninety degrees, it was a place where longitude was both undefined and irrelevant.

What the little party discovered upon halting on the exact bottom of the earth was that their sextant was missing. A sextant is a navigational tool, often used on ships, which measures angular differences between two objects to establish distance and position. After going through all of their gear and failing to locate it, the Lieutenant determined that it must've fallen off the sledge during their day's march since they'd used it before breaking camp in the morning. Ciaran and Owens volunteered to search for it while the Lieutenant and Hanes set up camp for the evening. The pair of enlisted men backtracked all the way to their campsite from the previous evening, which was much quicker and easier not hauling a sledge, but they were unable to locate the missing sextant. When they finally rejoined Hanes and the Lieutenant, the entire team was crestfallen.

The loss of the sextant wouldn't have hurt so much had it not been for the decision to depot the bulky, heavy theodolite along with other equipment deemed unnecessary on the polar plateau. This had been done at the bottom of Beardmore Glacier, more than a week's journey from where they now stood. Added to that was the fact that their sledge meter had stopped working at the top of Beardmore Glacier, shortly after the final support party had peeled off for home. So, instead of the precision of a sledge meter, they'd had to estimate distance traveled by pace count for the past week. What all of this meant was that they were unable to definitively establish their location, thus opening their claim of reaching the South Pole to questioning, much as what'd happened with Peary's claims of obtaining the North Pole several years earlier. And the truth of the matter was: without those readings even they couldn't be certain if they'd found the Pole or if they'd been off by a few miles.

Lieutenant Wellesley had kept up a brave face for the men, but Ciaran could see that it was killing him inside to have attained the South Pole with no way of proving it. It was killing all of them. Whether they cared to admit it or not, each man in the final party had devised intricate plans for his life to follow which relied upon the success of the mission. For instance, before landing command of this mission, the Lieutenant's career in the Royal Navy had stalled and he'd been confronted with the possibility of being retired without ever having made commander, much less captain. In spite of the Lieutenant's experience on two previous arctic expeditions, he hadn't been the Admiralty's first choice to lead this expedition, or even the second or third. But he'd campaigned hard and got it in the end. He was hoping that achieving the Pole would open a path to the command of an important ship, which previously had been out of the question.

Owens, a petty officer with more than twenty years in the Royal Navy, who, like Lieutenant Wellesley, was an artic veteran, planned to retire and open a pub in his native Wales relying on both the pay and the fame that he would accumulate from this mission. Of course, that plan was contingent on Owens not drinking and gambling all of that money away first.

Hanes, the only civilian member of the polar mission, had supplied the ponies for the expedition at his own expense. In addition to the ponies, Hanes had donated a large sum of his own money toward the expedition which ultimately enabled it to take place. An expert equestrian, he'd been included in the 16-man team that'd departed base camp two months earlier in order to tend to the ponies they'd employed for hauling supplies during the outward portion of their journey. The last of the ponies had died long before they reached the Pole, so Hanes could've returned with the final support party. However, in deference to the fact that he was the only member of the British aristocracy among a thirty-two-member shore party made up primarily of sailors from the Royal Navy, Lieutenant Wellesley had decided to include Hanes in the final four-man polar party. Of course, Hanes had a claim to inclusion in the final party on his own merits, as he was a tireless worker and possessed a good understanding of navigation from having previously served as an officer in the Royal Marines. Given the fact that he was independently wealthy, Hanes didn't have any financial aspirations pinned on the success of the mission. But he'd hoped to use the notoriety that success would create in order to bolster a run for parliament.

Ciaran, as the baby of the group, was the only one without definitive plans for what he'd do after the mission. He'd originally intended to remain in the Navy long enough to receive a pension. But some news he'd received from home prior to embarking for the Pole had changed those plans. Since reading that letter from Bridget, he'd begun to re-think the sailor's life—away from home for months, and even years, at a stretch. Then there was the threat of war in Europe that'd begun to rear its ugly head not long before their departure from England. He now seriously contemplated resigning from the Royal Navy upon their return to England and entering civilian life. Like the others, he'd begun to consider how to leverage the fame generated from reaching the Pole into furthering himself.

But the fatal combination of both lost and faulty equipment would render them, in the eyes of many, just one more group that had attempted the Pole. The queer, cruel irony of these men's existence was that while they were able to not only survive but to thrive in the harshest of environments, when left to their own devices in the civilized world they had a hard time just getting by. Lieutenant Wellesley didn't come from an important family, was socially awkward, and worst of all, had been judged by his superiors as having been less than competent in a couple of crucial junctures in his naval career. Owens drank. In the Antarctic, far removed from the pubs of London and Wales, and the bars of the various ports his ship might visit, he was trustworthy, highly competent, and effective. But he'd nearly drank himself off of the mission in New Zealand when he became so inebriated that he fell overboard and had to be fished out of the port of Lyttlelton. Only a heartfelt plea to the Lieutenant the next day, in addition to the fact that he was a polar veteran as well as the strongest man on the expedition, saved his spot on the mission despite a reduction in rank. Hanes ran the risk of all people born into vast wealth: the possibility of a banal and dissolute life of no redeeming social value spent frittering away an estate he'd never earned. Ciaran possessed a fiery Irish temper that'd caused him to be stripped of his rank on not one but two separate occasions, which was part of the reason he'd been so keen to join this mission—so that he could boost his pay grade back to where it should've been without the demotions. He'd actually been a last-minute substitute in the final party. Lieutenant Marvell, the expedition's first officer, was originally slotted to be part of the party that achieved the Pole. But Lieutenant Marvell was already demonstrating signs of advanced scurvy by the time they'd reached the Beardmore Glacier on their outward journey. He'd been sent back with the last support group, and Ciaran had replaced him in the final polar party.

  Away from the frozen wastelands of the Antarctic, the men of the polar party, in their own ways, were often lost. But here, in the worst place in the world, they excelled. That inability to adapt to the outside world had rendered their need for success on this mission all the more profound. If they could've come away with the laurel of the Pole, they very well may have found themselves set for life. Now, even though according to the Lieutenant's calculations—inexact though they were—they'd achieved the South Pole, they were unable to prove it definitively.

They camped that night at the Pole. It was supposed to be a celebration, but it felt more like a wake. They'd carried some cigars and brandy to celebrate their accomplishment. They still smoked the cigars and drank the brandy, but it all tasted flat and stale. It was a sedate evening where everyone contemplated what his separate future might hold now that their claims to the Pole had been put very much in doubt. They were all still relatively physically strong then. There was no sign of the scurvy that'd take Hanes, and was now taking the Lieutenant, with Ciaran not far behind him. The Lieutenant, Hanes and Owens sang "God Save the King," while Ciaran sang, "The Wearing of the Green."

The next morning, they took a number of photographs, hoping to verify their position in this manner. However, minus the sextant and sledge meter readings, it'd be hazy and highly questionable verification at best. It was a subdued group that broke camp that morning and turned back from the one spot on the globe where all paths lead north. The last thing they did was to plant a Union Jack in the permafrost and snap a group photo in front of it. No one had really thought about the return journey on their march to the Pole. It seemed somehow insignificant, paling in comparison to achieving the Pole. They'd all imagined the return voyage would simply be a repetition in reverse of the journey south. They were wrong.

*

That day at the Pole seemed lifetimes away now to Ciaran. At this point, any disappointment at not being able to verify that they'd reached the Pole had long since evaporated. With half of the polar party already gone and the other half on their way out, the goal had become much more modest. Survive.

County Kerry, October 1912

The keen starts deep in the diaphragm and only gradually makes its way up the throat to the vocal cords, then past the mouth. It is an articulation of grief in its rawest, most uninhibited form. The Catholic Church in Ireland didn't approve of keening, deeming it a pagan ritual. Fear of excommunication wasn't what prevented Eithne from joining the keen, however. She simply didn't possess the energy. Dressed in widow's weeds, with a veil extending down from her hat, she sat on a wooden chair staring straight ahead. Although the wall of the cottage, about eight feet in front of her, intervened, her gaze seemed to reach well beyond that —over the green fields of Kerry, across Dingle Bay, past the Blasket Islands. It traveled over the white breakers and gray waves of the North Atlantic, far out to sea, westward to Tír na nÓg, a land where the inhabitants never aged nor knew any death.

To Eithne's left sat David Patrick's sisters, a pair of silver-haired widows, also dressed all in black, who keened plaintively for the untimely loss of their baby brother. On Eithne's right, Father McGuire was doing his level best to ignore the cacophony. Behind Eithne, David Patrick lay stretched out in a pine coffin wearing his gray suit, the only set of dress clothes he'd owned. Seated around the table were Sean Ryan, Tim O'Reilly, and several of the other regulars from Ryan's shebeen, laughing and drinking whiskey to David Patrick's memory, impervious to the keening as though it amounted to nothing more than the melodies of street buskers. Bridget, also dressed in black, stood by the door watching little Ciaran David playing in the yard with some of his cousins.

"We can take comfort in the fact that he didn't suffer," the priest said to Eithne. Father McGuire, a man of average stature in his late thirties whose curly black hair made him look more Italian than Irish, spoke with a soft, melodic voice that'd never, truth be told, uttered any of the edicts Eithne had attributed to him in her arguments with David Patrick and Bridget. "Dr. O'Neill told me it would've happened quickly. The heart gave out, and he simply lay down in the field, as though he were going to bed of a night, and the Blessed Mother took his hand and guided him to eternal salvation."

"Aye," Eithne murmured absently.

"Had he complained about his heart at all?"

"What's that, Father?" Eithne asked, stirring herself to respond.

"I asked if himself had complained at all about his health—specifically his heart?"

"No, Father, he did not. But my David Patrick wasn't one to complain."

"Sure, he was one of the hardest working men in the parish. He was harvesting the potatoes from the new field when it happened, was he not?"

"The new field," Eithne repeated under her breath bitterly.

"He was a very enterprising man, your husband."

"Too enterprising, if you ask me, Father."

"And why would that be? If you don't mind my asking."

"If he hadn't been working in that cursed field, he'd still be with us, Father."

"I don't know about that, Mrs. O'Shea. If it hadn't happened in that particular field, it would've happened in another. They say that when the heart is weak, it's simply a matter of time."

"Aye," Eithne responded bitterly.

"Also, when our Father decides to call us home, then it doesn't matter where we are when He calls, Mrs. O'Shea. We must go home."

"I suppose so, Father."

"What troubles you, Mrs. O'Shea?"

"Sure, I wouldn't want to bother you with the likes of that, Father."

Father McGuire took Eithne's hands in his, looked her in the eye and said, "I wouldn't be much of a pastor if you couldn't share your troubles with me in time of need, Mrs. O'Shea. That's what the Church is here for—to lean on in times of trouble."

Eithne glanced around to see if anyone else might be listening, but between her sisters-in-laws' keening and the raucous conversation of Sean Ryan and his cronies, it would've been impossible to eavesdrop. She craned her neck closer to Father McGuire and confided in a hushed tone, "It's just I'm after hearing some things that trouble me greatly, Father."

"And what would that be, Mrs. O'Shea?"

"Well, Father, and I'm sure you'll think this daft, but the rumor used to be that there was a rath in that old bog that David Patrick drained, and the Good People had lived there before he dug it up."

"And by 'the Good People' you mean?"

"Fallen ones who become imps and live around us, Father."

"Would you be referring to some class of fairy, Mrs. O'Shea?"

"Aye, I'm referring to the Good People, Father. Their rath was smack in the middle of that old bog, so it was."

"I see. And it wouldn't be Mauve Rourke or Agnes Ahearn who told you of this?"

"It would, Father. But there were many others who said it, as well."

"And this is what's troubling you?"

"It's related to that, Father. It's something Mrs. Rourke claims to have seen."

Father McGuire rolled his eyes. "And what would that be, Mrs. O'Shea?" Seeing Eithne squirm uncomfortably, he added, "Come now, there's no use in holding back at this point."

"Well, if you insist, Father. Mrs. Rourke claims *that*," Eithne nodded over her shoulder toward David Patrick's corpse, "isn't my husband at all."

"What do you mean?"

Bridget wandered over from the door at that moment and paused close enough to eavesdrop on the conversation.

"Mrs. Rourke said she was passing by that field yesterday evening as the sun was going down," Eithne responded, "just when they say my dear David Patrick passed."

Bridget arched her eyebrows at hearing the words "dear" and "David Patrick" uttered in the same sentence by her mother.

"Mauve Rourke claims she saw one of the Good People, made out to look like a wee lad, leading my dear David Patrick away by the hand," Eithne continued. "She tried calling to David Patrick, but he couldn't hear her. They just kept going without looking back. And when they got to the end of the field, they just sort of disappeared, so they did."

Hearing the story, Bridget frowned, but said nothing. Father McGuire stared at Eithne, nonplussed.

"That," Eithne nodded toward the coffin, "isn't my David Patrick's body. That's simply an old log the Good People beguiled to look like David Patrick."

Father McGuire waited to ensure Eithne had finished, and then replied, "I don't properly know where to begin, Mrs. O'Shea. But allow me to assure you that this," he waved at the decedent, "is David Patrick's earthly remains. Dr. O'Neill examined him, and I can assure you that is not a log, or anything else of the sort. It's not your husband, I agree, Mrs. O'Shea. But that's because his immortal soul has shaken off these mortal coils. That," he nodded toward David Patrick's corpse, "is what remains of his earthly clay."

Eithne burst into tears, grabbed Father McGuire's hand and began to kiss it. Bridget, looking on, merely shook her head. "Oh Father," Eithne gasped between sobs, "Please tell me that's true. They say that once the Good People get a hold of a soul, they keep it for eternity so that it's never able to enjoy the eternal reward of heaven."

Father McGuire frowned: "I'm surprised that a good Christian woman like yourself could entertain such nonsense, Mrs. O'Shea. There's no such thing as the Good People or fairies or what have you. I'm certain that, as we speak, David Patrick is enjoying eternal bliss with our Father in heaven. Or at worst he's in Purgatory because he did like his drop."

Now Bridget frowned at Father McGuire. But Eithne sobbed from joy and began kissing Father McGuire's hand again: "Oh, thank you, Father, thank you. I couldn't bear the thought of my beloved David Patrick spending all of eternity in some sort of limbo, another stolen one whose soul was captured by the Good People."

Hearing the word "beloved" caused Bridget to frown and shake her head, but she continued to hold her peace.

"I must have a wee chat with Mrs. Rourke about spreading such nonsense," Father McGuire mused.

Eithne gripped the priest's wrist, "Oh please, Father, do no such thing. It'd go badly for myself if you did, so it would."

Father McGuire nodded, "I understand. Maybe I'll bring it up in one of my homilies. These supernatural beliefs amount to paganism and represent a threat to our immortal souls, Mrs. O'Shea."

Eithne, seemingly oblivious to the personal critique embedded in that comment, simply nodded: "Just please don't mention any names in your sermon, father."

"Of course not," Father McGuire replied, trying to not look bemused.

Bridget, afraid that she might snap at her mother or the priest or both if she listened to any more of their conversation, turned to walk outside. Opening the door, she paused to allow her eyes to adjust to the dazzling brightness of the late afternoon sun. She watched little Ciaran David, now more than eighteen months old, running after the older boys, laughing. He seemed particularly strong and athletic for a child of his age—David Patrick had often noted that. With the sun glinting off of his blond hair, his cheeks still chubby, he looked like a wee angel, she thought. She couldn't help but wonder what would become of the two of them. With David

Patrick gone, there'd be no one to mediate between her mother and herself, no one to intercede on Bridget's behalf. Of course, all would be well if Ciaran could somehow make it back to her. If they could only know for certain that Ciaran was going to return and make an honest woman of Bridget, then Eithne might be able to be reasonable. But if the reports from the paper had been true and he was…she couldn't bear to think of it. Until she knew otherwise with certainty, he was merely lost. Lost did not mean dead.

Stepping out into the yard, Bridget breathed in the crisp autumn air and was taken by the scent of fallen leaves. She'd always loved that smell. Now, with David Patrick passing, it'd just remind her of what it was—death. She walked around the back of the cottage to a spot under an elm beside the little stream where her father used to sit with her when she was a girl. She wondered why the tears wouldn't come. She'd felt frozen inside since learning that Ciaran was believed to be lost in the Antarctic. It was like some of that South Pole frost had traveled north along with the news and now clutched her heart and all of her emotions in its icy grip.

It was a frost that'd thaw instantly if only they'd locate Ciaran. She'd read every bit of news that she could lay hands on. The Murphys were very good about clipping the articles for her. In not one of the articles that she'd read had it been stated conclusively that Ciaran and the polar party were actually lost, properly speaking. That'd merely been a headline to sell newspapers. As of right now, they were late in returning, that was all. Their ship, the HMS Intrepid, an icebreaker that'd been specially fitted for sub-arctic travel, nevertheless had to sail from the Antarctic home base to New Zealand in mid-March in order to avoid being frozen in and forced to winter there. For all anyone back home knew, Ciaran and his mates had strolled into their base camp just as the Intrepid was steaming away and the lads were all sitting around a fire at this very moment, sipping hot cocoa and having a good laugh about it all. She was David Patrick's daughter in that she'd cling to any shred of hope until all hope was extinguished. But how could hope be extinguished when the relief ship hadn't even set sail to return to the Antarctic yet? At that moment it was harbored in Lyttlelton, awaiting the onset of the southern summer when the ice floes that encircled Antarctica would loosen their grip on that desolate land. Until the Intrepid returned once again to relieve the remaining shore party in the late spring or summer, nothing would be definitive.

*

Bridget thought of her last hours with Ciaran. It was the day he'd shipped out—a warm, late spring morning that they'd passed together on this very spot. He'd looked handsome in his navy uniform, even if it was the British navy. She'd worn her good white dress. Because she'd been worried about dirtying her best dress, he'd laid his pea jacket down on the cool, red clay for her to sit. The morning sun cascaded through the trees that lined the stream in golden rivulets. A soft breeze gently ruffled the leaves. Sitting beside her, Ciaran took Bridget's hand in his and smiled awkwardly. The intimacy of the previous evening had evaporated with the rising of the sun and now they were just a couple of shy kids again.

Several minutes passed in which the only sound was the soft gurgling of the stream. Finally, Ciaran cleared his throat and said, "If all goes well, I could be back here in a little over two years. Will yeh wait for me?"

"Of course, I'll wait for you," Bridget replied.

"In fairness, it could take longer—up to three or four years if the weather doesn't cooperate."

"I'll wait as long as it takes—forever if need be."

"I won't be forever, though it'll feel like that being so far away from yeh. But if I were to not make it back…"

"You *will* be back."

"I'm only saying don't wait forever. I want yeh to be happy no matter what."

Bridget gripped Ciaran's arm, "Please don't talk about that. I'm only going to be happy if I'm with you."

They were quiet for several minutes as they watched the stream trickle past. Finally, Ciaran cleared his throat and said, "When I do return, I'll have a lot of money in my pocket. Money we can get started with."

"I don't care about money,"

"I'll get promoted, too. I could make petty officer."

"I don't care about promotions."

"If we make it to the Pole, I could become famous."

"I don't care about fame, either. I only care about one thing."

"What's that?"

"You coming back to me safe and sound. Better a live donkey than a dead lion."

"What?" Ciaran laughed.

"You heard me. Better a live donkey than a dead lion. Come back to me. Don't take any unnecessary chances and, please God, don't volunteer for anything."

Ciaran leaned in and kissed Bridget on the mouth. They held the kiss for an eternity. When Bridget pulled back, tears glistened in her eyes as she breathed, "Come back to me."

Ciaran's guileless face betrayed not a trace of fear or doubt when he replied, "I shall."

*

That'd been more than two years earlier, but she recalled it as clearly as if it'd happened yesterday. Bridget picked up a dead leaf lying on the bank beside her and twirled it by its stem. She stared absently at it as it spun in non-concentric circles between her index finger and thumb. Mixed with the quiet, peaceful babbling of the stream were the laughter and shouts of the children playing in the garden behind her along with the piercing bray of her aunts' keening escaping from the cottage. Flinging the leaf away from her, she watched it flutter softly into the stream. The gentle current picked it up and slowly began to carry it away. As she watched the leaf recede, she repeated those last words softly to herself: "Come back to me."

New York, May 1947

When they worked on the ship, they rarely spoke. Sometimes they'd go for over an hour and not exchange a dozen words. After better than a month of dedicated labor the model yacht was starting to again look like a ship and not the detritus of some horrific maritime tragedy. Percy was now starting to believe that not only would they fix it, but that the ship really would be, as Mr. Patrick had promised, as good as new. It might even be better because the wood they were using was stronger than that which came with the kit, and they were adding a lot of new details as well.

Percy's boxing skills were progressing even more quickly. In fact, Mr. Patrick had told him on several occasions that he was a natural. That meant nothing to Percy as he loathed the very thought of fighting. Besides, he couldn't see the need for it. Marty and his flunkies had left Percy alone since they'd destroyed his model yacht. Maybe they decided that was enough for him and had moved on to the next victim. For whatever reason, the situation seemed to have resolved itself and Percy was happy to let sleeping dogs lie. He felt no desire for retribution whatsoever. He only wanted his ship fixed, and that was happening.

Mr. Patrick, who was busy sanding down a section of the hull, paused from his work and asked, "What do yeh know about yer parents, Percy?"

Percy was momentarily caught off guard. Mr. Patrick rarely spoke and when he did it was always about either boxing or repairing the ship. He never asked Percy personal questions, and Percy had been satisfied with that arrangement. Percy paused for a second, then replied, "Not much. My mother died when I was just a baby. Some of the kids say she was a whore, er, I mean a prostitute."

"Who says that?" Mr. Patrick demanded.

"Well, Marty Jones, mostly."

"That one's a prize poltogue."

"What's a poltogue?"

"A poltogue? It's that gobshite bowsy, Martin Jones. His picture's beside it in the dictionary. Anyway, didn't yer auntie never tell yeh nothing about yer mother?"

"Oh, sure. Aunt Martha says she was very beautiful, and that she was in the Rockettes at Radio City before I was born."

"Yeh wouldn't happen to know her name?"

"My mother?"

Mr. Patrick nodded.

"It was Mary, I think."

"Oh," Mr. Patrick replied, his voice betraying just the slightest hint of disappointment, though Percy didn't pick up on it.

"Mary Rita, that is. Her name was Mary Rita," Percy corrected himself.

"Mary Rita, eh? And what would her last name have been?"

"I assume it was the same as mine—Kelly. Why do you ask? Did you know her?"

"Eh?" Mr. Patrick replied, lost in thought for a moment. "Ah, no, no. I don't think so. What about yer father?"

"I don't know his name. I don't know anything about him, really. Aunt Martha says he disappeared before I was ever born and good riddance to him."

"Does yer auntie know who he was?"

"She says she doesn't know, that my mother wouldn't tell her."

They worked quietly for a minute, then Percy paused and asked, "Did you know your father, Mr. Patrick?"

"I knew the man. Betimes, though, I wished I hadn't."

"Why is that?"

"He was a good man when he wasn't on the drink. But he was always on the drink."

"So, he was a bad man?"

"Not a bad man, just a weak man—a weak man who would do bad things that he didn't mean to when he'd taken drink."

"Was it your father who taught you how to fight?"

"In a manner of speaking. I had to learn how to fight to defend me mam and sisters."

"Did you stand up to him and stop him?"

"I stood up to him, but it didn't stop him. It only made him madder."

"Then why do you want me to stand up to Marty?"

"Because I was a boy fighting a grown man. Yer just a lad fighting another lad, and I know yeh can take him. That right hand of yers has thunder in it. Yeh may not know it, but it does. Besides, this Marty's got nothin' inside him, just like me old fella."

"What ever happened to him?"

"Me da?"

Percy nodded.

"The drink took him."

"He died?"

"No, just disappeared, never to be seen again. I'm sure he's dead by now, though."

"I guess you could say we're both fatherless."

"Aye," Mr. Patrick smiled and patted Percy gently on the shoulder, "I suppose yeh could so."

Antarctica, February 1912

The Lieutenant came down with a high fever while they were tent-bound by the blizzard. His moaning had stirred Ciaran in the middle of the night and Ciaran never really got back to sleep. When morning at last broke, the storm that'd trapped them for the preceding three days had moved on, but at that point they couldn't. In addition to the physiological discomfort, the effects of the fever were causing the Lieutenant to fade in and out of lucidity. One moment he'd be chatting reasonably with Ciaran, the next he'd be raving.

As morning passed into afternoon, in a moment of rationality the Lieutenant, his weak voice quavering, had instructed Ciaran to: "Head for the One Hundred Stone Depot alone, Creagh. Leave me here."

"There's only one tent, sir," Ciaran objected.

"I know. Take it."

"But if I do, yeh won't…"

Ciaran couldn't finish the thought. But the Lieutenant understood: "I'm as good as dead either way, Creagh. Napoleon said, 'It requires more courage to suffer than to die.' My courage's run out."

"I won't let yeh give up, sir. I'll carry yeh on me back if I need to."

The Lieutenant paused for a moment, gathering all of his strength. Then he shook his head: "I'm already lost. You still have a chance. If you can get to the One Hundred Stone Depot right away, Ensign Brooks will be there with Lieutenant Donald and they can carry you back to base camp on a dog team."

"They'll carry *both* of us back on that dog team, sir. Yeh'll see."

His strength spent, the fever overtook the Lieutenant. His head dropped onto the pile of dirty clothes he used for a pillow, and his bloodshot, yellowing eyes rolled back in his head. Sweat beaded on his forehead in spite of the fact that the temperature inside the tent hovered around the freezing mark. His eyelids fluttered closed and the Lieutenant let out a long, guttural moan. Then he remained silent for several minutes.

*

Suddenly, the Lieutenant's eyes snapped open. The fever had provided him a path to surmount the strictures of time and space and he was now far away from their little tent. Back on the trail, they were working their way down the Beardmore Glacier during the early stages of their return journey. Shackleton originally discovered and named the glacier during his furthest south in '08. Others had since followed the path Shackleton navigated in their quests for the Pole. Filling a valley more than 125 miles long and 25 miles across between the Queen Maud Mountains to the east and the Queen Alexandra Range to the west, it was one of the few passages through the Transantarctic Mountains to the polar plateau. It was the key to reaching the Pole. They'd crossed it twice—on their way to the Pole, and again on the return trip when they'd more or less retraced their tracks from the outward journey.

Staring up at the roof of the tent, the Lieutenant's dilated pupils once again discerned a chasm suddenly tear open in the ice beneath their feet, causing Ciaran to plunge in. In a calm, yet decisive voice, he shouted, "Dig in men! If the sledge goes, we all go!"

Sitting beside him in a freezing tent that stunk of festering death, Ciaran knew exactly where the Lieutenant's fevered mind had transported him. It was a week into their return journey from the Pole. All four men of the final polar party were still alive and relatively healthy. Their progress had been slow and frustrating that day as they navigated through an enormous field of sastrugi. The hardened, irregularly shaped ridges of snow were extraordinarily difficult to man-haul over. So, like lab rats trying to negotiate a maze, they endeavored to work their way down the mountain following the grooves the sastrugi had created. With four grown men standing shoulder-to-shoulder, pulling a 500-pound sled behind them, this wasn't an easy proposition. Unfortunately, the group had more to contend with than merely navigating their way through the sastrugi. The primary challenge the returning polar party had negotiated were the crevasses, many of which plunged for miles beneath the surface and could be wide enough to easily swallow their entire four-man team.

The ancient glacier was veined with these crevasses. Most were visible, but some had been frozen over with a thin crust of ice that might appear on the surface to be solid, but would immediately collapse when any weight was applied to it. While the entire group kept a lookout for crevasses, the responsibility for finding a safe yet rapid route off of the glacier rested solely on the Lieutenant's shoulders. The weight of carrying three men's lives was written into the Lieutenant's lined and haggard soot-stained face, grown thin from hunger and worry.

They'd been on the march for close to four hours that day with only a few short stops for rest and no water since they'd broken camp that morning. Ciaran was running a leathery tongue along the inside of a parched cheek wondering how long before they stopped for tea when the world gave way beneath him. One moment he was sinking ankle-deep into crunchy snow, and the next moment he was dangling upside down in an eight-foot-wide crevice in the ice, the bottom of which he was unable to distinguish. His breath had been taken away by the unusual, almost surreal sensation of the ground literally evaporating beneath his tread. It was as though he'd stepped into a cleverly concealed trapdoor. In that microsecond during which there was nothing but frigid air supporting his one hundred and fifty pounds, a moment which seemed to stretch out into eternity, he'd had time enough to consider that his number was up. Then the rope that secured his harness to the sledge behind him became taut and he felt himself dangling in the air. His head pitched forward and his body slowly rotated until he was upside down. Chin in the chest, peering upward between his finnesko boots, he was blinded by the dazzling polar sun shining through the crack into which he'd slipped.

On the march, Ciaran had been stationed on the left end of the harness. Hanes was situated to his right, Owens beside him, with the Lieutenant on the far right. The idea was to have the two biggest men in the middle, with the smaller two on the ends. Fortunately for everyone, only Ciaran had broken through the ice. The others remained on firm footing, but Ciaran's weight was inexorably dragging the others toward the now-gaping mouth of the crevasse. The sledge, which was ten feet long and hauled a four-foot-high mound of equipment, pressed on the men from behind. It felt as if the crevasse was exerting the gravitational pull of a black hole on the group. They could've thrown Ciaran a rope, and then cut him and themselves loose from the sledge, but then the sledge assuredly would've plunged into the crevasse. Without their tent and sleeping bags, not to mention their food, primus stove and paraffin to fuel it, they were all as good as dead. So, cutting bait wasn't an option.

"Are you all right, Creagh?" the Lieutenant called, the struggle of maintaining the sledge telling in his voice.

"Fine, sir," Ciaran replied, trying to mask his anxiety with a chipper facade. It didn't help that he could hear his voice echoing deep into the bowels of the ice below him.

"Is there a ledge or anything you could step on, Creagh?"

"No, sir."

"Can you get a hold of the edge?"

"Not presently, sir. I'd say I'm a good few feet away yet."

"All right, men," the Lieutenant turned to the remaining two. "We're going to have to haul him out. Get low and take a step backwards on three. One...two...three!"

The three men grunted and sweat poured down their reddened faces with the exertion. After about fifteen seconds —which felt like hours to all of them, Ciaran included—they'd managed to move a step backward.

"Good," the Lieutenant, who was by far the smallest and physically weakest man of the group, panted. "Another couple steps and we should have him close enough to climb out."

"All right, let's try it again," the Lieutenant said after a few moments rest. He counted off and the men began to strain to push the sledge backward while at the same time pulling Ciaran out of the crevasse. Suddenly, there was a loud, cracking sound and Owens, who stood closest to the crevasse, called out in an urgent tone, "The ice is giving way, sir!"

"Disengage and pull the sledge from behind!" the Lieutenant panted.

Owens slipped out of the harness. The sledge immediately lurched hard toward the crevasse. Hanes and Lieutenant Wellesley strained to steady it, understanding that if they failed, they, along with Ciaran, would plunge to the bottom. Owens, selected for the polar party specifically because of his size and physical strength, scampered around the back of the sledge. Grabbing the runners where they curled upward in the rear of the sledge, he dropped into a squat and began to pulling. He was like a strongman at a carnival winning a tug-of-war against an entire team of opponents. The sledge began to slowly move backward, away from the crevasse again. Then it began to pick up steam and within moments, Ciaran was scrambling onto the ice. Once on terra firma, Ciaran disengaged from the harness and ran to the back to assist Owens. They moved the sledge onto firm ground and then all four men dropped to the snow, their backs resting against the sledge, panting.

Ciaran turned to Owens, who was sitting beside him gulping the frigid air, and said, "Thanks, mate."

Owens grinned revealing several gaps in his smile that were the result of a combination of poor oral hygiene and a tendency to get into dust-ups when he was on the drink. He slapped Ciaran on the back in a brotherly fashion and replied, "No worries, mate. What'd you see down there?"

Ciaran shook his head: "The rapture."

*

In the tent, the hallucinating Lieutenant, his mind still back on the trail, basked in the glow of their success, saying, "Good job, men. Good job."

Ciaran, concern in his eyes, sat up in his sleeping bag staring down at the Lieutenant. Looking directly into Ciaran's eyes, the Lieutenant said, "We nearly lost you, Creagh."

"Aye, sir," Ciaran replied, uncertain if the Lieutenant was in the tent with him, or still out on the trail somewhere.

Hell's Kitchen, July 1936

Large, picture windows with stained glass depictions of the saints filled the walls on both sides of the church. Broad columns that supported the high, arched ceiling lined both outer aisles. From the ceiling hung a number of long, tin lanterns containing electric lightbulbs. A wide, gray marble aisle led up the middle of the church to the altar. Behind the altar stood an ornate sacristy, over which hung a life-sized crucifix. Two-foot-high wooden statues of the saints peered down from pedestals adorning the walls. The scent of incense and burning candles hung over all of it. Kneeling in the front row, meticulously reciting the rosary over well-worn beads that each held in her right hand were two elderly women dressed in brown. Before a bank of flickering votive candles in the front corner kneeled another elderly woman, dressed all in black including the veil that covered her face, deep in prayer.

Davy and Paddy were seated in the rear pew. Paddy was wearing the same short-sleeved button-up shirt and loose khaki trousers he'd worn in the gym while Davy looked dapper in a pair of chinos, brown leather shoes, and white dress shirt unbuttoned at the neck. Over the back of the wooden pew hung Davy's sports coat. Neither man spoke, nor did they, for that matter, appear to be engaged in any form of worship. Both stared at three closed wooden doors situated almost side-by-side in the rear wall. Above the two outer doors red lightbulbs glowed. After several minutes the door on the left swung open and the lightbulb above it extinguished. From it emerged an elderly woman dressed in a simple gray house-frock over which she wore a tattered raincoat. Her iron gray hair was wrapped in a maroon scarf and her head was bowed piously.

Davy elbowed Paddy and whispered, "I wonder what gran there coulda had to confess."

Paddy frowned.

Standing, Davy began to walk toward the recently vacated cabinet. Before stepping in, he turned to Paddy and cracked, "I hope you brought something to read, Paddy. This could take a while."

"Just get in there yeh great, gassy bag of wind," Paddy snapped.

Davy laughed and pulled the door closed behind himself. The claustrophobic little room was smaller than a broom closet, with just enough space to hold one person. There was a low stool built into the corner and a padded kneeler on the floor. The divider separating the compartment Davy occupied from the middle room was made of thin wood, with a sliding partition situated at face-level when kneeling. Davy sat on the stool and waited his turn. From the other confessional, he could hear what sounded like the murmurs of an elderly woman, with what seemed to be occasional interjections from the priest spoken too quietly for Davy to make out. After several minutes, the murmuring ceased and he heard the outer door to the opposite confessional open. A few moments later, the panel that separated Davy's booth from the middle booth slid open. There remained a screen between his compartment and that of the priest which, when combined with the darkness of the booth, provided a sense of anonymity. Through this screen the profile of a middle-aged man wearing a priest's robes and collar became visible. The priest said nothing, apparently waiting for Davy to commence.

When Davy still hadn't said anything after several moments, the priest cleared his throat and said in a Cork accent that'd been watered-down and become more decipherable after many years in the United States: "Yes, my son?"

Realizing what was required, Davy muttered, "Sorry." Then he dropped onto the kneeler, performed a quick sign of the cross, and added, "Forgive me father, for I have sinned."

"Is that yourself, then, David O'Shea?" the priest asked in friendly manner.

"None other, Father Sullivan."

"So, you had the dream again, is it?"

"That's right, Father."

"Ah well, at least it affords you an opportunity to cleanse your immortal soul. You have a fight upcoming?"

"A big one, Father. I'm fighting Carvallo for the title at the Garden tomorrow night."

"Ah, that's right. I recall reading about that in the papers. Well, you'll need your rest tonight so I suppose we'd be well-served to start."

"Yes, Father."

A few moments of silence passed. Then Father Sullivan

prodded, "It's been…"

"Ah, right, Father," Davy said. "It's been…" He paused a moment to think. Then he shouted toward the exterior door, "When was the Washington fight, Paddy?"

A moment later, Paddy's muffled voice floated through the padded exterior door: "April."

"That's right," Davy replied. He started counting off the months on his fingers.

As Davy calculated, Father Sullivan called out to Paddy, "Is that yourself, Patrick Byrnes?"

"'Tis, Father Sullivan," Paddy replied.

"I haven't seen you at Mass these last few months."

"Sorry about that, Father. We've been pretty busy training for this Carvallo fight. I'll be in once it's over."

"Right so, Patrick," Father Sullivan replied.

Davy then said to Father Sullivan, "It's been four months since my last confession."

Davy paused again, so Father Sullivan prodded him, "Yes, my son, your sins…"

"Is having relations with a woman still considered a sin, Father?"

"'If you're not married to that woman, it is indeed, David. Just as it was the last time you took the sacrament of penance."

"Just making sure, Father. I thought the Bible said, 'Be fruitful and multiply'."

"It does, but that's referring to one's lawful spouse. If you're not married to the woman, then the act becomes the sin of adultery. Seventh commandment, David."

"I thought adultery was sleeping with a married woman."

"No, adultery is sleeping with anyone to whom one is not married."

"What if you don't use one of those rubber thingys, Father?"

"Are you asking is it still a sin?"

"I am, Father."

"It is a sin, indeed. Wearing a contraceptive device makes no difference with regards to whether the act is adulterous or not. It's true, the Church did ban the use of contraceptives. But considering the class of ladies—and I'm using that term liberally, mind you—that you consort with, David, not using a condom is just bad judgment."

"I see."

"So how many women have you slept with, my son?"

"Since my last confession, or in general, Father?"

"Let's just keep it to the women you've been with since your last confession."

"I'm not sure, to be honest, Father."

"Ballpark it."

"Okay…a dozen?"

"Twelve different women in four months, David?"

"I know that's less than usual, Father, but I've been seeing this woman Rita pretty steady for the past two months."

"And who is this Rita?"

"She's a swell gal, Father. She's Irish Catholic, as well, but born in America. And she's a Rockette."

"A Rockette? Do you mean the dancing girls?"

"That's right. You should see the gams on her, Father."

"Is she married?"

"No, Father. At least, I don't think so. She never mentioned it. I'm pretty sure she's not."

"Are you considering marriage?"

"With Rita, or in general, Father?"

"Either."

"No."

Father Sullivan shook his head and turned away so that Davy wouldn't see him smile. After pausing for a moment, he ran his hand over his face to wipe away any residue of amusement and asked, "David, you realize that if a bus would've hit you on the way over here, you would've died in a state of sin? Given the amount of sin you're carrying around on a regular basis, you'd be looking at a pretty long stretch in Purgatory. At best."

"That's why I'm here, Father."

"I can't offer you absolution if you're not truly repentant, David."

"I am repentant, Father. I truly am. I feel awful about it."

"About what?"

"About what?" Davy repeated, perplexed. "About all of it, Father. The whole works."

"You'll try to stop the womanizing? I thought you weren't supposed to do that sort of thing when you're in training, anyway."

"True, but I'm a weak man, Father."

"Is there anything else you'd like to confess?"

"No, that's about it, I suppose, Father."

"Why don't you say ten Hail Marys, ten Our Fathers, one rosary, and maybe drop a wee something in the Poor Box as penance for your sins."

"All right then, Father."

There was another pause.

"Say an Act of Contrition, my son."

Davy quickly made the sign of the cross, then he began to fumble for the words. Father Sullivan stepped in and got him started, "Oh my God…" He trailed off for Davy to pick it up from there.

"Right," Davy said, "Oh my God…"

He became stuck again and Father Sullivan suggested, "Let's just say it together. Eh, David? 'Oh my God, I am heartily sorry for all my sins'…" Davy falteringly followed along to the end.

When they finished praying, Father Sullivan said, "I hold you absolved for your earthly sins. Give thanks to the Lord for He is good."

"Amen," Davy replied, performing another sign of the cross. But rather than getting up, he simply moved back from the kneeler to the stool and sat there quietly.

"Is there something else that's troubling you, my son?" Father Sullivan asked after a short pause.

"Will this cover me for the fight then, Father? You know, just in case…"

"You mean in case your dream were to come true?"

"Yes, Father."

"As long as you made an honest confession, David, you're covered."

Davy looked uncertain.

"How many times have you had the dream now, if you don't mind my asking?"

"Not at all, Father. This last one makes twelve and a half."

"I'm just a simple parish priest, not one of these fancy psychiatrists, mind you. But did you ever consider that maybe the dream is telling you something apart from what literally happens in it?"

"Like what?"

"I don't know, that's for you to decide. Can you recall the first time you had the dream?"

"Not long after I turned professional, Father. Around eight years ago, give or take."

"Wasn't that about the time the cancer took your dear mother?"

"It was, Father. Do you think that's somehow related to the dream, then?"

"How did your mother feel about you boxing?"

"She didn't seem to mind the amateur fighting so much, but she wasn't too happy about me turning pro. I guess she believed the headgear and the bigger gloves in the amateurs would protect me. We had a big argument when I told her I was going pro. I remember she just kept saying this one thing over and over. It was the queerest thing."

"What was that?"

"Better a live donkey than a dead lion."

"Maybe she didn't want to risk losing another man."

"I suppose. She was always trying to baby me, always smothering me."

"Can you blame her after what happened to your father?"

"I don't know. All I know is all that babying was why I had to go out and learn how to fight in the first place."

"Did the other lads pick on you?"

"They did. They picked on me because I had no father, and they picked on me because they said I was a mama's boy."

"Children can be cruel. But I guess you showed them all, Davy."

"That I did, Father. That I did."

"What do you remember of your mother?"

"She was always working. And when she wasn't working, she was always tired. She seemed kind of hardened and bitter at life. She never discussed anything other than whatever happened that particular day. She never talked about my father, or life back in Ireland."

"Your mother had a difficult life—coming over here from Ireland, just the two of you, and having to raise you all on her own and work full-time. She wasn't always like that."

"Maybe not, Father, but that's all I remember of her." Davy paused and thought for a moment, then added, "It's like a part of her was trapped down there in the ice with him."

"I suppose there's a lot of truth in that, David. Hard times come to all of us eventually. They haven't come to you yet because you're still young…"

Davy interrupted him with a sound of dissent, but

Father Sullivan continued, "I understand you experienced some tough times growing up, but that's not what I mean. Eventually, something will come along that will test you, it will test your very being. You may find that after that you're no longer the person you thought you were—you're someone else entirely. Does that mean you failed the test? No. You only fail when you give up entirely. Your mother never did that."

"I wonder why she ever left Ireland."

"Ireland's grand, David, but it's a hard place for an unmarried woman with child."

"I suppose." Davy paused again, as though lost in thought. Then he added, "You know, I don't have any memories of Ireland, Father. I was too young when we left. The earliest memory of Mam I have was after we'd moved to New York. Whenever she had a little free time, she used to sit on the stairs of our fire escape sewing or sometimes just staring into space. She'd always face the same way, always downtown, never uptown. I noticed that because there was a lot less to see facing downtown than there was facing uptown. She'd do it spring through fall, so long as it wasn't raining. She said she liked the fresh air, though, as you know, Father, there's not so much fresh air to be had in the middle of Hell's Kitchen. I can see her now, just sitting there with her sewing on her lap, gazing off into the distance."

"That's a fine memory."

"Anyway, after a few years, she just stopped doing it."

"Why was that?"

"She never said and I never asked. But I figured it out on my own at some point. I realized it wasn't downtown she was facing at all. It was south. It was as though she was expecting my father to come marching up Tenth Avenue in his arctic parka, snow goggles and finnesko boots. Like what'd taken him so long was that he'd walked all the way back from the South Pole, as though that were even possible."

"We all nourish hopes deep within our hearts. Oftentimes, they're much more absurd than that."

"No argument there, Father. The thing is—when she hardened, my mother—it wasn't when we came over from Ireland. I have vague recollections of her being very different in our early days here. When she hardened was when she stopped sitting on that fire escape."

Eithne's Dream

In the dream, I recognize the cursed field immediately, so I do, even though I've never actually clapped eyes on it in my waking life, nor will I. Indeed, I've purposely avoided the blighted place since my dear David Patrick and Sean Ryan—the divil minds his own children—cleared it all those months ago. The land was nothing more than a bog on a slope, good for bricks of turf for the fire so long as a soul was careful to avoid the rath and that demonic trail set down by the wee folk. Thanks to those lads' industry, the ground is now leveled, tilled, and plowed, with spuds planted in neat rows. For the longest time I'd thought that the entire project was a ruse. I secretly laughed at the undertaking, so I did. I simply did not believe that David Patrick had the gumption to begin such a grand undertaking, let alone to complete it. Indeed, I was certain that the entire time David Patrick claimed to be working on the new field he was actually helping Sean Ryan with his still—both in the production and consumption of his filthy poteen. When they completed the new field, I couldn't help but admire my dear David Patrick's industry, ill-advised though it was.

What forced David Patrick to clear that damnable bit of land, against my own well-stated wishes, was the fact that farmland was much too dear to purchase, so it was. He couldn't lay hands on money enough to buy more. Even if he'd had the money, it was well known that any available land would go straight to the wee group of rich families, like the Grays and Nelsons, who dominated our county. Those big-house families took the rich farmland from them that couldn't afford to pay their bank notes. The usurpers would then plant over it with grass for the grazing so that wool could be produced for the bloody English. Aside from Sean Ryan's patch of farm to our north, we're surrounded by pastures on all sides, and soon enough they'll have our bit of earth as well—soil that five generations of David Patrick's family farmed. Since he felt he must expand because herself had to go and get in a family way with no husband to support her or the wee one, David Patrick decided he needed to put what he called his own unused land to work. But it wasn't unused, not at all. Nor was it truly his. The Good People owned and used that land and jealous of it they were.

*

The dream is the same every time, so it is. The late afternoon autumn sun is shining down, glinting off the windows of Sean Ryan's shebeen at the top of the hill. David Patrick pauses from his hoeing to straighten up and wipe the sweat from his brow with the forearm of his tweed coat. That's when he appears as if out of thin air. Immediately I know him —it's the same wee lad I'd seen when I was but a lass. Only he's taken on the form of a young boy in order to deceive my dear David Patrick, so he has. But I recognize the wee lad just the same. It's a well-established fact that once the Good People know you've seen them, they'll get you—even if it takes the rest of your natural life. Eternal beings they are, so fifty years is but a blink of the eye for them. Cast out of heaven they were, so they have no charity in them. What I can't understand is why they'd take David Patrick. It was myself who'd seen the wee lad all those years ago. Why not take me? But maybe they knew that taking my dear David Patrick would hurt me more.

When seen by the eyes of men, the Good People have a physical beauty far exceeding that of humans. And the wee lad's disguise in the dream is lovely—a child with an oval face, brown eyes with long lashes, and light brown hair that tumbles off of his head in curls. Only them with the second sight who can see through to the Good People's true being can perceive the hideousness that lurks beneath the surface of these lost creatures. Jealous the Good People are of their appearance, even if it's nothing more than an illusion. Whenever a rare human comes along who exceeds them in beauty, the Good People will snatch that lass or lad away in the bloom of youth. When I was but a child, it happened to Eileen O'Connor. The most gorgeous girl anyone in the village had ever seen—the toast of the entire county, so she was. One day she just disappeared. Some folks whispered that she'd run off with an English soldier. The constable had investigated a local farmer for foul play, but nothing came of any of that, of course. Eileen O'Connor was never seen nor heard from again and well we knew that it was the Good People behind her disappearance. Now they'd come for my David Patrick, just as they snatched away Eileen O'Connor those many long years ago.

The wee lad, in his disguise as a human child, barely comes past David Patrick's knee. He approaches David Patrick from behind and tugs at his coat. David Patrick, trusting soul that he is, breaks into a grand smile when he sees the lad. I'm standing on the edge of the field, maybe one hundred yards away. When I see this, I cry out in terror because I know. But no sound comes out. Again and again, I attempt to warn David Patrick, but my voice has been beguiled by the Good People, and it's silent I remain. Meanwhile, David Patrick drops his hoe, reaches down and takes the lad by the hand. They turn and start walking west, right into the setting sun. I try to chase after them, so I do, but I'm trapped in a muddy patch.

That bit of the old bog has obviously been charmed by the Good People and it won't release me. No matter how hard I churn my legs, I simply flounder in place as though I were sunk in quicksand.

Stuck, I'm forced to watch as David Patrick and the wee lad walk away, hand in hand. They stop at the crest of the hill, right where that old rath had been. Then, suddenly, they're gone. Vanished, so they have, just like Eileen O'Connor. Once they're after disappearing, my voice is freed and I let out a shriek that'd curdle the blood. I'm also able to break free of the muddy patch. Neither my house dress, nor my mud-caked boots, nor my painful bunions stop me from sprinting to the place where last I saw them. When I reach the spot, there's nary a trace left of them, nor of the evil rath itself. Frantic, I look all around for David Patrick and the wee lad, but they're gone. Gone forever, so they are. My chest heaving from the sprint, I fall to the ground. My cheek rests against the cool, moist earth. I can smell the recently turned soil. Pounding the ground where the rath once stood, I wail, "David Patrick! Let him go! I'm the one you want!" But what the Good People take they never return. Nor do they respond with anything but silence to the grievances of a mere mortals. Cold, awful silence.

County Kerry, April 1913

Eithne gasped for air and awoke with a start. She always snapped out of sleep at the same point in the dream. Practically every night for the past six months, ever since the dark day when they'd interred that log which the Good People had left behind in place of her husband, she'd had the same nightmare. The Good People had fooled Father McGuire, but they couldn't fool her. Or maybe they hadn't fooled him at all. Perhaps the priest had known that wasn't the remains of anything human over which he'd chanted the burial rights.

Only he couldn't admit he knew because it'd be admitting the failings of his blessed Church. There were things, dark things, that even priests could do nothing about and they couldn't allow anyone to know that fact or there'd be no need for them entirely. She'd been in church every Sunday and every holy day of obligation throughout her entire life, including the day after her Bridget was born. She hadn't missed weekly confession in all that time, either. Yet all of that faith and devotion was as nothing when weighed against a few stolen seconds as a child when she accidentally caught a glimpse of something she should never have seen. It was something the priests would have her believe didn't exist, but she'd seen it—seen it with her own eyes. But seeing it wasn't her fault, she hadn't wanted to see it. If anything, it was the fault of the wee lad. He'd made the mistake of allowing himself to be seen. But the Good People accept no blame. Nor excuses. It'd taken a lifetime to catch up to her, but they hadn't forgotten. All these years later she'd paid for it, and paid dearly.

What of David Patrick? His immortal soul was now trapped in some sort of limbo state, his body enthralled to the Good People until that dark day in the unimaginable future when God the Father finally deemed it was time for judgment. And how would David Patrick and the other stolen souls be judged? Would they even be permitted the opportunity of judgement? After being bonded to those unholy creatures for so many eons his soul would've worn away like the wispy, gray ashes of a fire long since spent. If anything of David Patrick's soul remained at all, it, along with the souls of those other unfortunate stolen mortals, would most likely be doomed to haunt limbo for whatever remained of eternity following Judgment Day.

And why? Because he'd been foolish enough to clear a field that contained one of their raths? Because he hadn't known any better and had refused to take Eithne's good advice? No. She had to admit it now, that wasn't why her

David Patrick had been taken. The Good People had their whims, and they were unpredictable, but they were also just. An eye for an eye our Lord sayeth, and they abided that much. They'd already taken their vengeance on David Patrick for clearing that field when the ice had consumed young Ciaran Creagh. That debt was paid. There was only one debt left unpaid. The debt of a young, foolish girl who'd had the misfortune to stumble upon one of them at his leisure. A debt that they'd carried on their books for half a century had finally been settled in full.

Eithne, now wide awake, stared at the thatched ceiling of the little cottage—the cottage her dear David Patrick had built with his own hands, along with his father and younger brothers. The air was still except for the low, rhythmic breathing of Bridget and her little one. Eithne only slept a few hours a night now. The dream invariably shattered her rest. Occasionally, she'd fall back into a fitful slumber. But more often than not she'd lie awake obsessing for the rest of the night. The Good People had taken her David Patrick in payment for her transgression, this much she had to admit. But what had stirred them? They'd lain dormant for half a century even though her cottage was only a stone's throw from their rath. They could've exacted their revenge upon her at any time, but they hadn't. Not until they'd been roused by David Patrick digging up that accursed field. And why? Why would David Patrick do such a thing in spite of all her warnings? Why had he not just let sleeping dogs lie?

There was only one reason driving David Patrick's desire to expand, of course. Being given a fourth mouth to feed with him already in his fifties was too much to ask. Dear David Patrick didn't complain, of course. That wasn't his way. He simply took on the extra work and said nothing of it. It was that additional mouth to feed and back to clothe that led him to clear that awful field. The thought of it would've never occurred to him had Bridget done the right thing and gotten married to anyone who would've taken her, thereby becoming another man's burden. Then that rath would've been left in peace. The Good People may've waited another twenty years to seek their vengeance on her, or they may've just forgotten it entirely, she thought. It was possible, she told herself. At the wake, Father McGuire had insisted that it was all nonsense, and she'd believed him at the time. At least, she'd wanted to. But there were things in this world that even priests couldn't understand. Old, dark things that'd been brushed aside by modern science, but which existed still, creeping in the shadows and appearing on moonless evenings.

She realized now that what the Church was selling was just fairy tales—fireside yarns told to children to keep them in line. Just like fairy tales, the Church's stories amounted to nothing more than cautionary fables. There was no power in the Church's stories, only suggestion. When it came to real magic—the old magic that still inhabited all of the dark corners in this supposedly enlightened world—the Church was powerless. Honest folk like herself and her dear David Patrick were on their own down here on Earth because God, way up there in heaven, sitting on His ivory throne, with legions of angels and archangels kissing His omnipotent arse, seemed disinclined to intervene. Thus, humanity was preyed upon by fallen ones that the Father, in His infinite wisdom, had banished from heaven and, in so doing, had unleashed upon the Earth.

The Good People? That made her laugh. They were devils, no different from Satan and his minions in that inferno below. People were just afraid to call them what they were, fearful of angering them. And the common folk were well-advised to be afraid, Eithne thought. The Good People were eternal and their memory was long. They never forget—or forgave—a debt. And woe to any misfortunate mortal soul who had the bad luck of incurring their spite. Still, Eithne couldn't help thinking that the Good People's vengeance upon herself might've been further postponed for years, decades even, if their rath hadn't been leveled. And it always came back to this: there was only one reason that rath was destroyed.

Eithne glanced over at wee Ciaran David, nearly two years old now, sleeping soundly in bed beside Bridget. He looked angelic with his curly blonde hair and red cheeks. It was hard for Eithne to feel bitter against him, even if he was the root of the trouble. She understood that the wee angel didn't bring himself into the world. He was brought. She glanced from the lad to his mother. Eithne's eyes narrowed. *He was brought*, she thought.

BOOK TWO

Davy Boy's Dream

The details sometimes change, but the dream itself is always the same. I'm in the ring, circling my opponent and everything is going gangbusters. The ring is engulfed in darkness—darker than usual, but I know that the joint is heaving because I can hear them. The crowd cheers every time my opponent connects. I don't know why, but they all seem to be rooting against me. The silence is deathly every time I land a punch. Paddy's in my corner, hollering instructions at me, as usual. And, as usual, I'm paying him no mind. Everything feels right, everything is good. I'm sticking and moving, fighting *my* fight. Then it happens. I never even see the punch. Those are the worst ones, the ones that really hurt you, the punches that you don't see.

Everything goes black.

The next thing I know, the world seems cockeyed, like I was watching a motion picture where someone came along and knocked the camera on its side while it was filming. So here comes the funny bit. When I open my eyes, I'm not looking up from the canvas. Instead, I find that I'm outside of my body, looking down on myself from fifteen feet in the air. I peer through the cigar smoke that hangs over everything like the morning mist clinging to the bogs in County Kerry when I was a kid. I can see myself stretched on the canvas, arms sprawled out above my head. My opponent has stalked off to a neutral corner, and I can see the referee standing over my body commencing the count. With each tick of the clock, he chops the air with his arm and shouts out the numbers. I can see his lips move, but I can't hear him. The delirious roar of the crowd, driven mad like sharks that've scented blood, drowns out everything. The ref, a short, bald man that I don't recognize from any of my other fights, counts to ten and then waves his arms to signal the end of the fight. My opponent jumps in the air, and the crowd roars.

All the while, I'm hovering above, lighter than the ether, looking down on all of this. For some reason I feel strangely disconnected from it all. That I've lost is clear, but I just don't care anymore. The ref bends down to take a closer look at my face as I lay stretched-out on the canvas, but I can only make out the back of his head. He turns and waves frantically to the ring doctor. The ring doctor, an old croaker who pulled bullets out of mobsters on the hush before he lost his license, rushes into the ring. In his right hand he carries a black physician's bag. Around his neck he wears a stethoscope like a necklace. When the crowd sees this, the cheering stops. My opponent pauses from his celebration to look over at my fallen body with concern. The doctor places the buds of the stethoscope in his ears and kneels down beside me. The arena is silent as a crypt now, but I'm too far away to hear what's said. I can read the lips of the referee, however, when he says to the doctor: "He ain't breathing."

The croaker nods and places the stethoscope's diaphragm in the center of my chest and listens. I don't feel the touch of the cool, metal disc on my bare skin, just as I didn't feel the pain of the shot that dropped me, nor the impact of my limp body collapsing onto the canvas, nor the concussion of the back of my head slamming against the hard ring apron. I was out before I hit the mat. Now, I'm looking on from above as though I was watching someone else up on a screen at a picture house. I can't see the ring doctor's face as he hunches over my body, moving the stethoscope around my chest. The croaker removes the eartips of the stethoscope, turns to the ref, and shakes his head. As he's doing this, a couple fellows dressed in white hoist a stretcher into the ring. The croaker says a few words to them and they nod. Then they bend over and transfer my body onto the stretcher.

They lift the stretcher and begin carrying my body out

of the ring. I can hear someone cough from the upper seats of the arena, that's how quiet it is. Suddenly, I feel myself being pulled away. I try to fight it, but I can do nothing—the pull is too strong. Below me, I can see the medics passing the stretcher which carries my body through the ring ropes. I can see them, but they're growing farther and farther away by the moment. I'm near the roof of the arena now, hovering in a cloud of cigarette smoke, and still I can feel myself being pulled away. I want to cry out "No!" or "Stop!" but nothing will come out. The smoke grows thicker and thicker until I can no longer make out anything. It's suffocating me, forcing me to fight for breath.

*

Usually the dream ends here and I awaken in a sweat. But occasionally it continues. In those ones, I remain in the cloud, but it's no longer smoke. Instead, I'm outside now and the smoke has turned to fog. I can only see a foot or two around myself. Everything is white and cold, impossibly cold. I know what I'm doing now—I'm searching for my father. I search for him even though I've never actually clapped eyes on him, not even a photo. I search for him even though I realize that if I find him, he won't recognize me. I search for him, telling myself: *He'll know. He'll just know.*

I keep moving, keep searching. I trudge forward, one foot after another, fully aware that I may simply be walking in circles, the fog is so thick. None of that matters. I have to find him although I'm not sure why. I push on blindly for what seems like hours, days even. All the while, I keep calling out to him, "Da! Da!", until my throat grows raw from the strain of it. One thing keeps me going. I don't know how I know this, but I'm certain that if I find him, it'll somehow save him—save us both. I go until I can walk no further and I drop to my knees in the cold, wet snow. I call out to him over and over again with a faltering voice, but he never appears. I never find him.

County Kerry, October 1913

The entire Murphy clan attended—the children: Colm, Niamh, Ronan, Aideen, and little Eoin. Mrs. Murphy, eight months pregnant with their sixth was present, as was Mr. Murphy who'd taken off work early to be there. And, of course, Eleanor was there. It was the first party ever thrown in her honor and Bridget was more embarrassed than pleased to be the center of attention. Of course, whenever little Ciaran David was around she'd never truly be the center of attention. He was the nexus of the universe wherever he went—a bright, shining little star who, like a star, exuded a gravitational pull that drew everyone within his orbit toward him. At the moment he was out in the yard playing an impromptu game of footie with the Murphy children. The Murphys, being the richest Catholic family in the village, owned a proper, store-bought football. It was a rare delight for Ciaran David to get to play with a real football, so he was showing off, amazing the young Murphys with his skill and dexterity dribbling and shooting.

Bridget and Eleanor sat at the kitchen table with Mr. and Mrs. Murphy. Bridget found herself a bit ill-at ease owing to the fact that she'd never been in the Murphys' house except for work. Eleanor, on the other hand, seemed right at home, perhaps because she lived there. Mrs. Murphy poured Bridget yet another cup of tea, in spite of Bridget demurring. A stout, well-meaning but distracted woman in her mid-thirties who'd always treated Bridget with abstracted kindness, Mrs. Murphy had never wavered in her support of Bridget, even after she'd become the primary topic of village gossip during her pregnancy. "I'm sorry your mother can't make it," Mrs. Murphy said, setting the teapot on the table. "Is she quite well?"

"Quite well, missus. Thank you for asking. Mam said she couldn't come because she's in mourning."

"Ah, yes, I've noticed she's still wearing the weeds. How long has it been since your dear father's passing?"

"A little over a year now, missus."

Mrs. Murphy shook her head. "A year already? My goodness. Well, I guess some people never really stop mourning."

Eleanor and Mr. Murphy both studied Bridget with concern, understanding how close to home this comment hit given Bridget's other, perhaps dearer, loss.

"I suppose that's true, Missus." Bridget tried to play it off but couldn't help grimacing a little.

Mrs. Murphy continued blithely, "He was a good man—your father. A bit fond of his drink…."

"Now, Acushla," Mr. Murphy interrupted her.

"I was only saying we all have our faults, dearest."

"I suppose that's true," Mr. Murphy nodded. A moment or two of uncomfortable silence passed. Mr. Murphy cleared his throat and asked, "Where will you go in America, Bridget?"

"New York," Bridget replied, taking a sip of her tea, even though she felt like a dam about to burst. "I've a cousin on my father's side there."

"Ah, New York. It's a grand place, I hear."

"We hope to visit there someday," Mrs. Murphy interjected. Turning to look at her husband she added, "Isn't that right, dearest?"

Mr. Murphy, a man of middling height with thinning hair who reminded Bridget of her father, replied after a short pause, as though awoken from a reverie, "Sure, sure, Acushla. Someday. When I can get away from the business." He paused for a moment, then added, "and the children are grown."

"I suppose we'll come over to see you someday, Bridget," Mrs. Murphy said, rolling her green eyes. "When we're both grandmothers."

Bridget laughed uncomfortably.

"What will you do in New York?" Mr. Murphy asked.

"Oh, I don't know," Bridget replied, nibbling on a scone. "Same thing as here, I suppose. My cousin said she could help me to find a position."

"There's no shortage of work in America, I can tell you that," Mr. Murphy replied, his tone turning admiring. "Those Yanks know how to do it. You're your own man in America," he paused for a moment, then added, "Or woman. You're only judged on what you do, not on if your grandfather was a bad farmer."

"Now don't bring that up again, dearest," Mrs. Murphy chided him. "Your grandfather was a bad farmer—facts are facts. But, you're a wonderful businessman."

Mr. Murphy shook his head but held his peace.

Bridget looked from Mrs. Murphy to Mr. Murphy to Eleanor, who'd been surprisingly quiet throughout. Setting down her tea cup, Bridget pushed herself to her feet, saying, "This has been lovely, Mr. and Mrs. Murphy. Thank you both very much for all of it, but I really must be going."

Mr. Murphy sprung to his feet, then helped Mrs. Murphy to stand. With some effort, Mrs. Murphy walked around the table to embrace Bridget. "When does your ship depart?"

"In two days, missus," Bridget replied, nervously hugging Mrs. Murphy, afraid that she might induce labor. "I leave for Cork first thing tomorrow."

The embrace lingered for several seconds, then both women stepped away and dabbed their eyes with handkerchiefs. Mr. Murphy stepped in and handed Bridget an envelope with a ten-pound note in it—the equivalent of two year's wages for Bridget—saying, "This should help get you and little Ciaran David started."

Bridget accepted the envelope and burst into tears anew. Mr. Murphy now stepped back and rubbed at the corner of his eye, as though he'd suddenly gotten something lodged in it. Mrs. Murphy, still dabbing at her eyes with her handkerchief, said, "You have our address. I expect you to write us when you're settled and tell us how you're getting on."

Bridget sniffed and wiped her eyes again. Eleanor threw her arm around Bridget and steered her toward the kitchen door, "I'd best get you out of here before we're all rolling on the floor blubbering and gnashing our teeth."

Bridget nodded and allowed Eleanor to lead her away to a chorus of goodbyes from Mr. and Mrs. Murphy. Outside, they paused on the back porch for a moment while Bridget collected herself. The early autumn sun, still far above the horizon, shone down red and orange and pink from a cerulean sky. In the yard, the children laughed and continued their game. Bridget watched as Ciaran David stole the ball from Ronan, who was nearly three years older but only an inch or two taller. Ciaran David then dribbled past Niamh and fired a kick at the goal as the last defender to beat, little Eoin, fell over backward into the grass laughing riotously. Bridget shook her head and smiled.

"You'll have a professional footballer on your hands someday," Eleanor remarked with a laugh. "Just watch."

"Anything but an explorer would be grand," Bridget dabbed her eyes. "Better a live donkey…" She trailed off.

Eleanor nodded. They were both quiet for a moment and watched as Colm demonstrated to Ciaran David how to dribble the ball in the air using his knees. Eleanor added, "So, what does herself think of you leaving?"

"She hasn't said. In fact, she didn't react at all when I told her we'd be leaving for America. But I imagine she's happy. She's made it very clear that she blames me for everything."

"Blames you?"

"Aye, if it wasn't for me having Ciaran David, Da would never have plowed the new field and the wee folk wouldn't have spirited him away."

"Then they did take him?"

Bridget turned to Eleanor, nonplussed. "Don't tell me you subscribe to that nonsense?"

Looking embarrassed, Eleanor quickly replied, "No. I mean, I heard it from Mauve Rourke. I didn't believe it. Although Agnes Ahearn had told me years ago that there was a rath in that field. And the Good People…" Now it was Eleanor's turn to leave a thought unfinished.

"It wasn't fairies, or elves, or leprechauns or any class of mythical creature. My da had a heart attack, plain and simple. So, stop repeating that nonsense."

"Sure, you're right. Nonsense it is. Only, please don't speak of the Good People disrespectfully. Just to be safe. Please."

Bridget stared at Eleanor and then shook her head. A few moments of uncomfortable silence passed, then Eleanor cleared her throat and asked, "Did you talk to old man Creagh, like said you were going to?"

Bridget was quiet for a moment, then slowly nodded.

"What'd he say?"

"He's no better than me mam. Refuses to even acknowledge Ciaran David without Ciaran himself telling him he's his son." Her eyes started to tear up. She looked away for a moment, shook her head, then added, "I wish I'd never gone. I wanted nothing from him. Only for him to acknowledge his wee grandson..."

Eleanor threw her arm around Bridget and hugged her, saying, "The older ones—they're funny."

"The younger ones are, too."

"True."

At that instant, Ciaran David spotted her. He cried, "Mammy!", and charged toward her.

Eleanor, removing a handkerchief from her pocket and dabbing her eyes, said, "This place won't be the same without the two of you."

"That's where you're wrong," Bridget replied. "It'll be exactly the same. This place will never change."

Bridget then walked down the three steps to the ground and caught Ciaran David just as he was leaping into her arms.

New York, May 1947

It was a cramped, yet orderly and clean, one-bedroom flat on the 6th floor of a walk-up building. The bedroom was Aunt Martha's. Percy slept in the living room on the couch. While the little apartment lacked a radio—which Aunt Martha considered a waste of one's valuable time—there was no lack of niceties such as lace doilies on the tables and a real oriental carpet in the center of the living room. And though Aunt Martha was, by necessity, frugal, Percy never wanted for anything. He sat at the breakfast table completing his homework while Aunt Martha cooked dinner. Aunt Martha, a stout, matronly woman who'd once been attractive—though, not quite beautiful like her sister, the dancer—worked as a secretary for some big-wig lawyer downtown.

She entered the room carrying two steaming plates, announcing, "Put your books away, child. Time for dinner."

She placed before Percy a plate of fish, rice and green beans. Percy curled his upper lip back in disgust: "Fish?"

"Of course, fish," Aunt Martha retorted, setting her own plate down and dropping into her chair. "It's Friday."

"My friend Anthony is Catholic and they only eat fish on Fridays during Lent."

"Anthony?" Aunt Martha paused to tuck a napkin into the Percy's shirt, then she sat down opposite him and placed her own on her lap. "Sounds Italian."

"I don't know."

"Come Judgment Day your friend Anthony can answer to God the Father as to why he didn't eat fish every Friday. You won't have to—not as long as you're in my keeping." She punctuated this statement with a quick sign of the cross.

"Are you saying Anthony will go to hell for not eating fish every Friday?" The terror was apparent in Percy's voice.

"Well," Aunt Martha relented somewhat, "maybe not hell. Probably just Purgatory." After a pause, she added, "Anyway, our Lord died on the cross for us. You can't eat fish once a week for Him?"

"Yes, ma'am," Percy replied glumly, pushing the fried cod around his plate with his fork.

They ate in silence for a few minutes after this. When he'd almost fought his way through the codfish, Percy looked up sheepishly and asked, "Aunt Martha, do you have any idea who my father was?"

Caught off-guard, Aunt Martha placed her knife and

fork on her plate she looked at Percy seriously. "I've told you before, Percy. Your mother never told me who your father was. I'm not certain that she even knew for sure. Why do you ask, child?"

"Mr. Patrick asked. The way he asked, it seemed like he thought he knew who my father might be."

"And who is this Mr. Patrick?"

"He's the school custodian. He's helping me re-build my ship."

"What happened to your ship?"

"I told you, Aunt Martha," Percy replied, unable to mask his frustration. "I dropped it walking down the steps of the subway and it broke."

"Don't take that tone with me, child!"

"I'm sorry," Percy replied. Downcast, he returned his attention to his plate.

After a few moments of silence, Aunt Martha said in a gentler tone, "My sister was a kind, caring, wonderful woman, but she had bad judgment when it came to men. She always consorted with the wrong type—gangsters and entertainers and athletes and such." She paused for a moment, then added, "In my opinion, it's probably for the better that you don't know who your father was. It would just disappoint you."

"But if I knew who my father was, maybe the kids at school wouldn't make fun of me so much."

"They make fun of you?"

"Yes—for not having a father."

"You know who else didn't have a father, child? Jesus Christ, our lord and savior. Tell the children at school that the next time they try to make fun of you."

"But Jesus did have a father, Aunt Martha," Percy protested, "God. And he had Joseph, too! Jesus had two fathers!"

"Maybe it's not the lack of a father that causes the other children to pick on you," Aunt Martha replied in a withering tone. "Maybe it's that smart mouth of yours."

"Yes, ma'am," Percy returned his attention to his plate once again, deflated.

"Perhaps it would be for the best if you didn't spend so much time with this Mr. Patrick."

"But we haven't finished re-building the ship!"

"When you finish, tell Mr. Patrick you no longer have time to spend with him. Tell him your Aunt Martha said so,"

"Yes, ma'am."

Hell's Kitchen, July 1936

The fight was only six hours away and either Paddy or Tommy, or both, had been Davy's constant companion for the preceding three days. Tommy had actually slept on the couch in Davy's less-than-hygienic flat the past three nights. This was all at Jake's insistence. Jake wanted to make sure that if Davy had that goddammed dream again he wouldn't up and pull a Houdini. As he constantly reminded Paddy, Jake had a lot riding on this fight. Having the middleweight champion of the world in his stable of fighters would bring fame to his gym. They might actually be able to start competing with Stillman's and Gleason's for some of the other top fighters in the city. Then his joint wouldn't be populated by Davy and a bunch of punch-drunk ham-and-eggers.

The fact was they all had a lot riding on this fight. Paddy knew that if Davy were to take the title, as the head trainer of the middleweight champion of the world—the most popular division after heavyweight—his own career would be set. Henceforth, he'd always be known as the trainer of the middleweight champ which meant that he'd never have trouble getting work moving forward. Plus, he'd get paid more for that work. He might even generate enough cache to finally split from Jake and open his own gym. That'd always been Paddy's dream since he'd retired from fighting. And Tommy, green as he was, might be able to find a head trainer job somewhere after working the corner of a middleweight champion. Therefore, Paddy and Tommy didn't complain about the extra duty. After all, Davy couldn't become middleweight champion if he didn't show up for the fight.

They were on high alert the day of the fight. Jake figured the closer it got to fight-time, the more likely Davy was to rabbit. He issued strict orders to both Paddy and Tommy not to let Davy out of their sight until he stepped through the ring ropes later that night. So, when Davy wanted to stop by to see Rita on his way to the Garden, Paddy and Tommy insisted on accompanying him. The lift in Rita's tenement was still out of service, so Davy, Paddy and Tommy were forced to climb six flights of stairs. Because it was a particularly hot day, they'd all broken a sweat by the time they reached Rita's floor. As they were strolling down the darkened hallway to Rita's apartment, Paddy turned to Davy and asked, "Are yeh sure it's a good idea to be breaking a sweat like this and the fight still six hours away?"

Davy, wearing an expensive checkered sportscoat and pleated khaki slacks, but no hat—Davy's vanity didn't allow him to cover his wavy, blond hair—turned to Paddy and replied, "I'll thank you to keep your thoughts to yourself until fight time, Pads." After a short pause, as an afterthought, he added, "In fact, why not just keep 'em to yourself altogether?"

At the end of the hall, they stopped before Rita's door.

Paddy turned to Davy and asked, "Are yeh sure she's even in at all?"

"She's there," Davy responded. "She always comes home and has a nap between the matinee and evening shows." Davy then pounded on the door and called, "Open the door, Rita. It's me."

After a few moments, her voice groggy from sleep, Rita called back through the closed door, "Who's 'me'?"

"Who do you think?"

"How should I know? I got louses coming around here bugging me all the time."

"Open the door, would you, please? I gotta have a word."

"Why should I after how you talked to me the last time?"

"So you do know who it is," Davy chuckled. "The fight's tonight and I wanna make sure we're square, you and me."

"You wanna make sure we're square? Then apologize for all them mean things you said to me."

"C'mon, baby, you know I didn't mean those things."

"Then apologize."

Davy turned to Jake and Tommy: "Take a powder, boys."

Tommy looked nervous, but replied adamantly, "Jake said we wasn't supposed to leave you alone, Davy."

Davy shook his head in disgust, "What am I gonna do, Tommy? Climb out the window? This is the sixth floor. Use your head, man!"

Paddy patted Tommy on the shoulder, "It's okay, Tommy. We'll wait at the end of the hall." Turning to Davy, he added, "No funny stuff—it weakens the legs."

"I know," Davy rolled his eyes. "Disappear already, I'm getting tired of smelling the two of you."

Tommy reflexively dropped his nose to his right armpit and took a sniff. Paddy clapped his hand on Tommy's shoulder and said, "C'mon, Tommy." Paddy turned to walk away and nodded for Tommy to follow. Tommy looked from Paddy to Davy and back to Paddy. Then he turned and reluctantly followed.

As he was walking away, Paddy called over his shoulder, "Yeh got five minutes, Davy. Fight's in less than six hours and we don't have time for this nonsense."

"Would you just blow already?"

Davy waited until Paddy and Tommy had receded from sight, then he leaned his cheek against the apartment door and intoned coolly, "Rita?"

"I'm still waiting for that apology." She sounded impatient.

"I'm sorry for those hurtful things I said, baby," he replied in a tone just above a whisper. "I didn't mean none of 'em. I blame the influence of Paddy Byrnes. He's a terrible man."

Several long seconds of complete silence followed. Then the bolt slid unlocked, the doorknob turned, and the door opened inward with a creak. Rita, ravishing in a brief nightgown in spite of a hairnet and cold cream liberally slathered on her face, stood in the doorway trembling slightly. "Don't ever talk that way to me again," she said.

"I won't," Davy replied. "You have my word."

Still blocking the door, Rita peaked her head out and looked down the hall, "What happened to those other two mugs?"

"I told 'em to take a powder."

"Well, c'mon in, I guess," Rita stepped back and waved Davy in.

Davy stepped into the room, closed the door behind himself, fastening the bolt lock.

Walking over to the bureau, Rita picked up a three-quarters empty bottle of whiskey and asked, "Care for a highball?"

Davy shook his head, then walked over and had a seat on the edge of the bed. Mopping the sweat from his brow with a handkerchief that he'd produced from his coat pocket, Davy replied, "I'm fighting Carvallo in six hours."

Rita poured herself a stiff drink and took a gulp of it. Then, still holding her glass, she walked over and had a seat on the edge of the bed beside Davy. Her mostly exposed right thigh brushed against Davy's left. "So, you're still going through with that, huh?"

"As Jake said, a man doesn't get too many opportunities like this. You gotta seize 'em when they come."

"In spite of the dream?"

Davy grimaced. "I talked to Father Sullivan about it and he said it's just a dream and it could mean anything." He paused for a moment until his face cleared, then continued, "Besides, I had it eleven and a half times before and nothing happened. No reason to think it'll be any different this time."

"Yeah, but you weren't fighting the champ them other times."

"Sure," Davy replied uncertainly. Then, mustering some bravado, he added, "And the champ wasn't fightin' me then, neither."

"That don't make any sense."

Davy shook his head, "Look, Rita, don't worry about none of that. I come here to make sure we're square, just in case. I really care about you, Rita."

"If you cared about me, you wouldn't fight tonight."

"What's that supposed to mean? Don't you want your man to be champ?"

"I don't care about none of that. I want my man to be with me and not dead or punch-drunk, that's all."

"But the dream doesn't mean anything. Father Sullivan said so,"

"I don't believe in that silly dream, either. But Carvallo nearly killed Johnson in his last fight and Johnson's a pretty good fighter. And I don't know if you've been reading the papers, but Carvallo's been saying he's gonna put you in a box."

The color drained out of Davy's handsome face, "Don't say that kinda stuff, Rita. It ain't helping none."

"I'm not trying to help, you chucklehead. I'm trying to get you to not fight. Can't you see I love you, you big lummox?"

"I love you, too, Rita. But I gotta fight. Can't you see that? This is my one chance at the big time! I'm tired of being a nobody."

"I'd rather have a living nobody than a dead somebody."

"Stop saying stuff like that!" Davy shook his head and stared at Rita. Rita drained her glass, then stood up and poured herself another.

Just then, there was a loud knock at the door. Paddy's muffled voice floated through the door, "We gotta get going, Davy. Weigh-in's in one hour."

Davy looked at the door desperately, then turned to Rita. Catching his glance, Rita turned her back on him. Davy stood and removed something from his coat pocket. Placing it on the bed, he said, "I got you a ticket for tonight, Rita. Ringside."

"I can't go," Rita replied curtly, her back still to him. "Got the evening show."

"I'll leave it here for you all the same." Davy took a couple steps toward the door. Gripping the knob, Davy said, "Wish me luck?"

Breaking down in tears, Rita turned and ran to Davy. Throwing her arms around him, she kissed his face repeatedly, sobbing, "Just come back to me in one piece you big, dumb Irishman."

"You have my word."

*

As they were walking down the hall, away from Rita's flat, Davy turned to Paddy and asked, "Did you know Carvallo's been saying he's gonna sell me the farm?"

"Saying something don't make it so," Paddy replied calmly. "If it did, Jake Scanlan would be the most honest man in New York."

"Carvallo's just trying to sell the fight, Davy," Tommy put in.

"No, Tommy," Paddy interjected quickly, "Carvallo's scared." Turning to Davy, Paddy added, "Carvallo's never been in the ring with anyone like yeh, Davy. He's trying to mask his fear with that nonsense. Take my word for it. He's scared—plain and simple."

"I suppose," Davy replied, lost in thought.

Antarctica, February 1912

Lieutenant Wellesley's fever had broken by the next morning, and he was both rational and chipper again. While he seemed physically no stronger, the Lieutenant assured Ciaran that he was fit for travel. Ciaran rose at what would've been sunrise, though the sun hadn't actually risen or set in months. He went outside the tent to assemble the theodolite, which they'd retrieved at the bottom of Beardmore Glacier on their way back from the Pole. The Lieutenant remained in the tent to melt some ice and then heat breakfast. The weather was mild for that time of year with the temperature hovering around -20 Fahrenheit and no wind to speak of. Compared to what they'd traveled through a few days back, it'd be like a spring day in County Kerry.

The theodolite was made of brass. To operate it one sighted through a telescope mounted on two rotating circular axes that allowed it to move on horizontal and vertical planes. The principle driving the theodolite is that a beam of light must travel in a straight line. If the length of one side of a triangle is known, then by measuring the angles of the corners using reflected beams of light, one can precisely determine location. Obtaining a reading was a long and cumbersome process that, including setting up and breaking down the equipment, could take up to an hour. An excellent tool for surveying, the theodolite wouldn't have been the first choice of most travelers. But after the loss of their sextant—a much smaller, lighter, easier to manipulate piece of equipment—they had no other choice, compasses being useless.

Ciaran had no idea how a theodolite worked when they'd first set out for the Pole all those months ago. But the Lieutenant, understanding the need to prepare for all contingencies, had taught all of the men on the return party how to operate it. Ciaran, being the last man standing, had gotten the most training. From his reading that morning, Ciaran determined that they shouldn't be much more than a three-day march from the One Hundred Stone Depot. Of course, that three-day pace was predicated on a four-man team hauling at full strength. From the looks of the Lieutenant, Ciaran reckoned they were down to a one-man team—himself —pulling at, maybe, half-strength. But that was the situation and, he thought, the road would rise up to meet them whether it was just himself pulling or a dozen stout men.

Ciaran shielded his eyes and gazed overhead. A bright yellow sun shone down from a clear blue sky. Perfect conditions. But after more than two months trekking across this desolate continent, Ciaran knew the weather could change by the minute. After stowing the theodolite on the sledge, Ciaran pushed his way into the tent to see about breakfast.

As they were eating their hoosh, spiced with the extra sugar and cocoa rations that would've gone to their two lost companions, Lieutenant Wellesley announced, "I think I'm good for pulling today, Creagh. I feel much fitter."

Ciaran looked at the Lieutenant dubiously. Down thirty pounds from the weight he'd carried when they'd set out from home base, the Lieutenant appeared to be nothing more than oversized clothes hanging off of some rickety sticks. It reminded Ciaran of the scarecrows the old fellow would set up in the barley field on their farm. "I don't know, sir," he respectfully replied. "Maybe to start I can pull the sledge and yeh can just walk along beside. After all, yer just after getting over a fever."

"Nonsense, Creagh. I feel fit as a fiddle."

"I don't know, sir."

"Don't make me pull rank, Creagh."

"Aye, sir."

Two people pulling would be better, Ciaran admitted to himself. But it was too much to hope that the Lieutenant could pull his weight in the harness. And, if Ciaran ended up pulling both the sledge and the Lieutenant, that'd be more work than simply pulling the sledge alone and having the Lieutenant walk alongside. But the Lieutenant was C.O. More than that, he'd become like a big brother to Ciaran. He ceded to the Lieutenant's wishes.

*

Packed, the sledge weighed approximately two hundred and twenty pounds at this point. It was significantly less than what it would've weighed had their four-man team remained intact, as they'd removed the equipment and personal gear of both Owens and Hanes. Anything else that wasn't absolutely crucial had been jettisoned ages ago, but they still had to haul their own gear, the food, the tent, the theodolite, as well as the other essential equipage. Two hundred and twenty pounds wouldn't be difficult for two healthy men to drag, assuming level ground and good snow. But, of course, neither of those conditions prevailed in Antarctica. The ground was constantly undulating and the surface was frequently dappled with sastrugi, the wave-like ridges of hardened snow brought about by powerful blasts of Antarctic wind. And with each step they took they'd break through the hard, crunchy surface of the snow and sink to mid-calf.

In spite of the challenging terrain, not to mention often having to march into fifty mile-an-hour winds, a healthy four-man team would be able to cover fifteen miles in a ten-hour day. Indeed, on the outward journey before sickness and accidents had decimated them, they often exceeded that average. The depots had been situated with the idea of a twelve-mile per day average march. Because it took so much effort to haul the supplies, the amounts were limited to just enough to sustain a team from one depot to the next with very little wiggle-room. While it was true that Ciaran and the Lieutenant had extra food rations owing to the deaths of Hanes and Owens, they consumed the same amount of paraffin fueling the primus stove for two people as for four. On top of that, they were far behind schedule and first sunset was now only a few days away. While the sun would dip below the horizon for only about ninety minutes that first night, it signified that the polar winter's long night was not far off. There'd be no surviving the polar night away from the comfort and protection of base camp.

Ciaran finished stowing the last of the gear on the sledge and tying it down. He walked to the front of the sledge to find Lieutenant Wellesley struggling to secure himself in the harness. Gently removing the harness from the Lieutenant's hands, Ciaran strapped him in like a father tying his toddler's shoes. After strapping himself in, Ciaran turned to his right and looked at the Lieutenant. It was impossible to see either of their faces owing to the scarves, masks, and snow goggles that protected them from exposure. No part of their bodies could be exposed or it would result in almost instantaneous frostbite. Ciaran raised his gloved right hand and gave the Lieutenant a thumbs-up. When the Lieutenant returned it, Ciaran leaned forward into his harness and took that first agonizing step forward.

*

The Lieutenant was okay for the first half-hour or so. He wasn't pulling his weight, but he was pulling some. By the one-hour mark he was pulling even less. At two hours, Ciaran glanced over to see that not only was the Lieutenant not pulling, he wasn't even walking. He'd fallen almost to his knees and was being dragged forward, the harness suspending him. Ciaran stopped pulling and unbuckled his own harness. He took a few moments to rub his aching shoulders. Then Ciaran removed the harness from Lieutenant Wellesley, causing the Lieutenant to immediately drop onto the crunchy snow. This, in turn, brought the Lieutenant back to consciousness, shouting, "Pull, lads!" from the seat of his pants.

Too tired to move the Lieutenant, Ciaran left him where he'd landed and walked to the back of the sledge and grabbed two biscuits from the supply tin. Returning, he handed the Lieutenant the biscuits: "Here, sir."

Accepting the biscuits, the Lieutenant looked at them for a moment and said, "It's too many. We shouldn't even eat one so early."

"We're grand for the supplies, sir," Ciaran replied, guided more by his unflagging optimism than any realistic inventory. "And yeh need yer strength."

The Lieutenant looked at Ciaran dubiously, then removed the scarf covering his mouth and took a bite of the biscuit using the left side of his mouth, having already lost several teeth from the right side. After a few bites, he glanced at Ciaran and asked, "Where's yours, Creagh?"

"I ate mine already, sir," Ciaran lied.

The Lieutenant knew Ciaran well enough by now to know when he wasn't telling the truth, but they'd long ago tacitly agreed to accept whatever fabrications they told each other in order to keep going. So, the Lieutenant finished the biscuits, then asked, "How far have we traveled this morning?"

"By my step count, I'd estimate about half a mile, sir."

"Half a mile, only? How long have we been at it?"

"Two hours, sir."

"I'll have to pull harder."

"About that, sir. I think yeh should just walk along beside the sledge today. Just until yeh get yer strength back. That fever took a lot out of yeh."

"I can't let you pull the entire sledge by yourself, Creagh."

"It's no problem, sir, really. Just until yeh get yer strength back."

The Lieutenant pondered it for a moment, and then said, "All right, Creagh. All of our hopes rest on you now."

"Aye, sir."

Ellis Island, November 1913

After her pregnancy, Bridget had sometimes felt like her little village—with their superstitious, close-minded ways, not to mention the begrudgery, back-biting and gossip—was something like hell on earth. But life in steerage forced her to reconsider. Nearly a thousand emigrants from all over Europe had been jammed into that lower level situated immediately before the bulkhead of the great cabin and just below the quarter-deck. The steerage passengers were treated little better than the cargo stowed in the closed hold beneath them. With almost no ventilation and no way for the passengers in steerage to wash themselves or their clothing, the air was foul, and the stench became more intolerable with each passing day. No one cleaned the space, so Bridget and Ciaran David were constantly forced to dodge puddles of vomit and excrement left behind by sea-sick passengers. Because of the strict caste system established by the shipping line, they weren't permitted to leave the steerage area and mingle with passengers of other classes. In spite of the squalor prevailing in steerage, little Ciaran David, two and a half years old now, seemed mostly unaffected by it. He'd complain about the food and would occasionally comment on the queerness of some of their fellow passengers, yet his spirits never seemed to waver.

For the seven days and nights that the journey lasted, they slept in a hold that contained 300 passengers. The berths were arranged in two tiers with less than two and a half feet separating the upper and lower bunks. The five rows of bunkbeds were jammed so close together it almost looked like one enormous bed. No separation was made by the shipping line between families, single women and single men. Rather, everyone was thrown in there willy-nilly, forcing the steerage passengers to fend for themselves. Meals, rather than something to look forward to, were a cruel joke. The food served in steerage most days was a watery gruel, the taste of which varied between bland and disgusting, accompanied by bread crusts that, often as not, were moldy. The caloric content and nutritional value of this repast was barely sufficient to keep spirit joined to body for the weeklong passage. In the worst moments, Bridget had wondered if steerage was what the leper colonies in Jesus's time had been like. Thus, Bridget came to realize that her village wasn't hell —steerage was. This came into broad relief for Bridget on their fifth night out.

*

Bridget and Ciaran David were sleeping in the same narrow upper bunk that they'd occupied since the first night out. Because she didn't want Ciaran David out of hand's reach at any time during the voyage, Bridget didn't bother trying to find the boy his own berth. The snug conditions atop the bunk didn't bother Ciaran David in the least and he slept like a log every night. However, the arrangement was a bit too cramped for Bridget to ever secure a decent night's sleep, no matter how tired she was. The bunk below theirs was occupied by an older man from Derry named Martin who was traveling to the States to stay with his daughter and son-in-law in upstate New York. It was the middle of the night when Bridget awoke with a start as a large, foul-smelling hand covered her mouth. That was quickly followed by an equally large, calloused hand darting under her dress. Bridget's eyes opened wide and she attempted to scream, but the hand smothering her mouth completely muffled any sound. A soot-covered, angular, Eastern European face hovered over hers, whispering something in a language that Bridget had never heard before. His breath reeked worse than the hand.

She glanced down at Ciaran David, still sleeping peacefully at her side. As the hand made its way up her dress, Bridget clamped her thighs shut tight and thrashed around wildly, trying to create as much noise as possible. But the symphony of snoring which filled the hold continued unabated. The hand under her dress at this point had made it to her crotch and was fumbling with her knickers. Desperate, Bridget sunk her teeth into the meaty part of the hand covering her mouth and bit as hard as she could. The hand immediately drew away from her face as her assailant grunted in pain. She immediately screamed, "Help!" as loud as she could.

This awoke Ciaran David, who rubbed his eyes, asking, "What is it, Mammy?"

Her assailant, more agitated than hurt, immediately reached for her again. This time it was with both hands, as though he was going to strangle her. Channeling the boxing lessons David Patrick had given her as a girl, Bridget sat up in bed, balled her right hand into a tight fist and smashed it into her assailant's nose. Blood spurted from his nostrils as he uttered what were undoubtedly curses. The commotion managed to arouse Martin in the lower bunk. He sat up in bed, demanding, "What's all this now?"

The assailant grabbed Martin's hair and drove a knee

into his face, knocking him unconscious. The distraction gave Bridget and the now wailing Ciaran David a chance to roll off the other side of the bunk and scream bloody murder. This finally awakened the sleeping hold, and a handful of men clambered out of their bunks to see what was causing the commotion. After beginning to follow Bridget to the other side of the bunk, the assailant suddenly slunk off before anyone arrived. Ciaran David, between sobs, asked Bridget, "What happened, Mammy?"

Bridget kneeled down and hugged him, whispering in soothing tones, "It's alright, Asthore. There was a bad man..."

"What bad man?" he interrupted, swinging his head around in a wild search.

Bridget glanced over his shoulder at the shadows layering the large room and involuntarily shuddered. "Don't worry, love. He's gone now."

"I'll protect you from the bad man, Mammy," Ciaran David asserted between sobs.

"I know you will, love."

*

For the next two nights, Bridget didn't sleep, constantly fearing a return of her attacker. But he'd either learned his lesson or, more likely, had moved on to easier prey. Bridget didn't see her accoster again until their final day aboard. Just before noon on that day word reached steerage that the ship was about to enter New York Harbor. There was a great rush to the section of deck between the bow and the bridge where steerage passengers were permitted. By the time Bridget and Ciaran David managed to squeeze outside, the number of souls on deck was greater than the entire population of her village. Unwashed bodies were pressed shoulder to shoulder like sheep in a holding pen. Emerging on deck, Bridget found that she couldn't see past the first wave of bodies halted just outside the steerage door, much less all the way to the rail. Only twenty yards away, that rail may as well have been on another continent owing to everything that stood between her and it. Yet Bridget was determined that young Ciaran David should see what they'd suffered the most miserable week of their lives in order to reach. Picking him up, she gripped him tightly to her breast with both arms and began to fight her way toward the rail. Nearly ten minutes elapsed as Bridget wriggled through the crowd, absorbing both curses and physical abuse along the way. Protecting Ciaran David being her only concern, she left herself exposed throughout the gauntlet to elbows to various parts of her body and to having her dainty feet stomped on mercilessly.

At last, the only thing standing between her and an unimpeded view was a tall, broad-shouldered man with greasy black hair wearing a shabby, brown suit. His back to her, Bridget paused as she tried to figure out how to get around this giant. As she was considering her options, she noticed something on the palm of his right hand. It was a red mark in the shape of teeth. Bridget recoiled in recognition and attempted to back away. But it wasn't easy to enact a quick getaway pinned within that throng as they were. Sensing that someone was looking at him, the giant spun his head around. Catching sight of Bridget, he turned completely around and grinned malevolently at her. Their eyes locked for a moment, then Bridget pushed hard to her right and was absorbed by the crowd. When she turned to see if he was pursuing them, she'd only made it maybe five feet, but that meant that at least a dozen bodies now intervened. Enough separation to allow her to breathe again. She was further relieved to see that he'd already turned his back on her and was focused on the sight of New York harbor.

She looped around and was able to wriggle into a front row spot about twenty feet further down the rail. Just as she was wedging her way into a few free inches along the rail, Bridget heard a shout go up: "There it is!"

Following with her eyes the path blazed by the several hundred arms pointing to the port side, Bridget caught her first glimpse of the New Colossus towering green with hints of copper above the gray waves of New York Harbor. Hidden from view by the crowd pressing against the ship's rail were Liberty Island and the great stone pedestal on which the colossal statue perched. But Bridget had a clear view of Lady Liberty from the knees up. Hoisting up Ciaran David for a better view, she asked, "Do you see that, love?"

"Yes, Mammy," he replied, his blue eyes opened wide. "What is it?"

"The Statue of Liberty, love. We made it."

"We're in America now?"

"Aye, love. What do you think of it?"

Ciaran David couldn't take his eyes off of the statue, replying in a dreamy voice after a moment's reflection, "It's grand."

Bridget gripped Ciaran David tightly with her right arm so that she could wipe the tears from her eyes with her left hand. A slight catch in her voice, she replied, "Aye."

*

As they approached the Great Hall at Ellis Island, Bridget and Ciaran David found themselves pressed among the fifty score immigrants from their ship, who were, in turn, merging into an even larger line consisting of thousands more immigrants from other ships. They were shuffled into a great maze of metal rails and fencing that reminded Bridget of cattle being led into the shambles located just outside of her village. After inching forward for several hours, they made it to the medical examination room. The immigrants filed in by the dozen and were prodded and poked by several teams of doctors and nurses. The sick travelers were separated from the rest, often to be immediately repatriated to their country of origin. As Bridget awaited her and Ciaran David's turn, she heard a piercing wail. Turning, she saw a girl of no more than nine being led away from her parents. The parents had to be restrained by several burly guards. They struggled and pleaded with the guards in a language Bridget didn't understand. But the language barrier wasn't the problem. The problem was the parents were beseeching men whose hearts had been turned to stone by the tremendous amount of misery that constantly confronted them. Bridget shuddered and looked away.

Once they'd passed the physical, Bridget and Ciaran David were led into another room where a different kind of examination was being held. They were placed before a low-grade civil servant wearing round spectacles and a cheap, rumpled gray suit. His first question was: "Do you need an interpreter?"

"No sir," Bridget replied, sitting up straight in a hard-backed wooden chair with Ciaran David on her lap. "We speak English."

Glancing down at the ship's manifest, the civil servant asked, "You are Bridget and David O'Shea?"

"Yes and no," Bridget replied nervously. "That is to say, sir, I'm Bridget O'Shea. My son's name is Ciaran David O'Shea."

The civil servant removed his spectacles and wiped them with a ragged, black necktie. Replacing the glasses on his nose, he looked at the manifest again: "It says only David O'Shea here, madam."

"The clerk at the shipping line was an English lad. He didn't know how to spell Ciaran, so he left it out entirely."

"Do you have a birth certificate, madam?"

"No sir."

"Do you have anything that could verify your son's name?"

"Nothing, sir."

"Then I'm afraid that, for now, it will have to remain David only. I'm not authorized to correct mistakes made at the port of embarkation without some form of documentation. Now, I have a series of questions that I'm required to ask of you."

"It's just sir…" Bridget put in, but then trailed off.

"Yes?'

"Ciaran was his da's name. His da may be, em, lost. The name's the only thing the wee thing might have left of him."

"He has his surname, madame."

"No sir. You see, his da was lost before we were ever able to get married properly."

"I see," the civil servant frowned and looked over his glasses at Bridget. "Well, perhaps he'll be found again. I understand that is a not infrequent occurrence with Irishmen."

Bridget bit her lip and nodded.

"In any event, I must get on with my questionnaire. Have you ever been incarcerated, in an alms house, or an institution for the insane?"

Her mind still dimly aware of what was going on, Bridget answered the questions perfunctorily. But her heart —her heart was in a cold and barren place whose winter-long night had just ended, searching for a man who'd now, finally, had the last thing left for him to give stripped away.

New York, May 1947

When Percy opened the door, sunlight streamed into the shed, glinting off of the tools hanging on the opposite wall. Seated at the worktable, Mr. Patrick, wearing reading spectacles, was going over all of the ship's seams with a flashlight. Seeing Percy enter, Mr. Patrick removed his glasses and set them on the table. Gently hoisting the ship from the workbench, he turned and held it toward Percy. Although he'd been working side-by-side with Mr. Patrick throughout the entire process, Percy still couldn't help but marvel at the finished product. Not only was the ship now completely repaired, it was better than it'd been before. First of all, the hull was stronger because they'd used sturdier wood to repair the rents and reinforce the remainder. The finish was better, too. Mr. Patrick had found a stain that was deeper and darker than the original paint, and he'd shellacked the entire thing so that it was not only more realistic in appearance, it was more water-tight. They'd also added details. Mr. Patrick had painted the ship's name on the hull and, where there'd only been a captain before, an entire crew was now fastened securely to the deck.

"The glue's dried," Mr. Patrick said, carefully handing the ship to Percy. "She should be fit for the open seas."

The sunlight streaming through the open door reflected off of the shiny surface of the ship. Mr. Patrick extended it to him. Accepting it, Percy ran his hands over the hull. It felt smooth and sturdy. "Have you tested it in water yet?"

"I thought I'd leave it to yerself to see if she's seaworthy. Though, there's nary a doubt in my mind that she is."

"I'm going to take her to the boat pond at Central Park right now. Can you come?"

Mr. Patrick shook his head, "Sorry, lad. I've something I must do."

Percy looked crestfallen, "But she's as much yours as she is mine now, Mr. Patrick."

Mr. Patrick walked over to Percy and patted him on the shoulder, "Another day, I promise. Yeh'll tell me all about it tomorrow, eh?"

Percy nodded glumly.

Mr. Patrick put his arm around Percy's shoulders and led him to the door, saying, "Don't look so down in the mouth, Percy. Yer about to launch yer ship again!"

Percy stopped before crossing the threshold. Turning to Mr. Patrick, he asked, "What if I run into Marty and those fellows?"

"Ah. So that's what's troubling yeh?"

Percy nodded.

"Well, if those bleeding eejits turn up, yeh do what I taught yeh. Do yeh remember?"

Percy nodded uncertainly. Mr. Patrick leaned down and removed the ship from Percy's hands and placed it gently on the work bench. Then he returned to Percy and squatted on his haunches. Holding his hands up, his palms facing Percy, he said, "Give me a right."

Percy balled his little fist and threw a half-hearted right cross into Mr. Patrick's left palm. Mr. Patrick looked at Percy, shook his head in disgust, and said, "Yeh wouldn't manage to dislodge a fly from day-old shite with that punch." Nodding to Percy's feet, he barked, "Set yer feet!"

Percy stepped into a boxing stance, left-foot forward. Then he raised his fists in a defensive posture. "That's it. Now get angry. Think what them thick apes done to yer ship."

A fire flashed in Percy's eyes briefly. He nodded.

"Now let's see a proper right!"

Percy planted his right foot and drove a hard right into Mr. Patrick's left hand.

"That's it! Another!"

Percy landed another punch, even harder this time.

"Left, right!"

Percy drove a left into Mr. Patrick's right hand and a right into his left.

"Left, right, left, right, left!"

Percy delivered the requested five-punch combination with speed, accuracy and power, looking like he wanted to keep swinging after it was finished. Mr. Patrick stood up and shook out his hands as though in pain. "If yeh hit 'em like that, yer troubles with them thick-skulled gobhawks will be over."

Mr. Patrick fetched the ship from the workbench and handed it to Percy again: "There. Now go Christen her. Tomorrow, yeh'll tell me how she sailed."

New York, May 1947

Mr. Patrick got off of the subway at 42nd street and followed 7th Avenue uptown. Possessing no clear idea of where to look, he was forced to scour all of the side streets and alleys that threaded their way through the Times Square area. It'd been a couple months since Mr. Patrick had seen him, but Mr. Patrick figured that if he was still around, he'd be in this area. He'd been searching for nearly two hours when Mr. Patrick came across a balding man in tattered clothes who could've been anywhere from thirty-five to fifty-five years of age. His face and clothing covered in grime, the man was sprawled out and snoring on a cardboard box near some garbage cans situated against the wall of a tenement building. Mr. Patrick walked over to him. Beside the man was an empty bottle of cheap whiskey.

Mr. Patrick squatted beside the man and observed him for a few moments. Glancing at his feet, Mr. Patrick noticed that the man's boots were mismatched. He shook his head sadly, then leaned over and gave one of those boots a hard smack. The man immediately sat up and threw several punches at the air in front of him, muttering in a voice thick with phlegm and whiskey, "Back off if you know what's good for you!" He paused and hocked a loogie onto the filthy cobblestone beside himself, then muttered, "Can't a fellow grab a wink in this city without some jerk coming along and kicking him?"

"I see the right's still working." Mr. Patrick smiled.

The man took a moment to rub the sleep from his eyes, then turned to Mr. Patrick and said in a groggy voice, "Is that you, Paddy Byrnes, you bandy-legged bastard?"

"The same, Davy," Paddy replied. "I'd ask how yer doing, but that's apparent enough."

"Did you come here after all these years to simply insult me?"

"Years?" Paddy asked. "It's been two months since last I seen yeh."

"Let it be another twenty years before I have to clap eyes on your ugly gob again, you punch-drunk, little shoemaker."

Paddy chuckled, "I see yeh haven't lost yer gift of gab either, Davy."

"And you haven't lost the gift of boring me, Paddy."

Sitting fully upright, Davy extended his hand palm-up toward Paddy, adding: "Now that we're all caught-up, make with a pint of rye or fuck off."

"I have something I want to discuss with yeh, Davy."

"Oh, you want to discuss something? What say we discuss what you did to me, Paddy. Shall we discuss that?"

"I've done nothing to yeh, Davy O'Shea, and well yeh know that. We've been over this and over this. It was all Jake's doing. I knew nothing of it. And when I tried to expose it, Jake got me blackballed out of boxing. I've been working as a janitor these past ten years."

"And, as you can see, I've been prospering, as well. In fact, I got me a place in midtown."

"Look, going over all of that again benefits neither of us. I've something serious to discuss with yeh, Davy. A minute's all I need."

"What's in it for me?"

"Same old Davy," Paddy shook his head and smiled. "Nothing, maybe, I don't know. But if I'm right, something more valuable than all the money in the world."

"And what would that be?"

"Redemption."

"Redemption?" Dave burst into a hearty laugh which was soon overtaken by a hacking cough that shook his entire body. When he'd finished coughing, he turned to his right and hocked out a thick clump of mucus, then added, "That and a nickel will get you a cup of coffee. I got no need for redemption. What I do have a need of is whiskey. So, if you're not standing me a pint of rye, please fuck off."

Paddy reached into his back pocket and removed his

wallet. Producing a bill, he held it up and asked, "Will a fiver do yeh?"

Davy's eyes widened. He reached for the bill, but Paddy pulled it back, saying, "Yeh've gotta answer me a few questions first."

Davy slid his body backward until he was able to rest his back against the wall of the tenement building and, in a resigned voice, replied, "All right. I'll answer your damn questions if it'll stop you from tormenting me."

"Do yeh recall a lass named Rita that yeh used to go with back in yer fighting days?"

"You'll have to be more specific than that, Paddy. I ran with a lot of skirts in my fighting days."

"Aye, but yeh stuck with this one longer than the others. Leggy blonde, danced with the Rockettes. She was yer girl at the time of the Carvallo fight."

"Oh, Rita." A wisp of a smile fluttered across Davy's face, revealing a number of gaps where teeth should've been. The teeth that remained were stained a dark brown. "Rita," he repeated almost dreamily. Snapping back to the present, he growled, "What of her?"

"What became of her?"

"No idea," Davy shook his head. "We parted ways after the Carvallo fight. She said the fight changed me—that I wasn't the same person no more." Davy paused for a moment, then added, "I told her she was nuts. People don't just change. But now... now, I don't know...."

Paddy looked at Davy. The reply to that statement was too obvious to warrant giving voice to it, so he let it pass. "Yeh've heard nothing of her from that point?"

"Nothing." Davy seemed lost in thought again for a

moment, then looked at Paddy suspiciously, "Say, what're you getting at, anyway?"

"I'm not sure. I'll let yeh know when I am."

"I'm all on pins and needles. Now fork over the fin."

"Let me take yeh to the St. Vincent de Paul to get yeh some clean clothes and a hot meal."

"That's one idea. Here's another: gimme the dough you promised, then fuck off."

Paddy reluctantly handed Davy the five-dollar bill, saying, "Please don't spend this on drink, Davy."

Demonstrating remarkable hand speed for a man in his decrepit condition, Davy snatched the bill away from Paddy, replying, "I'll use it as I see fit, thank you very much. Now go on back to the Lollipop Guild."

Madison Square Garden, July 1936

Wearing a white terrycloth bathrobe, the slippers on his feet flapping with every step he took, Davy, with Paddy and Tommy flanking him, wended his way through the bowels of Madison Square Garden. Arriving at their dressing room door, Tommy pushed it open and they entered. It wasn't the team locker room used by the Rangers hockey club, but rather was a smaller space designed to house fighters, wrestlers and the like. With just Davy and his corner occupying it, the windowless room was plenty spacious. Already seated on a folding metal chair adjacent to a rubdown table against the far wall was Jake Scanlan, puffing on a cigar. Stopping just inside the door, Davy reached into his bathrobe pocket and removed the medal that Rita had thrown at him. Handing it to Paddy, he said, "Hold onto this for me Pads."

Nodding, Paddy accepted the medal.

"Keep that thing with you during the fight," Davy directed him.

Dropping it into his vest pocket, Paddy replied, "Don't I always?"

Patting Paddy on his cheek, Davy said, "You do a good job of looking out for me, Paddy."

"Somebody has to."

Spying Jake, Paddy shook his head in disgust. Walking over to him, Paddy removed the cigar from Jake's mouth, threw it to the floor, then ground it out with his foot.

"What the hell'd ya do that for, ya crazy mick?" Jake demanded.

"Davy's fighting in three hours. He doesn't need to be breathing yer stinking stogie smoke, Jake."

"I'd've put it out," Jake whined, looking disconsolately at the twisted remnants of his cigar. "Ya didn't have to go and destroy it."

"Where've yeh been, anyway?" Paddy demanded. "Yeh missed weigh-in."

"I had things to take care of," Jake responded defensively, his tone still aggrieved. Turning to Davy, he asked in a more chipper voice, "Did ya make weight, kid?"

"Yep," Davy responded, climbing onto the padded rub-down table. Laying down on his back, he cradled his head within his laced fingers.

"Did ya have to cut?"

"Nope," Davy replied lazily, gazing at the ceiling. "Came in a quarter pound under."

"Ya cut it pretty close, kid" Jake said, still staring wistfully at his crushed cigar.

"What're you talking about, Jake?" Davy demanded with a laugh. "I didn't even have to take off my underpants!"

"Under's under, Jake," Paddy interjected in a testy voice. "Now he can just rest instead of having to sweat off weight."

"All right, Paddy, all right. Don't get so aggravated over everything—it'll give ya high blood pressure."

Paddy bit his lip and scowled. Jake smiled and reached in the breast pocket of his rumpled, double-breasted suit coat. Realizing he had no cigars left, it was now Jake's turn to scowl. Paddy grabbed a folding chair and dragged it across the room until it was adjacent to the head of the rubdown table. "Scram, Jake. I gotta get Davy ready."

"Loosen your corset, Paddy. Ya got three hours 'til fight time. I wanna talk to my boy."

Seeing the look of anger that crossed Paddy's face, Jake grinned, knowing that he was now winning their constant game of who could irritate the other the most. Turning to Davy, he inquired, "How ya feelin', Davy?"

"Like a million bucks, Jake," Davy replied with a yawn, as though he had not a care in the world.

"You're only a two-to-one underdog, kid. That's the best odds any contender had against Carvallo since he won the belt. How much money should I lay on ya?"

"Every penny you got, Jake," Davy replied with a laugh. "I'll make you a rich man. Maybe you can start buying a better class of stogies."

"Maybe I will, kid," Jake laughed. "Ya feel good, huh?"

"Never better."

"Ya gonna win us that champeenship?"

"It's as good as ours, Jake."

"That's what I wanna hear, kid." Jake sat back and instinctively reached for a new cigar, only to once again be disappointed. "Carvallo won't know what hit 'im."

"He can read about it in the funny papers."

"Ya seem loose—confident, kid."

Davy's only reply was to stretch his arms above his head and let out another enormous yawn.

"Boy, I hope ya can stay awake for the fight, kid," Jake laughed. After a short pause, he added, "So ya haven't had that dream no more?"

Davy stopped in mid-yawn. He dropped his arms to his side as the blood drained out of his face. Paddy leapt to his feet, looking like he might go after Jake. Tommy quickly stepped between them. His face red with anger, Paddy took a moment to compose himself. Then, through clenched teeth, he snarled, "Outside. Now. Jake."

"Whaddaya gettin' all worked up over, Paddy?" Jake replied, innocently. Waving at Davy, who no longer had the calm relaxed look that'd suffused him only moments earlier, he added, "The kid knows it ain't nothin' but a dream and that it's all nonsense. Don't ya, kid?"

Davy nodded without conviction, the aura of undaunted confidence having been punctured.

"Outside now, Jake," Paddy repeated in clipped tones.

"I'll leave when I'm damn-well ready," Jake replied icily, the jocular sparring now over. "He's my fighter. I own him."

"Yeh own his contract, Jake. Not him."

"Same difference," Jake shrugged.

"Well, yeh may own Davy's contract, but yeh don't own mine."

"Don't need to. I can fire ya whenever I please. In fact," turning to address Tommy, he continued, "Tommy, how'd ya like to run the corner for a middleweight champeenship fight?"

Tommy's eyes got wide, as though he'd suddenly been confronted with some unspeakable horror. He took a step back and waved his hands as though he were under attack by a swarm of hornets.

"Don't put Tommy in the middle of this, Jake," Paddy replied more calmly. "Tommy's gonna be a great trainer someday, but he's not ready for this now." Pointing toward the door with his thumb, he said, "Let's discuss this in the hall."

"As long as we understand each other, Paddy."

"We understand each other, Jake."

Pushing himself to his feet with a groan, Jake patted Davy on the shoulder, saying, "Good luck, kid. I know you're gonna do us proud."

Davy nodded mutely. Brushing past Paddy, Jake growled, "Let's talk."

Paddy watched Jake exit the dressing room, then said, "Don't pay none of that any mind, Davy." Turning to Tommy, he added, "Get started with Davy's rubdown. I'll be back in a minute."

Tommy nodded. Paddy turned to leave. Tommy called after him, "Paddy..."

When Paddy turned to look at him, Tommy said, "I wouldn't have..."

Paddy brushed the thought away, "I know yeh wouldn't, Tommy. That's just Jake blowing gas, trying to show everyone who's boss."

Tommy nodded sheepishly and Paddy turned and exited the dressing room. Once both Jake and Paddy were gone, Davy turned to Tommy and asked, "Why'd Jake have to go and bring up the dream?"

Tommy shrugged, "Dunno. Flip over, champ. I gotta rub you down."

*

The hallway outside the dressing room was dark and wide, with a high ceiling from which hung fluorescent lights. Jake stood in the middle of the hallway looking at his watch. Paddy closed the door and walked up to Jake until they were almost nose to nose. Nose to chin, anyway, as Jake stood several inches taller. "I oughta slug yeh," Paddy said in an even, though menacing, tone.

"Take your shot, tough guy. That don't sweat me none," Jake replied nonchalantly. "You're forgettin' I seen ya fight."

"What's yer angle, Jake?" Paddy demanded.

"Whaddaya talkin' about, Paddy?"

"Why the hell'd yeh bring up the dream? Yeh know it scares the shite out of Davy."

Jake shrugged, "He looked fine to me."

"Now I gotta spend the next hour talking him into fighting again instead of going over strategy."

"He'll be fine. Ya said it yourself, he's in the best shape he's ever been in. That kid's lethal."

"What'd yeh get yerself mixed up in, Jake? Where were yeh earlier?"

"I told ya, I had things to take care of. Not that it's any of your business. Don't forget who's boss here."

"How could I? Yeh keep reminding me." Paddy turned and placed his hand on the doorknob. He started to turn the knob, and then stopped. Spinning around, he said, "Davy ain't taking no dive, Jake."

"You're like a broken record, Paddy."

"If we're fighting, then we're fighting straight up—to win."

"No one's askin' anyone to take no dives."

Paddy eyed Jake for a moment, as though trying to read his thoughts. Then he shook his head and reached for the doorknob again. Just then, a man with thinning white hair combed over a bald spot on top, wearing a white shirt with the sleeves rolled up to the forearms, and slacks held up by suspenders, approached the two. "The commission needs someone from Davy's corner to come down and inspect the fight gloves."

"I'll do it," Paddy replied, taking a step toward the man.

Jake grasped Paddy's elbow, "It's okay, Paddy. I'll take care of this."

"I always check the gloves."

"Ya need to take care of Davy. I'll do it this time."

"But yeh never done it before, Jake! How would yeh know…"

"It ain't brain surgery," Jake interrupted him. "I just gotta make sure the gloves is okey-dokey."

"Well, one of you needs to do it and I don't give a damn who," the man from the commission interrupted sternly. "I don't got all night."

The man from the commission turned and started to walk away. Jake followed him calling back to Paddy over his shoulder, "Make sure Davy's head is straight. This is our big chance!"

With that, Jake turned and scurried after the man from the commission. Paddy watched him until he disappeared into the murkiness further down the hall. Paddy rubbed his chin as he listened to Jake's disembodied footsteps echoing fainter and fainter. When the final echo died away, Paddy turned and opened the door to the dressing room.

Antarctica, February 1912

Ciaran knew that the people from his village would never understand Antarctica or the allure it held for him. They saw it only as a cold and barren place—a land unfit for human existence. And they were right about that much. But what they didn't understand, what even he didn't know until he got there, was the breathtaking, unsullied beauty of the place. On clear evenings in the winter it seemed that every star in the universe was visible—the night sky being a sea of white with slivers of black filling the interstices. The auroral displays on winter nights were stunning—a cross between a fireworks display and an impressionist painting. He'd heard of the aurora before coming here, but what he'd heard hadn't come close to doing justice to the spectacle of it. There were fog bows, which were white rainbows composed of fog that stretched from one end of the horizon to the other. In the winter there were moon dogs, or paraselenes—lunar halos caused by a refraction of moonlight by ice crystals. These moon dogs were so large, and hung so low in the sky it seemed that if you just jumped you could touch them. In the summer the sun dogs, or parhelions, came out. These were like moon dogs, but flanked the sun so that it seemed there were three suns. Iridescent clouds, colorful optical phenomena appearing in the proximity of the sun or moon, often appeared in the sky, as though God the Father had decided to add some pastel colors to the crisp blue and white Antarctic sky.

Then there was the landscape. Near the base camp were Mt. Terror and Mt. Erebus, dormant volcanoes on Ross Island that towered twelve thousand feet above sea level, the tops of which were almost always wreathed in mist, and possessed an awesome primordial beauty. During their march to the Pole they'd passed Mount Discovery and Mount Morning, lying at the head of the McMurdo Sound, part of a panorama of mountain ranges. Beardmore Glacier, which ran miles deep, had waterfalls made of ice hundreds of feet high that made it look like a glittering ice palace. He knew that even if he returned home minus a leg and no teeth (in addition to the scurvy causing his teeth to fall out, the cold had shattered those that remained) he wouldn't regret his decision to join the expedition. Even the sastrugi, when one wasn't struggling to haul heavy sledges across them, had a gripping beauty—like waves on a sea of nearly pure white. People back home sometimes called Ireland God's country, and loving his home island, Ciaran admitted that it did have its own unique charm. But Antarctica was truly God's country. It was desolate of biological life, perhaps, but every inch of it was infused with an artistry that could only be called divine. God had used the cold, along with the inaccessibility of the place, to keep it all for Himself. After all, only a handful of mortals had ever glimpsed it, much less set foot on it.

Ciaran thought about all of this while he sat in the tent watching the Lieutenant writhing in what Ciaran knew to be his death throes. Two days previously, too weak to pull, the Lieutenant had begun walking along behind the sledge. But even this seemed too much as he kept falling farther behind as the day's march wore on. They'd only made it three miles that day with Ciaran pulling alone and having to constantly stop to allow the Lieutenant to catch up. The next day it was apparent the Lieutenant would be unable to even walk, forcing Ciaran to pack him on the sledge and haul him along with the food, supplies, and gear. Despite starvation and disease having whittled him down to a shadow of his former self, the Lieutenant and his cold weather gear still added more than ten stone to a load that at least two healthy men should've been hauling.

When they stopped at the end of that day, the Lieutenant was burning with fever and was clearly unfit to be transported in -30 Fahrenheit weather with gusting winds registering force 5 on the Beaufort Scale. So, in spite of conditions that were more than adequate for hauling that next morning, they stayed in the tent while Ciaran nursed the Lieutenant as best he could. Ciaran realized that at this point the care he was offering was merely palliative. In addition to fever, the Lieutenant would occasionally be wracked with seizures so bad that Ciaran was forced to sit on his frail chest in order to control the convulsive writhing. The Lieutenant's moments of lucidity were fleeting. In one of them, Ciaran had offered the Lieutenant morphine from the medicine kit to ease his suffering, but the Lieutenant refused it.

In his final moment of clarity, the Lieutenant's eyes snapped open. Cold sweat beaded on his forehead in spite of temperatures within the tent that hovered around 0 Fahrenheit. Gasping, the Lieutenant croaked in a voice wrecked by cold and dehydration, "Go, Creagh. Leave me!"

"No sir. Yeh'll be fit presently," Ciaran replied.

"We both know that's untrue," the Lieutenant weakly shook his head. "Go. Our companion will look after you."

Ciaran looked at the Lieutenant, astonished. "Companion, sir?"

"Yes, the third traveler—the one who's followed along with us since we got on the Ross shelf."

"You've seen him too, sir? I thought it was only meself

seeing him." Ciaran paused for a moment and then asked, "Who do you reckon it is, sir?"

Lieutenant Wellesley smiled weakly, "Ministering angel."

Ciaran sat back, shaking his head at the shock of learning the Lieutenant had seen the third traveler as well. It wasn't just a figment of his imagination. He stared at the Lieutenant, who seemed to muster all of his strength just to utter a few words.

With one final effort, the Lieutenant said, "I already have Hanes's and Owens' deaths to answer for. I won't have yours, as well. Go, Creagh. It's an order."

Ciaran shook his head, "I'll have to respectfully disobey that order, sir."

A look of steely determination came to the Lieutenant's watery, bloodshot eyes. With great effort the Lieutenant raised his head. He looked like he was about to bark an order. But then his eyes fluttered, his head dropped back onto the sleeping bag and the fever overtook him again. Ciaran watched as he writhed in pain, thinking back to their first meeting in London when he'd volunteered for the mission.

*

Ciaran's ship, the HMS Dreadnought, was anchored in Portsmouth when the call for volunteers for a polar mission went out. Though Ciaran knew nothing of Antarctica and had little experience with seriously cold weather, he was lured by the offer of extra pay and rapid promotion. But, more than that, he was drawn to the adventure of it. When he arrived at the office that Lieutenant Wellesley and his backers had established in South Kensington, there was a line of volunteers stretching around the block. Ciaran discovered later that nearly three thousand men had volunteered for thirty available positions (many spots had already been filled by specialists and former polar explorers). It took most of the day, but Ciaran waited patiently until he was ushered into the tiny, musty office that served as Lieutenant Wellesley's headquarters.

They started off talking about Ciaran's background—the village he grew up in, life on the farm, and Ciaran's abbreviated school career. The conversation then turned to Ciaran's naval career. The Lieutenant had spread out before him on his desk Ciaran's service records. Glancing them over, the Lieutenant asked in a diplomatic tone, "I see here you've been demoted twice, Creagh."

"That's true, sir."

"Can you explain what happened?"

"The first one happened when I was only sixteen, not long after I'd shipped out the first time. I got in a dispute with an older seaman and I didn't handle it well. But I've learned me lesson, sir."

"Well, you were young and the report indicates the other seaman was at least equally at fault, so perhaps we can overlook that one. This second demotion is more troubling to me as it's for insubordination to an officer."

"I admit I did disobey an order, sir. It was on the Cadmus, a sloop assigned to the China fleet. We was sailing in the South China Sea. The officer was a newly minted midshipman. I was a bos'n's mate with six years of service time at that point. I was standing watch on the fo'c'sle when the midshipman ordered the helmsman to turn her hard to port because of some shoals that were visible far off in the distance to the starboard. The problem was, sir, there were wicked shoals hard to our port. They weren't quite visible, but I knew they were there from having sailed the route several times. I called up to the helmsman telling him to belay that order and turn the wheel to starboard instead. The midshipman, being a new officer and anxious to establish authority, ordered me to stand down. We were close to that shoal and I was worried the shoal would either rip a hole in our hull or, at best, that we'd ground and be left high and dry.

"I rushed up to the bridge and told the helmsman to turn to the starboard before it was too late. When the midshipman ordered him to maintain his course, I grabbed the wheel and turned us to starboard and I didn't let go until we were well clear of the danger. By that time, the midshipman had summoned a couple marines who clapped me in irons. Luckily, the ruckus drew the captain to the bridge. When what'd happened was explained to him, the captain told the midshipman that what he was trying to do would've lost the ship, for sure. The captain spoke to me later. He said I was right to do what I done, that in doing what I done I'd saved the ship and his command both. But he had to demote me all the same because I'd refused a lawful order by an officer."

"Yes, I see in the report that there were extenuating circumstances." The Lieutenant tapped the pen he'd been taking notes with on his chin. As he did so, Ciaran noticed that there wasn't even a hint of whiskers on it. He began to wonder how old the Lieutenant might be as he didn't look much older than himself.

After a short pause, the Lieutenant continued, "On a mission such as this, it's important that everyone do their jobs and follow orders, whether they agree with them or not."

"Aye, sir."

"At the same time, even though this will ostensibly be run as a naval mission, it'll be much more democratic in procedure. If someone can think of a better way of doing something, whether he be from the upper or lower deck, I'm always open to new ideas. In a place like the Antarctic, it's important to have a clear, firm plan from which to operate. But, at the same time, we must be able to adapt as circumstances dictate. And in the poles, circumstances very often dictate."

Ciaran nodded respectfully.

"You received a sterling recommendation from your current commanding officer, Captain Newburn. That recommendation carries more weight with me than anything, as Captain Newburn happens to be the first officer I sailed under after receiving my commission." The Lieutenant paused again and tapped his pen on the notepad spread out before him on the desk. "I need to know now, though, that there will be no more quarreling or insubordination."

"No sir, there'll be none of that. I promise yeh."

"Good. I've found that in polar exploration, the one quality above all others that'll dictate success is self-control in the expedition members."

"Aye, sir."

"And after that selflessness, courtesy and optimism. You'll never reach the Pole with pessimists."

"That makes sense, sir."

Their interview had been going on for nearly an hour, whereas most of the interviews were finished in a matter of minutes. Closing his notepad, Lieutenant Wellesley said, "I have a good feeling about you, Creagh. Based on that and Captain Newburn's glowing recommendation, I think we can find a spot for you on the ship party."

"Thank yeh, sir."

The Lieutenant stood, extended his hand across the desk and Ciaran shook it. "Welcome to the mission, Creagh."

THE THIRD TRAVELER

"Yeh won't regret it, sir. I promise yeh."

*

Ciaran had only been assigned to work on the ship. After the base camp was landed, he was to remain with the ship, returning to port in New Zealand in the fall, and then returning to Cape Evans with new supplies for the base camp in the spring. But Ciaran's performance aboard ship and in establishing base camp was so exemplary that he'd been added to the shore party. Based on his performance on the initial fall sledging journeys when they'd set up the supply depots for the polar run, as well as on some smaller sledging missions in the spring, he'd been added to one of the support sledging teams. Initially slotted in the last supply team, which was only to go as far as the Beardmore Glacier and return home, he'd been added to the polar party when scurvy had rendered Lieutenant Marvell unable to continue. Now, the last member added to the polar party was about to be the last man standing.

During a lull in the fits wracking the Lieutenant, Ciaran dug out the letter he'd received from Bridget just before departing for the Pole four months earlier. He'd initially kept it in the breast pocket of his fur-lined jacket. But between sweat and melting snow, the ink was starting to run and the paper had begun to decompose. So instead, he now kept it in his pack with his few personal belongings, tucked into the one book he'd brought—the Seaman's Handbook. He removed the letter from the book and gently unfolded it on top of his sleeping bag. Then he began reading for the three hundredth or four hundredth time that fist that he loved so dearly:

10 Feb. 1911

Mo shioghra,

I'm hoping that this letter finds you well and not perishing with the cold. I got your letter telling me that the Lieutenant added you to the polar support party. I wish you hadn't volunteered for that as it seems a terrible risk to me. You told me that any letter I wrote would take at least 6 months to get to you, so I'm hoping this will reach you before you leave for the pole. Everything is mostly the same as usual at home. Nothing ever changes here. Your da and brothers are well. Tiernach is getting married to Siobahn Flaherty, but I'm sure you already knew that. And I heard that Ailill is moving to Australia. So you might stop by and see him on your way back.

There is one big piece of news that I've been dreading to tell you. I'm pregnant. The baby is due in one month. So when you return from the south pole you'll have a son or daughter waiting for you. I hope you find this good news. Please write back as soon as you can and let me know what you think.

I miss you powerfully.

Love always,

Bridget

Ciaran kissed the letter and carefully folded it back into his book. He wished he'd had an opportunity to respond, but it'd only arrived the day before they departed for the Pole and there'd been no time. Now he regretted his lack of foresight in not writing a reply during the outward journey and sending it back with one of the lads on the support teams. But there was nothing to be done about that now. He glanced at the Lieutenant, whose sleep had become a bit more restless.

The letter made him think of the diary that he'd seen the Lieutenant scribbling in throughout their journey. He decided to go through the Lieutenant's personal bag and remove the diary and anything else that the Lieutenant might want Ciaran to carry back.

After digging the various documents out of the Lieutenant's bag, Ciaran glanced at the diary. There were some empty pages at the end. Tearing a page out, Ciaran decided to write Bridget a letter and carry it with him. Just in case.

New York, December 1913

The one-bedroom flat had been designed to hold four people comfortably. Roisin, Bridget's third cousin on her father's side, her husband Ardan, and their three children, Brendan, Colin, and little Deidre were already there. Now added to that mix were Bridget and Ciaran David, whom she'd taken to simply calling David to avoid confusion after the shipping company had arbitrarily changed his legal name. Roisin's family slept in the bedroom, all crammed onto one double-bed, while Bridget and little David slept together on the davenport. The furniture in the flat was strictly second and third-hand. The only decorations the tiny apartment contained were cheap paintings of the Sacred Heart of Jesus, and of the Virgin Mary. So thin were the walls upon which those paintings hung that Bridget often felt as if she were sitting in the middle of their neighbors' conversations and, as was more often the case, arguments. It was quite an adjustment for Bridget. The old homestead back in County Kerry had been snug—much snugger, indeed, than this apartment. Yet, aside from the chirping of cicadas and the occasional bleating of sheep in the summer, her father's home had been still as a church graveyard at night. Then there was the climb to get to Roisin's flat. It was on the top-floor of an eight-story walk-up tenement. It felt like hiking to the top of Cnoc na Piseog every time she returned home. And the weather—it was cold in New York in December, much colder than Ireland. Bridget, knowing little about world meteorological patterns, wondered how much colder the South Pole could possibly be as compared to New York in the winter.

Those first few weeks in Roisin's flat were a difficult transition for Bridget. Her sole comfort was that there was no call for homesickness because there seemed to be more Irish in Hell's Kitchen than in counties Kerry, Cork, Limerick and Clare combined. Of course, the heavily Irish presence carried negative implications with it as well, as the judgements she'd fled her village to escape were being rendered here in America as well, just more muted. Little David, on the other hand, had no trouble whatsoever adapting to his new surroundings. Indeed, after only a month it seemed as if he'd forgotten Ireland entirely. His cousins, who ranged in age from six to ten, became like the siblings he'd never had. Only they were better than siblings, they treated him like he was the center of the universe. In the eyes of Brendan, Colin, and Deidre, not to mention Roisin and Ardan, little David was a golden child.

Nights were the hardest for Bridget. It was then she'd think of Ciaran. She knew the polar party had been reported lost. Her hopes all rested on the chance that the reports had been premature. Perhaps the polar party had turned up, just too late for word to get out. After all, it took half a year to get messages into or out of that godforsaken place. Maybe they'd found a cave in which to pass the winter and were living off of penguins and polar bears. Did they even have polar bears in the Antarctic? She was uncertain. If they didn't, there was surely something down there they could consume to survive the winter. When they got thirsty, they could simply eat snow. The possibilities of what could've become of them were endless, death was only one option. It wasn't crazy to think that they might yet be alive. Surely it wasn't, of that she was certain. Well, mostly certain.

Roisin did her best to help Bridget make it through the nights. They'd wait until everyone had gone to sleep and then Roisin would boil a pot of weak tea from the leaves left over from supper. Then they'd talk late into the evening in the tiny kitchenette.

Roisin poured Bridget a cup, then pushed a nearly empty bottle of milk toward her. After pouring herself a cup, Roisin dropped a lump of sugar into it, then she collapsed into the rickety wooden chair with a groan. The round, pock-marked breakfast table was only large enough to hold four people, so at dinner the adults ate there while the children sat at their own little folding table. Electricity having not yet made it to their building, the flickering light was provided by gas lamps mounted on the walls.

"Any word at all from the South Pole?" Roisin whispered in a Wexford accent that'd been only slightly watered down by nearly a decade in America.

"No," Bridget shook her head and took a sip from her tea. "I reckon if there is any news, you'll know as soon as I because it'll be all over the papers."

"How long had..." Roisin, having caught herself, continued, "em, *have* the two of you been together?"

"Four years, though I'd known him my entire life. His da's farm was just over the hill from ours."

"How'd you get together?"

"He was home on leave from the navy. I saw him in his dress whites and that was my heart gone."

"When did he propose?"

"The night before he left for the Antarctic. The night wee Ciaran David was conceived. But he couldn't afford a ring at the time, so it was unofficial."

"And he knows about the wee angel?" Roisin made a point of using present tense verbs when discussing Ciaran.

"I'm not sure. I sent him a letter, but I never got any response. I don't even know if he would've gotten it before he left for the Pole."

"Well, when he returns I'm sure he'll be delighted to find he has such a fine son as wee Davy...Ciaran David."

Bridget merely nodded. After a short pause, Roisin asked, "Have you heard from herself at all?"

"Not a word," Bridget shook her head. "Nor do I expect to. I've no doubt that she felt well rid of us. Sure, she didn't even bother seeing us off."

"Maybe it hurt too much to say goodbye. You were all she had left after David Patrick passed."

"You mean after the Good People took him," Bridget corrected Roisin acidly.

"Sometimes people tell themselves such things because it's easier to cope with. It's not as final as death. If the wee folk have him, then it's possible she'll see him again in this life."

"If you listen to Mam, it's worse than death. It's all eternity they'll have his soul."

Roisin shook her head, "I don't miss the superstitious ways of the old country. And you can throw the priests right in there with it. It's all of one piece."

"It's different here?"

"There's still superstitious ninnies here as anywhere. But in America progress is their religion, and people don't focus on the past, they focus on the future."

"The future?" Bridget gazed dreamily at little David, sleeping peacefully on the ottoman. "Wouldn't that be lovely? The past is always done. It may not be completely gone, but it's done, for better or worse. But in the future, there's still a chance for all of us."

*

A little later, after Roisin had gone to bed, Bridget climbed onto the davenport beside David and pulled the blanket over them. David rolled over and looked up at her, his eyes bleary with sleep. He stretched, yawned and asked, "Mam, do you think da will ever come back, like the man at the island said?"

Bridget stroked his soft blonde hair and asked, "Did you overhear what Aunt Roisin and I were saying."

David nodded, "Some of it. I couldn't sleep."

"It's possible that your da could return. We don't want to give up hope yet. But it's not so simple as the man at the island made it out to be. The South Pole is a long way away."

"Don't worry, Mammy. If Da doesn't get back soon, I'll go down to the South Pole and find him myself."

Bridget sniffled as the tears filled her eyes and then began to escape.

"Why are you crying, Mammy?"

"Because I love you so much, an leanbh."

New York, May 1947

As he made his way down the crowded sidewalk, Percy had both arms wrapped tightly around the ship like a mother clutching her babe. Still a couple blocks away, he could make out the sign for the Hudson Yards Station over the heads of the pedestrians jamming the sidewalk. As people passed, many would stare at the three-masted wooden sailboat in his arms, and some even gave him nods of approval. Percy would smile back without ever making eye contact, his gaze fixed firmly on the 47th Street entrance, now one block away. Percy wished that Mr. Patrick could've come along so they could witness together the triumph of the repaired ship's official launching. A clear sunny day with a light breeze, Percy was thinking how perfect the conditions were for boating. He kept imagining seeing its sails fill up with wind and the ship shooting across the Central Park boat pond.

Then, from somewhere over his left shoulder he heard something that chilled his heart and turned his legs to jelly: "Hey, it's Pussy Kelly!"

Percy paused, afraid to turn around, but also too scared to continue walking. He heard Marty call again, "Hey Pussy, wait up!"

Reluctantly, Percy turned. Half a block away he saw Marty, with Michael at his right side and the Pinto brothers padding dutifully behind, starting to cross Sixth Avenue, making a beeline for him. Percy froze, unsure how to proceed. He recalled Mr. Patrick's advice: land the first punch and don't stop punching until he was sure he'd won the fight. Now, with the storm about to descend upon him, all of those words, uttered in the safety of the school groundskeeper's shed, felt like ashes that would crumble and blow away in the first stiff wind. If only Mr. Patrick had been there to watch over him Percy might've found the courage to fight. But Mr. Patrick wasn't there. It was him alone on the street against four boys, two of whom—Marty and Michael—were much bigger and more aggressive than him. It's easy to hit an inanimate object like a punching bag. A bag doesn't have a face. A bag doesn't bleed or cry when hit. And, most of all, a punching bag doesn't punch back.

Seemingly oblivious to the traffic rushing by, Marty and his little gang blithely sauntered across the street, forcing a cab driver to slam on his brakes to avoid hitting them. When the cabbie yelled at them, Marty paused in the middle of the street, gave the cabbie the Italian forearm jerk and replied, "Up yours, pal!" Amazed at Marty's nerve, Percy became even more frightened. After all, if Marty wasn't even afraid of adults what chance did a kid have?

Once they were on the same sidewalk about twenty feet from Percy, Marty noticed the ship. Elbowing Michael, he said, "Look, Mikey, Pussy's got himself another ship."

Michael nodded in reply. Marty continued, "What'd ya make this time, Pussy? The Lusitania?"

The Pinto brothers cackled appreciatively at Marty's lively banter. Percy was too petrified to even respond. Marty glanced at the Pintos and nodded ever-so-slightly in Percy's direction. The Pintos, knowing what to do, split and began to casually saunter in a wide circle on either end of the sidewalk in order to get behind Percy. Aware that he was about to be flanked, Percy fell back on an instinct ingrained in humans even more deeply than the impulse to fight. Flight. Clutching the ship tightly to his chest, he turned and sprinted in the other direction as fast as his legs would carry him. Seeing this, Marty scowled and barked, "Get him!"

The Pintos took off after Percy, followed closely by Michael and then Marty. Percy made a beeline for the stairway that descended into the 50th Street Station. He knew that trying to elude them on the surface would be futile. He was faster than all of them, but something was bound to eventually impede him if he stayed on the sidewalk—a traffic signal, a passing car or bus, or perhaps a pedestrian on the crowded midtown sidewalk. So, he made for the subway station. Percy didn't entertain any fantasies like serendipitously slipping onto a train just as it pulled away. That only happened in the pictures. Rather, Percy wanted to make his pursuers think that such was his intention. The 50th Street Station had more than a dozen different exits to the surface. He could lose his pursuers in the crowded station and then slip up to the surface.

Taking the steps two at a time, he could practically feel the Pintos nipping at his heels. He didn't dare look back for fear that he'd take a header and finish the job for them —beating himself up and destroying the ship with a tumble down the steep concrete stairway. When he reached the bottom, he juked right then turned left. The station was more crowded than the surface, so he had to pick his way carefully through the throngs of commuters in order to protect the ship. As he plunged into the crowd, he swiveled his head and looked behind himself. He saw the Pinto brothers reach the bottom of the stairs and pause to scan the crowd for him. One of them pointed at him and Percy lowered his head and scampered down a busy corridor.

He wanted to stay out of the fared areas because most of them were dead ends. So, he stuck to the passageways in the mezzanine, outside of fare control. He knew there were a number of these tunnels linked together under Rockefeller Center, so that became his destination. Breaking free of the crowd outside the platforms, he entered a long tunnel down which he sprinted. He was panting hard and beginning to perspire when he reached the end of the tunnel and paused to glance back. He saw Michael enter the other end of the tunnel, but the other three weren't visible. He decided to take the stairs up the closest exit. Emerging adjacent to the RCA building, Percy began to weave through the crowd on the street. Ducking into the nearest alley, he glanced behind himself to see if any of his tormentors had pursued him onto the surface.

As he did so, he tripped over the legs of a hobo who appeared to be passed out. Percy tumbled forward, and as he did so all he could think was that it'd been all in vain. He was about to smash the ship to pieces himself. In an effort to save it, he spun around in midair and held the ship aloft at arm's length from his body. He landed on his back with a thud. The impact from the cobblestone pavement drove the air out of his lungs. He stiffened his neck to prevent his head from whiplashing into the brick. Skidding backwards into some nearby trash cans, he managed to keep the ship unscathed. Immediately rolling over and jumping to his feet, Percy scrambled behind the trash cans. As he did so, out of the corner of his eye he saw the perplexed hobo rouse and shout, "Back off if you know what's good for you!"

Ignoring the hobo, Percy rapidly shifted the garbage cans around so that he was fully concealed. Then he squatted behind them, the ship still cradled in his arms, his back resting against a brick wall. Concerned that his heavy panting would give him away, he tried to calm his breathing. Taking slow, deep inhalations through his mouth, he glanced at his elbows. Both were bleeding from his fall. A quick survey of the ship confirmed that it remained completely intact, so he didn't mind the elbows so much. The hobo, hardly having budged, made a cursory visual search for his perceived assailant. Seemingly satisfied that whoever had run into him had since departed, he lowered his head and immediately resumed snoring.

Percy wasn't sure how much time had elapsed when he detected the sound of footsteps on cobblestone. It felt like hours but probably, in reality, had only been a few minutes. The steps were light and measured. Glancing through a crack between the garbage cans, Percy gulped when he saw Michael silently searching the alley. Percy cursed himself for taking refuge in a dead-end. The problem was that at the time he'd ducked in here he'd thought they'd been hot on his heels. Now he was trapped and his only hope was that Michael wouldn't notice him. Percy closed his eyes, held his breath and silently mouthed a "Hail Mary."

It didn't work. He opened his eyes to see Michael, squatting down and peering at him through a crack between the garbage cans. They locked eyes for a moment. They'd been friends once, but that was long ago, before Michael had taken up with Marty. They stared at each other for several seconds without either saying a word when Percy heard Marty's voice from the entrance to the alley shout, "You see him, Mikey?"

Percy gave him a pleading look. Michael glanced away. Straightening up, Michael turned to Marty and replied, "Nope. Nothing here."

Marty walked over and kicked the hobo in the feet, rousing him again. "Did you see a kid with a model boat come by here, pops?" Marty demanded.

"Fuck off, you little prick," the hobo snarled. "Before I get up and give you the cuffing your old man should've."

"Up yours, you dirty old bum!" Marty snapped. Nevertheless, he turned and fled the alley.

Percy could hear Michael follow Marty out of the alley. Then he leaned back against the brick wall. It was a hot day for May, and the cool wall felt good. He waited nearly fifteen minutes before abandoning his place of refuge. Stepping from behind the garbage cans, he saw the hobo stretched out in the same place, snoring. Percy paused for a moment at the man's feet. Clearing his throat, Percy said in a timid voice, "Thanks, Mister."

The hobo stopped snoring for a moment, but without stirring or even opening his eyes, snapped, "Fuck off!"

Madison Square Garden, July 1936

Davy sat on the massage table, his legs hanging over

the side. The color seemed to have drained out of him, though it was difficult to tell with his pasty Irish complexion. On a stool before him sat Paddy. A dozen white strips of adhesive tape hung from the edge of massage table. Paddy slowly, methodically wrapped gauze around Davy's hands, periodically taking a strip of tape from the edge of the table to secure it. Tommy stood behind Paddy, soaking in Paddy's every move. A radio in the corner blared big band tunes. Paddy worked in silence, like a watchmaker consumed by the intricacies of his work. It took five minutes to complete each hand. When he put the last strip of tape on the right, Paddy sat back and said, "How's that feel?"

Davy opened and closed his left fist several times. Then, balling it up, he slammed it half-heartedly into the open palm of his already-wrapped right hand and replied, "Good."

Still leaning forward in his chair so that they were almost face to face, Paddy looked up at Davy and said, "Let's go over the fight plan again."

"Okay," Davy replied absently.

"Carvallo likes to finish his fights early. At opening bell he's gonna come charging out of his corner like a bull what's been kicked in the bollocks. What're yeh gonna do when that happens?"

"Move, slip, jab," Davy replied, as if reciting from rote.

"Let him burn up all his energy the first couple rounds chasing yeh. We got fifteen rounds to win this thing. It's what?"

"A marathon, not a sprint," Davy replied robotically.

Paddy nodded: "Once yeh've calmed him down, what do yeh do?"

"Feed him a steady diet of jabs."

"That's right. Yeh got three inches on Carvallo. Keep him right at the end of yer jab the entire fight. Every time he tries to work his way inside, yeh bust him in the gob with the jab."

"Okay."

"What do yeh do when he manages to get inside yer jab?"

"Uppercut and spin him."

"And if spinning him don't work?"

"Clinch and wait for the ref to separate us."

"Aye, clinch," Paddy nodded approvingly. "But never drop yer guard. Carvallo's famous for getting up to nonsense in clinches. And because he's the champ, the ref will probably look the other way."

"Okay."

Paddy stared at Davy for a minute, sizing him up. Then he sat back and demanded, "What's troubling yeh, Davy?"

Davy shook his head and was silent for a moment. Then, tentatively, he asked, "Why'd Jake have to go and bring up the dream?"

Paddy shook his head. In a measured tone, he replied, "Because Jake's an arsehole. Who knows why Jake does anything he does?"

Davy didn't reply, so Paddy added, "It's just a dream, man! How many times have you had it?"

"Twelve and a half."

"Aye, twelve and a half," Paddy replied, starting to get heated. "And how many times has it come true?"

"Zero," Davy responded. Then, after a pause, he added,

"But that's just for the first eleven and a half times."

Paddy spun his upper body around and looked at Tommy, as if soliciting a solution. In response, Tommy merely shook his head and shrugged apologetically. Paddy turned back to Davy, "Yer gonna get in the ring with the middleweight champion of the world in a little over an hour. I gotta know that yer gonna fight like I know yeh can or I want no part of this. Carvallo ain't gonna have no sympathy for yeh because yeh had a dream."

Davy only shrugged.

Paddy jumped to his feet, knocking his chair over backward as he did so. "Listen to me, Davy. Yer the finest fighter I ever trained. Hell, yer the finest fighter I ever seen, and I've seen 'em all. Are yeh gonna fight him or do I call it off?"

Davy shrugged once again.

Paddy glanced at Tommy again, but there was no help to be found there. Shaking his head in disgust, Paddy began to pace the room. He walked back and forth in silence for several minutes while Tommy watched him and Davy stared at the floor. Finally, he stood before Davy again and, in a calm, quiet voice, said, "Listen to me, Davy."

Davy looked up and Paddy continued, "If yeh wanna call this fight off, we'll call it. I'll say yer sick. Jake won't like it much, but Jake can kiss my arse. But hear me, man."

Davy nodded slightly, and Paddy continued, "This is the one chance yer ever gonna get at this. If yeh back outa this fight now, yeh may as well hang up the gloves forever. Yer never getting another shot at a title. Never."

Paddy paused and looked at Davy meaningfully, then added, "If yeh wanna do that, I'll support yeh. But it'll be a damn shame because I've never been sure of much in my life but the one thing I am certain of is that yer better than

Carvallo. A damn sight better. Yeh can walk out of here tonight as the middleweight champion of the world if yeh want to. But yeh gotta want to."

Davy said nothing. Paddy glanced at Tommy, who shrugged. Paddy rubbed his forehead and began to pace the room again. After several moments of this, he returned to Davy and asked, "Who is Carvallo, eh? Tell me that?"

Davy still didn't reply and so Paddy answered the question himself. "I'll tell yeh who he is. He's a brawler from the Bronx who landed a lucky punch and won the title and has fought nothing but stiffs since that night. That is, until tonight."

"He's the champ all the same, Pads," Davy finally responded. "Who am I?"

"Who are you? Dammit, you're Davy O'Shea, the terror from County Kerry and the finest fighter I ever clapped eyes on." Paddy paused. Removing from his vest pocket the medal that Davy had entrusted to him earlier, Paddy held it before Davy and growled, "Yer a lion, man. A lion born of lions!"

Davy replied flatly, "Better a live donkey than a dead lion."

Paddy stared at Davy for a moment, utterly perplexed by this statement. Then he added, "Great feats is in yer blood! Yer da walked all the way to the bloody South Pole, man!"

"Yeah," Davy replied. "And he died walking back."

Pocketing the medal, Paddy threw his hands up in the air and turned away from Davy. But then he immediately spun around and drove a hard right cross into Davy's chest. The impact of the punch against Davy's bare chest sounded like a watermelon being dropped on concrete from a second-floor window. Even though Paddy didn't hold back on the punch, it only caused Davy to fall back slightly. A look of consternation crossed Davy's face. After taking a moment to recover his senses, Davy glared at Paddy and demanded, "What do you think you're doing, Paddy?"

In response, Paddy hauled back and drove another right into Davy's chest, even harder this time. Then he replied, "If yer not fighting, Carvallo, yer fighting me because I'm well tired of yer shite, Davy O'Shea."

Tommy, who still stood behind Paddy, looked on, unsure what to do. Paddy turned to Tommy and winked. A wisp of smile parted Tommy's lips. Davy, who was not amused, dropped onto the floor and raised his hands in a fighting posture and demanded, "Don't push it, Paddy. If you know what's good for you."

Paddy said nothing. Instead, he feinted another right, then dropped down and dug a left hook into Davy's right oblique.

Davy let out a grunt, a look of shock on his face. Then he straightened up and said, "You asked for it." As the last word left his lips, Davy threw a thundering straight right at Paddy which, luckily, he was able to slip. Paddy's ducking out of the way of his punch made Davy even more enraged and he followed Paddy as he backpedaled across the dressing room.

"Yeh wanna fight, do yeh?" Paddy asked as he stumbled backwards, trying to stay outside of Davy's reach.

Davy pursued Paddy to the other side of the room. Feinting a right, Davy whipped a left uppercut that, had it connected, would've taken Paddy's head clean off. As it was, it missed by about an inch and Paddy, bolting away, held up his hands and said, "I don't wanna fight yeh, Davy. I'm no match for yeh and yeh know it. I want yeh to fight Carvallo and take the goddam title from the bum!"

Tommy smiled and nodded appreciatively. Davy, finally

understanding what'd just happened stopped pursuing Paddy. Paddy, seeing his life was no longer in imminent danger, stepped forward and said calmly, "Now let's get warmed up. Carvallo ain't gonna know what hit him!"

A grim look of determination on his face, Davy rolled his neck, nodded at Paddy, and banged his right fist into his left palm so hard that the sound of it rang throughout the bowels of Madison Square Garden.

Paddy's Dream

Me da never saw me fight. For that matter, he never even clapped eyes on me as an adult. I was fourteen when he did his flit. Went to work one morning and never came back. Dunno what could've happened to him. Don't really care, either. He was sound enough when he was sober, but he was never sober. When he was scuttered, which was most times, he was a bloody terror. Hit Mam so hard she lost most of her teeth plus the hearing in one ear. Blessed was the day that he didn't return from work, even if Mam was destroyed by it. Keened over it like he'd died some tragic death instead of just fecking off. I saved up and emigrated to America when I was eighteen. I joined the Army not long after that, just as the Great War was drawing to a close. That's how I became an American citizen. It bothered me that I wasn't able to bring the old wan with me, but when I'd earned enough to send for her, she wouldn't come. Said she couldn't bear to leave the old country, but I know what she was about. Waiting for that bastard of a husband to come back. He never did.

I had a secret hope—so secret that I never even admitted it to meself. It was that Da would read about me in the papers and one day he'd come to see me fight and he'd respect me—respect the man I'd become. A foolish hope, that. The red-nosed bastard, always with the smell of Arthur Guinness on him. Why should I care what he thought? But care I did, and that was the problem. I've heard there's this Swiss doctor, Jung is his name, who tries to make sense of yer dreams and can solve all yer problems that way. Who knows? Maybe he can and fair play to him for it. But I don't need to go all the way to Switzerland to know what my dream signified. It was about me da, plain and simple.

Unlike Davy, the dream that haunts me isn't some daft thing like me dying in the ring to some mystery opponent. The dream is about the Mitchell fight, and the dreams only started well after the fight had occurred. Henry Mitchell was the third-ranked featherweight contender and I fought him with the possibility of meeting Canzoneri for the undisputed championship on the line. A loss for Mitchell probably wouldn't have been that big of a deal. Boxing insiders would've seen it as a fluke. But for me a loss would've meant the first step on the road to Palookaville. No fighter wants to get put on that road. Yeh only get so many shots at the brass ring in the fight game. Usually, the number of those chances ranges between zero and one. The Mitchell fight was me one chance, and I knew it.

Mitchell was a major step up in competition for me. Me record going into the fight was 22-2, but most of those bouts were against club fighters. I'd headlined a couple cards, but they were smokers in small-time venues for piddling purses. This was Sunnyside Garden that Mitchell and meself would be topping the card at that night. Sunnyside wasn't *The* Garden, but it was a major fight venue—much bigger than any place where I'd appeared up to that time. Of course, it wasn't me who made us the main event at Sunnyside Garden, it was Mitchell. Mitchell was big-time. He'd been in the ring with some of the best featherweights of the era. Some he'd beaten and some he'd lost to, but Mitchell was always in it to the end and he always put on a good show.

Mitchell was a sound bloke. I knew him because I'd been

brought in to spar him a few times and he always treated his sparring partners with respect. He was a colored boy, and it was hard for colored fighters to make it those days—too much prejudice. I empathized because Americans treated colored people the way the English treated the Irish. If yeh wanted to make it in their eyes, yeh needed to be twice as good as the best of them.

From the perspective of Mitchell's promoter, I was nothing more than a warm-up—a way for Mitchell to break a sweat and make a few bucks while he waited for his shot at the belt. I think his people handpicked me for that match because I'd sparred with Mitchell and they didn't see me as a threat. What they didn't know was that while I never failed to give Mitchell a good workout, I was always holding something back—just in case I ever fought him for real someday. Mitchell was slick and had a powerful right hand as the twenty-three knockouts in his thirty fights attested, but he had holes. I didn't take advantage of many of those holes when we'd sparred, but I'd taken mental notes. I cataloged and filed 'em away, just in case we ever fought for real. For instance, Mitchell loved to hook off of the jab. Drop yer right a little while he was poking a jab in yer gob and he'd be sure to jam a hook in yer right ear where yer glove shoulda been. Or when yeh had him against the ropes, he always dropped his right in order to spin yeh. If yeh knew that was coming, it was a gift-wrapped left hook to the jaw. I could've done it when we sparred, but instead I kept it in me back-pocket, just in case. There were other tells and little chinks in Mitchell's armor, too—loads of 'em. I was great at spotting openings, tendencies, and flaws. I just wasn't always so great at taking advantage of 'em. That's why I became a better trainer than fighter.

*

Since it was the main event, our fight was scheduled for ten rounds. I'd fought ten rounders twice before and both fights had gone the distance, so I knew that I had the wind to see it through. Mitchell had a powerful right, which I'd tasted sparring and knew I had to avoid if I was to have any chance of winning. I never had a tremendous amount of power, even for a featherweight. Only six stoppages in those twenty-two wins prior to the Mitchell bout. But I was crafty, and I was at my craftiest that night. I'd frustrated Mitchell for nine rounds and was ahead on all three judges' scorecards by simply counterpunching and moving. It was in the tenth that I ran into trouble and the dream was always about the tenth.

The problem was I'd done so good of a job avoiding Mitchell's right that I suppose I'd lost that healthy fear of it. Also, Mitchell was the contender, I was a nobody. I worried that just beating Mitchell on points wouldn't get me in the ring with Canzoneri. A decision would get me noted, but probably not a shot at the title. There was a long list of contenders ahead of me all waiting their turn. I needed to stop Mitchell —send up a flare to the boxing world that Paddy Byrnes was worthy of a title shot. So, rather than getting on me bicycle in the tenth round and coasting to a victory, I decided to go for the knockout. Where I'd stuck and moved before, I now stood me ground and mixed it up. Mitchell immediately sensed the change in tactics and must've known this was his chance to salvage a win and, along with it, his shot at Canzoneri. The entire fight he'd seemed kind of tired and listless, but this change in the flow of the fight ignited a fire in him.

For the first minute of the tenth round, I was able to slip every punch of consequence. The ones that he did land I rolled with, depriving them of their power. Then he dropped a left hook on my liver that paralyzed me momentarily. While I was frozen, he threw a right uppercut. The uppercut only grazed me forehead, but straightening up to avoid it left me open. Mitchell immediately followed the uppercut with another left hook, this time to the head. Landing square on the button, it sent a message that traveled from me chin, up the jawbone, straight to the old brain. The message it sent was that it might not be a bad time to take a kip. Nevertheless, I somehow managed to remain upright, hanging on for dear life. But he immediately drove a short right into the other side of me jaw that sent me on a one-way trip to la-la land. That was it. I got up at the count of eight, but the ref could see that the light was on but nobody was home. He waved the fight over, making it a technical knockout rather than a pure knockout. Not that such a wee distinction mattered at all.

The dream always centers on that last exchange because I had the fight wrapped up right until that final barrage. The thing was: I knew he liked to hook off of the uppercut. He'd done it several times when we'd sparred and I'd taken note of it. The uppercut only grazed me, it was the left hook to the chin that did me in. In the dream, I keep me right up high like it shoulda been and block that second left hook. Then I lean in and clinch before he can unleash the short right that finished me. When the ref tells us to break—in the dream—I get on me bicycle and avoid him for the last two minutes, sewing up the decision. And maybe I'd even have done that if given the opportunity. If I'd've seen what mixing it up with Mitchell would lead to I'd've probably stuck with the original fight plan and danced to a victory. After the fight, I learned that I was far enough ahead on all three judges' cards that I could've lost the tenth and still won the fight. But in the fight game things can change quickly, and that's a fact. No other sport is like that. Yeh can go from winner to loser, or loser to winner in a matter of seconds. That's what the dream always focuses on—those seconds when the Mitchell fight went from a unanimous decision win to a TKO loss. In those few fleeting moments I took a hard turn from up-and-coming, soon-to-be contender to opponent status. And all it would've taken to change that was keeping me right up to protect me jaw and then clinching.

That's what happens in the dream—in the dream it always goes down the way I felt it should've gone down. I block the hook, clinch, then dance to a victory. After the decision has been announced and the ref raises me hand, I spot me father seated ringside. In his eyes I see pride.

Now that I think of it, it may be that my dream is dafter than Davy's after all. Think of it. Da was nothing more than a no-account rumpot who beat Mam and deserted us. Yet I care if the bastard's proud of me? But I do. Bedamn me, but I do.

New York, May 1947

When Paddy arrived at the sixth-floor landing he had to pause to catch his breath and then mop the sweat from his brow. Nearing fifty, he didn't have the wind he'd possessed in his fighting days. In his twenties, he could go ten rounds and barely break a sweat. Now, a few flights of steps left him gasping. Once he'd stopped panting, he strolled down the hall until he located the flat. He paused before the door to remove his cloth cap and straighten his tie. It'd been so long since he'd worn a tie, he'd forgotten how uncomfortable the damn things were. He knocked three times, then waited. A reply was so long in coming that he was preparing to knock again when a woman's voice wafted through the closed door.

"Who is it?" the voice demanded. Judging by her tone, Paddy figured that she probably thought he was a salesman or bill collector.

Paddy cleared his throat and replied, "Patrick Byrnes, missus."

There was another pause, then Paddy heard the bolt lock slide open. The door opened inward to the extent that the chain lock permitted. The round, matronly face of Aunt Martha—divided into halves by the chain—appeared in the crack. "I don't know any Patrick Byrnes." Her voice was curt. "State your business."

"I'm a friend of Percy's, missus. You would be Aunt Martha, I presume."

"You presume correctly. How, exactly, are you friends with my Percy?"

"I work at the school, missus…"

"It's not Mrs.," Aunt Martha interrupted him. "It's Miss."

"Beg pardon, Miss. As I said, I work at the school—I'm the groundskeeper. I've been helping Percy repair his ship."

The door was pushed shut in Paddy's face. He stared at it, perplexed. Then he heard the chain slide off and the door opened wide. Before him stood Aunt Martha. She appeared formidable with her square jaw jutted upward in a haughty position and her gray eyes fixed unblinkingly on him. In spite of the fleshy face and the fine web of wrinkles in the corners of those eyes, Paddy was certain that he caught a glimpse of Rita in them.

"So," she drew the word out. "You're Mr. Patrick."

"I am," Paddy forced a smile, unsure why she seemed so peeved about it. "May I come in? I wish to have a word with yerself, if that'd be possible."

"Yes, I wish to have a word with you, too," Aunt Martha almost growled. She stepped aside and waved Paddy in and then directed him to sit at the breakfast table. After Paddy had seated himself, Aunt Martha closed the door and walked over to him, asking with forced courtesy, "Can I get you something to drink, Mister…"

"Byrnes," Paddy filled in the blank for her. "A glass of water would be grand."

Aunt Martha nodded and walked into the kitchen. As he listened to her retrieve a glass from the cupboard and fill it, Paddy glanced around the room. Everything was neat and in its proper place as if she were expecting company, although she obviously wasn't. It was nothing like the tenement in south Dublin where he'd been raised. That was only one room for six people—five after his father left. He glanced over at the couch—it was covered with a plastic sofa protector. He was able to see into the bedroom and it only contained one double bed, so Paddy wondered where Percy slept. Before he'd had an opportunity to ponder the matter further, Aunt Martha returned from the kitchen with a glass of water which she placed on a doily on the table before him.

Paddy glanced up at her and said, "Thanks Missu…". She glared at him and he stopped before he completed the second syllable.

Aunt Martha sat down, then looked Paddy in the eyes: "What is it I can help you with, Mr. Byrnes?"

Paddy took a sip of his water and set the glass down. Wiping his mouth with the back of his hand, he replied, "I've gotten to know Percy a bit over these past few weeks. He tells me yeh've raised him since his mam died."

"Yes, I took Percy in when my sister passed. What of it?"

"I merely wanted to complement yeh on the fine job yeh've done raising him on yer own. Percy's a grand lad—polite, respectful, intelligent. I know it was difficult. Me own mam had to raise meself and me three sisters after Da left."

Aunt Martha nodded in recognition of the compliment and seemed to soften, ever-so-slightly.

"I was wondering if yeh could tell me Percy's mam's name?"

"What business would that be of yours, Mr. Byrnes?"

"Call it curiosity, Miss."

"Prying is what I'd call it, Mr. Byrnes. If you only

came here to satisfy idle curiosity, I'm afraid you're going to be disappointed. Now that we've settled that, I have a few questions for you, Mr. Byrnes."

Paddy held up his hands in an appeasing gesture. "Actually, Miss, we haven't settled it. Yeh see, I believe I know who his mam was. Her name was Rita and she danced in the Rockettes."

Aunt Martha sat back, looking shocked. "How did you know that?"

"I pieced it together from what the lad told me. Yeh see, I knew Rita back before she had Percy. I didn't know her that well, but I liked her. She had a great spirit."

"How did you come to know my sister?"

"She was a friend of a friend."

"What do you want from me?"

"I was wondering if it was possible if yeh knew who Percy's da was?"

Aunt Martha was starting to become indignant again. "What business is it of yours who that poor child's father might be?"

"Because I think I know who it is."

Aunt Martha started to rise. Flustered, she said, "I've heard just about enough out of you, Mr. Byrnes!"

Paddy held up his hands in a calming gesture. "Please, Miss, hear me out."

Aunt Martha glared at Paddy for a few moments. Then she nodded, settled back into her chair, and said, "You've got one minute, Mr. Byrnes."

Paddy nodded. "I wasn't always a groundskeeper, Miss.

I was a professional boxer in me youth and when I hung up the gloves, I started training fighters. About ten years ago I had this middleweight—best fighter I ever trained, hands down. Yeh might've heard of him—Davy O'Shea?"

Paddy paused from his tale and eyed Aunt Martha. Her face flushed slightly at the mention of Davy's name, but she recovered quickly and stared back at him impassively. "I know nothing about boxing or boxers, I can assure you, Mr. Byrnes. A brutal, nasty business, if you ask me."

"It can be both of those things, I'll give yeh that, Miss. But it's also a way for a lad who came from nothing to maybe make something of himself. It did that for Davy O'Shea. Davy fought for the middleweight championship of the world right here at Madison Square Garden. He was seeing yer sister Rita at that time because I had to drag him away from her on a couple occasions so he could train. Did yer sister ever mention Davy at all? Did she say if he was the father?"

"I've never heard of this Davy character," Aunt Martha had resumed her haughty disposition.

Paddy eyed Aunt Martha skeptically. "The reason I ask is Percy's the spitting image of Davy O'Shea. And Davy and Rita were an item right about the time I figure little Percy, em, came into being, if yeh'll pardon me French."

"How dare you speak to a lady like that, Mr. Byrnes?"

"I apologize for that, Miss. Didn't know any other way to touch on it. The funny thing about Davy, Miss, is he grew up without a Da, too."

"Do none of you Irishmen stick around to raise your children?"

"It wasn't like that with Davy's da. He died in the Antarctic, returning from the South Pole with Lieutenant Wellesley. Yeh've heard of that expedition?"

Aunt Martha seemed to soften somewhat. "I read about it in school, I believe."

"Davy never got to meet him. His da shipped out for the Antarctic before Davy was born. Davy never talked about it much, but yeh could tell it hurt him."

"Where are you going with this, Mr. Byrnes?"

"Yer doing a fine job, of raising Percy, Miss. But a lad needs his da. A da can teach him how to ride a bicycle, or catch a baseball, or throw a punch."

"I won't have my Percy fighting. It's Neanderthal. Jesus never threw a punch."

"Aye, but Jesus was the son of God. The rest of us gotta make do as best we can."

"What do you want from me, Mr. Byrnes?"

"I only wanted to confirm what I believe to be true, that Davy is Percy's da."

Aunt Martha got up and paced the floor without saying anything for several moments. She stopped and looked Paddy in the eye, "I lost my father, as well, Mr. Byrnes. Cancer. I was ten and Rita was five when he passed. I've often wondered if Rita might've turned out differently had Father lived. Let me ask you a question, Mr. Byrnes."

"Go ahead," Paddy nodded.

"What was your father like before he left?"

"If I'm being honest, Miss, he was a holy terror. Abusive when he was drunk and he was always drunk."

"So, you'll agree with me that no father is better than a bad father?"

"It was true enough for me, I suppose."

Aunt Martha sat back down. "I was a bit disingenuous with you earlier, Mr. Byrnes. You see, right before the cancer took her, my sister did tell me who Percy's father was. I even tried to find him after Rita had passed. But he was a fallen man. A man who'd been overcome by vice. I decided then that, as you yourself admit, no father was better than a bad one."

"True. But, yeh know, Miss, people can change."

"They can, I agree. But tell me, in your experience have you ever seen that happen?"

"Can't say that I have, personally," Paddy nodded, "but that doesn't mean it can't happen." Grabbing his cloth cap from the table, he rose, saying, "Thank yeh for the water and for yer time, Miss."

Aunt Martha rose and walked Paddy to the door. Before opening the door, Aunt Martha thrust her right hand toward Paddy, saying, "You know, Mr. Byrnes, when I found out who you were I was going to forbid you from seeing Percy any more. But, having spoken with you, I find you're correct. A boy does need a father figure. You are welcome to continue spending time with him."

Paddy shook her hand. "Thank you, Miss."

Antarctica, March 1912

Ciaran fashioned a cross using Lieutenant Wellesley's skis, then he drove it deep into the permafrost with a mallet. He'd bundled the Lieutenant into his sleeping bag and had buried him as best he could in the frozen tundra. Once he'd finished covering the Lieutenant, Ciaran mumbled a Pater Noster and several "Hail Mary's". Feeling like he should eulogize the Lieutenant as the Lieutenant had done for the others, Ciaran cleared his throat and said, "Here lies Lieutenant Wellesley. He always treated me fair and with respect. A good leader—what happened to us was no fault of his. Just bad luck. He was a good man, even if he was English."

Ciaran performed a sign of the cross and then turned to the sledge. He'd already removed everything of the Lieutenant's that could be discarded and had packed the remainder. Depoting the Lieutenant's gear hadn't cut the load in half. Because Ciaran still had to carry the tent, cooker and utensils, theodolite and various other equipment, the subtraction of the Lieutenant's things had only saved twenty or thirty pounds. The sledge and its contents now weighed just over two hundred pounds. That was a challenging amount to pull for a healthy, rested man. Ciaran was neither. To help him along, he erected a makeshift sail using a side of the tent held aloft by bamboo poles.

Four straight hours he marched that morning. Ciaran probably would've stopped for a breather once or twice, but the wind was light and steady from the south—the wind almost always came from the south this close to the Pole—and the sail kept pushing him forward. According to his pace count, which was far from precise, he'd traveled nearly seven miles by the time he stopped for lunch. This was a tremendous increase in productivity given that he'd only been making six miles a day on average during the Lieutenant's final week. And he accomplished that distance in spite of the tendrils of agony that began in his toes and ran up past his knees with every step he took on his blackened, gangrenous foot. If he were able to maintain this pace, he might just make the next supply depot. Hopefully the rescue team would still be awaiting him at the Hundred Stone Depot.

The weather was clear and unseasonably cold. The sun goggles that he hated to wear because they were always steaming-up were strapped to his face. Once, during the journey outward, he'd gone snow-blind from the sun's glare. Almost everyone from the final two parties experienced it at one time or another. Not only was snow-blindness agonizingly painful—and the pain didn't subside, even when he slept—it'd rendered Ciaran completely sightless for two full days. In a sledge party of four, one man could be guided by the other three. Snow-blind on his own was another matter entirely. It was a death sentence, plain and simple. A man alone in the Antarctic faced a lot more peril than any individual member of a team of four, or even two. He was glad he was off Beardmore Glacier so that he didn't have to contend with its minefield of crevasses. With a four-man team, if one member plunged in the crevasse, the others could rescue him, as the Lieutenant, Hanes and Owens had already done for Ciaran during the return journey. If he were to fall into a crevasse alone as he now was, even if the sledge remained on solid ground, it'd be very challenging to extricate himself. Especially given his diminished physical capacity.

As he was undertaking the morning march, he contemplated the fact that it'd been several days since he'd last seen his companion—the third traveler who'd shadowed their steps since Beardmore Glacier. The Lieutenant had thought he was their guardian angel. If that were the case, a fine guardian he was, given that the Lieutenant was now buried in the ice, several miles back. Since Ciaran still hadn't gotten a clear view of this shadowy figure, he wasn't willing to commit to who or what it might be. One thing he felt certain of was that it wasn't a mirage. Mirages were quite common in the Antarctic. On a number of occasions Ciaran had been dead certain that he'd spotted things that eventually turned out to be simple optical illusions. For instance, on the Barrier the Lieutenant and he had both often thought that they'd seen a large body of water in the distance when the nearest water was hundreds of miles away. A week earlier, they both thought that they'd seen a dog camp in the distance, raising their hopes that they'd been discovered by a rescue party. But the rescue party turned out to be nothing more than a discarded biscuit tin. The difference between these mirages and the third traveler who shadowed him was that the mirages he'd apprehended from a solely visual perspective. In the case of the third traveler, while Ciaran was constantly spotting him in the periphery of his field of vision, he also *felt* its presence. He didn't need to see his companion to sense that he was with him. That wasn't the case with mirages.

Back home, Ciaran had always laughed at talk of the wee folk, leprechauns, fairies and the like. People in his village were superstitious. His time in the Royal Navy had taught Ciaran to place his full trust in science and technology. He now considered himself an entirely modern, twentieth-century man. Yet his old gran had told him on more than one occasion that there were things in this world which couldn't be explained by science or logic. Old things—much older than the human race. The third traveler that'd been shadowing Ciaran's journey back from the Pole perhaps fell into this class of being. It may've been a ministering angel watching over him, as the Lieutenant had believed, and it could've been the Grim Reaper haunting him. Between those two choices, however, Ciaran tended to believe it was the former. The third traveler's failure to appear, therefore, had created an existential crisis for Ciaran.

Given the many concrete problems with which he had to contend, it seemed absurd that his mind might be troubled by existentialist dilemmas. Yet it was. The inexplicable disappearance of the third traveler had caused Ciaran to wonder if the dream of the grim reaper from a week earlier wasn't actually reality. Perhaps he was already dead and this march was the penance he'd been assigned to fulfill in Purgatory for his earthly sins. In truth, he'd been far from a perfect man. It'd been nearly five years since his last confession. As a boy he was constantly nicking apples from old Moran's orchard. He'd quarreled with his father often—the last blow-up leading to his running off to join the Royal Navy.

Last, but not least, he'd gone and gotten Bridget in a family way and then set sail for the Antarctic, abandoning her. Granted, he hadn't known Bridget was pregnant when he left. But he'd convinced her to do the deed that resulted in her being in that condition. And there were loads of other sins—mostly venial, but some, perhaps, mortal. Were these transgressions enough to damn him to eternal perdition? He hoped not. Purgatory was no great shakes, but there was a limit to one's sentence there, unlike the other place.

*

After five hours in the harness, Ciaran stopped for lunch. The midday meal was a long, tedious process that now took two hours instead of thirty minutes because there was only himself to perform all of the requisite tasks. In order to eat and drink, he had to pitch the tent, then prepare the cooker to melt the ice for water and to heat the frozen chunks of pemmican. Setting up and breaking down the tent was so much work that he'd have simply leaned against the sledge and eaten a biscuit for lunch, cold as it was. The problem was if he wanted to drink, he had no choice but to set up the cooker to thaw ice. And in order to use the cooker, he needed the protection of the tent around it. In spite of the frigid weather, the effort to drag the sledge caused him to perspire freely. Without water, he'd die of thirst in less than two days. Thus, he was forced to go through the entire process of setting up and breaking down camp twice a day.

After eating lunch, he took a theodolite reading in order to confirm his position. That added another thirty minutes to his stop, but it was essential. Since most of their tracks from the outward journey had been effaced by snowstorms, he needed to be certain that he was following the correct route. If he was off by even half a degree, he might miss the One Hundred Stone Depot, and that'd be the end of him, full stop. Once he'd plotted his coordinates and determined his route, he broke down the tent and loaded the sledge. Feeling rejuvenated for the afternoon march, Ciaran did the math in his head. Counting the seven miles he'd covered in the morning, by his reckoning he was approximately fifty-one miles from the One Hundred Stone Depot. It could be done. If he could keep up this pace, he'd be there in four more days. With the Lieutenant gone, he had food enough to carry him there on full rations with a few days to spare.

But maintaining his pace assumed a number of factors that hadn't prevailed thus far during the return march. First, the wind would need to remain calm so that he could employ the makeshift sail. He'd have a hard time covering the distance to One Hundred Stone Depot merely man-hauling. Second, the temperature couldn't dip much lower. During one of the bi-weekly winter lectures back at base camp they'd been informed by Dr. Appleby that the colder it got, the more calories the body burned in order to maintain a healthy core temperature. Third, there couldn't be any blizzards which would force him to remain in the tent, getting sicker by the day and using up precious supplies. And, finally, his body would have to hold up.

Like Lieutenant Wellesley, Ciaran had lost nearly thirty pounds since setting out from base camp four months earlier and he was evincing many of the symptoms of advanced scurvy. His gums were swollen and spongy, his teeth were loose, and the backs of his knees and his ankles were swollen and painful. Then there was the frostbitten foot. It'd turned gangrenous and the blackness had spread to above his ankle. He was now certain that he'd lose that leg at the knee—at a minimum—if he survived. In addition to the pain of marching, it took him nearly half an hour to remove his boots at night, and then another half hour in the morning to get them on again, even after slitting them down the side to render easier access.

Despite these concerns, Ciaran began to feel guardedly optimistic about his chances owing to the progress he'd made during the morning march. The wind velocity had picked up to force 3 since the morning, but it was still good sailing weather. If anything, it'd push him along faster. After raising the sail, he stepped into the harness and resumed his march. As he pulled, he thought back to the day he'd first met Bridget.

*

It was at the annual dance sponsored by the Gaelic League at Michael Dwyer's barn. He'd just turned twenty at the time and was home on leave for the first occasion since enlisting in the Royal Navy more than four years earlier. The barn that housed the dance was massive, larger by far than the C-of-E Church which was the next largest structure in the village. Michael Dwyer went all-out at these events, hiring musicians and providing a spread of food and drink the likes of which most of the village only saw once a year—at Michael Dwyer's party. For Michael Dwyer, it was what in more modern times would be referred to as a public relations event. He was the richest man in town by a long shot and this was his way to try to keep the rest of the town from begrudging his success. For this reason, he allowed the Gaelic League to sponsor the dance, even though they hadn't laid out one penny toward it. The presence of the Gaelic League helped to gloss over an ugly little fact that was never truly out of mind for anyone in the village: Michael Dwyer was Protestant because in order to qualify for English relief during the Great Hunger his antecedents had turned their back on the one true Church and converted.

Michael Dwyer's house sat atop the hill opposite Cnoc na Piseog. It overlooked the valley containing David Patrick's farm, as well as the village. In spite of the great resentment most of the town bore Michael Dwyer, the vast majority of those young and/or healthy enough to attend did so to eat

Michael Dwyer's food, drink his whiskey, and dance to his band. Some of Ciaran's old mates convinced him to tag along with them to the event. Ciaran decided to wear his dress uniform, even though he knew it'd probably inspire animosity in the ranks of the Gaelic Leaguers. And while the Royal Navy uniform did elicit some grumbling, particularly among the older men in attendance, it never progressed beyond that. It was a festive night and no one wanted to spoil the party. Besides, most people understood that there was no work to be had for a young man in their village. Or anywhere else in Ireland, for that matter.

Ciaran had been at the party for not quite fifteen minutes—enough time to drink a glass of stout and eat a sandwich—when he noticed her. She was standing on the other side of the barn with Eleanor and a couple other girlfriends. Although they'd been practically neighbors, Ciaran didn't recognize Bridget because she was still a child when he'd left for the navy. Now, at nearly sixteen years of age, she'd developed into one of the most beautiful girls in the county. He elbowed Tommy Molloy who was in the process of shoveling stew into his mouth. Tommy, short and stocky with red hair and freckles, grunted between bites, "What do you want, man? Can't you see I'm eating?"

"Aye," Ciaran shook his head and laughed. "And if yeh keep lashing stew into yer gob like that, Michael Dwyer will mistake yeh for one of his pigs and stick an apple in yer mouth."

"Sure, I haven't eaten all day. Been saving up for this."

"Well, look up would yeh, please?"

Tommy paused from eating for a moment and looked up. "What is it that's so important it can't wait for me to finish my stew?"

Nodding at Bridget, Ciaran asked, "Who's the lass over

there in the blue dress?"

Tommy wiped his mouth with the back of his sleeve and replied, "Bridget O'Shea."

"Bridget O'Shea?" Ciaran's eyes opened wide with wonder. "Do yeh mean David Patrick's little girl?"

"The same." Tommy gulped down a mouthful of stew. "Ain't so little anymore, eh?"

"Is she spoken for?"

"Not as I'm aware." It was a small enough town that everyone was aware of the relationship status of everyone, so Ciaran took that for a hard *no*.

"Why the devil not?"

"How should I know? It's probably because she's the daughter of David Patrick, so everyone assumes there'll be no dowry."

"Dowry?" Ciaran laughed. "That's like asking someone to pay yeh to take the Crown Jewels. She's dowry enough for me."

"Then go and talk to her and stop tormenting me!"

Ciaran shook his head and laughed. Then he pushed himself to his feet and sauntered over to Bridget and her friends. He walked slowly, hoping she'd take notice of him before he arrived. It worked. While he was still twenty paces away, Eleanor elbowed Bridget, whispered something to her, and giggled. Bridget looked up at Ciaran, momentarily freezing him in his tracks. A doubt crept into his mind as to whether he possessed the courage to speak to an ethereal creature like this. Then, reminding himself of the many dangers he'd braved in the Royal Navy, Ciaran recovered his confidence and strode boldly forward.

Stopping before them, Ciaran ignored the three giggling girls flanking her and said to Bridget, "Could this be little Bridget O'Shea?"

Bridget blushed and glanced away momentarily, replying only, "'Tis."

"Yeh probably don't remember me…"

"You're Ciaran Creagh," Bridget interrupted him.

"Aye," Ciaran grinned, feeling his confidence fully return.

"That's a beautiful uniform you're wearing," Bridget said, causing the other girls to giggle. "You might want to give the Gaelic League lads a miss, though." Bridget nodded to a handful of young men in their teens and early twenties drinking in a corner of the barn. This caused Eleanor and the other girls to burst into laughter again.

Ciaran eyed the girls, wishing they were gone. "I'm not concerned about them lads," he replied confidently.

This last statement, for reasons Ciaran was completely at a loss to divine, sent the girls, Bridget excepted, into the greatest fits of laughter yet. The band started playing a ballad, *Eiblin A Run*. Ciaran grabbed Bridget's hand and asked, "May I have this dance?"

Bridget nodded and he led her to the dance floor to the accompaniment of her friends' shrieks of laughter. Ignoring this, Ciaran took Bridget in his arms and spun her lightly around the floor. When they'd completed their dance, Ciaran asked, "Can I see yeh again?"

"Yes," Bridget replied breathlessly.

*

Ciaran remembered the night with a smile as he

strained all of his weight against the harness. A tear might've come to his eye, had there been enough moisture in his body to produce one.

Hell's Kitchen, May 1917

All of the talk around town was of the Great War. One month earlier the United States had agreed to enter hostilities alongside its allies Great Britain and France. President Wilson had managed to keep America out of Europe's internecine squabbles for more than two and a half years. The Irish of Hell's Kitchen supported Wilson's policy of neutrality, having no great desire to help their longtime oppressors in England. But once it was discovered that Germany had offered to aid Mexico in regaining its lost territories, not to mention the U-Boats sinking American merchant vessels, Wilson's hand was forced. Although U.S. troops wouldn't begin arriving in numbers at the Western Front until 1918, the United States was now involved.

Ciaran David, now just Davy, was only dimly aware of world events. At six years of age, the only brawls that concerned him were those taking place in the environs of PS 51. On this particular day, he came home crying with a bloody nose. They'd been living in their own flat, a few blocks over from her cousin Roisin's, for several years now. Located on West 49th not far from the river, it was an efficiency apartment, which meant a living room and a kitchenette jammed together into one claustrophobically small room. They shared a bathroom down the hall with the six other families residing on their floor. It wasn't the most convenient or pleasant arrangement, but at least they didn't have to venture outside and face the elements when visiting the privy as they had back in Ireland. The flat was sparsely furnished with pieces that, like Roisin's place, were mostly third-hand—gifted to her by other Irish who no longer wanted or needed them. There was a davenport that doubled as Bridget's bed, a small breakfast table, and one overstuffed chair which, owing to a rip in the upholstery, was rapidly downgrading into merely a stuffed chair. There was a folding cot that Davy slept on which they kept tucked away in their one closet.

Bridget had just returned home from a long day of scrubbing other people's floors. As she often did on warm days, she was seated on the rusty metal fire escape, located just outside of their one window. She'd left the window propped open so that the spring breeze could refresh the stale, stuffy air that'd hung in the apartment throughout the cold winter months—of which there were several more in New York than there'd ever been County Kerry. Facing down 12th Avenue, from her perch on the fire escape she was able to see westward all the way across the Hudson to the Jersey side, and to the south she could see down to the Hudson Yards. Sometimes she'd take some sewing out there with her, but on this day she just sat gazing absently over the railyards.

Davy, a blood-stained handkerchief jammed into his left nostril to staunch the flow, opened the door and quietly slipped into the flat. He'd been able to master his tears for the seven-block journey home, but seeing his mother, the floodgates released and he wailed, "Mammy!"

Bridget immediately snapped out of her reverie. Seeing Davy crying in the middle of the living room, she climbed through the window and went to him. Wrapping her arms around him, she asked, "What happened to you, love?"

Davy, who moments before wasn't even crying, was now bawling as though it'd just happened. He choked his sobs long enough to spit out, "They…beat…me…up!"

Hugging Davy and stroking his hair, Bridget demanded, "Who did this to you, love?"

"Mickey…and…Ralph."

"I don't know those names."

Davy was starting to calm down now, having rid himself of the horror of the attack that'd sprung up anew upon glimpsing his mother, "They're older boys at school."

Bridget took a moment to examine Davy. There was the bloody nose and a welt under his left eye that looked like it'd probably blacken. Drops of blood had stained his white shirt collar which she'd have to scrub out that night if he was to wear it to school the following day. That was it, though. Superficial injuries—he'd survive. "Why'd they beat you up, love?"

"They were making fun of me because I don't have a da. They called me a bastard." He paused, then asked, "What's a bastard, Mammy?"

"It's what those two lads are, love."

Davy looked at her, perplexed.

"Where'd it happen?"

"Walking home from school."

"Were there no adults around?"

"Mr. Fitzpatrick came by and stopped them, but not before they got their licks in."

Bridget nodded and hugged him again. As she did so, a few stray sobs slipped out. Putting her hands on his shoulders, she pushed him away in order to look him in the eye. Davy sniffled and wiped the snot away from his nose with the back of his hand.

"Right, so. I'm going to teach you how to fight."

"What do you know about fighting, Mammy? You're just a girl."

"From your Gran-da. He was county champion when he was young—before Mam got her hooks into him."

"Why'd he teach you to fight?"

"Because he wanted a boy. He'd never admit it, but I could tell. He taught me to fight, play footie, fish and hunt, just like he would've taught a son. I only ever had to use it once—fighting—but I can remember everything he taught me."

Bridget stood up and faced Davy. "All right, spread your feet to shoulder-width apart, left foot forward."

"But Mammy, Sister Mary Barbara taught us that we should always turn the other cheek—like Jesus."

"Aye, just keep turning that cheek until eventually they crucify you."

Davy looked at Bridget, perplexed. She decided it was time for tough love. "Get your feet apart like I told you!" she snapped. When he did so, she used her left foot to kick his feet a little further apart to give him a solid base. Then she curled her fingers into fists and held them up in boxing posture. "Hold your hands up like this!"

Once she'd positioned him, Bridget went through with him step by step how to throw a proper right cross. After he'd practiced it thirty or forty times, she said, "All right, if those bullies pick on you again, you walk right up to the biggest one and bust him in the gob, just like that. Don't wait for him to push you or throw the first punch, just hit him and don't stop hitting him until you're sure he's not going to hit back."

"What if the other lad jumps in?"

"You just keep hitting the bigger lad 'til he's done in. Then worry about the other one."

A steely look of determination entered Davy's soft, blue eyes. He nodded. Bridget nodded back, saying, "All right, let's practice that some more."

Madison Square Garden, July 1936

"One, one, two, three!" Paddy called out.

Davy, a fine sheen of sweat covering his body, performed the combination Paddy demanded, then dipped and pivoted away.

"One, one, three, two!"

Davy jabbed twice, threw a left hook off of the jab followed by a straight right. Then he bounced lightly away.

"Shine shoes!" Paddy commanded.

Davy, as he pivoted in a circle, began pumping out short uppercuts with both hands, his fists firing up and down like pistons as though he were polishing wingtips. When he'd thrown 20 or 25 mini-punches, Paddy shouted, "Time!"

Davy rolled his neck, shook out his arms, and stalked away. Paddy turned to Tommy, who was standing beside him in the dressing room, "What do yeh think?"

"I think Davy got his mojo back," Tommy grinned.

Paddy smiled: "Carvallo won't know what hit him."

There was a knock at the door. Without waiting for a response, a man in his thirties wearing a rumpled white shirt and a bow tie, with a pair of red boxing gloves tucked under his left armpit, walked in. "Commission, fellas," he announced.

"How's tricks, Lenny?" Paddy grinned.

"Can't complain, Paddy."

Nodding at the gloves, Paddy inquired, "Jake check 'em out?"

"Yep," Lenny nodded. Handing the gloves to Paddy, he added, "Lace 'em up, fellas. It's go-time."

"About time," Davy, who'd been in the corner of the room throwing slow, easy punches, growled. He walked over to the other three.

Lenny patted Davy on the shoulder and said, "Good luck, Davy." Turning to Paddy, he added, "They're getting ready to sing the anthem."

Paddy nodded, understanding that opening bell was imminent.

"Good luck to ya," Lenny said to Paddy, then turned and exited the room.

Once the door closed, Paddy turned to Davy and said, "All right, Davy. Moment of truth. Yeh ready?"

"I'm ready," Davy snarled.

Davy hopped onto the trainer table and extended his wrapped left fist at Paddy, palm up, to receive the glove. Paddy pulled the glove until the laces were part-way up Davy's forearm. Tightening the laces, Paddy knotted and then double-knotted them. Finally, he taped the laces down so that they wouldn't fly free. He then repeated the process with the right fist.

Once Davy was gloved, Paddy asked, "How they feel?"

Davy looked down at his hands. He banged his gloves together, fist to fist. Then he popped off of the table, took a few steps away from Paddy and Tommy, and fired off an eight-punch combination at the air. When he finished, he nodded his approval.

"Grand," Paddy replied. "They're about to touch Carvallo's face about four hundred times."

Davy shook his head, "No. It won't take that many."

Paddy grinned, "That's the Davy Boy I know." Turning to Tommy, he said, "Robe."

Tommy removed a kelly-green satin robe with white trim from a hook on the wall. On the back of it in white lettering was stitched: "DAVY BOY". Beneath that was a shamrock, with: "O'SHEA" underneath. After helping Davy pull on the robe, Tommy tied it off in front. With Paddy and Tommy flanking Davy, the three men formed a tight circle, bowed their heads, clasped hands and said an "Our Father." When they finished the prayer, Paddy looked Davy in the eye. He wanted to make sure there were no residual effects from Jake's hare-brained mention of the dream. Davy stared back at him without an ounce of fear or trepidation. Paddy grinned and said, "Let's go take that title!"

*

Standing in the mouth of the tunnel that led into the arena, Davy, Paddy and Tommy waited while a famous crooner standing in the middle of the ring sang "The Star-Spangled Banner." Davy kept his head bowed but skipped from foot to foot and shook out his arms in an effort to keep warm while the performance lasted. When the national anthem ended, another singer stepped into the ring and performed the Irish National Anthem, "A Soldiers Song", in its original Gaelic. The singer was quickly joined by the voices of ten thousand drunken Irishman lustily stumbling along in mostly broken Irish. When this song finished, the crowd went wild. Paddy and Tommy looked at each other wide-eyed, realizing that at least two-thirds of the crowd would be pulling for Davy. If Paddy had been concerned about Davy's mental state following Jake's slip-up, his fears were allayed. Davy would feed off of the energy of the crowd as divas always do.

The emcee stepped into center ring and grabbed the

microphone. As he was beginning to announce the fight, Jake walked up and stood next to Paddy. Paddy turned to him and demanded, "Where the hell yeh been?"

"That's no concern of yours," Jake snapped, reaching for a stogie in his breast pocket. Seeing Paddy glaring at him, he dropped the hand and added, "I'm here now,"

"Did yeh check the gloves?"

"Yeah, I checked 'em," Jake growled defensively. "Course I checked 'em."

"Everything okay?"

"With the gloves?"

Paddy nodded.

"Hunky dory. Why're ya so worried about the gloves? Did ya ever in your life have a problem with the gloves?"

"No," Paddy admitted, "and I don't wanna start tonight."

"The gloves are fine. Worry about Davy."

Paddy glanced over at Davy, dancing and shaking out his arms. Davy's head was up now and he was staring at the ring, with seemingly no cognizance of the raucous crowd. The ring announcer finished giving Davy's record and bellowed dramatically, "DAVY …. BOY… O'SHEA!!!!"

The crowd erupted into delirious cheering. Turning to Tommy, Paddy locked eyes and then nodded toward the ring.

Tommy stepped out of the tunnel onto the walkway and began making his way to the ring. Davy, all business now, followed, appearing impervious to the adoring crowd. Paddy and Jake fell in at the rear. They didn't rush, making a grand entrance. They'd only traveled a few steps when the Irish tenor standing in the ring began a slow, soulful rendition of "Danny Boy", only the lyrics had been altered slightly:

"Oh, Davy Boy, the pipes, the pipes are calling

"From glen to glen, and down the mountainside."

Paddy immediately turned to Jake and demanded, "Who changed his entrance song? It's supposed to be 'The Wearing of the Green'!"

"I did," Jake snapped, "and it was my idea to change the lyrics." Jake grandiosely waved at the crowd who were all drunkenly singing along. "Look at 'em. Those stupid, goddam micks are lapping it up!"

"Do you even know what that song is about?"

"I don't know—some dumb Irishman named Danny?"

"It's about dying young, Jake."

"You goddam Irish are so morbid! Do ya have any songs that ain't about dying?"

Just then, Davy, his face drained of all color, turned and looked at Paddy, almost plaintively.

"Just ignore it, Davy!" Even though they were only separated by a few feet, Paddy was forced to shout to be heard over the lusty, off-key crooning of ten thousand Irish voices.

Davy, looking much less focused than when he'd commenced his march only moments earlier, dropped his head and continued the long trek to the ring.

Paddy turned to Jake and said, "Now look what yeh've done!"

Shrugging and turning his palms upward, Jake asked innocently, "What'd I do?"

Antarctica, March 1912

The sun had set the day before for the first time in four

and a half months. It was up again in under two hours, but the inexorable commencement of the long winter's night had begun which meant that nearly five months of total darkness was now only weeks away. No one could survive the frigid Antarctic winter alone on the tundra with no more shelter than a tent. Ciaran was well aware of this. It'd been three days since the Lieutenant passed and Ciaran found himself none the better for no longer having to carry and tend to him. Rather, Ciaran felt like he was going off his head in the tent by himself at night with no one to talk to. And having to do everything himself—the hauling, the assembly and disassembly of the tent, the cooking of the food—was wearing on him. Luckily, his shadowy companion hadn't forsaken him. The third traveler had accompanied Ciaran throughout his marches each of the past three days, its comforting presence perceptible just out of the corner of his eye. Thanks to the makeshift sail and favorable winds he'd made nearly forty miles by the end of the third day. But it looked like the assistance he was receiving from the sail was about to end, as the wind had picked up in force considerably, rendering a sail impracticable. That night the wind rattled the tiny tent so violently that Ciaran feared it might be torn out of the ground —an event that assuredly would mark the end of him. But it somehow held fast.

On the fourth morning following the Lieutenant's death, after cooking and eating his hoosh and packing away everything within the tent, Ciaran pushed the tent flaps out of the way and emerged to a frigid, gray morning. As he stood before the tent stretching, Ciaran thought he saw something move to the Northwest, maybe a quarter of a mile from where he stood. Nothing lived in the Antarctic, so the motion had to have been caused either by a person or perhaps some refuse from their outward journey being played upon by the winds. Ciaran was certain that this movement wasn't caused by the third traveler—it was always cloaked in brown and the form that Ciaran thought he could vaguely make out was gray. Ciaran squinted to get a clearer vision of this figure. What he perceived was a grayish splotch which seemed to be about the size that a man should appear from that distance. Thinking it might be a scout from a rescue party, Ciaran jumped up and down, waving his arms and shouting, "Hullo!!!"

The figure turned and began to move away from him in a northerly direction. Fearing his rescuer hadn't seen him, Ciaran took off at a sprint after the gray form, shouting all the way. The pursuit took Ciaran across a field of sastrugi, forcing Ciaran to leap over the waves of foot-high, hardened snow as though he were running hurdles. When his lead foot would land on the other side of a sastrugi, the leg would sink almost to the knee in the crunchy snow. When his gangrenous foot touched down every other step, tendrils of agony—which he was only able to overcome through sheer force of will—would shoot up his left leg all the way to the pelvis. Ciaran's hot breath converted to miniature ice crystals almost as soon as it was exhaled. The air he pulled into his lungs burned with cold. In spite of his weakened condition, Ciaran had dashed a quarter mile in good time, all things considered. Yet, after traveling that distance he found he'd drawn no closer to the ever-receding gray figure.

Unable to even narrow the gap, Ciaran began easing to a stop. That's when the snow gave way beneath him. His lead foot landed on the far side of a sastrugi and just kept sinking. As he burst through the thin layer of snow concealing a narrow crevasse, Ciaran desperately reached for something to cling to. Fortunately, his momentum pulled him forward and his left forearm came down on solid ground on the other side. With nothing to latch onto, the left arm immediately started sliding backward toward the abyss below. He quickly threw his right arm onto the far side of the crevasse alongside the left. His right hand came to rest on a rock protruding from the permafrost. This bought him time to feel around desperately under the snow for something to grip with his left hand. Luck was with him as he came upon another rock. Clinging to the edge of the crevasse, his legs dangling free, Ciaran tried to look below to see how far he was from the bottom, but no floor was visible.

With firm handholds he could attempt to extricate himself onto solid ground. Yet he didn't immediately. Not fighting to the last breath might seem unnatural to someone who's never been faced with such privation, but the truth was he'd been dying by degrees for months. Now the weakened, precarious physical state that his body had attained very much resembled his current predicament. Alone, slowly starving, his body wracked by scurvy, his gangrenous left foot turned into a festering open sore by frostbite, Ciaran understood that he was clinging to life by his fingernails and was quickly losing his grip. In such a state, death wasn't something to be feared. Instead, it'd come more like a peaceful sleep after a long day's work. It meant the cessation of pain and suffering. How could that be a bad thing? He hadn't thought much about his own demise until the Lieutenant succumbed. But since he'd been on his own, in his weaker moments Ciaran found his thoughts often drifted to the release that death offered. In those moments he began to consider that what was actually unnatural was continuing to desperately cling to life—fighting a battle which was almost certainly going to end with him dead.

It'd be so easy to just let go—to disappear into the nothingness. Instead of frightening him, the thought of such an end actually gave Ciaran peace. It might hurt momentarily when he landed, but the cold would quickly numb him and then whisk him away. Or perhaps he'd land on his head and it'd be over immediately. It wouldn't even be suicide, not really, so he didn't have to worry about perdition. But then he remembered Bridget's letter and the wee one who awaited him back home. He realized he couldn't give up, he had continue fighting for them. It was probably a losing battle, but he was bound to fight it to the end.

Mustering all of his strength, he pulled himself up until his right armpit got to ground level and he was able to fling his right elbow and upper arm onto the ground. He then repeated the process with his left arm. Once he had both of his arms entirely on the ground, with almost superhuman effort, he pulled himself upward until his chest rested on the other side. Once his upper torso was partially on solid ground, he kicked his right leg up until his right foot landed on solid ground. Pivoting off of the right foot, he managed to get his entire leg on the ground. Then, with one final supreme effort, he kicked his game left leg up and rolled onto solid earth, safe at last. The entire process had taken less than a minute, but it'd seemed an eternity. Completely spent, he lay in the snow panting.

After several minutes, he'd recovered enough to try to stand. Pushing himself onto his knees, he was taken aback by the sight of three figures appearing before him. Only it wasn't a rescue party. Rather, it was Owens, Hanes, and Lieutenant Wellesley. Recognizing them, Ciaran's eyes grew wide and he half-gasped, half-croaked in an unsteady voice: "Owens! Lord Hanes!" Their only response was to turn and walk away, evanescing after a few steps, leaving only the Lieutenant.

Ciaran held his hand out toward the Lieutenant, pleading, "Please help me, sir!"

The Lieutenant, his eyes filled with equal parts pity, anguish, and guilt, took a step toward Ciaran, extending his hand. Before Ciaran could clasp it, the Lieutenant evaporated just as Owens and Hanes had. Ciaran called, "Lieutenant!" But the Lieutenant was gone. Ciaran looked about himself, there was nothing but white as far as the eye could see. The emotion of everything that'd happened overtook him and, for the first time since he was a child, he began to weep. The sobs that wracked his body were dry, as he was too dehydrated to work up even one tear.

*

Ciaran slowly, carefully returned to the tent, which fortunately he had not yet broken. He'd thought there were no crevasses on the Great Ice Barrier, but obviously some existed. He'd have to be more careful when he pressed forward, which would only slow his progress. When he got to the tent, he set up the cooker and melted some ice. He was too parched after his experience to begin his march without a drink. Down to his last bottle of paraffin, he shook it before adding the oil to the cooker. Enough remained for one, perhaps two more days. With the Lieutenant gone there was plenty of food. But once the paraffin was depleted, he'd only survive a day or so before dehydration took him. After he'd melted enough ice for a good drink, he went outside and grabbed the theodolite. Painstakingly setting it up, he took a careful reading. According to the theodolite he was still on track to find the One Hundred Stone Depot. He figured there were sixteen or seventeen miles left to go—the exact distance being unclear owing to the lack of a sledge meter. Still, with a little luck, he could make the depot before he'd used all of his paraffin. A rescue party should be awaiting him at the depot. Or so he hoped.

Ciaran broke down the theodolite and the tent and loaded them onto the sledge. While the wind had calmed enough for him to march, it was too strong to employ a sail. But at least it was at his back. Thinking of Bridget and the wee one, he climbed into the harness, gritted his teeth, and strained forward against the onerous load. The first few steps were always the hardest.

Bridget's Dream

The dream never changes, though I'm unsure if it might

not be more proper to call it a nightmare. It always starts off hopefully. I spy him, plain as day, a duffle bag slung over his right shoulder, wearing the dress whites that he wore the night of Michael Dwyer's 'do. He's marching up 12th Avenue, that same sweet grin he always wore plastered across his face. When he's about a block away, he sees me, five stories up and sitting on the rusted fire escape stairs. He drops his bag and waves. I can't believe my eyes. For a moment I just sit there frozen to the spot, too stunned to know what to do. Then I leap up, step through the window, and cross the flat in three steps. I throw the door open and don't even bother closing it behind myself. I sprint down the hallway and take the five flights of stairs down to street level two steps at a time.

I'm breathing hard and my heart feels like it's going to beat out of my chest when I burst through the front door. As I step outside into the cool, grey early fall day, Ciaran is just arriving. He drops his bag on the pavement and stands there looking at me, shyly and sweetly. I throw my arms around him and smother him with kisses. After what seems like an eternity of kissing, still holding him tightly, I draw my head back and whisper, "You're back."

Ciaran slowly nods: "I been searching a long time for yeh, but I didn't know where yeh were. I was worried I might never find yeh."

"You've found me now," I reply, tears of happiness in my eyes. Then I lean forward and breathe into his ear, "I waited for you, Ciaran. There's been no one else. I knew you'd return to me."

Ciaran smiles shyly, then asks, "Where's that wee one of mine?"

I suddenly become troubled because I realize I've no idea where little Davy is. I can't even recall the last time I saw him. But who should appear just then but himself, wearing his wee school uniform and carrying his books cinched together with a belt. Seeing me, he beams that brilliant smile of his and exclaims, "Hi Mammy!"

I'm almost in tears when I bend down and tell him, "Davy, this is your da."

"Da?" He repeats in shock and wonder.

"Aye, your da," I reply.

Davy turns to Ciaran and asks, "What took you so long, Da?"

Ciaran laughs and replies, "The South Pole's a long ways away, an leanbh."

"I told Mammy if you didn't turn up soon I was going down there myself to find you."

Ciaran smiles, then squats down until he's eye-to-eye with Davy. Placing his hands on his son's shoulders, Ciaran says, "I'm sure yeh would, me lad. Yer a fine, strong gossoon. Yeh remind me of me brother, Tiernach. He was a tall and fair-haired one as well. Yeh've got some Viking blood in yeh."

A cold breeze blows down 12th Avenue, rustling my dress and causing me to shiver. I put my hand on Ciaran's shoulder and he jumps, I don't know why. "Let's go inside, mo shioghra," I say. "There's a cold wind blowing."

A look of fright grips Ciaran's face and he just shakes his head. David looks up at him, puzzled. I reach for Ciaran's hand, saying, "Come with me."

But Ciaran simply shakes his head again. I become concerned and ask, "What's wrong, mo shioghra?"

"I can't come in until I locate the other lads."

"The other lads?" I repeat. "I thought they were…"

I can't finish the thought because I know that if they were, then he was, too. I shake my head, stamp my foot, and say, "No. You're staying with me and your son."

I grab his hand, but he's already slipping away. It's as though something is pulling him from me. His fingers slide out of my grip. There's a sad look on his face—one I've never seen before. A frigid northerly wind, this one with the force of a hurricane, blows down 12th Avenue. It tears him away from me. As he begins to disappear, I cry to him, "Come find me again! I'll be here. I'll wait for you, no matter how long it takes!"

But he's gone before the last words part my lips. I stand shivering in the street searching for him, but he's nowhere to be seen. I've lost him.

Hell's Kitchen, February 1919

Wearing his thin woolen winter jacket and a fourth-hand tweed flat cap too large for his head, Davy skipped up the five flights of stairs to their apartment whistling, "Molly Malone". It'd been a good day. He'd spent the afternoon playing with his cousins Brendan and Colin, and Aunt Roisin had fed him a nice tea. They'd sent him home for supper with the previous day's newspaper, which he carried under his arm. On the street he'd passed Mickey and Ralph, the boys who'd bullied him the previous year, and they didn't say a word to him. This wasn't surprising after the thrashing he'd given Mickey in front of the entire school using the boxing techniques his mother had taught him. All in all, things were good.

Walking down the hallway, he passed the Reilly's apartment. The door hung open and, glancing inside, he saw Mr. Reilly sitting on the couch in his boxer shorts and a sleeveless t-shirt drinking a bottle of beer. Spotting Davy, Mr.

Reilly raised his beer and asked, "How's things, Davy?"

"Grand, Mr. Reilly," Davy replied with a grin. The strong Irish accent he'd entered the United States with was now watered down considerably. Holding up the newspaper, he said, "Did you hear they burned President Wilson in effigy?"

"So I heard. It was the Woman's Party did that."

"Where's Effigy?"

Mr. Reilly choked on a gulp of beer. Grinning, he replied, "Somewhere in Jersey, I think."

Davy nodded thoughtfully, then said, "Well, so long!"

"Stay outa trouble!" Mr. Reilly called after him good-naturedly.

Arriving at their flat, Davy removed the key from his pocket. After fitting it into the lock, Davy discovered the door was already unlocked. Thinking that his mother must've gotten off work early, he threw the door open and stepped inside. Holding the newspaper aloft, he announced proudly, "I got you a newspaper from Aunt Roisin, Mam. She already did the crossword, though."

Bridget, seated at the breakfast table staring vacantly ahead, didn't react to Davy's entry. The window behind Bridget was open, causing the yellowing piece of lined paper that she held loosely in her right hand to flutter. From behind her, the sounds of 12th Avenue drifted in: a siren wailed and honking horns wafted in on a current of cold air. He took a couple of steps toward Bridget. Noticing that her eyes were red and puffy and her face was streaked, Davy froze in his tracks. After a few moments pause, he approached her uncertainly: "Mammy?"

But Bridget continued gazing off into space. Davy became frightened at his inability to get through to her. He'd never seen his mother like this. Deducing that whatever was wrong probably had something to do with that paper in her hand, he took a couple more steps in her direction. Before he reached her, his attention was wrested by a piece of white stationary lying on the floor at her feet. Dropping the newspaper, he kneeled down and picked it up. Flipping the paper over, he saw it contained handwriting. He glanced up at his mother to make sure he wouldn't catch a scolding for reading it, but she was still off in her own world. Turning his attention back to the piece of paper in his hand, he could feel that it was heavy, embossed stationary. The message was written in black ink in a tight, neat fist:

My Dear Bridget O'Shea,

My name is Commander Reginald Marvell and I had the privilege of serving with your fiancée, Petty Officer Ciaran Creagh, in Lieutenant Wellesley's Antarctic Survey Expedition. I had originally been slotted for the final, polar party in Lieutenant Wellesley's ill-fated journey. But I became too sick to continue and was forced to return to base camp with the last supply group, turning around one hundred and twenty miles short of the Pole. Your fiancée took my place on the polar party. I can't properly express to you the remorse I feel over this. It should've been me, not Creagh. But the scurvy had weakened me too much to continue and Creagh was the fittest man to take my place. Your fiancée was one of the finest sailors I ever shipped with: loyal, diligent, untiring in work and unfailing in optimism. I can tell you from personal experience and from the diary that Lieutenant Wellesley left behind that Creagh served with courage and valor to the bitter end.

When I recuperated from my illness, I volunteered

to captain the relief ship that sailed in the spring of 1913 to pick up the entire expedition and return them to New Zealand. When I arrived at Ross Island, however, I learned that Lieutenant Wellesley's polar party had never returned. We waited as long as we could, but then had to depart to avoid being frozen in, leaving behind a contingent to await their return. I was to sail back in the spring of 1914, but then the Great War intervened. My duties only recently allowed me to return to the Antarctic to endeavour to recover the remains of the lost party.

The only member of the polar party whom I was able to locate was your fiancée, Creagh. Fortunately, he carried with him all of Lieutenant Wellesley's documents, so we know what happened. The polar party dropped off one by one until the only man left standing was Creagh. On his own, in the worst place on earth, fighting hellish conditions, he made a heroic effort to make it back, falling just short. I know it will be of little solace to you, given your immense loss, but perhaps someday you'll be able to reflect with pride on the fact that to the very end he never gave up trying to return to you, dying in the harness.

The reason for my writing you is two-fold. First, I wanted to inform you that I put P.O. Creagh up, posthumously of course, for the Meritorious Service Medal, which he was, deservedly, awarded. The medal is supposed to go to the next-of-kin, but P.O. Creagh made a note that all of his earthly belongings should go to you. Unfortunately, the Royal Navy didn't recognize this as a legal document, and, therefore, you are not entitled to collect survivor benefits or any back pay owed to P.O. Creagh. I, however, retained the personal effects recovered with his body and thus, along with the Meritorious Service Medal, I enclose his pipe and his copy of the Seaman's Handbook

The second reason I am writing is that there was a letter addressed to yourself from P.O. Creagh that he'd written during the final days of the return journey, which I recovered from his person. It has been of the utmost importance to me to see this letter delivered to you owing to the great service rendered by P.O. Creagh not only to the British Crown, but to Lieutenant Wellesley and to myself. I apologise for any delay in getting this to you, but it took me some weeks to locate you. I offer you my deepest condolences for your loss. Having served with P.O. Creagh, I understand only too well how great that loss is. Please do not hesitate to contact me in the future if ever I may be of service to you in any way.

With Kind Regards,

Cdr. Reginald Marvell, RN, DSC

Davy was only able to comprehend about half of the vocabulary. But he understood enough to glean the import of the correspondence and the impact it would've had on his mother. Davy looked up at Bridget—her position remained unchanged. She still stared vacantly at something far off in the distance. The yellowing letter remained gripped loosely in her right hand. Standing up, he glanced at the table and noticed for the first time an open box lined with black felt in which rested a bronze medallion the size of a dollar on which was depicted the bust in profile of a man whom Davy didn't recognize. The medallion was suspended from a ribbon made up of red and white stripes. Setting Commander Marvell's letter on the table, he placed the box containing the medal on top of it to weigh it down against the wind. Then he carefully removed the medal from the box. He held it up before his face and stared at it in wonder. The weight of it was impressive, and it was, hands down, the most beautiful thing he'd ever clapped eyes on. It was the first palpable proof he'd seen of his father's existence and he found himself in awe of it.

Davy realized that he hadn't thought of his da in ages. Never having met him—or even seen a photograph of the man—his father had loomed in his childish imagination like a mythological character of old—a Finn McCool or Cuchulainn. Mythological characters couldn't die—could they? But his da had died, proving only that he was a man, nothing more, nothing less. When Davy was younger, he'd entertained fantasies of traveling to the South Pole to find his father and fetch him back. Even though the entire polar party, his father included, had been reported lost, Davy had been certain they'd managed to locate a safe, warm place to survive the winter and they just needed someone to come and find them. As the years passed, he'd clung to that fantasy, unwilling to believe his father could've passed from the earth without his ever having met the man. Those were childish thoughts, he realized. Now, he was no longer a mere child—he was a second-grader and the man of his little family.

He glanced at his mother again. Even though she never mentioned it, he realized that, just like himself, she'd continued to hold out hope that she'd be reunited with him in this world. As he thought of it, he came to understand that was the reason his mam always sat on the fire escape gazing south. She was looking for his return. Now they knew for certain there'd be no return. His father would remain merely a memory for his mam, and a fantasy for himself. In some ways that meant his da would be more than a mere mortal because the legend is always greater than the man. Yet he'd also be less than mortal because of a fact that should've been abundantly clear years ago—his father would never again walk this earth. Davy would never be able to kick a football with him, or catch baseball, or wrestle like other boys did with their fathers. Davy felt like he should cry for this loss, but it was hard to mourn something that he'd never had. His father had never been anything more than an idea to him. The only change was that now Davy knew for certain that he'd remain so.

Davy decided to have a look at the paper in his mother's hand. She hadn't moved one iota since he'd entered the room, appearing almost comatose. He stepped in front of her and bent at the waist in order to look her in the eye, but her eyes were blank spaces. Reaching down, he lightly grasped the paper, saying gently, "Here now, Mammy."

He slid the paper out of her hand without a struggle. Once he held it, he could feel how brittle it was. Gently lifting it before his eyes, he saw that it only contained a few fading, scribbled lines. The fist was much less neat and certain than that of Commander Marvell. Yet he understood that this flimsy, yellowing bit of paper was the thing that'd crumbled the rock that was his mother. He had to squint in order to read the whisper-thin print:

Mo shioghra,

I'm writing you now because Lieutenant Wellesley's dying and I'm soon to be the last. I just wanted to let you know that I got your letter and I couldn't be happier about the wee lad and it is the thought of him and yourself that keeps me going. I'm giving it my all to get back to you, know that. But if you're reading this letter then that means... Anyway, always know that I love you and that wee one, and it was the thought of you both that kept me going. I miss you powerfully, as well.

Love Always,

Ciaran

Davy gently placed the letter with that of Commander Marvell under the box containing the medal. So, his father had known that Davy existed. That was something. Now he knew for certain that he had a father and that his father knew he had a son. No one could ever again call him that dirty "B" word. He had a father who'd loved him.

Taking Bridget's arm, he said, "Come on, Mammy. Lie down on the couch while I make some tea."

Like a calf being led into the barn, she allowed Davy to help her to her feet, and then guide her to the couch. He moved her into a sitting position, then lifted her feet up. Putting a pillow under her head, he helped her lay her head down and covered her with a blanket. He walked over and closed the window, then went into the kitchenette to make tea, understanding that at eight years of age he was, in truth, the man of the house.

New York, May 1947

Paddy leaned against a rail, staring across the Rockefeller Center skating pond at the statue of Prometheus. From the backdrop of an azure blue sky, a brilliant orange sun peaked through the skyscrapers, glinting off of Prometheus's gold plating. In Greek myth, Prometheus was a Titan who'd had the audacity to steal fire from the gods and present it to humankind. As a reward for his troubles, Zeus had Prometheus bound to a rock where eagles would peck out his liver every day only to have it regenerate overnight to begin the process anew. The inscription on the sixty-foot-high sculpture stated that Prometheus had provided "mortals a means to mighty ends." Paddy chuckled, thinking a quote from his countryman might be more appropriate: "no good deed goes unpunished." Paddy, too, had tried to bring light to something and his reward was the loss of everything, followed by a life of obscurity and near poverty. He wondered if it really was the gods who conspired to ruin the lives of mere mortals, or if we actually did it to ourselves and merely blamed the gods because we didn't want to be held responsible for our own failings.

Paddy exited the plaza and crossed 49th Street heading southwest. Passing the Time-Life building, he caught a look at himself in a plate-glass window. He paused momentarily to survey the damage. There was the crooked beak, a remembrance of the Walker fight in '26 when his nose got busted in during the 4th round. In spite of it, he'd gone on to win an eight-round decision. He could still clearly recall how painful it was every time Walker connected on his nose after it'd been broken. He'd never known jabs could hurt so much. Glancing at his ears, which protruded from under his cap, he noted the cauliflowering from all those years of training and fighting without headgear. There was the large, jagged scar on his forehead from the night of Davy's title bout. Then there were the smaller scars from his fighting days around his right eye, both on the cheekbone and above the eyebrow. The problem with scars, which he knew both from fighting and training, was that they opened up a lot quicker than healthy skin. Scars were supposed to be stronger than healthy skin, but that wasn't really the case. When boxing gloves were applied to a scar repeatedly and with great force the only thing the scar could do was split apart and become worse. It was a vicious cycle. He'd seen scars end more than one fighter's career.

Then there were the marks left on him not by fighting, but by Father Time. From the corners of his brown eyes spread fine spider webs of wrinkles, and his forehead was deeply furrowed. Though it was covered by a gray, tweed cap, he knew that his hair, once thick and brown was now gray and thinning, with a bald spot slowly forming on top. His cheeks had become hollow and gaunt. The one good thing he could see was that he was still trim—just ten pounds over his old fighting weight. In his mind he was still the lad of twenty-seven fighting for an opportunity at a title shot against Canzoneri. This old man standing before him was a stranger to Paddy.

Shaking his head at the reflection, Paddy turned and continued on his way. The streets around Rockefeller Center were teeming with businessmen wearing suits and fedoras. Paddy, in his grimy workman's pants, shabby tweed jacket and flat cap, felt self-conscious around men of importance like that. Shoving his hands in his pockets, he continued down the street whistling "Chattanooga Choo Choo" to himself. He'd only made it half a block when a shoeshine boy called out to him, "Hey, Mister! Shine your shoes?"

Paddy looked down at his dusty work boots, grinned, shook his head and replied, "Yeh don't have enough polish to fix these."

Turning down an alley, Paddy hoped that Davy hadn't moved on during the weeks that'd elapsed since their previous meeting. The city played a game of musical chairs with the homeless. Periodically New York's finest come around, roust the indigent and make them move along to the next spot. Occasionally, though, there wouldn't be enough seats. Then one of the hobos would get run-in, only to be turned out again as soon as the short vagrancy sentence had been served. What it added up to was a never-ending cycle of shuffling the homeless from place to place without ever finding a home for them. Fortunately for Paddy, the next round of musical chairs had not yet commenced and Davy was stretched out, slumbering, in the same alley.

Standing over Davy, Paddy had trouble believing this could be the same man he'd trained for a championship bout only ten years earlier. Back then, Davy had movie star good-looks and the physique of an Adonis. The man lying before Paddy now was almost unrecognizable. His face was bloated, but not in a healthy sort of way. Like Paddy, he'd begun losing his hair, only the process had begun for Davy about a decade earlier than it had for Paddy. Davy's mouth hung open as he loudly snored. Glancing inside it, Paddy noticed Davy had more gaps than teeth. A few of them had been knocked out while boxing. The rest could be attributed to years of life on the streets. Davy was still wearing the same clothes he'd had on a few weeks earlier, but that was hardly surprising. When you're being rousted from block to block every other week you can hardly maintain a robust wardrobe.

Paddy couldn't help but feel some responsibility for Davy's current state. Sure, it was Jake who'd done it. But Paddy was his trainer. As soon as he began to suspect something funny was afoot, he should've stopped the fight. He should've thrown in the towel and then immediately demanded a commission investigation. He should've exposed what happened to the press. He never should've kept his mouth shut and followed "proper channels", as Jake had urged. Instead, he'd let Davy fight on. It was a championship fight, after all. Most fighters only get one shot at that brass ring, if they even get that. It would've been much better for Davy if he'd been knocked out clean in the first round. Instead, Paddy let Davy fight on. He'd absorbed an unimaginable amount of punishment at the hands of Carvallo. And for what? The fight had been dirty from the jump. The truth was Davy never had a chance and he, Tommy, and Paddy were the only ones involved not to know it.

Looking at him now, sprawled out on top of a cardboard box snoring loudly, Paddy couldn't believe how far Davy had fallen. But it was understandable, given what Davy had been through. Paddy wasn't about to judge him. He'd fallen, too. Shaking his head sadly, he approached Davy. Staying well clear of his hands, Paddy kicked Davy's right foot. Hard times had found Davy, but that didn't mean he couldn't sting someone in a time of need. At one time not so long ago, Davy had been the finest fighter Paddy had ever seen. All of those years of training were still stored in his muscle memory. If push came to shove, no doubt he could rise far above what might be expected of him by anyone who'd only encountered him in his current state. The fact that Davy had survived on the streets alone for so long attested to this fact. Paddy waited, but Davy didn't react to the first kick. So, Paddy reared back and booted Davy's foot harder. This time, Davy sat straight up, threw a left-right-left combination, and growled, "Back off if you know what's good for you!"

"Calm yerself, boyo," Paddy grinned. "It's me."

Still not fully awake, Davy demanded in a groggy voice, thick with sleep and drink, "Who's me?"

"Paddy Byrnes, Davy. Have yeh forgotten me so quickly?"

Rubbing his head as if it pained him, Davy licked his parched lips and replied, "Well I'd like to forget you, but you insist on haunting me like some sawed-off banshee."

"Still making friends and influencing people. Eh, Davy?"

Sitting up, Davy rubbed his head some more and replied, "Fuck off."

Pulling a deli sandwich wrapped in white paper from his jacket pocket, Paddy handed it to Davy and said, "Eat something, Davy. Yeh look like week-old shite."

Davy looked at Paddy, annoyed, and replied, "Did you come here just to insult me, Paddy Byrnes?"

"No, I came for something else, as well." Nodding at the sandwich, he added, "Eat."

"My mouth's too dry to even think about eating that."

Removing a ten-ounce bottle of Coca Cola from his jacket pocket, Paddy produced an opener from his hip pocket. Snapping the cap off, Paddy handed the bottle to Davy, saying, "I assume yeh still like soda pop."

"When I can't lay my hands on anything stronger." Accepting the Coke from Paddy, Davy raised it to him, saying, "Sláinte." Davy then downed half of its contents in one gulp. Setting the bottle on the pavement, Davy began unwrapping the sandwich. Once he'd removed the paper surrounding it, Davy attacked the sandwich with the gusto of a man who hadn't eaten in some time. Paddy waited patiently while Davy devoured the sandwich. Once it was gone, Davy picked up the Coke and downed the remains. Emitting an enormous belch, Davy wiped his mouth with the back of his hand and said, "Okay, what do you want from me?"

"Can I not just bring yeh a sandwich?"

"Stop pulling my leg, Paddy. Not after all we been through."

Paddy squatted down so that he was eye-to-eye with Davy: "Right so," he chuckled, "yeh got me. There's something I'd like to ask of yeh."

"Here is comes," Davy rolled his eyes.

"I'd like yeh to take a walk with me."

"Where?"

"Central Park."

"Central Park? Are you nuts? That's at least ten blocks from here!"

"More than that to where we're going. But I'll make it easy on yeh. We'll take a cab."

"Why should I go anywhere with the likes of you, Paddy

Byrnes?" Davy squinted at Paddy. Then, leaning back against the wall of the alley, he added, "I'm comfortable right where I am."

"I can see that," Paddy responded, glancing around the alley in disgust.

Seeing Paddy's look, Davy demanded, "You don't like my midtown flat, Pads?"

"It's grand, Davy. Listen, I don't wanna bicker with yeh. I've something important to show yeh. Something that's bigger than the both of us."

"What might that be? My middleweight champion's belt, maybe?"

"Davy," Paddy shook his head sadly. "Yeh gotta let go of that, lad. That's in the past. If yeh insist on living in the past, yeh'll have no present nor future."

"In case you hadn't noticed, Paddy," Davy waved his arm grandiosely around the alley, "the present's not so great for me, and the future...I don't even wanna think about that."

"Do yeh believe in redemption, Davy?"

"There's that word again," Davy responded, shaking his head. "I'm not sure what that's supposed to mean, but I know it's a load of shit."

"So yeh won't come with me then, Davy?"

"No," Davy chuckled bitterly, "I'm content just where I am."

Paddy shook his head sadly and stood up. He turned to walk away, but paused. Turning back to Davy, he asked, "What if I were to offer yeh a fiver to come along with me?"

Davy scrutinized Paddy, then replied, "You're not gonna take me to one of those homes for wayward souls, are you?"

"No," Paddy chuckled, then held his right hand up, "I swear it's nothing of the sort."

"You're not gonna leave me be 'til I go along with you, are you?"

Paddy smiled, shook his head, "Indeed, I am not."

"Make it a ten-spot."

"Deal," Paddy quickly replied. Then he extended his hand to Davy to help him up.

New York, May 1947

Dazzling sunlight forced Percy to squint as he emerged from the darkness of Aunt Martha's apartment building. Perched on the stoop, his model ship under his right arm, Percy peeked in each direction to ensure that Marty and his crew weren't around. As he had to pass in the direction of the school on his way to the park, he'd decided to wait until Saturday to attempt to launch the repaired ship in the hopes that they wouldn't be lurking about. Seeing the way was clear, he stepped onto the sidewalk, bowed his head and embarked on a circuitous journey to the subway entrance which gave the school as wide a berth as possible. The streets were crowded. Then again, they were always crowded. He avoided Ninth Avenue as that was where Marty and his flunkies had nearly captured him a few days prior. Instead, he crossed through the theater district.

Navigating his way through swarms of theater patrons rushing to beat the matinee curtains, Percy took note of the young parents holding hands with their children, all of them decked-out in their Sunday best. He liked to imagine himself walking down Broadway holding the hand of his mother on one side and his father on the other. In his fantasy the three of them were dressed to the nines, off to see a show and then an early supper at a nice midtown restaurant. It was a hazy sort of daydream since he couldn't really remember his mother and his father was essentially a null set to him. But being a nullity meant that Percy could fill him with anything he wanted. His father could be a senator, a ship's captain, a spy—the only limit was his own imagination. For some reason, his imagination usually chose businessman for his father's profession. He liked to see the businessmen who marched around midtown in their crisp woolen suits, tweed overcoats, and gray felt fedoras, seemingly always hastening toward someplace important. They had the look of success, importance, and most of all, solidity. Something about them bespoke reliability to Percy. His father the businessman would be at the breakfast table every morning drinking coffee and reading his paper, and he'd be home again at night for supper. He'd take them on a vacation to the Jersey shore for a week every summer. Percy wondered what that'd be like—a vacation. He'd never been on one. Money was too tight and Aunt Martha was always working.

He made it to the 47-50th Streets Station without incident. In another twenty minutes he was walking through Inventor's Gate at the 72nd Street entrance to Central Park. Having made it as far as the park without incident, Percy began to let his guard down as he followed the path that'd take him to Conservatory Water. It was a beautiful spring day— warm enough that he didn't need a windbreaker, only a cotton shirt and dungarees. The flowers lining the path were all in bloom, encompassing nearly every color in the crayon box at school. He passed through the lush green trees that encircled Conservatory Water. When he stepped onto the walkway surrounding the model boat pond, Percy was amazed at the number of ships afloat. It looked like the Spanish Armada had invaded Central Park. The borders of the pond were lined by spectators, enjoying the day and taking in the spectacle of the miniature regatta.

Percy selected a relatively secluded spot in the southwest corner. Setting down his ship on the concrete bank of the pond, Percy eyed the surface. Small ripples created by a light southeast breeze rolled across the green water. Lifting the ship, Percy said under his breath, "I christen thee..."

Before he could finish that thought, he was struck violently from behind. It felt as if someone had kicked him in the small of his back. Lurching forward, Percy was forced to drop the ship in the pond in order to prevent himself from plunging headfirst into the water. He watched nervously as the ship bobbed wildly from side to side after crashing to the surface. Then it righted itself, the southeasterly breeze filled its sails, and his model ship began to make its way tentatively toward the center of the pond. As he was breathing a sigh of relief, another kick landed on his back—this time between the shoulder blades. The air was driven from his lungs with an involuntary grunt. Again, he pitched forward. This time, though, he was low enough that he easily stopped himself from tumbling into the water. Realizing that ducking him in the water seemed to be his unknown assailant's intent, Percy rolled to his right so that his back was to the water. Quickly he gained his feet and faced his antagonists.

To his right he saw the ferret-faces of the Pinto brothers. Posted on his left was his former friend, Michael. Before him, leering like a feral cat that's cornered a wounded mouse, was Marty. Clearly, it was Marty who'd just given him the boot in the back twice. Percy glanced from one to the others nervously.

"Why, look who it is, fellas," Marty exclaimed, feigning surprise. "It's Pussy Kelly!"

Michael's face remained impassive while the Pintos chortled at their leader's lively banter.

Percy gulped, but said nothing.

"Watcha doing, Pussy?"

"Sailing my boat," Percy responded weakly.

"Your boat?" Marty feigned surprise. "I thought it hit an iceberg."

The Pinto brothers snickered. His eyes desperately searching the environs for someone who might come to his rescue, Percy replied, "I fixed it."

"You fixed it! How'd ya do that? That thing was in a million pieces. Did ya get your old man to help ya? Oh wait, you ain't got no old man. Do ya, Pussy?" Marty, his eyes glinting with delight, glanced over at the Pintos who snickered dutifully.

A look of annoyance crossed Percy's face for the first time. "What do you want from me, Marty?"

"Can't a guy just shoot the breeze, Pussy?" Marty paused a beat, and then added, "But since ya brought it up, where's that boat of yours?"

Percy nodded behind himself, but said nothing.

"I sure would like a gander at it. Why don't ya wade out there and bring it to me so's we can have a look-see?"

Percy glanced around. Seeing no rescue imminent, he weakly shook his head.

"No?" Marty asked. It was hard to tell if he was feigning shock or really was shocked. "You're hurting my feelings, Pussy." He paused a moment, then added, "Speaking of hurting my feelings, why'd ya run from me the other day?"

Percy shook his head.

"Come on now, Pussy, don't tell me ya don't remember? Ya ran into the 50th Street Station like your pants was on fire!" Marty took a step toward him, forcing Percy backwards until the backs of his knees were touching the concrete bank of the man-made lake. The Pintos and Michael held their ground, as Marty was now almost chest-to-chest with Percy. Marty, standing a head taller than Percy, leered down at him. It wasn't that Marty was particularly tall, the difference in height was explained by the fact that Marty had flunked twice prior to landing in Percy's grade. Marty dropped the façade of gentility, snarling, "When I tell ya to do something, Pussy, ya do it. Got me?"

Percy stared at Marty, wide-eyed. Marty growled, "Now go get that boat for me, like I told ya."

Percy shook his head.

Marty became infuriated, "I told ya, go get it!"

This final statement Marty punctuated with a hard two-hand shove to Percy's chest. The crest of the bank operating like a fulcrum against the backs of his knees, Percy's eyes got wide as he felt gravity pulling him backward into the pond. Desperately, he flailed for something to arrest his fall. The closest thing was Marty, so Percy snatched a hold of Marty's shirt with both hands. But the shove was too forceful. Instead of Percy righting himself, he took Marty along with him, back end over teacups, into the pond. The Pintos gasped as Percy and Marty plunged into the water with a giant splash.

Marty was the first to his feet, followed in short order by Percy. They stood several feet apart, both dripping wet. An infuriated look on his face, Marty hissed, "Now ya went and did it, Pussy!"

Madison Square Garden, July 1936

Carvallo entered the ring to much less fanfare than one would expect to greet a defending champion. There could be no doubt that it was a solidly Davy Boy crowd. Carvallo wore black shorts with red trim, to Davy's white shorts with Kelly green trim. Carvallo was a study in contrast to Davy. Where Davy was tall and blond, Carvallo was short and dark. Davy's face was unscarred and it appeared as if he hadn't started shaving yet. Carvallo seemed to have a permanent five o'clock shadow and his forehead was knotted with scars as Carvallo was notorious for head-butting opponents during clinches. While Carvallo was squat and heavily muscled, Davy possessed a lean, chiseled physique. The differences in body type resulted in very different fighting styles, as well. Although he had plenty of pop, Davy was a slick fighter who liked to jab, move and counterpunch. Carvallo tried to set up camp in his opponent's hip pocket from the opening bell to the end of the fight, delivering devastating body blows and short powerful hooks.

Once they were in the ring Tommy removed Davy's robe and Paddy popped Davy's mouthguard in. Davy did a double-take when he saw the referee, a short, bald man wearing a white shirt, black bow tie and black slacks. A troubled look crossed Davy's face as he muttered, "It's him."

"What's that?" Paddy asked as he smeared gobs of petroleum jelly on Davy's face.

"It's the ref from my dream!" Davy replied, horrified.

An annoyed look clouded Paddy's face, "Don't be daft, man! We don't have time for that nonsense."

Before Davy could respond, the ref called the two fighters to the center of the ring to issue the fight instructions. Davy looked hesitant, so Paddy gave him a shove.

Ring instructions were patently unnecessary at this level given that the rules were always the same—no punching off the break, no punching below the belt or rabbit punches, etc. But since the instructions were part of the spectacle, they did it, even though neither of the combatants listened to a word of it. Carvallo used the opportunity to glare up at Davy. This sort of gamesmanship would've usually caused Davy to burst out laughing in his opponent's face, but not this time. Jake's entrance song combined with the referee's resemblance to the ref from his dream. seemed to have gotten to him as he simply stood there staring at Carvallo's feet. When he finished his spiel, the referee told Davy and Carvallo to "Touch gloves and come out fighting." Carvallo slammed his gloves down on Davy's in another attempt to intimidate him. Davy didn't react to this provocation, he simply retreated to his corner.

Paddy awaited Davy in his corner. When Davy returned, Paddy looked him in the eye and said, "This is yer one shot, Davy. Yer not getting another. Forget about that dream nonsense and just fight yer fight. If yeh do that, there's no way yeh can lose. Carvallo ain't in yer class, and well he knows it. Take that title from him—it's yers!"

Davy noddy absently. Shaking his head at Davy's reaction, Paddy stepped through the ropes that Tommy held open for him, then retreated to the ground outside the ring with Tommy following.

The bell rang and the fight got off to a quick start. As Paddy had predicted, Carvallo charged out of his corner like a rodeo bull. Clearly, he was trying to make good on his promise to put Davy away early. While Paddy had advised Davy to expect this during their preparations for the fight, Davy nevertheless seemed taken aback by the ferocity of Carvallo's initial assault. As the first round progressed, Davy often found himself backpedaling while Carvallo charged after him, throwing everything but the kitchen sink. Watching from ringside, Paddy was alarmed at how flat Davy looked. It appeared as if he wasn't trying to win the fight, but simply wanted to survive it. Turning to Tommy, who stood beside him adjacent to their corner, Paddy shook his head and shouted over the roar of the crowd, "Jake had to go and change our entrance song." Then he turned and glared at Jake, who was sitting in the first row, ringside. Sensing Paddy's stare, Jake looked him in the eye and shrugged, as if to say, *What?*

The first round went to Carvallo. Paddy was amazed at Carvallo's hand speed. That was one area where Paddy had been dead certain Davy held a clear advantage. The power was a wash, and Carvallo was physically stronger and more experienced, but Davy was a slicker and much faster boxer than Carvallo. Yet Carvallo somehow kept beating Davy to the punch. Paddy couldn't figure out if it was just because Davy was so flat, or if Carvallo, at the age of 29, had somehow found a way to markedly improve his hand speed. When the bell rang ending the first, Paddy placed a low wooden stool in their corner, then slipped through the ropes into the ring. Tommy followed Paddy up the ring steps carrying a metal spit bucket which contained a water bottle and tools for mitigating cuts and swelling.

Paddy didn't like Davy's body language as he trudged to the corner after the bell. His shoulders were slumped and his head bowed as though he'd already lost. Paddy studied Davy's face as he approached. The amount of damage Carvallo had done to Davy in only one round was startling. Seeing how red and lumpy Davy's cheeks were, Paddy would've sworn he'd already gone the full fifteen.

Plopping himself on the stool, Davy panted, "I can't believe how hard his punches feel! It's like he ain't wearing any gloves!"

"Quiet yourself," Paddy commanded. "Don't be wasting yer breath on talking."

Davy slung his arms over the ropes on each side of him. Knowing that propping the arms up in that way only fatigued the arms and shoulders more, Paddy slapped Davy's arms off of the ropes and onto his lap. Paddy then sprayed water from his bottle on Davy's face. Wiping the water and perspiration from Davy's face with a towel that he'd slung over his shoulder, Paddy then squirted water into Davy's mouth, saying, "Don't drink any."

Davy swished the water around, then spit it into the bucket that Tommy held before him. Looking in the bucket, Paddy noticed the spit was tinted pink by blood. Paddy glanced at Tommy, who shook his head and shrugged. Turning his attention back to Davy, who was slumped on the stool panting, Paddy thought he'd never seen Davy look so worn out following a fight, let alone after only one round. Realizing that what was draining Davy was more than the battering he was receiving in the ring, Paddy decided to address the elephant in the arena.

"Yer still here, lad," Paddy looked Davy in the eye and stated bluntly.

"What?" Davy replied, baffled.

"It's that bloody dream taking the pep out of yer step."

Davy looked down and didn't reply.

"It hasn't happened. Yer fine, man."

"The dream never said what round it happens. We got fourteen more to go."

Becoming angry, Paddy shouted, "This is yer one shot, man! Yeh ain't gonna get another. Don't let some bloody dream scare yeh outa taking what's rightfully yers!"

Davy still said nothing. The timekeeper banged on the ring apron to signify that ten seconds remained until round two. Davy stood up. Tommy grabbed the stool and ducked through the ropes. With the water bottle, Paddy rinsed off Davy's mouthguard, then shoved it back in Davy's mouth, saying, "Stop mixing it up with him so much. Stay on the outside and feed him the jab."

Davy nodded. The bell rang. Davy limply banged his gloves together and strode toward center ring like a condemned man climbing the gallows.

Paddy immediately spun around and looked at Jake, who was sitting back smoking a stogie. Catching Jake's eye, Paddy shouted, "Did yeh check them gloves like yeh said, Jake?"

Jake, looking annoyed at having his attention wrested from the blonde seated beside him, snapped, "Course I checked 'em. Worry about your fighter, Paddy!"

"I am. Davy's getting busted up."

"Maybe ya shoulda taught him how to slip a punch!"

Paddy shook his head and turned away. Looking at Tommy, who was standing on the arena floor beside him, Paddy asked, "Could Carvallo do that much damage if the gloves were right?"

Tommy shrugged and replied, "Possibly."

*

The second round was more of the same. The crowd, which had been delirious with enthusiasm for Davy at the start of the fight, now appeared deflated. By the end of the second, the cheers for Davy had turned weak and uncertain. It was as if his fans were trying to figure out what'd happened to the Davy Boy they knew. When the bell rang ending the round, Davy returned to the corner looking more bruised, swollen, and disheartened. On the plus side, no cuts had opened yet. He'd lost both rounds so far, but there were thirteen more to go. Thus, in theory, Davy had plenty of time to recover. But recovery seemed out of the question the way things were going.

The problem, Paddy realized, was Davy wasn't just

fighting Carvallo, which was tough enough. He was also fighting the ghosts of his dream and that was one fight he seemed incapable of winning. In spite of that mini-bender that he'd gone on during the penultimate week of training, Davy was prepared. Sparring throughout the week leading up to the fight, Davy had been sharper than at any other time in his career. His strength, wind and reflexes were honed to the highest degree. Even after Davy's moment of doubt in the locker room, Paddy had brought him around. At that point, Davy had looked like a man who was about to go out and win a world title. Then Jake had to pick that maudlin treacle for Davy's entrance music. In a matter of seconds, it'd undone everything Paddy had accomplished in the dressing room.

*

About halfway through the third round, the moment of truth arrived. Davy had continued to plod through the fight and Carvallo kept after him like a starving wolf, constantly beating Davy to the punch. There was an exchange in the middle of the ring that at first appeared innocuous. Both men landed jabs and missed with rights. As Davy was backing up to break contact, Carvallo caught him with a left hook, flush on the chin. Davy never saw it coming. The punch sent a message straight up Davy's jawbone and into his brain. The message was: *fall down.*

Davy dropped to the canvas in a heap. It was the first time he'd been knocked down in his career. The entire arena went silent as a tomb. For a moment, Davy could feel himself hovering weightless above the ring. Looking down, Davy saw himself sprawled out on the canvas. He felt himself being pulled away. Davy's eyes snapped open to see the referee standing over him counting. Uncertain how he'd gotten to be in a prone position, Davy sat up and shook his head to clear the cobwebs. When he glanced up at the ref again, the count was to seven. Pushing himself to his feet, Davy held up his gloves in a fighting posture to demonstrate that he was prepared to continue as the ref's count reached nine. The ref looked in Davy's eyes to ensure someone was home. Satisfied, he took Davy's gloves in his hands and wiped the striking surface on the front of his shirt. The crowd emitted a collective sigh of relief.

Once the ref signaled for the fight to continue, Carvallo, who'd been waiting in a neutral corner, charged at Davy in an effort to finish him quickly. Forgoing the jab, Carvallo waded in throwing bombs with both hands. Davy was able to keep his arms up and fend off Carvallo's wild shots. Continuing the onslaught, Carvallo backed Davy against the ropes. When Carvallo got close enough, Davy got him in a clinch and tied him up, just hoping to survive the round. As he was leaning back against the ropes, trying to hold onto Carvallo, something in the audience caught Davy's eye. Squinting over Carvallo's hairy shoulder, Davy saw a figure in a white dress whom he recognized. It was Rita, sitting in the ringside seat he'd provided her. She'd come after all, although, judging by the tears filling her eyes, she probably regretted it.

Something within Davy changed at that moment. He realized that he'd become unmanned and had already given up before even entering the ring. He thought of how, in front of Rita, he'd allowed himself to be battered around the ring for three rounds like some punch-drunk sparring partner. The thought of that did something to him. It made him angry. Paddy was right, he was throwing away his one shot at the title because he'd been frozen by fear. And it was the fear of nothing more than a dream—a dream which he saw now was just that, a dream, not some premonition. He'd given away three rounds. There was nothing to be done about that now. He wasn't giving away any more.

*

The ref separated Carvallo from Davy and signaled for

them to continue. Given how quickly Davy had gone for the clinch, Carvallo undoubtedly assumed that his opponent was merely hanging on by a thread. That being the case, putting Davy away would only require a little push. Carvallo charged back in wailing haymakers from his ankles, eschewing even the most basic pretense of defense. Since the punches were so wild and looping, Davy was easily able to block or slip them. Stepping inside Carvallo's punching distance, Davy uncorked a vicious left uppercut that snapped Carvallo's head back. He followed this with a straight right that drove Carvallo back into the neutral corner from which he'd emerged. The crowd roared deliriously. Pursuing Carvallo into the corner, Davy was about to unleash a combination when the bell rang, signaling the end of the round.

The cheering swelled to an almost deafening level. This was the Davy Boy the crowd had all paid to see—the Terror from County Kerry. Davy dropped his hands and stalked back to his corner. On the way, he glanced over at Rita. Catching her eye, Davy winked to let her know everything was okay. When he got to the corner, Tommy set the stool down, but Davy refused to sit. Paddy climbed into the ring and barked, "Seat yerself!"

But Davy merely mashed his gloves together and shook his head. Paddy studied Davy for a moment. Deciding he liked what he saw, he said, "Suit yourself." Then he held out his hand so that Davy could spit his mouthpiece into it.

Hell's Kitchen, August 1921

Thanks to Ardan's promotion to foreman at the waterfront, Bridget's cousin Roisin and their family had been able to move into a new flat. It was still in Hell's Kitchen, but it was bigger, nicer and cleaner. It even had an actual kitchen—not a sink and oven tacked onto the end of a living room. Although it was located on the sixth floor, this wasn't a negative as the building actually contained a lift. The luxury of it was almost unimaginable to Bridget. She could only dream of not having to climb five flights of stairs on her return from a hard day's work. Roisin, pregnant with their fourth, poured a cup of tea for Bridget and herself, then sat down at the small, circular breakfast table. As Bridget blew the steam from her cup, the fine web of wrinkles emanating from the corners of her eyes fanned out. Not yet thirty, care and toil seemed to have aged Bridget beyond her years. Her hazel eyes had lost the sparkle of their youth. While work had kept her figure trim, she moved like someone much older. Nonetheless, she remained exquisitely beautiful.

"I don't know what I'm going to do about Davy," Bridget mused after taking a sip of tea.

"What class of problems could you possibly have with the wee angel?"

"More like a fallen one. I'm in the principal's office every other week for something the wee ruffian's done."

"Such as?"

"Fighting mostly. I never should've taught the gurrier how to throw a punch, except for he was getting picked on at school. I never thought he'd take to it so much."

"He's getting picked on?"

"He was. No more. Now it seems Davy's the one doing the picking. He never saw a scrap he didn't like, so says the principal."

"He needs a da."

"That he does. But his da…" She drifted off.

Roisin was silent for a few moments. Then she cleared her throat and said, "You could always…you know."

"Find a man?"

"Sure, you're still young. If you had someone, maybe you wouldn't have to work so hard. Plus, there'd be a man around for Davy. A gosoon needs a da."

"But it wouldn't be a da. Ciaran David only has one da, and he's buried in the South Pole."

"Aren't you lonely?"

Bridget thought about this for a moment. "Sometimes." She paused again, then added, "But I have Davy. He's all I need."

"You won't be young for much longer…"

"I haven't been young for a long time, col ceathrar."

"So, you're just going to remain alone for the rest of your life?"

"I'm not alone. I have Davy. But if you're asking if I'll be taking up with another man, the answer is no. Do you recall the story of Diarmuid and Gráinne?"

"The old myth?" Roisin took a sip of her tea and then shook her head, "I remember learning it in school, but I can't recall the particulars."

"Gráinne was the daughter of the high king, Cormac. King Cormac promised her hand to Finn McCool, leader of the Fianna. At their wedding feast, Gráinne saw Diarmuid, a young warrior in Finn's band, and she instantly fell desperately in love with him. The two ran off so that they could be together. But Finn was jealous and angry, so he pursued them. Eventually, Finn caught up with the lovers and sent word to Diarmuid that he only wanted to reconcile. Against Gráinne's wishes, Diarmuid went to make it up with his former chief at which point Finn murdered him so that he could possess Gráinne. But Gráinne never did give herself to Finn. She kept putting him off, telling Finn she needed time to grieve Diarmuid. Before Finn could ever possess her, Gráinne grieved herself to death."

"That's just a story."

"Aye. But our lives are stories, too. Stories that we try to write ourselves. We all hope that there'll be a happy ending. But the truth of the matter is we have no control over the ending—it always writes itself. Sometimes, we wind up like Gráinne."

"Are you going to grieve yourself to death, then?"

"Maybe. But slowly."

"If Ciaran was everything you told me he was then he'd want you to be happy."

"He would. This is my choice. Ciaran was with no one else. That I know. I also know that, just as Gráinne was eventually reunited with Diarmuid, I'll see Ciaran again in the next world. When I do see him, I want to be able to tell him that I've been with no one else, either."

"But that might not be for another fifty years."

"If fifty years it's to be, then fifty years it'll be."

New York, May 1947

Paddy and Davy entered Central Park through Inventor's Gate. The pathway that led to Conservatory Water was perfumed by the tulips and germaniums that were bursting into bloom. The chirping of sparrows and wrens filled the air. Crowded with people enjoying the spring weather, the path seemed as congested as the mid-town sidewalks at rush hour. Paddy and Davy were an odd pair: a middle-aged man dressed in dusty work clothes accompanied by a man of indeterminate age wearing a soiled overcoat far too heavy for the mild spring weather, with unruly, matted dirty-blond hair and a scarred face that looked like it hadn't been washed in years. As a result, they elicited curious, and sometimes frightened, looks from passers-by.

After five minutes of walking, Davy turned to his left and asked, "What is it you're so damned insistent I see?"

"Yeh'll see," Paddy replied.

"Do you have to be so goddammed mysterious?"

Paddy grinned, "Isn't it nice to get a bit of fresh air?"

"Fresh air I get plenty of. I'm outside 24 hours a day, man. What'd be nice would be some whiskey." Davy paused for a moment, then muttered, "You better have that ten-spot of mine if you know what's good for you."

Paddy glanced over at Davy and chuckled. A few minutes later, they were approaching Conservatory Water. When they arrived at the walkway that lined the man-made pond, they paused while Paddy scanned the environs. Spotting what he was looking for, he led Davy to a bench under a massive, old oak tree that overlooked the pond. Paddy waved for Davy to have a seat. Collapsing onto the bench with a groan, Davy complained, "How far did we walk?"

"About a quarter mile give or take." Paddy seated himself beside Davy and grinned, "I can remember, not so very long ago, yeh could run ten miles and not even breathe heavy."

Davy started to respond, then stopped and shook his head. "Did you bring me here to watch the boats sail?"

Paddy nodded toward Percy, who was standing about fifty yards away, unaware of them, about to place his model ship in the pond. "I came to show you that."

Davy followed Paddy's glance. His back to them, Percy bent over to place his ship in the water. As he was doing so, he was accosted from behind by Marty and his crew. Davy arched his eyebrows and turned to Paddy: "You brought me all the way here to watch a group of hooligans beat up some mama's boy?"

"I brought yeh here to see him—the mama's boy, that is, as yeh described him with that colorful vocabulary of yers." As he was saying this, Marty shoved Percy in an effort to knock him into the pond, only to have Percy pull Marty in with him. They landed in the water with a massive splash. Both boys got to their feet quickly, separated by six feet of water. As far away as they were, Davy and Paddy still clearly heard Marty bellow, "I'm gonna kill you!"

"You know that blond kid?"

"Aye," Paddy nodded.

"Might not be a bad idea to break it up before that big kid murders him."

"He'll be okay."

*

After threatening to kill him, Marty charged Percy. Realizing that the moment of truth had arrived, for a split-second Percy was frozen with fear. He had two options open to him: fight Marty and maybe put an end to the cycle of bullying and intimidation, or he could allow Marty to pound him, hoping Marty would take it easy on him if he didn't fight back. He didn't have much time to decide as Marty was rushing Percy, his fat right fist balled up and ready to strike. For some reason, Percy suddenly felt calm. He allowed the training that Mr. Patrick had given him to take over. He stepped toward Marty, planted his feet and threw the hardest right that he could muster. Combined with Marty's forward momentum, the punch landed on Marty's nose with a sickening thud, causing it to spurt blood. Marty bent over and held his nose in pain. Straightening up, Marty glanced at his right hand, stained a deep red with blood.

"I'm going to kill you for that, Pussy!"

Marty lurched at Percy, hands outstretched in an attempt to drag him down. But Percy, emboldened by the success of his first punch, stepped forward and threw a jab, straight right, left hook combination, all of which landed. The hook finished him. Marty dropped, sinking into the cool gray water of the man-made pond. Percy got in his fighting stance and studied the water warily. He expected that at any moment Marty would burst to the surface like an enraged Kraken. When several moments had passed without that happening, Percy became concerned. He waded over to the spot where he'd seen Marty sink and felt around for him under the water. Getting his hands under Marty's armpits, he hoisted Marty's head and shoulders out of the water. When he broke the surface, Marty gasped for air, then his eyes snapped open.

Percy dragged him to the water's edge and leaned Marty against the concrete shore. Marty coughed out some dirty water and blinked several times, as though trying to figure out what'd hit him. Once he'd gathered his senses, he turned to the Pinto brothers and Michael, all of whom stood, mouths agape, at water's edge. "Don't just stand there gawking," Marty snarled at them. "Get him!"

The Pinto brothers looked at each other. Clearly, they weren't anxious to be on the receiving end of what Marty had just absorbed. The elder of the two shrugged and said, "Sorry, Marty. Our dad would kill us if we got our clothes wet." With that, they turned and began walking away.

"Come back here, ya cowards!" Marty hollered. But the Pintos kept walking without turning back. Marty then turned to Michael and commanded, "Get him, Mikey!"

Michael looked at Percy, an apology in his eyes. Then he turned to Marty and locked eyes with him. He slowly shook his head, then turned and walked away. "Come back here ya yellow bastards!" Marty screamed. But by that point they were already gone.

Percy climbed out of the pond and stood there dripping onto the pavement. He looked across the water and spotted his boat, sailing majestically in the middle of the pond. Then he glanced down at Marty, who was in the same position muttering something about "rats." Percy extended his hand to Marty and said, "Come on, Marty. It's over."

Marty eyed Percy with resentment, but he accepted the hand and allowed Percy to help him out of the water. Once he was on dry land, he turned to Percy and said, "It ain't over 'til I say it is, Pussy."

Percy balled up his right fist, took a step toward Marty, and replied evenly, "My name is Percy."

Marty threw his hands up in a gesture of mollification: "All right, it's Percy."

"Is it over?" Percy took another step toward Marty, fists at the ready.

"Yeah, yeah, it's over." Marty glanced around to see if anyone had witnessed his comeuppance. Satisfied that no one had, he turned and shuffled away. Once Marty had left his field of vision, Percy turned back to the pond to search for his boat. Spying it, its sails filled with wind as it made its way around the pond, the smallest hint of a smile curled the corners of Percy's mouth.

Madison Square Garden, July 1936

Davy came back and knocked Carvallo down in the sixth and ninth rounds. But Carvallo, tough and possessed of the determination one would expect of a champion, never stopped attacking. Davy took a terrible beating. Even though he'd landed a lot more punches, Davy appeared much the worse for wear than Carvallo. Deep cuts had opened under both of his eyes and along his right cheekbone. The gash over his left eyebrow was the one that hindered Davy the most because every time Carvallo opened it, it bled down into Davy's left eye, blinding him on that side and thereby rendering him susceptible to straight rights. When he looked Davy over in the corner, Paddy figured it'd probably take close to two hundred stitches to mend the wounds he'd accumulated. Following every round from the tenth on, the referee would inspect Davy and then threaten to stop the bout over cuts. But Paddy was able to work magic with his cold metal press and petroleum jelly, always closing the cuts by the start of the next round. Still refusing to sit, between rounds Davy would stand mashing his gloves together and glaring across the ring at Carvallo.

During the break before the fifteenth round, after Paddy had removed his mouthguard, Davy asked, "How'm I doing?"

Paddy rinsed off the mouthpiece and handed it to Tommy to hold. As he did so, Paddy's and Tommy's eyes met. They'd calculated that Davy should be up by two or three points on the three judges' scorecards. But they also knew that judging fights was very subjective and not always honest. To take a championship belt, a contender had to thoroughly defeat the champion because the benefit of the doubt always went to the title-holder. Furthermore, in the case of a draw or majority draw, the champ retained the title. Knowing all of this, Paddy replied, "It could go either way. Yeh gotta win this last round convincingly. No doubts."

Davy nodded, then Paddy squirted some water into his mouth from a bottle.

"Make him eat that jab. Keep him at arm's length. Don't go mixing it up if yeh don't need to. Just score points. Pitch a shut-out."

Davy swished the water around his mouth, spit it out, and nodded. The timekeeper pounded on the ring apron to signal that ten seconds remained. Paddy popped in Davy's mouthguard. The referee came over to examine Davy's cuts. Nodding that it was okay for Davy to continue, the ref moved to the center of the ring and signaled for Davy and Carvallo to come out. Davy glanced over at Rita, still seated at ringside. She looked as though she were about to burst into tears at any moment. Meeting his eyes, she forced a brave smile and nodded encouragement. Davy nodded back and attempted to wink, but his eyes were too swollen to pull it off. Instead, it looked more like a grimace of pain.

Davy and Carvallo stood surveying each other in the center of the ring, two exhausted but proud warriors. The referee said, "Final round, fellas. Touch gloves and come out fighting."

Carvallo extended his left toward Davy, grudging respect in his eyes. Davy nodded to Carvallo, then touched the punching surface of his left glove to that of Carvallo's. Both fighters retreated to their corners and awaited the bell to start the round. When it sounded, the crowd, already collectively hoarse, nevertheless found the voice to urge Davy on for one final round. The action of the fifteenth round was understandably slow, as both men had suffered a lot of abuse and were understandably exhausted. Although Carvallo continued to plod forward after Davy, his rushes no longer contained the ferocity or doggedness of earlier rounds. Davy followed Paddy's instructions and force-fed Carvallo the left jab throughout. Although the jab no longer snapped Carvallo's head back, as it had in previous rounds, Davy was piling up points.

The only real action came after the timekeeper banged the ring apron to signal ten seconds remained in the fight. Perhaps hoping to finish Davy, Carvallo stepped forward and threw a long, looping right. Davy dipped, stepped inside of Carvallo's right and drove a short right of his own into Carvallo's chin. Carvallo's knees buckled and he fell forward onto Davy, draping his arms around Davy's neck in order to maintain verticality. Realizing that Carvallo was out on his feet, Davy began to desperately throw short punches at the sides of Carvallo's head in an effort to break Carvallo's grip on his neck. If he could only get Carvallo to release his grip, gravity would do the rest and Carvallo would fall flat on his face at Davy's feet. But the bell ending the bout rang with Carvallo's arms still wrapped tightly around Davy's neck.

The referee immediately stepped in and shouted, "Break it up, fellas! Fight's over!"

Davy tried to disengage from Carvallo, but Carvallo wouldn't let go because the fact of the matter was that Davy was the only thing keeping him on his feet. Perceiving this, the referee stepped in and helped the wobbly Carvallo weave his way to his corner. Davy raised his arms triumphantly over his head and strutted to his corner. Sensing that a victorious decision for Davy was imminent, the crowd went wild.

Paddy and Tommy climbed into the ring. Paddy threw his arms around Davy, hugged him, kissed his cheek and said, "Well done, me lad." Turning to Tommy, he instructed, "Cut his gloves off."

Tommy nodded, then slapped Davy on the shoulder. Paddy disengaged, crossed the ring and entered Carvallo's corner. Paddy had to push his way through the throng of cornermen, attendants, and hangers-on surrounding the champion's corner. He found Carvallo seated on his stool. His head trainer, a white-haired, pug-nosed Italian was hastily cutting off Carvallo's left glove while an assistant trainer ran smelling salts under Carvallo's nose. Paddy bent down, grabbed Carvallo's right glove. Carvallo looked at Paddy blankly as he shook Carvallo's hand and said, "Great fight,

Champ."

As he was shaking, Paddy felt the punching surface of the glove. Pressing down lightly, he felt the clear outline of Carvallo's taped knuckles. As he'd suspected, there was almost no padding left in the punching surface of the glove. It'd somehow been removed. Whether that'd occurred after Jake had checked the gloves or before, Paddy couldn't say. But without question the gloves had been tampered with. That's why Carvallo seemed so fast. It also explained why Davy had so much more damage on his face than Carvallo. Carvallo had a mouse under his left eye from all of the jabs Davy had landed and some general swelling and redness, but that was it. Meanwhile, Davy looked like his head had been used as a hurley ball, and it was evident that he'd have to spend the next few nights in a hospital.

Clinging tightly to Carvallo's right glove, Davy shouted, "The padding's been removed from these gloves! Ref, get over here!"

Carvallo's trainer pulled off the left glove and handed it through the ropes to a man in a black suit standing outside the ring. Nodding at Paddy, the trainer growled, "Get him the fuck outa here!"

Two burly, dark-haired, olive-skinned thugs in black suits grabbed Paddy's arms from behind and pulled him back forcefully. Paddy spun his head around to look at his accosters, then shouted more frantically than ever, "The gloves! Check the gloves!"

The larger of the two leaned in and whispered in a menacing tone, "If ya know what's good for ya, you'll shut your potato-hole, Paddy," employing the moniker as an ethnic slur, without actually knowing that Paddy was, indeed, his name.

As they dragged him to the center of the ring, Paddy saw someone outside of the ring slip a pair of replacement gloves through the ring to Carvallo's trainer, who then handed back the right glove which he'd just cut from Carvallo's hand. Paddy could see the new gloves had been stained with sweat and taped, just like the fight gloves that'd been removed from Carvallo's hands. "The gloves!" he shouted one last time, knowing that it was already too late. The ref went over and checked the new gloves, then turned and shouted across the ring at Paddy, "The gloves are fine!"

Paddy spun around, looking for Jake. Davy's corner was relatively empty compared to Carvallo's, with only Tommy, Jake, and Davy standing in it. Jake, smoking an enormous stogie, slapped Davy on the back and said, "Great fight, kid! That belt's as good as yours!"

Paddy approached Jake from the side, put his hand on Jake's shoulder and spun him around, saying, "I thought yeh checked the gloves, Jake!"

A surprised yet innocent look on his face, Jake replied, "I did check 'em. I told ya that. Why're ya bothering me about that now?"

"Cause the gloves they just pulled off of Carvallo didn't have any padding over the knuckles!"

"What?" Jake at least appeared shocked. "How do ya know?"

"I just felt 'em. There was nothing in there."

"They were good when I checked 'em. Where are they?"

"Gone. The gloves they have over there now I'm after seeing a lad slip into the corner once they cut the real fight gloves off. We gotta tell the commission, Jake. Can yeh go find Lenny?"

"Now?" Jake replied, nonplussed. "When they're about to crown my boy here middleweight champeen of the world?"

"We gotta do it now while the gloves are still in the building."

The referee walked over and guided Davy into the center of the ring, then stood there between Carvallo and Davy awaiting the decision. Davy glanced over at Carvallo, who had his head down and still seemed out of it. Davy stood there shaking out his arms and rolling his neck, as though he were ready to go another fifteen rounds.

Jake waited until Davy was out of earshot, then asked, "You saw them hand the gloves out of the ring?"

Paddy nodded.

"Who'd they hand 'em to?"

"Some lad in a black suit."

Jake nodded toward Carvallo's corner at a man in a gray suit with salt-and-pepper hair and cold, brown eyes. "Ya see that mug?"

"Aye."

"Ya know who that is?"

Paddy shook his head.

"It's Frankie Carbo."

"Yeh got mixed up with Carbo?" Paddy demanded angrily.

"It's not like that, Paddy. Carbo got himself mixed up in this. He owns Carvallo. Didn't ya know that?"

Paddy shook his head.

"Let me give ya a bit of advice, Paddy. If Frankie Carbo wants to do something, ya let 'im do it. Otherwise, you're gonna find yourself singing with the choir invisible. So, if ya know what's good for ya, you'll let it be."

Jake glanced at Paddy, who seemed unconvinced. "Look," Jake added placatingly, "Let's see what the decision is. If Davy wins, then there's no harm done."

"No harm done? Take a look at him, Jake!" Paddy nodded at Davy in the center of the ring. His face red and swollen, with both eyes nearly closed and a series of cuts held together only by petroleum jelly, Davy didn't look like a man about to be awarded the middleweight belt. He looked like a victim of an aggravated assault. "A beating like that can ruin a fighter."

Jake was about to reply when the emcee stepped into the ring holding a microphone. The announcer, a dapper looking silver-haired man in a tuxedo with a mellifluous voice, bellowed into the microphone, "Ladies and gentlemen, we have a split decision."

Paddy shook his head, "Split decision? Davy won by a minimum of four rounds. What fight were they watching?"

A buzz ran through the crowd, which was quickly suppressed so that the announcement could be heard. The referee grabbed both Davy's and Carvallo's wrists, preparing to raise the arm of the winner, as they both stood with their heads bowed, awaiting the decision. Paddy held his breath while Jake puffed furiously on his stogie. The announcer, reading from a card, boomed, "Judge Randolph Gates scores it 142-140 for Carvallo."

This was immediately greeted by a large wave of boos from the predominantly Irish crowd. But it was quickly stifled as, given that it was a split decision, everyone already knew at least one judge had ruled for Carvallo. Though the vacancy light was still lit in his eyes, Carvallo glanced up and grinned briefly. Davy, head bowed, didn't react. Paddy merely pursed his lips and shook his head.

The ring announcer continued, "Judge Harold

Goodnight scores it 143-139 for O'Shea."

The crowd immediately erupted into an enormous cheer of approval. Paddy allowed the hint of a grin to form around the corners of his mouth, while Jake pounded him on the back. Davy glanced up enough to catch the eyes of Rita at ringside. Although she still looked like she was about to burst out weeping, she held up both hands to show him her crossed fingers.

The ring announcer waited a few extra beats to build the suspense before bellowing, "Our final judge, Wendell Schmidt, scores the fight 142-141 for the winner...and still the champion..." The ref raised Carvallo's arm and Carvallo threw the other arm up with it. "Rocco Carvallo!"

At that moment it seemed as if all the air had been drawn out of the arena. The place was deathly silent for a few beats while the audience tried to assimilate the decision. It was probably the most subdued initial reaction by a crowd after a champion retained his crown ever. Davy, crestfallen, stood with his shoulders slumped in the middle of the ring, staring at the canvas flooring. Paddy cursed, "Carbo owns at least one of those judges!"

The cigar dropped out of Jake's mouth and began smoldering on the canvas until he looked down and ground it out with his wing-tip. Then he muttered, "They said the fix wasn't in, that the judges was clean. Whoever won won, so long as I..." Jake caught himself and immediately dummied up.

Paddy turned on him: "So long as yeh what, Jake?"

Jake said nothing, and Paddy repeated, louder still, "So long as yeh WHAT, Jake?"

Jake shook his head. Paddy was about to demand a third time when a half empty beer bottle zipped past his head and exploded into a thousand pieces on the concrete ringside floor. The crowd erupted into apoplectic boos. That was soon followed by more refuse being hurled into the ring. Paddy glanced around and recognized that a riot was breaking out. Forgetting his previous line of enquiry, he turned to Jake and said, "We gotta get Davy out of here before he gets hurt!"

Looking spooked, Jake quickly nodded assent. Tommy, who'd been standing over Jake's shoulder listening in, ran to the ring apron. Stepping on the middle rope until it was depressed to ankle height, he held up the top rope and shouted, "Come on, Davy! We gotta get outa here!"

Hearing his name, Davy, still standing in the center of the ring—now alone—turned and stared at Tommy without any hint of recognition. Meanwhile, Carvallo and his entourage were spilling out of his corner like rats leaping off of a sinking ship. Seeing that Davy hadn't budged, Paddy went over and grabbed him by the elbow, saying, "C'mon, Davy."

Jake ducked through the ropes where Tommy held them open and, not bothering to wait for the others, made a beeline for the tunnel which led to the locker room. Paddy steered Davy toward Tommy. Pushing down on his head so that Davy didn't catch it on the top rope, Paddy guided Davy through the ropes, then followed behind. After descending the small set of wooden steps that led to the ring, Tommy hopped down and grabbed Davy's robe. Holding it over Davy's head to protect him from the flying debris, Tommy followed as Paddy led Davy away from the ring by the arm. As they passed Rita, standing by herself in front of her ringside seat, Paddy, with his free arm, grabbed her by the elbow and dragged her along. At this point, it was pandemonium. The inadequate police presence had fanned out and were trying to contain the mayhem. Unsuccessfully.

The little group had made it about halfway to the exit tunnel when a fan jumped over the barricade and stood on the concrete walkway in front of them, screaming in a distinctly

Irish accent, "They fecking robbed yeh, Davy!"

Paddy shoved him out of the way and they pressed forward. They were within twenty yards of the exit when a flying bottle clipped Paddy square in the forehead, shattering upon impact. Paddy immediately dipped his upper body down, clapped his right hand to his forehead and cursed.

Tommy paused to wait on Paddy. After a moment, Paddy looked up. His hand was pressed to his forehead as the blood was gushed out from between his fingers. Looking at Tommy, he barked, "Go, man!"

Tommy threw his free arm around Davy, who seemed completely oblivious to the conflagration raging around them, and said, "Come on, Davy."

Shell-shocked, Davy allowed Tommy to lead him forward. Still clinging to Paddy's arm, Rita said, "Come on, Paddy. We'd better am-scray!"

Paddy nodded and allowed Rita to guide him out of the arena. When they finally reached the safety of the tunnel to the dressing room, they paused to catch their breath. Paddy, his right hand still pressed to his wound, glanced around and asked, "Anybody seen Jake?"

Tommy and Rita shook their heads. Davy just stood there looking bewildered. Removing his right hand from his forehead momentarily, Paddy examined the thick coating of dark red blood on it. Clapping it back on his forehead to staunch the flow, Paddy muttered, "The bastard sold us out!"

Rita disengaged from Paddy and walked over to Davy. Tears filled her eyes as she surveyed the wreck of his once handsome face. Gently touching his right cheek, she said, "Aw, look what they done to you, Davy."

Davy pressed his right hand, still taped, against hers. Fully cognizant for the first time since the decision had been announced, he replied, "I'm fine, baby. A few days rest and I'll be right as rain."

Throwing her arms around him and sobbing, Rita could only say, "Oh, Davy!"

Paddy looked at the two of them. Tears in his eyes, he turned to Tommy and quietly said, "He'll never be the same after that beating."

Tommy glanced at Davy. The swelling on his cheeks had nearly closed his eyes, his face was covered by a web of future scars. Turning back to Paddy, he sadly shook his head in accord.

Ciaran's Dream

We'd have a wee gaff on the hillside, not far from the old fella's farm. From the front door yeh'd see Cnoc na Piseog towering over the valley that contained David Patrick's farm, the wee stream that ran through the bottom of it, and at the far end of the valley, the village. It'd be the entire world open to us at a glance. I'd use the bit of land to farm for our own use—spuds and vegetables mostly. I'd open me pub just outside of the village. There was an old, abandoned house out that way that I could convert, or maybe I'd just build it meself from scratch. I'd constructed enough buildings at base camp, not to mention putting up that barn for the old fella, so I knew what I was about when it came to carpentry. My days I'd spend in the pub beside a warm stove, summer and winter. Everywhere I went—home, the pub, to visit the old fella—there'd always have to be fires going regardless of the season. In the afternoons, I'd go home and have tea with Bridget and the wee lad. I can just see him. He'd have brown hair and hazel eyes like his mam, and he'd be tall and straight like meself. Bridget would be in a new dress, always of the latest fashion, that I'd buy with me back pay. The most beautiful girl in County Kerry deserved to be dressed in duds as pretty as herself.

On the way back from the Pole, when we'd been sharing the old craic in the tent of a night, Owens used to love to go on about all the parades and parties that'd be thrown in our honor once we returned triumphant. We'd made it to a Pole, after all. Not many can say that. Owens was looking forward to the fame it'd bring. Personally, I never cared a fig for fame. The money would be nice because it'd fund the life that I hoped to live. But when I got back to Ireland, I'd want nothing more than a quiet life, out of the spotlight. I looked forward to seeing mam and da and the brothers, and David Patrick and Eithne, as well. I dreamed of teaching me son how to hunt rabbits and farm. More than anything, I wanted to get into a warm bed every night with me own loving one, Bridget. I wanted what most men want: a bit of land, a wee family, and the portion of happiness that they say everyone is supposed to be entitled to. It wasn't much to ask. Was it?

Antarctica, March 1912

Once the sun began to set, Ciaran would search for a place to make camp. It was important that he be in the tent before nightfall, as the temperature dropped precipitously after sundown. Every day the hours of darkness increased and would continue to do so until, in a matter of weeks, there'd be nothing but night. Unremitting blackness that'd stretch on for months. Aside from the drop in temperature, it was too dangerous to travel in the darkness because without the sun to guide him Ciaran might fall into another crevasse. Or he could lose his way, which would kill him the same as a crevasse, just slower.

It was now the seventh morning after the Lieutenant's

death and things were grim. The lack of human contact had gotten to him and Ciaran feared he was beginning to crack. Alone in the tent at night, he found himself holding conversations with the Lieutenant, Owens, and Lord Hanes. Deep down, he knew they were all gone, but he went on chattering away as though they were seated on their lumpy sleeping bags alongside him. Adding to his woes, Ciaran had used the last of the paraffin the previous night. There'd be no water to drink and nothing but dry biscuits to eat until he found the depot. Already dehydrated, he figured he could survive a day or so without water. He was surrounded by a sea of frozen fresh water, but without the paraffin to melt it, it may as well have been granite. The one bit of good news was that by his calculations he was only three miles from One Hundred Stone Depot. Of course, with all of the previous depots on the return journey, it'd taken some searching to finally locate them. Sometimes it'd taken as much as half a day, and that was with two or more people (when the Lieutenant, Hanes and Owens were still alive) looking.

Ciaran waited until the sun had been up for a couple hours to emerge from the tent. The previous evening's rest had left him unrefreshed because the combination of bitter cold and his physical pain prevented him from sleeping properly. Instead, he rolled from side to side all night in hopes of stealing a few winks. The sky that greeted him that morning was slate. As he threw open the flaps of the tent and stepped outside, a gust of wind nearly blew him over. Steadying himself, Ciaran shivered and stamped his right foot to get the circulation going. The temperature had been dropping steadily for the past week, ever since the sun had begun setting. He glanced at the thermometer attached to the sledge. It read negative 45—that meant 77 degrees of frost, without even taking into account windchill. As if on cue, another blast of frigid air howled across the tundra, knocking him off balance once again. It troubled him that a bit of wind could toss him about like a dried-out leaf. That wouldn't have happened a month ago. The cold was getting to him more now, as well. Having shed every ounce of fat, his clothes were the only things insulating his battered, reed-thin body. The clothes alone, however, weren't enough in this kind of cold. To maintain a core temperature sufficiently warm to survive, Ciaran required the exertion of hauling the sledge.

Glancing to the east, he didn't like the look of some of the dark clouds massing on the horizon. It was all the more reason to be on his way and find that depot. The depot had been dug into the ground, then surrounded by thick, ten-foot-high walls of hard-packed snow, like an igloo. In addition to containing the life-giving necessities of food and paraffin, the depot would offer extra shelter against the worsening weather. Most importantly, there was the hope that the relief party awaited him there.

Before he could set out, he needed to get a theodolite reading. Without proper bearings he'd be sailing blind, so to speak. The process took nearly half an hour, about ten minutes more than it had earlier in the journey because his fingers had become far less nimble. Attempting to manipulate the intricate dials and knobs, he found himself constantly fumbling, as though the hands that he was trying to operate were somebody else's. Like all of his joints, his fingers were swollen around the knuckles and ached constantly. Whether it was the cold or something else causing it, Ciaran's hands just wouldn't do what he told them to do. *Daft hands*, his father would've called them.

Once he'd completed his theodolite reading, Ciaran packed everything onto the sledge. The wind was too strong to employ his makeshift sail. Instead, he took one of the bamboo poles that he'd been using for the sail and affixed to it a red pennant similar to the ones that marked the supply depots and equipment drops. Understanding that he was carrying all of the polar party's records, he wanted to ensure that they'd be located by a recovery party. Just in case he didn't make it, he tried to tell himself. Deep down, though, he knew how it was going to go.

The first few steps of a sledging journey were always the hardest, not only owing to Newton's first law of motion but also because of the blinding pain those steps triggered in Ciaran's frostbitten left foot. After a few minutes on the march, thanks to the numbing effects of the snow, the pain at least became tolerable. Once he'd broken the inertia of rest and started the sledge moving forward, he glanced to his right and was relieved to see that the third traveler was once again accompanying him. Ciaran was now convinced that it was indeed, as the Lieutenant had posited, his ministering angel. As he marched, he had to fight to maintain concentration on the trail. He felt as though his spirit had retreated into a tiny corner of his mind, and he was peering out at the world as though through the wrong lens of a telescope. His breathing was labored and sounded to him as if it were emanating from someone else entirely.

He'd been on the march for an hour and had only covered half a mile when he found himself drifting off. The lack of rest and general exhaustion were causing him to, literally, fall asleep on his feet. He started slapping himself in the face to stay awake, knowing full well that to fall asleep outside of the protection of the tent was to die. But the urge to sleep proved too strong. One moment he'd be trudging forward, and the next moment he'd snap back to attention only to find that he'd stopped moving. In those instances, the only thing that kept him from face-planting into the snow was the harness attaching his body to the sledge. After each unexpected stop, he had to put that extra effort into getting the sledge started again, which was becoming more and more difficult. Knowing that he was as good as dead without the necessities the sledge carried, Ciaran understood that leaving it wasn't an option. What good would it be to get to the paraffin stored in the depot if he had no cooker in which to employ it? Reminding himself of how close he was to the One Hundred Stone Depot, he reasoned that it was just a matter of pushing on. And, who knows? Perhaps the rescue party that was supposed to be waiting at the supply depot would venture out and find him.

As the second hour of marching stretched into the third, and he'd only gained another mile, Ciaran began to think wistfully about how easy it'd be to just stop. It goes against human nature not to struggle for life. But once a person has suffered enough, no matter how strong mentally that person may be, any sort of release becomes an object of intense desire. It'd be so simple and relatively painless, Ciaran thought. He'd drift off, and that'd be the end of it.

Or would it? His mind was so addled by malnutrition, dehydration, lack of sleep, and both physical and mental exhaustion that he'd fallen into that ontological doubt once again that made him question whether or not he was even animate. He recalled learning about Dante's Inferno from the Christian Brothers during his brief academic career. For Dante, Purgatory was essentially an endless mountain-climbing expedition. Ciaran pondered if his penance was to trudge across the frozen tundra of Antarctica for centuries until his immortal soul had at last been purified. When these mystical conundrums would begin to torment him, Ciaran was forced to dismiss them quickly, realizing that if he began to truly accept that he actually was in Purgatory there'd be no way to make himself go on. Then again, if he was in Purgatory, he wouldn't have a choice.

Although Ciaran was determined to complete the mission, the mission itself had become meaningless to him. Indeed, in his present condition he was finally able to clearly see the folly of all human endeavor. People who set out to achieve great deeds were simply trying to secure some sense of immortality for themselves. But immortality was never the lot of humanity. We're all born with our graves already dug. Even the most enduring human fame is like the flicker of a candle. For an average, everyday person like himself, the most that could be hoped for was for a child or children to carry on one's legacy for a brief time after one's death. His mind turned to his son. It was the thought of the lad and Bridget that kept him going. Ever since he'd read Bridget's letter telling him that he was a father he'd determined that he'd make it back to them or… But now the "or" portion of that vow seemed to be the only real possibility. He'd tried. He hoped they could know that. He never gave up.

*

The sun felt warm on his face. Looking down, Ciaran spied his bare forearm, reddened by the sun. Marveling at it, he wondered how he could survive the Antarctic in just his shirt sleeves. Then he glanced up and realized he wasn't in the Antarctic at all. Below him lay a field of barley on a gently sloping hill, leading into a valley with a little stream cutting through it. He recognized the place. But it couldn't be.

"It's ready for the reaping." He heard a voice that he recognized address him from over his right shoulder. Unable to believe his own ears, Ciaran turned and saw his father standing just behind him, big as life. His frayed tweed, flat cap covered his head, with the gray hair in the back visible. The old fellow wore the same black vest and white shirt that he always seemed to have on. As Ciaran stood there gawking, his older brother Tiernach emerged from the barn carrying a long scythe. Ciaran blinked several times to ensure he wasn't hallucinating. But they remained—his father and brother.

"Get yourself a scythe, lad."

Reflexively, Ciaran replied, "Aye, Da."

But he didn't move. Instead, he just stood there gaping, unable to grasp what was happening. A wind blew down the hill, causing the rows of golden yellow barley to ripple like waves on the ocean. It was a cold wind—unnaturally cold for Ireland—and it caused Ciaran to shudder.

*

Ciaran's eyes snapped open. Like a man drunk with sleep after unexpectedly being roused, he had no idea where he was. Glancing down, he saw nothing but white and realized that he was suspended above the frost-covered ground by his sledge harness. With his neck slack, his head drooped down in an unnatural manner. As he came to, he could feel the harness straps digging into his shoulders, causing them to ache. More. Blinking, he slowly, methodically worked his way to a standing posture. The change in positions caused knives of pain to slice down his neck and shoulders. His mouth was so dry it hurt. To relieve it he tried to run his tongue around his cheeks, but it was thick and dry as leather. He simply had no saliva left to wet it. Once he was fully upright, he felt dizzy and nauseous. His joints were stiff and throbbing, causing him to wonder how long he'd been out. If he was being honest with himself, he had to admit he wished he'd remained out. It probably wouldn't have taken much longer. Then his troubles would've been over.

But he'd awakened, and since he had he knew that he must struggle on. Glancing around, Ciaran tried to figure out how far he'd traveled. But he was engulfed in an ocean of white. It was the exact same landscape he'd been looking at since entering the Great Ice Barrier ages ago. Taking a deep breath which, even through the scarves covering his face, caused his lungs to ache, he leaned forward and tried to start. But nothing happened. It felt like he was single-handedly trying to drag Blarney Castle off of its moorings. Pausing so he could gather himself, he put forth another mighty effort. The sledge budged—barely. Feeling this, he surged forward. First one step, and then another. The sledge loosened and he began moving forward. After traveling a dozen paces, he noticed something: his left foot didn't burn with pain anymore. Indeed, he couldn't feel either of his feet at all. It was a peculiar sensation—feeling his upper legs propel his feet forward, but never sensing those feet touching ground. But he was moving, and that was all that mattered. His eyes shifted to the left to see if the third traveler still accompanied him. Spying a nondescript brown figure flitting along slightly behind him, Ciaran let out a sigh of relief. He wasn't alone.

After a while, Ciaran began to wonder how far he'd traveled. He'd lost his pace count ages ago, so he was forced to estimate the distance based on how fast he was moving and how many hours he'd sledged. The problem was he'd fallen asleep several times during the journey, and he was unsure how long he'd been out during those intervals. Thus, any estimate of distance covered was going to have a rather large margin for error. His best guess was a mile and a half or, if he was going to be optimistic, a mile and three quarters. In another hour he'd stop, unhitch himself from the harness and take a look around for the depot. But, at the moment, it was too soon. Owing to the overcast sky and the manner in which the gusty wind was stirring up the snow, visibility was poor and it would've been futile trying to search for it at this distance. So, he pressed onward.

*

Ciaran opened the door and immediately felt the warmth of the fire within. Once again, he was bewildered. Had he somehow stumbled upon the depot without realizing it? But who'd built the fire? The rescue party? If so, where were they? Blinking several times, Ciaran realized he wasn't in any depot. It was a tiny, thatch-roofed cottage. But it was unfamiliar to him. At the far end stood a large bed and, alongside it, a smaller, lower bed. In the center of the room was a large, wooden table beside which squatted the black, cast-iron stove from which the heat emanated. Emitting the most wonderful aroma, a covered pot cooked on a burner. He recognized the smell of stew immediately. Ciaran felt his empty stomach rumble. Salivating, he stepped inside the cottage and made his way over to the pot. When he lifted the lid, Ciaran was overwhelmed by an intoxicating rush of steam fragrant with the scents of mutton, carrots, onions, and potatoes.

As he was breathing in the delicious aroma, he heard the doorknob turn behind him. Dropping the lid back onto the pot, Ciaran spun around and stared at the door in trepidation. What would the owners say when they found he'd invaded their home? He felt like Goldilocks about to be pinched by the three bears. The first thing to pass through the door was dazzling sunshine, accompanied by the chirping of birds. That was immediately followed by the most beautiful woman he'd ever seen. Behind her trailed a boy of perhaps two. It was Bridget and his son. He stood there, mouth agape.

"You're home, then?" Bridget asked with a smile.

The only response Ciaran could muster was to nod mutely.

"You're early. Did you leave Richie in charge of the pub?"

Still unable to find his voice, and uncertain how to respond, Ciaran nodded again.

"Have you lost your voice?" Bridget asked with a laugh. She was wearing a white sun dress, and the boy was in short pants and a short-sleeved shirt.

"Is it yerself?" Ciaran finally gasped. His voice sounded to him like it'd come from miles away.

"Who else would it be? You're the queer one, today,"

Bridget replied. As she was answering, the young boy broke away from her side and made a beeline for Ciaran. "Give your wee son a kiss."

Tears in his eyes, Ciaran dropped to one knee and caught the child in his arms. Kissing the boy on his head, Ciaran gasped, "I made it back to yeh."

Bridget gave him an odd look: "Made it back to us? Sure, it's only ten minutes walking to the pub."

Squeezing the lad tightly to himself, Ciaran looked at Bridget and replied, "I dreamed I was still there."

"Still where?"

Before he could answer her, Ciaran felt himself being ripped away. He clung desperately to the child, hoping that would somehow keep him anchored. But it wasn't enough.

*

The cottage fell away and Ciaran found himself once again staring at the frozen earth of the Antarctic. Feeling nothing but disappointment at the change in environs, Ciaran blinked several times in an effort to clear his head. Straightening up was even more painful than the last time, but that didn't stop him. Ciaran fought his way once again to an upright position. Still somewhat out of it, he glanced around, wondering how much distance he might've covered since his last unplanned stop. Glancing at his watch, Ciaran determined an hour had passed since the last time he came to. How far had he made it? That all depended on how long he'd been out this time. His eyes searched the northern horizon, but he was unable to make out the pennant marking the One Hundred Stone Depot. Of course, he also realized he could no longer trust his eyes. Up close, his vision was fine. But when he attempted to scan the distance, everything became jumbled and collapsed.

Gazing westward, Ciaran saw that the sun was rapidly moving toward the horizon. If he was going to make camp, he thought, he should do it now. But, without paraffin, he had no way of generating water. If he still possessed the strength to set up camp, he'd die in his tent. Of that he was certain. He was so dehydrated that he understood on a cellular level that only a few hours remained to him without water. He decided to push on. Probably, he would've been better served to detach himself from the sledge and search for the depot on foot. But he wasn't thinking clearly enough at this point to reason it out. Like his field of vision, everything in his brain felt muddled and confused. Summoning all of the strength left to him, he leaned into the harness and pulled. After five seconds of struggling, he hadn't budged the sledge at all. He stopped, placed his hands on his knees, bent over and panted.

As he was catching his breath, Ciaran began to wonder if the runners of the sledge had iced over. When the polar party still had its full contingent, Owens or himself had made a point of cleaning the runners every time they stopped. Even up to the last few days with the Lieutenant, Ciaran had cleaned the runners when they camped every evening. But once he was the last man standing, cleaning the runners became a luxury he had neither the time nor the energy to undertake. For a moment, he contemplated removing himself from the harness and examining the runners, just in case. Then he realized that if the runners were iced-over, he didn't possess the strength to unload the sledge and turn it onto its side in order to clear away the ice. Instead, he straightened up, breathed deeply, and then leaned into the harness. Calling on whatever strength remained in his bandy, scurvy-ravaged legs, Ciaran managed to take one small step forward.

That first step was followed by another, and then another. He was moving! Slowly but surely, he was pulling the sledge forward. After he'd taken a dozen steps, he glanced to his left. In the muted light of the Antarctic loaming, he thought he saw a brown shape gliding along just behind him. If he'd had the strength, Ciaran would've smiled. The third traveler hadn't abandoned him. He wasn't completely alone on the desolate, frozen expanse of the Barrier.

His legs now felt numb from the knees down. If not for a tiny jolt of pain that ran up his gangrenous left leg each time his left foot planted, Ciaran wouldn't have been able to tell that he was moving at all. The wind had picked up since he'd set out in the morning. Judging by the howl of it, as well as the manner in which the pennant affixed to the top of the sledge whipped around, Ciaran estimated that the wind had increased to force 6. Conditions were becoming treacherous, and he wondered if another blizzard was on its way. However, there'd be no waiting out the weather as they'd done throughout their journey. He'd assuredly expire from dehydration long before any storm passed. The bottom line was: if he ceased moving forward, he was dead.

He glanced to his left again. The third traveler continued to shadow him. His sheltering angel, Ciaran thought. Or was it? His mind and body were far too exhausted to contemplate the metaphysical ramifications of this mysterious companion of his. He'd been moving for fifteen minutes now and he estimated that in another forty-five minutes he could stop, unhitch himself from the sledge, and search for the depot. He was certain that the depot was nearby. It had to be. Night was coming on quickly. And while night was still relatively brief at this time of year, Ciaran understood that he'd be unable to survive the cold of the Antarctic night exposed as he was, even for just a few hours. Yes, the depot was close. He'd be okay if he could just keep moving.

Another ten minutes of marching had passed when he noticed that he was seeing two of everything. Because the landscape around him was a tedious stretch of white uniformity, it'd taken a while for him to recognize that he was experiencing double-vision. But when he looked toward the northern horizon, he could discern the outline of the peak of Mt. Erebus. Right beside it he could see its identical twin— which he knew did not exist. Tired and scattered as his mind felt, he realized this was a problem. If he managed to get close enough to spy the pennant for the One Hundred Stone Depot, the double vision meant he'd see two of them. What if he pursued the wrong one? It could mean the difference between life and death. Then again, at this point literally everything meant the difference between life and death for Ciaran. He could only push on and hope for the best.

*

Ciaran found himself staring at a man with a thick, gray beard smoking a pipe. Unable to place the man, Ciaran became confused. No one in the shore party was that gray. Indeed, the oldest man in the party had been Owens, and his beard had only contained a sprinkling of salt. Could it have been someone from the relief ship? If so, where were the others? Ciaran took a couple steps backward and tried to take it all in. He recognized that he was in a dark, close building, but he now realized that it wasn't the One Hundred Stone Depot. The room was filled with a warm, earthy aroma of burning turf that he remembered well from his younger days. Combined with the comforting scent of peat were the smells of poteen, sour stout, and sweat.

Glancing around, Ciaran realized that he was in a pub. It was snug enough. The floor space couldn't have been much more than twenty by twenty. The thatched ceiling was so low that a man of six feet like himself would've been forced to tilt his head along the edges where the roof met the walls. Before the short, pock-marked oaken bar stood several empty stools. The man with the gray beard was seated in the center of the pub, right next to the large, cast-iron stove that heated the place. Ciaran could feel the warmth emanating from it. It was lovely. Once he'd acclimated himself to the dark, Ciaran crept a few steps closer. The man with the beard glanced up and their eyes met. The face of the man was deeply lined. There seemed to be sadness around his eyes, yet mirth peeped out from the corners of his mouth. Ciaran gasped, realizing finally that it was himself he was looking at.

Himself as an old man.

A self that would never exist in this world.

*

Ciaran's eyes snapped open. It was dark outside now, and so cold. He'd drifted off again and the sun had set. Every part of his body had gone numb. His mouth was so dry that it hurt. Marshalling his strength, he raised his head so that he was looking up. When he did so, a sharp pain knifed through his neck, in spite of the general numbness. He was greeted by a supermoon, so full and low it looked like another planet about to crash into the Earth. It lit up the sky so that it was almost like day. Its rays glittered and sparkled along the surface of the ancient snow that engulfed him.

Dangling over the ground by his harness, Ciaran endeavored to rise into a standing position. His first attempt failed before it'd even begun. But he didn't give up. Focusing all of his will on the act of rising, Ciaran somehow made it to his feet. Yet he felt as wobbly as if he had twelve pints of brown in him. Thinking of Bridget and his young son, he leaned into the harness and tried to take a step, but he failed. Perhaps the runners had iced over. Or maybe he'd simply exhausted the last bit of strength left in his frail, emaciated body. He tried again. Leaning all of his weight into the harness, he attempted to take a step forward with his right foot.

But the sledge didn't budge and he lost his footing and slipped. Once more, he found himself drooping over the ground, suspended by the harness that moored him to the sledge. From the corner of his left eye, he saw something move. Lit up by the supermoon, the snow betrayed the shadow of a figure gliding across it and into his field of vision. Now, for the first time, Ciaran saw his companion—the third traveler—standing directly before him. For a moment he stared wide-eyed, uncertain if he was asleep or being tricked by another polar mirage. He attempted licking his blistered lips, but found he had no saliva left. He tried to speak, but he was too parched to even clear his throat. He tried again, but the words failed to come out. He ended up silently mouthing, "It's you."

A solitary tear, the last bit of moisture remaining in his desiccated body, rolled out of the corner of his right eye. It made it halfway down his hollow, sunken cheek, then froze in place. Staring rapt at the third traveler, Ciaran's eyes said more than his mouth could've ever hoped to. A calmness overtook Ciaran. Suddenly, he felt at peace. He knew he didn't have to struggle anymore. It was okay. He could finally rest.

Not taking his eyes off of the third traveler, Ciaran drew in a low, shallow breath. The frozen air no longer burned his lungs. He exhaled. Breathing in again, he breathed out one last time. Slumping forward, his body hung limply, suspended just above the ground by his harness. A fierce wind blew up from the south, ruffling the deer fur that lined his hood. It howled savagely as it passed over his body. No longer possessing the power to injure him it moved on, dying away somewhere off in the distance. Glittering down on it all was what seemed like a billion pinpoints of light—each one millions of years old.

Hell's Kitchen, October 1923

A cold wind blew up 12th Avenue, causing Bridget to shiver. It'd been a warm, early autumn day, but now that the sun was preparing to set, the weather had turned nippy. The completely rusted-over fire escape, always a little wobbly when she first stepped onto it, would invariably steady once she'd situated herself. First, she'd spread out an old blanket both for comfort and to prevent the rust from the stairs from wearing off on her dress. Then she'd take a seat two steps up with her feet resting on the platform below. This allowed her to gaze southward about twenty blocks down 12th Avenue. She could also, through some gaps in buildings, just make out the Hudson River to the west. Mrs. Reilly from down the hall had told Bridget that she was mad to venture onto "that rickety old thing." But Bridget liked it out there. It was pleasant in spring and autumn. And in the summer when the heat was sweltering within the flat, she could come out here and maybe catch a refreshing breeze. Sitting on the fire escape had always made her feel somehow connected, but to what she'd never been certain. Perhaps it connected her to her adopted city. Or, maybe it reminded her of home—the feeling of looking down on things like when she'd sit atop Cnoc na Piseog with Eleanor.

Eleanor. Bridget hadn't thought of her in years. There'd been a few letters that first year after she'd emigrated, then nothing. Most likely Eleanor had found a man of her own and no longer had the time or energy for pastimes like writing letters. She couldn't blame Eleanor for the break in communication, realizing the fault was as much her own. Between work and raising Davy, she'd been too tired to write anyone those first few years in America. Bridget wondered if Eleanor was still in the employ of the Murphys after all these years.

The Murphys. Bridget hadn't heard from them, either. At her going-away party, they'd said they'd come and visit her. But that was just something people say. She knew there was very little chance of that ever happening. Still, the Murphys had always treated her well and they'd gifted her the money that gave Bridget her start in America, so her memories of them would always be fond.

At the end of the day, she didn't want news of the old country because she knew that eventually someone would mention *herself*. Her mother. There'd been nary a word from her since Bridget and Ciaran David had undarkened her doorstep a full decade earlier. Eithne was still alive, of that Bridget was certain. Her mam was just too mean to die.

*

As she further pondered what drew her to the fire escape, Bridget realized it was neither connections to her adopted city, nor tenuous links to the old country that beckoned her. If she was honest with herself, she had to admit she was searching for something. No, someone. Five years after receiving that letter from Commander Marvell she was well aware now that the someone she'd been hoping to see wasn't coming. Would never be coming. Yet for five years she'd continued to drag herself out here to gaze wistfully southward. She'd known for five long years—actually, several years longer than that if she was honest with herself—that there'd be no reunion. Not in this life, anyway. She'd meet him in the next life. But how long would that take? Fifty years? When compared to the billions of years that scientists now said that the universe had existed, half a century was less than the blink of an eye. But that was from the perspective of the universe. To one tiny person, fifty years was a lifetime—two lifetimes, if you based it on Ciaran's abbreviated existence.

Sometimes she wondered if she could take it—fifty more years of this. Lapsed Catholic though she was, she nevertheless clung to the notion that if she did something to expedite their reunion, she'd never meet him. She'd been taught by the Benedictine Sisters that suicide was a mortal sin and, furthermore, a sin for which no repentance was possible since the act itself obviated the possibility of contrition. Besides, she had Ciaran David to look after. Davy, which is what everyone had taken to calling him, was the only thing that'd kept her going these dozen years gone by. She couldn't leave him an orphan. Sure, he'd become a handful lately, always either mitching school or, when he went, getting into trouble fighting with older boys. Yet she couldn't bring herself to blame him. Deep down, he had a heart of gold. The problem was he'd had to grow up without a father, and that'd been hard on the lad. When she'd lost her da, Bridget had been an adult. She still recalled the pain and emptiness that David Patrick's parting had caused her—still caused her when she thought about it. Her mam never did accept it, blaming the wee folk for his loss. With the perspective granted by time and distance, Bridget realized that attributing David Patrick's passing to the "Good People" had somehow made the parting bearable for Eithne. But it'd also made Eithne unbearable.

  Bridget shook her head to change her line of thinking. Her friends had told Bridget that she should start dating. She was thirty-one, which to Bridget felt ancient. In reality, though, it wasn't so old. Work had kept her figure trim. But heartbreak and stress had worn lines that Mrs. Murphy hadn't possessed at the same age into Bridget's once ethereally beautiful face. The Murphys were rich, though. Why would the rich have worry lines? What'd they have to worry about? Bridget had never taken seriously her friends' suggestions that she find a man. Sure, there'd been fellows interested.

  Short of actually announcing it, Mr. Green, the clerk at the market where she shopped, had done everything in his power to let her know how he felt. He was about her age and had a kind face which reminded Bridget of David Patrick. Yet, he was a bit pudgy around the middle and not at all dashing like Ciaran. Maybe it was nitpicking—many was the time that Roisin had advised Bridget that beggars can't be choosers. But Bridget didn't see herself a beggar—one wasn't a beggar until she'd actually begged something. Bridget had begged for nothing, nor would she. So, she couldn't see herself with Mr. Green. It wasn't that she didn't think that Mr. Green would be a worthy spouse. Rather, it would've been unfair to him to only receive the meager scraps of her affection that remained after Ciaran and Davy. If she was honest with herself, her heart had been frozen and may as well have been buried in that icy grave that Commander Marvell had dug for Ciaran in the South Pole. And just like Ciaran's, there'd be no melting her heart until the end of days.

There was a change taking place inside of Bridget that'd been going on for some time now. She could feel herself hardening. It'd begun back in Ireland when she'd glimpsed that first newspaper article stating that the polar party hadn't returned. How long had that been now? Bridget furrowed her brow in thought. David Patrick had still been alive. That meant it'd been—she counted it off on her fingers—eleven years. Had it been so long? All that time a shell had been gradually forming around her. The shell was hard, like a turtle's. But unlike a turtle, there was no soft, exposed underbelly. The shell enclosed her completely. As the years to come passed, it'd only grow thicker and harder. Eventually, it'd become impenetrable. Was there anything she could do to arrest this process? Probably, but she knew she'd never do it.

Hearing a horn blare, Bridget glanced down at 12th Avenue. Studebakers and Model Ts were vying with horse-and-buggies for command of the road. Bridget felt like a fledging draft horse: already obsolete, but with a long and uncertain life of thankless toil stretching out before her. Shifting her glance toward the heavens, Bridget noticed that even though the sun had not yet set, the outlines of a full harvest moon, hanging just above Manhattan, were visible. She recalled those days long past when, seeing the moon, she'd think that the same moon was shining down on Ciaran. Bridget realized now that that particular fancy had been misguided, given the fact that the sun didn't set for nearly six months in the South Pole. And now? Now the moon didn't shine on Ciaran at all, just the grave that Commander Marvell had dug for him.

*

Another cold wind caused Bridget to shudder once again. She decided to move inside. Davy would be home any minute now wanting his supper. *Fifty years*, she thought. It was a long time. But now that she was thirty, maybe it'd only be forty years. Or, even thirty, who knows? Picking up her blanket, she stepped through the window into the flat. As she closed the window, she decided she wouldn't sit on the fire escape any more. Mrs. Reilly was right—it was mad to sit on that rickety old thing. Plus, now that cars were replacing horses, the air was no longer so fresh anymore. And fifty years? It was a long time.

Percy's Dream

It's not a dream, really—just something I like to think about sometimes when I'm sad. We'd live in a little house in the country, away from the smoke and noise and dirt of the city. Just the three of us—my mother, my father and me. Aunt Martha wouldn't live with us. She could visit from the city and have Sunday dinner with us every week. Or, maybe every other week. Not Fridays. The rest of the time it'd be just the three of us together. Our house wouldn't be a mansion, but it'd be large enough that I'd have my own room with an actual bed. We'd have a neat, little front yard with grass, and flowers lining the walkway up to a front porch with a swing on it. In the backyard there'd be a big maple tree which I could climb and also sit under to read during the summer. Behind our place there'd be a little pond where I could sail my ships. I could just step out the back door, cross the backyard and it'd be right there—no subway journeys and no walking block after block through the city. And best of all, no bullies.

Mommy would be beautiful in a dress and apron. Aunt

Martha has shown me snapshots of her. She had kind, sparkling eyes, blonde hair, and was glamorous like a movie star. She used to be a dancer in the Rockettes before she got sick. But in my dream, she's healthy and strong, and she'd be all done with the dancing once I'd come along. She'd stay home and just be a regular mom. She'd be nice and patient, unlike Aunt Martha who was always grouchy because she worked so much. In the mornings, mommy would walk me to school. When school was done in the afternoon, she'd be there waiting to walk me home. She'd be a great cook and wouldn't make me always eat fish on Fridays. Every time she saw me, she'd smile a smile that'd light up a building.

I have to use my imagination to picture my father because I've never even seen a snapshot of him. Aunt Martha told me she had no idea who my father might've been. She'd get angry when I'd bring it up because she said that my mother used to "run around" with a lot of bad men and it was better that I didn't know who my father was. But I'm not so sure of that. Sometimes I think a bad father would be better than no father at all. In my dream, my father is tall and handsome and strong. When he hugs me, I feel like there's nothing in the world that can hurt me. He's a businessman and always goes to work smelling of aftershave and soap, wearing a gray suit and one of those hats all the businessmen wear. On weekends, he takes me fishing, or works on my boats with me, or tosses baseball with me. The other boys wouldn't be able to say that I threw like a girl because my father would teach me how to throw properly. Aunt Martha had no idea how to throw and didn't care to learn so that she could teach me. And, anyway, there was nowhere to have a catch near our apartment even if she'd wanted to.

In the evenings, the three of us would sit down to dinner together. My father would talk about his day at work, and my mother would smile and serve us the food. There'd always be something good for dessert—peach pie or apple cobbler with ice cream. After dinner we'd sit around the living room by a fire—my mom sewing, dad reading the paper, and me listening to my programs on the radio. When it was time to go to bed, they'd both tuck me in and read me a story. Before switching off the light, they'd each kiss me on the cheek, wish me good night, and tell me they loved me.

*

Aunt Martha says I'm too much of a dreamer—that I need to get my head out of the clouds. Maybe she's right. But when you never had a mother or father, the best you can do is dream ones. It's not much, I'll admit, but it's better than nothing.

New York, May 1947

Standing tall, the ship made its way over the gently rolling waves to the center of the Conservatory Water. A light southeasterly breeze kept the sails filled as the ship sliced through the green water. Percy was amazed that it hadn't been struck by another ship, there were so many out there. It was as if the tiny captain and crew that Mr. Patrick had glued to the deck were somehow steering it. Still dripping wet from his fight with Marty, Percy thought of Mr. Patrick. He couldn't wait to tell Mr. Patrick about the ship's successful maiden voyage. And he wanted to tell Mr. Patrick about how he'd stood up to Marty—how he'd used what Mr. Patrick had taught him and he'd won! Percy's chest swelled with pride. He'd accomplished a lot this day. Would he tell Aunt Martha about the fight? No, he decided not. She wouldn't understand.

A bright orange sun shone down through the treetops that surrounded Conservatory Water, warming Percy and drying his clothes. Watching the ship sailing majestically across the miniature boat lake, the beginnings of a smile began to crease the corners of his mouth. Yes, he thought, he would have to tell Mr. Patrick.

*

As Marty walked away in defeat, leaving Percy standing alone at water's edge watching his ship sail, Davy, seated on a park bench, turned to Paddy and asked, "You brought me all the way out here to watch some corner boys scrap?"

Paddy smiled and shook his head, saying, "Take a look at the lad."

"The mama's boy?"

"Does he not look familiar to yeh at all?"

"I've never seen that kid in my life, Paddy."

"That's not what I meant. Does he not remind yeh of anyone?"

Davy leaned forward and squinted at Percy. After a few seconds, he shook his head.

"Come on, man. Look at the blond hair and the blue eyes!"

In response, Davy merely shook his head again.

"Did that right hand of his not remind yeh of anyone?"

"He did have a good right for a kid," Davy admitted. His eyes grew wide. Turning to Paddy, he demanded in a subdued voice, "Say, what're you trying to tell me?"

"Do I have to spell it out for yeh?" Paddy smiled and shook his head. "He's Rita's boy…"

"Rita?" Davy interrupted him.

"Aye, Davy. Rita." Paddy paused for a moment, then added softly, "He woulda been conceived at the time yeh was going with Rita."

"But she never told me."

"The two of yez were after breaking up by the time she had him. Besides, after that Carvallo fight, nobody could tell yeh nothing."

"Rita," Davy mused. "I haven't thought of her in ages. She was the only girl I ever loved, you know, Paddy."

"I believe that."

"What's she up to?"

Paddy patted Davy on the knee, then replied gently, "She's dead, Davy." Nodding at Percy, he added, "She died while the lad was just a wee one."

"Dead?" Davy fell back against the bench. "How?"

"Not sure," Paddy replied. "She got sick."

"Rita," Davy breathed.

Paddy glanced over and saw a tear roll out of the corner of Davy's left eye and then cut a path through the dirt encrusting his cheek. So that Davy wouldn't know he'd witnessed his moment of weakness, Paddy snapped his head immediately to the forward. Focusing on the boats crisscrossing Conservatory Water, Paddy tried to figure out which one was Percy's. It took him a while, but eventually he was able to pick it out. Sails full of wind, it'd traversed the center of the pond and was breaking out of the pack. Shifting his eyes to his right, he stole a glance at Davy, who was still concentrating on Percy, fifty yards away. A long time passed in silence. It felt like hours, but Paddy realized it must've only been about ten minutes. At last, Davy stirred from his reverie, turned to Paddy and said, "You know, I grew up without a father."

Paddy nodded, "I do." Paddy didn't want to push things. It was a lot to take in—learning in one go that he had a son and that the only woman he'd ever loved was dead. He wanted

Davy to come around to it in his own time, no matter how long that took. Paddy stole a glance at Davy and saw he continued to study Percy in wide-eyed wonder.

Another five minutes had passed when Davy sat back, a light of recognition entering his eyes. Recalling a dream he'd had what seemed like a lifetime ago, he murmured to himself, "*If I find him, it'll somehow save me—save us both.*"

"What's that?"

Davy took several moments to reply: "A boy needs a da."

"Aye." Paddy allowed a few more minutes to pass, then asked, "Do yeh want to meet him?"

Davy looked at Paddy, aghast: "Not like this." Glancing down at his filthy clothes and grimy hands, he added, "I couldn't have him see me like this."

Paddy nodded. Another five minutes passed, then Paddy asked, "Well, do yeh want yer tenner?"

Davy shook his head, "Do you think you could take me by the St. Vincent de Paul, Paddy? I'd like to get cleaned up."

Paddy smiled, "Right so." He slapped his hands on his knees and started to rise, saying, "Well, no time like the present."

Never taking his eyes off of Percy, Davy reached his left arm out and held Paddy down, saying, "Not yet. I wanna stay here awhile."

Paddy nodded and sat back down.

They both sat on the bench, watching the miniature ships float lazily across the pond. It was a beautiful spring day. A light breeze ruffled the leaves of the trees surrounding the Conservatory Waters. The brilliant sunlight caused the miniature waves flowing across the pond to sparkle like glitter.

Laughter and shouts of joy from children at play could be heard all around them. Percy, unaware of the presence of Paddy and Davy, stood dripping at water's edge watching his ship navigate the large pond.

A crooked grin on his face, Paddy followed the progress of their ship. Davy didn't budge, his gaze was fixed on Percy as if he were a unicorn. Another ten minutes passed. A light of recollection entered Paddy's eyes and he reached into his jacket pocket and removed the medal Davy had given him to hold the night of the Carvallo fight. The decade that had intervened had caused the medal to tarnish and the red and white ribbon to fade and begin to curl. Holding it up to Davy, he said, "I believe this is yers. I been holding onto it since…" He faded away, afraid that speaking the name Carvallo would trigger Davy.

Davy looked at the medal. His eyes widened, "My da's medal! I'd thought I'd lost it." He took the medal from Paddy and stared at it, his eyes glistening. After a minute, he handed it back to Paddy, saying, "You hold onto it for me a bit longer."

Davy went back to watching Percy. Another five minutes passed. Without taking his eyes from Percy, Davy said, "You've always looked out for me, haven't you, Paddy?"

Paddy's eyes were fixed on Percy's boat. There were lots of model ships out there, but Percy's was the best. Grinning, Paddy replied, "Somebody had to."

***

ABOUT THE AUTHOR

Stephen L Graf

Stephen L Graf has more than thirty publication credits for short fiction and creative non-fiction including: Philadelphia Stories, Cicada, The Southern Review, The Chrysalis Reader, Fiction, New Works Review, The Broadkill Review, SNReview, and The Black Mountain Review in Ireland, among others. His short fiction has won several Editor's Choice awards, and has twice been nominated for the Pushcart Prize. He lived in Ireland for 2 years while earning an MPhil in Anglo-Irish literature at Trinity College, Dublin. He holds a PhD. in 20th-century Irish literature from the University of Newcastle in the UK. He currently resides in Pittsburgh with his son Declan and teaches English literature.

To see more of his work, please visit his website:

stephenlgraf.com

Made in the USA
Middletown, DE
10 May 2024